DO UNTO OTHERS

DO UNTO OTHERS

Robert C. Varney

FOREST WOODS
MEDIA PRODUCTIONS
WASHINGTON, D.C.

First Edition. First Printing
Do Unto Others
Ccpyright © 2012 Robert C. Varney

Anyone familiar with the State of New Hampshire knows that there are no "County Courts," no "Hadley" or "Windsor," no "Lake Wasoka" or "Wasoka Club" and no "Hadley County," just as any Philadelphian knows there is no law firm called "Wharton Biddle" and anyone who has attended the University of Pennsylvania knows that, while there was a Zeta Psi, a Delta Psi and a Phi Kappa Psi at Penn in the sixties, there was no fraternity named "Phi Psi," no "St. Michaels" and no "Alpha" sorority. These and the people who inhabit them live only in fiction.

No part of this book may be reproduced without the express permission in writing from the publisher.

Published by Forest Woods Media Productions

Cover art by Margot Skelley
Book design by Janice Olson
Printed by Lightning Source

Library of Congress Control Number: 2012934404
International Standard Book Number: 978-0-938572-57-2

For Joyce

I would never have written this book without the encouragement, assistance and example of my mother, Joyce Varney Thompson, which is why this book is dedicated to her. I also wish to thank a number of others. First, my wife, Maria, a first reader who knew how to encourage and make suggestions at the same time; my friends Steve Bennett, Jay MacLaughlin and Glo Bulloch, who did much the same; my daughters Hope, Margot and Paige, who each lent an ignorant old man her surprising expertise at critical moments; and most of all, Diane Jordan, who, ably assisted by Margaret Cassidy from time to time, faithfully and patiently typed and re-typed this manuscript until she surely knew it by heart, all while simultaneously proving to be the best secretary a lawyer ever had.

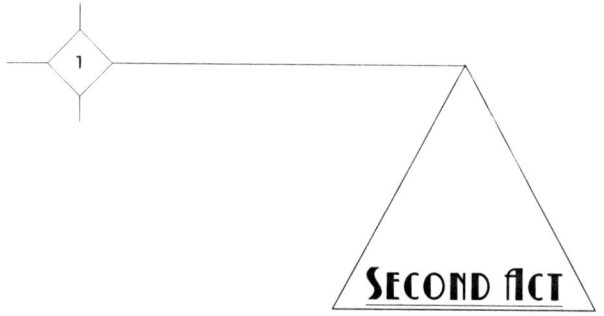

Second Act

He should have seen it coming, but that was no excuse. No, as usual, even when he saw trouble closing in, he had shied away from the hard, the necessary choice. It was a failure of nerve, not judgment. As a judge, he was used to watching sins recast as mistakes. "Must we ruin a man's life for a single bad decision, Your Honor?" But he knew better. The words would sound just as hollow coming from him.

Squinting into the bright, thin November sunshine, he could pinpoint exactly when it began. A week ago. No, this was Saturday. It was more than a week, eight days.

Eight days. Eight days ago he had the usual worries. Life's clock was running down, more minutes counted than coming, the usual bouts of angst of the sane and satisfied. Fifty years gone and little to show for it. Outside of the tiny State of New Hampshire and a small collection of college era friends, no one had, no one would, hear very much of Harry Warren.

For some years now, he had turned first to the death notices in the *Pennsylvania Gazette*, Penn's alumni magazine. He knew what his would say: "Hon. Harry Warren; New Hampshire County Court Judge. While at Penn, Judge Warren was a member of Phi Psi and Masque & Wig, in Windsor, New Hampshire, of ....."

He looked up at the bulk of Langdon House gleaming down on him. He scowled. Even now he was failing to concentrate. The dog at his knee felt neglected and pushed her wet nose against his hand.

He lowered himself onto a sun warmed boulder at the corner of two stone walls. Well, he'd had twenty five years in that house. With its grounds and gardens, terraces and trees, it was everything he had wanted, everything a man could want. Even the fact that it wasn't his had sharpened his pleasure in walking the grounds, observing it from different angles and prospects. He did this so often that Emma wouldn't suspect that this morning's sudden desire for a walk was anything more than another periodic exercise of this privilege.

But of course she would have to know soon. In the past half hour he had committed at least two felonies and broken God alone knew how many judicial canons. They would hear about him now, but instead of a decorous announcement in the *Gazette*, it would be "New Hampshire Jurist Indicted" or "Disgraced Judge Disbarred."

In the distance a hurried 'pop, pop, pop' signaled the death of another whitetail deer. "Lucky deer," he thought but flinched just the same. He had always been a coward. It should have been no surprise that cowardice had done him in.

Once he had asked his mother, "Barbara, why am I so afraid?"

"Harry, you're little. When you're six you're allowed to be afraid."

"But I'm afraid of balls, of frogs, the dark." He ticked these off on his fingers. "I don't think I'll ever be brave."

"I'm afraid of all those things, Harry, so you see, it's all right." She had looked down at him her hands still busy kneading bread dough on the counter top.

Relieved, he had hugged her around her waist.

Well, it wasn't all right at all. In sport, in war, in his profession, even in love: his default response to danger was to shy or shirk. He suffered much for this in the small hours of the morning when remorse is the only currency, but he had never paid for it in the daylit world where a well placed lie or two could do wonders. Time after time he had slipped the noose. Until now.

He petted the golden brown head of the dog. "Poor Harry," he said softly to his uncomprehending listener.

EIGHT DAYS BEFORE, his chambers door had opened about a foot and Grace Carroll's bullet-proof blue hair appeared just as her voice—a feminine baritone manufactured from equal parts American whiskey and American tobacco—announced, "Lady to see you, boss. Your cousin, Jordan Baker."

Harry looked up from the order he was about to sign. It was midway through Friday afternoon. Miller time. Time to go home, not time for a walk-in appointment. When he heard the name though, what began as irritation descended into something more like fear. No, it would be okay. If she meant trouble, she would have used her real name.

"You okay boss?"

"Yah, sure. I, ah … just a little surprised to hear from Mrs. Baker. Didn't know she was coming." Well, that, at least, was true.

Grace could always detect his moods and came into the room completely now, tiny and elegant in her tartan suit. A hundred smile lines melted from her face as it slackened to concern.

"I don't remember her, do I?" she asked.

Grace had grown up in Massachusetts so she didn't have the Hadley, New Hampshire native's knowledge of local families like the Warrens. She wouldn't know the cousins.

"My second cousin, actually," Harry said, adding a degree of separation just to be safe. "Is she …" He gestured toward Grace's own office on the other side of the door.

"No, still out in the courtroom with Russell," Grace said. "Send her in?"

Harry could picture how that was going. Russell Chase, his loyal, taciturn bailiff of a dozen years, would be providing one syllable responses to the new woman's nervous busts of conversation.

"Well, of course … sure," Harry said.

Grateful for a moment alone, Harry got up, went to his closet and put on the blue blazer hanging there. He inspected himself in a wall mirror. Then, feeling warm, he took it off and laid it on his black judicial robe already thrown over the back of a chair. He sat back down, got up, and was back down again when Grace returned with a blonde woman in dark slacks and a tweed jacket.

"Jordan," he said, rising. He was certain his voice sounded artificial, probably because it did.

The blonde presented him with two hands and a cheek. "Hi cuz." She accepted his kiss. "Sorry to drop in, but we were in Hadley and I thought I'd come by. It's been a long time." The skin bunched at the corners of her eyes like it always had when she made the familiar lopsided smile. Maybe this wouldn't be so bad after all.

Grace said "I'll hold your calls, Judge," and began closing the door. Harry nodded and watched the door click shut.

As he turned back he was staggered by a stinging slap. She'd had time and room for a full swing and gave him the whole hand. For a moment he saw stars and instinctively shrunk back, one hand rising.

"I've waited eight years for that," the blonde said then, her voice bright with insincerity. Then she shrugged and laughed softly. "Did it hurt? It felt great to me."

"WELL AT LEAST you remembered about Jordan Baker," she said. "That's something, I suppose."

He had seated her on the opposite side of his small conference table. Harry touched his cheek. "How could I forget. I read *Gatsby* again last summer."

"Jordan Baker" had been their fallback name for her if she and Harry ran into anyone he knew unexpectedly during their weekends together. She had been quite practical about it, recognizing that adulteries which relied solely on spontaneity were likely to be short lived. She had argued for "Daisy Buchanan," but Harry had dismissed it as too obvious.

Now, as she surveyed him, Harry reflexively drew in his stomach. In her case, like most unattached women, the years between thirty and forty hadn't left much of a mark. Her ash-blonde hair was still pulled back in that simple wave that took such discipline to achieve.

Her clothes were just what a proper Main Line matron would wear for a day of riding or shooting or visiting country courthouses.

"You look great, Ephne," he said, using her real name.

"I do, don't I. I'd say the same, but, well let's not get into that."

"You're not going to slug me again are you?"

"I haven't decided." She reached into a pocket and pulled out a pack of Parliaments. Taking one out of the box, she saw his hesitation.

"Look Harry, I'm nervous enough. You're not really going to tell me I can't smoke? I mean, you are the boss around here, aren't you?"

In no mood to explain where power really lay at the Hadley County courthouse, he went to a window and opened it a foot. A gust of late October air came into the room smelling of leaves and mown grass. Walking back, he retrieved a small demi-tasse saucer from the sideboard for her to use as an ashtray.

Ephne lit up and gratefully pulled in the smoke. She turned her attention to the room.

"I can see it now," she said, gesturing with her cigarette. "When I drove up and saw this crummy little courthouse with its WPA murals and those miserable looking people in the lobby, I thought 'Jesus, he threw me over for this?' But now," she gestured again, "I think I get it."

Most of his fellow judges' chambers were noteworthy for diplomas, family pictures, and shabby cast-off furniture. Not this one. Judge Harry Warren usually enjoyed the reactions of new visitors to his own rooms, but not today.

"Hepplewhite," she said, bringing a knuckle down on the table. "If I'm not mistaken, that's a Champney." She pointed at a painting of a mountain gorge discharging mist and rushing water into a forest pool. "And this Bokhara must be a hundred years old." She traced a circle on the rug with her foot.

THE BARELY REPRESSED emotion behind the words and the unfriendly laugh that followed was enough to warn him away from a response. She took another long pull on her cigarette. "Any of this yours?" Bits of smoke came out as she spoke.

He turned his palms up. "Alas," he said.

"It does have the Llewellyn look, that Emma Llewellyn Warren touch," she said. Of course she would get around to Emma. He had no reason to be surprised.

"But you do fit in, Warren." She nodded at the silver coffee service. "It's obvious your good wife has excellent taste in accessories."

"Look, Ephne..."

"No, no. I'm done," she said stubbing out her cigarette. "I'll be good, okay?" Outside a lawn mower started up. "Actually, I need a favor." She looked down and rubbed the table with a finger. This was the same old Ephne, with her mix of cynicism and vulnerability.

"You can't have the table," he said. With some relief he saw her smile for real. "Mmm" she said looking up. "No, I need to ask you about ... you remember that case you talked about the last weekend ... the last weekend we were together?"

Harry frowned, partly in concentration, but only partly. He remembered the weekend of course, the Inn, the sounds and smells of frantic lovemaking, and the languid exchange of confidences afterward in the ruined bed. But what she remembered was a lawsuit.

"I, ah, don't ..."

"Oh cut it out Warren." She could always see right into him. "The fucking was fine. It was very good in fact. The earth moved, okay? Remember it was you who dumped me. I need your help here, okay?" She leaned forward and spoke softly. "You were telling me about a will that was being challenged by a kid who'd been cut out by his grandfather. Something about appointments." She lit another cigarette.

"Powers of appointment," he said.

Harry did remember. The Endicott case. He even remembered lying naked in bed with her, sharing a cigarette while he recounted the trial between Arthur Endicott's grandchildren.

Endicott had had two daughters who died young, both predeceasing him. The older daughter had three children of her own. The Endicotts had money and these kids, Arthur Endicott's grandchildren, had grown up expecting it would all come to them.

The trouble was that Arthur Endicott's second daughter was every parents nightmare; alcohol, drugs, prison—all ending with her death at thirty in a Boston crack house. Along the way, however, she had borne a child, a boy, and though he was in foster care, between jail sentences and rehabilitations, she'd found time to visit him and fill his head with stories about her rich father. The kid remembered this and when he turned eighteen he went looking for his grandfather and found him just before he died.

Endicott had held a power of appointment over a multi-million dollar trust. He couldn't get at the Trust himself, only the income, but he could designate, or "appoint," the shares that his children and grandchildren got after his death. He hadn't known about the boy so he had never bothered to exercise the power, and by the time the grandson showed up he had third stage Alzheimer's.

Just before he died, Endicott's granddaughters learned they had a cousin. One of them went to a lawyer and, after some scrambling, they got the old man to sign a paper exercising the power and cutting the boy out of any share of the Trust.

"*But by then it was too late,*" Harry had explained.

"*How come?*"

"*Because he wasn't competent.*"

Ephne had turned toward him, she lay on her side her breasts bunched together against her upturned elbow. "*So you gave this kid everything?*"

"*No, just the share his mother would have got. He gets half.*"

"*Half? You said there were three other grandchildren. Why not a quarter?*"

Harry had turned toward her. "*You know, this is a very strange conversation.*" Sweat still shone on her forehead.

"*No, I'm interested.*"

"*Well, the boy gets half because the trust said if Endicott didn't exercise his power to appoint, the money would go to his heirs at law. The boy's mother's share was half. He gets her half share. His cousins split the other half, the share their mother would have got.*"

"So he ends up with more than the others?" She had giggled then. For an adopted girl this was a happy ending.

◆△◆

IN THE PRESENT Ephne broke in on his memories. "You said you have to be competent to exercise this power, power point ..."

"Power of appointment."

"Uh huh. And you have to sign something, right? It has to be written?"

Harry considered. "Sure, nearly always."

"So, what if two people have to agree on this power thing?" She played with the burning end of her cigarette.

"Agree?"

"Yah. If both people don't agree, does the heirs' business kick in?" She asked.

"I guess if they both don't agree, there's no exercise and it descends to the heirs." Harry puzzled for a moment. He was seeing his lover for the first time in eight years and he was giving her a primer on intestacy.

"Now, if one of them was crazy, incompetent?" She let the words hang. A question.

"If it takes two to exercise the power, there's probably no exercise. I'd have to see the document, Ephne."

She seemed to take this in. Then she said, "Okay, I got it." A wall clock began to chime. Ephne gave him a long look, pursed her lips and nodded. She collected her cigarettes and lighter and stood.

"Well," she said looking down on him.

"You're leaving?" Over the past eight years he had come to believe he would never see her again, but it hadn't been a certainty. Now in an instant it was.

As usual, she read his mind. "Leaving?" she said, imitating his voice. "Maybe I could drop in for dinner with you and the good Mrs. Warren. Say, seven?"

He made a gesture of resignation. The Westminster cycle ended with three soft notes. "It's just that after..."

"I know," she said. She seemed to relent then, maybe remember. "How do you think I feel?" She pursed her lips. "I'm sorry I sprung this on you. I wanted to see you, I guess. Now it doesn't feel like such a great idea."

"Think what you saved in legal fees."

She was moving toward the door now. The lopsided smile returned with sideways eyes.

"I feel so used," he said when they reached the door.

She looked down. "Don't go there, Harry," she said her hand on the door knob.

"Sorry."

"Uh huh." She turned the knob but let him open the door for her. When Grace looked up, Ephne had replaced the visiting cousin mask.

"Nice to see you Harry, we'll try to drop in on you and Emma on Sunday if we get the chance." Again the cheek.

"Okay Jordan, give us a call."

And she was gone. He closed the door gently then, and fool that he was, he leaned back against it with his shoulders and blew out in relief.

A HALF HOUR LATER, Grace Carroll and Russell Chase, secretary to and bailiff for the Honorable Harry Warren, presiding judge of the Hadley County Court for the State of New Hampshire, went about their separate end-of-the-day chores, happy to be finishing another week an hour early. Down the hall in Judge Steven's chambers an obsolete copier whined and the phones still rang. There were advantages to working for Harry Warren, a man who knew that nothing worthwhile ever happened after three thirty on a Friday afternoon.

"Well, the boss cleared out real fast after that lady left," Grace said. This was really a question, but Russell only continued to dry the small saucer that had held two forbidden cigarette butts, whistling as he did so. He was a big man, more than a foot taller than Grace even in her heels. Outside, Russell saw the large silver-colored German sedan, a recent present to the judge from his generous wife, cruise out of the courthouse parking lot.

"The man lives in a house that has its own name. Where would you rather be?" Russell was referring to Langdon House, the Warren's, or more properly, Mrs. Warren's sprawling hilltop home.

Grace smiled. She would accept any reasonable excuse for her judge's failings, even his persistent belief that he could fool her. "Well Russell, take the rest of the week off," she said as she did most Fridays.

"I think I will." He closed the closet and surveyed the judge's office, his "chambers," satisfied everything in his part of it was in its place.

"What are you doing for Halloween?" Grace asked.

"Same as always. Nothing. Maybe give out candy to the kids." Like most ex-cops, Russell hated Halloween.

"You be in Monday?" The coming Monday, the first of November, was the beginning of hunting season. In New Hampshire it ranked as one of the last of the high holy days and was the cause of widespread "illness" among court bailiffs and sheriff's deputies.

"Sure," Russell said. "Gettin' too old for chasing deer. I'll be here."

Grace gathered up her things and snapped out the lights.

"You ever see that lady before?" she asked as they crossed the empty courtroom.

"Nope."

"Me either," Grace said. "Funny thing. She said she was going to drop in on the family, but Mrs. Warren is out of town. Won't be back until Monday."

"Guess she'll be disappointed then." Russell's bland expression told her he considered the subject of the suspicious visitor closed, and the two didn't mention it again as they left the courthouse together. But then Russell was a New Hampshire boy, Hadley born and bred. He knew all of the Warrens. He especially knew there was no Warren cousin named Jordan Baker.

Grace didn't know that, but she did know her boss was wrong if he thought he was the only one in the office who read Scott Fitzgerald.

2

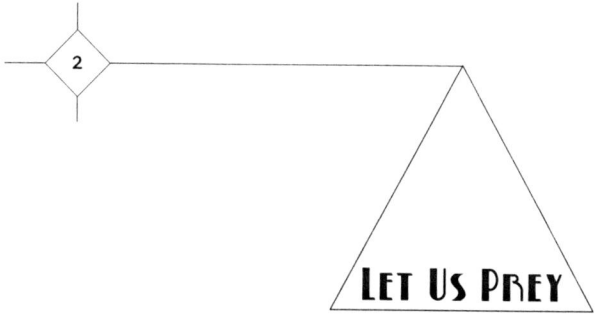

LET US PREY

Three days later, thirty miles west of the Hadley County courthouse, and thirty miles north of the Beaux Arts country home called Langdon House, it was at last the first day of New Hampshire's deer hunting season. Four men, including Oscar Leighton, sat crowded together in a mud-splattered Jeep as it made its way uphill along a logging road.

Now anyone given the name Oscar is bound to be a pessimist, and thirty-four years had taught Oscar Leighton that discomfort was usually a preview of disaster. Like the way he discovered that Tori had given him crabs just two days before she told him she was pregnant.

So when Oscar's head bounced him awake against the window, his face was already set in a frown. As he came to, the Jeep's front tire crunched through a skim of ice with a wet splash. The Jeep lurched and Oscar's head hit the window again, hard.

"Jesus," he said, resettling himself on the narrow back seat so not to fall against the snoring, open-mouthed man beside him who could sleep through anything.

Up front Oscar could see his two other companions give each other a look he'd seen before.

"We wake you up, Oscar?' the driver said, his eyes meeting Oscar's in the rear view mirror.

"Uh huh," Oscar said. He stared back as long as he could, then looked away. The engine whined and pulled. Stump sprouts and blackberry bushes scraped finger-on-the-blackboard noises on the fenders.

Oscar knew where they were. They had hunted here last fall, but the owner had clear-cut his land over the winter and now it was thick with new hardwood stump sprouts shoulder high. It looked like long gray grass through the window, too thick for walking. They'd hunt the far side of the ridge this morning.

The road ended at a stone wall and they skidded to a stop. The man next to Oscar came awake then and stretched. "Good-fuckin'-mornin' everyone." They all smiled, even the driver. Outside first, Oscar opened the back hatch and handed out rifles to the other two passengers through a cloud of exhaust swirling grey and pink in the ruby gleam of the taillights. Taillights, up close, always made Oscar think of Christmas. It was that or the novelty of his own new gun that made him forget to keep hold of the back hatch. It came down hard. That brought the driver's window down.

"Jesus, you think you could slam it any harder, Oscar?"

"Sorry," Oscar said, turning away. He made a face where he couldn't be seen, then snapped in the pre-loaded magazine and released the slide. The rifle jerked in his hand as a round slid into the chamber. He clicked the safety, on keeping the barrel pointed down and away from the others.

Turning back Oscar asked, "Anyone got a cigarette?"

"You know, you're allowed to buy 'em, Leighton." But the man was reaching in his pocket as he spoke and handed the pack over.

The hunters shared a lighter flickering yellow against their unshaven faces, then turned back to settle the afternoon pick-up with the driver. "Well, don't shoot yourselves," he said, rolling up the window. "Be careful with that new cannon, Oscar."

The three watched the Jeep out of sight saying nothing, enjoying the first smoke of the day. By the time they were ready to put the butts out, pulling them apart as they did, the sky above the trees had turned pink. As Oscar stripped his, he delivered a long musical fart.

"Well, Leighton, we're all glad you got that off your mind."

"Scare off the deer."

"No," Oscar said, "Just stun 'em a little." Oscar smiled and made settling movements like a girl. "Least I waited."

The three started together into the uncut stand of trees while spreading out to about a hundred feet apart. The light was coming on but it was still dark in the forest. Somewhere leaves rattled. Oscar felt there was something different about today. Almost enough to make him stay back. He spotted a white cardboard notice on one of the first pines. "No Hunting or Trespassing."

"Hey, they posted this land." Oscar had to raise his voice to be heard over the wind.

"So what?" the man nearest to him called back.

Oscar ripped the notice down without thinking.

"Jesus, Oscar, take his damn sign, why don't you. Maybe you can leave him a note, 'sure-shot was here.'"

Oscar started to answer the man, but he was right. Well, too late now. He let the notice go. Caught in the wind, it cartwheeled into the brush behind them.

An easy hour's walk down the east ridge brought them full sunlight and views of Lake Wasoka, now the color of a new pair of jeans. Clouds, puffs of white against the softer blue of the sky, made good time in the stiff breeze. Their shadows followed each other across the lake and onto the grey-green of the forest surface. Oscar never could see why the shadows always seemed to move faster than the clouds that made them. They did though.

Even the downhill walk had left him out of breath and his bright orange cap had already raised a furious itch in his scalp. His red hunting coat fit good last year, but it felt tight now. He undid two buttons. His hands bare, his gloves back in his pockets, he breathed deeply, raised the orange cap and gave his head a good scratch.

It wasn't easy keeping up, bad right knee and all, but he knew the rules. Each man had a sector. No shooting allowed inside or behind the shallow triangle they made. Break that rule, even once, and from then on, you hunt alone.

The woods seemed empty today. No forest birds with their color and calls that he liked to watch and listen to on breaks from working his uncle's backhoe. Sometimes he watched them through an old pair of binoculars he hid under the seat. Winter birds didn't sing worth a damn, like the pair of unseen crows making a racket nearby.

Pushing to keep up, Oscar stepped onto a sloping shelf of granite ledge. It looked wet so he shifted his weight and led like he always did with his good left leg. But instead of taking hold, his foot flew out from under him and he only just saved himself from falling completely flat with his free left hand. He swore first in surprise then in pain as he slid on the seat of his pants down the face of the rock. Instinctively, Oscar stuck the rifle out to brake and it scratched and banged on the stone surface. He yelled as his free hand was scraped up on the rock.

He came to rest in soft leaves at the foot of the ledge. The pain in his hand was so bad he thought he'd cry.

Shifting the new rifle to his left hand, Oscar cursed the new deep yellow gouge in the stock and laid his head back flat. He hadn't got his deer for three years and his friends—some friends—were calling him "sure-shot" at the Legion after work. This new gun was supposed to bring him luck. He waited for the others to start in again about how clumsy he was.

But they didn't say a thing. Oscar hitched himself halfway upright on his elbows and saw why. The point man was cracking and softly swearing his way through a tangle of blown-down grey birch, too busy to hear. The other was out of sight. Well, that was a break. Oscar sucked on the pink and red wound and held his hand out to look at it. Not that bad. He pushed himself upright.

The fall had deepened the headache that started in the Jeep, and last night's beer and cigarettes sat heavy in his mouth. He coughed up a satisfying thickness, turned his head and spit.

The man in the brush had turned still as a statue, rifle up, his narrow body leaning forward. Twice Oscar saw him look up from the rifle, level and lethal in front of him. Oscar knew it was certain death for any deer to walk into those sights.

But no. Nothing. The hunter lowered the gun and started forward again. Oscar breathed out and re-examined his hand still wet from his mouth. Time to get going, but now what he really needed was a piss.

Oscar set the new rifle against the crotch of a bull pine and fully unbuttoned his coat as the need turned fierce. He had sense enough to step around the pine to get out of the wind but then Oscar pulled too quickly at his zipper and caught it on the fly flap. Shit! Making half steps and small groans now, he jerked the zipper back and forth and got it open just in time. His shoulders sank in pleasure and he settled back on his heels with a sigh, sending out a satisfying stream watching it steam as it hit the leaves and pine needles. He shivered then and looked up.

She was sitting twenty feet away against the smooth grey trunk of a solitary beech. Her head was cocked down on her right shoulder, her mouth open in reproach. Her outstretched left hand lay open and empty, as if expecting to receive something. Her right was clenched and held in close. Birds had been at her and the darkened pits where her eyes had been stared at Oscar, black and unblinking. Her blonde hair blew up slightly with a gust of wind. Small dried brownish stains fell across her cheeks, like dark tears. The crows sensed Oscar's interest and began to hop away.

Oscar jerked straight up and screamed. He made a high-pitched cry for a big man, and at this, the crows left off their hopping and flapped into the air. Oscar later admitted he screamed "kinda high," but only because he'd caught his foreskin in the zipper. And this was true. But though he had managed to release the offended member and even get his dampened pants closed up before the others made it over to see what the hollering was about, Oscar was still making "ahh-ahh" noises and pointing at the woman when they got there.

By then the crows reached adjoining branches high on the bull pine. Here they adjusted themselves with stiff, abrupt shifts of weight and claw, the way crows will. They looked at the scene below, then away, and then briefly at one another as if ashamed for the screaming man.

◆△◆

SERGEANT GREGG LEAVITT gave up trying to match the conservation officer's pace halfway up the mountain. Though the man in the distinctive red woolen coat of a New Hampshire "fish cop" was old enough to be Gregg's father, he showed no sign of fatigue, not a drop of sweat though the mid-morning sun had brought the temperature up from the freeze of the night before. The man made no wasted motion, just kept a steady rolling pace, assisting himself occasionally with the five-foot pole he carried, or using it to hold branches from snapping back onto the sweat-shined faces of the two state policemen trying to keep up.

They had gone a mile uphill without stopping when the man turned and gave them a shiny Gallic smile, his teeth bright against his weathered face. It was less than an hour since they got the call. He was giving them silent permission to rest.

"Not so bad, eh?" He gestured back at the expanse of blue water just becoming visible over the tree-tops.

"Real pretty," Gregg said, careful to keep the breathlessness out of his voice. The conservation officer glanced then at a second trooper, just coming up, puffing hard and beyond shame. The older man straightened his red coat and played with his stick.

"You boys don't get in the woods much, eh?"

"'Nuff to suit me," the second trooper said as his panting subsided.

"They' up there," the conservation officer gestured with the pole. "You hear?"

Gregg cupped his hand next to his ear against the wind. It was true. He could hear faint voices. Gregg realized then the man had stopped to give them time to catch their breath. Gregg didn't know the officer, but he knew he was a friend of his Uncle Russell. "Homer" something-or-other.

When they'd rested long enough, Gregg nodded for the white-haired man to lead them off again, uphill in the direction of the voices. Just as they got to where the voices became distinct, the conservation officer held a branch for the other two and stood back to let them go first into a clearing. At one end three hunters, all in red and orange, sat talking to each other in the overly cheerful tones of men keeping up their courage. At the other, Gregg saw the reason why.

Gregg waited for the other trooper to pull out his camera before going over to take the hunters' statements. He thought he remembered one of them from long ago basketball court confrontations between Hadley High and Lakes Regional. That man looked back at him and gave a confirming shake of the head and a smile of recognition.

"Leavitt, right?" The man separating himself from the others may have remembered, or maybe he'd just read his name tag. They shook hands. Gregg saw the lines in the other man's face. Did he look that old? Probably not, country boys aged fast.

"Uh huh."

The two turned together toward the woman in her stillness. Without looking back at the others, Gregg said, "You didn't move her—touch anything?"

"Nope. She's just like we... like Oscar, found her." As he said this, a stout, shorter man shambled over. His cap was pushed back on his head. Gregg could see that the front of his pants were stained.

"We didn't touch nothin'," Oscar announced. He offered his hand which Gregg took after a momentary hesitation. The third hunter came up but said nothing.

"Shooed away the fuckin' crows, that's all," Oscar continued. At this, a gust of wind raised the woman's hair. Gregg frowned.

Remembering himself, Gregg introduced the second trooper who only nodded as he got the camera ready. The hunters already knew the conservation officer and the three accepted his smile of recognition with the downward glances and shifting feet of men for whom the fish and game laws were an unwanted, and much ignored, intrusion into the settled patterns of their lives.

"When'd you find her?" Gregg asked.

"Just 'fore we called," Oscar said holding up a cell phone. Then he added, "Called the Sheriff."

Gregg looked at him, detecting the qualification in the announcement. "You call anyone else?"

"Yah. We called the Chief, 'course." He gave Gregg a sideways smile. "Afterwards."

Seeing Gregg's reaction, Oscar said, "Well this is West Harbor," he said. "'It's his town, our town."

"Sure. Good thinking," Gregg said, knowing his tone conveyed the opposite of his words.

"Anything we can do?" Oscar asked then, gesturing toward the woman.

"Yeah, little later. We may need some help carrying, if you're willing. Don't mind waiting?"

"Sure. Don't feel much like gunnin' anymore today," Oscar said. "We'll just stay outta your way over here. Call us when you need us."

The other trooper by now had snapped filters and a flash attachment onto his camera. As he approached the woman, he began taking pictures from different angles. Close-ups of each hand, each foot. He knelt down and clicked away at her face and torso.

Gregg stood just away, careful to stay out of the pictures.

After a dozen pictures, Gregg motioned to the trooper who stood back as Gregg knelt next to her. She was a small woman. She had some kind of comb that still held most of her hair behind one ear. Close to the roots Gregg could see the hair was dark brown, with a little gray, but a quarter inch up, it lightened to a mixture of yellow white and light brown. A patterned yellow scarf was knotted at her neck and contrasted with the brown tweed of her jacket.

She wore simple gold earrings on pierced ears. Her hands were scratched but her nails looked unbroken. They were cut short and coated with clear polish. No rings. Reaching into her coat pockets Gregg found a pack of Parliaments, three cigarettes left, seventy-eight cents in change and some tinsel paper. A faint mint odor came from the paper. No wallet. Only one shoe. His hand brushed her chest as a gust of wind raised a lock of hair from her forehead. He felt himself jerk back, but it was only hair. Her ruined eyes continued to ignore him.

Gregg used his pen to pull her jacket away from her body revealing a blackish-brown stain on the white shirt underneath. There was a pattern of small holes in the stain just above her dark slacks.

At this the conservation officer made a soft whistle behind him. Gregg turned his head. He hadn't heard him come up.

The man smiled an apology, then said, "That's for sure bird shot, eh?" There was the touch of an accent in the words, a French Canadian. "Omer," Gregg thought. "His name is Omer."

Gregg looked down again. This was only his third 'fatal.'

"Uh-huh," he said trying to put as much of 'of course' as he could into the two syllables.

"Bird season over, month ago."

"Mmm," Gregg said.

"She ain' been here no month."

The man bent past Gregg and, without touching the woman's shirt, traced his finger in the air just above the pattern of small holes. "Tight shot group," he said. "She was shot close-in."

As he said this the sound of cracking and snapping wood came from behind them. Gregg looked up a rock face. Blue uniforms were emerging from the forest above. He regretted his sigh of resignation as soon as he made it.

Then there was a thud and exclamation of breath followed by a loud "ahh … shit…" and the sound of leather, cloth and metal against rock. The familiar form of the West Harbor Chief of Police emerged feet first and sliding on his back down the rock face to land in a heap at the bottom.

One of the hunters got over to him first, offering a hand to help him up. As he did he said, "Not so smooth as she looks, is she chief?"

The two other hunters hid their smiles and looked away as the red-faced man stood and re-adjusted his gun belt below his paunch. Two other blue-clad men came down the rock in a crab-like crouch. Setting his hat, the chief glowered at the three hunters before turning and walking to Gregg Leavitt. He walked over a wet patch of leaves and several stuck to one boot.

"What we got?" he asked as if nothing unusual had just happened.

The conservation man took a step back, exchanging a nod but no words with the chief.

"We got a probable homicide, Chief," Gregg said to the exhausted, red-faced man, glad he hadn't joined in the merriment.

"When they call you?" the chief waved in the direction of the hunters.

"Don't know Chief," Gregg said. "We took a call from the Sheriff"s office."

"Uh-huh." The chief nodded down to the small, unmoving form at their feet. "ID?"

"Nope."

"Any of these three assholes know her?" He jerked his thumb at the three hunters and gave them an 'I'll see you later' look.

Hearing this, all three said in unison.

"No ..."

"Not from round here ..."

"Never seen her before."

The chief silenced them with his hand. Taking in the knotted silk scarf, the tailored tweed jacket and the one slipper-like shoe, the chief said. "Looks like one o' those Wasoka Club folks."

Gregg saw the conservation officer make an upside-down 'u' of his mouth and nod twice. Gregg hadn't thought of that either. The chief had his uses.

Gregg knelt down next to the woman again, probing beneath the knotted scarf. No marks, no bruising.

The last shooting he'd investigated was a woman. They found her slumped onto the dinette table in her trash-filled trailer. Her boyfriend had shot her right through the face. He tried to kill himself afterward, but he couldn't bring himself to do more than a couple of cowardly scalp wounds. When Gregg realized the woman was six months pregnant he wished he'd been there to help the guy along.

At least this new lady had died in a clean place, wearing nice clothes. Except for the missing shoe and the heel protruding from the thin white fabric of her stocking, she could have been out for a walk in the woods. Bringing his face close to hers, Gregg tried to smell for alcohol. Nothing. Nothing left anyway.

The Wasoka Club. Sure. That country club on the north shore of the Lake for rich people from the city. She had the look, that 'Don't you know who I am?' look the members gave him when they got pulled over drunk, or speeding. But they were summer people. This was November.

A cloud shadow fell over the clearing and Gregg felt himself shiver. As he straightened up the shadow passed and the morning sun hit his back again warm and bright. That was when he saw a glint from her closed hand. Gregg bent back down and probed the hand with his pen revealing a gold colored strip beneath the thumb. Pushing further, Gregg got the top of the pen under this and levered it out of her grasp. A tiny gold signet ring with a face half the size of a dime fell onto the leaves beside her. The wind through the empty branches of the beech tree made something like a sigh.

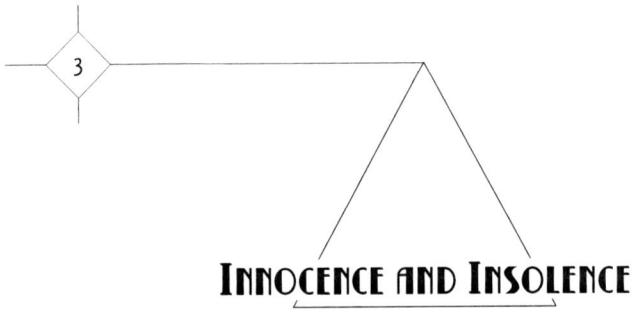

3

INNOCENCE AND INSOLENCE

Since becoming a judge, Harry Warren never minded Mondays. The tyranny of deadlines over sloth and its trinity of consequences—apprehension, shame, and resentment—were things of the past for him. A lazy student who got by on the head start of early childhood reading and the inexplicable beneficence of the Educational Testing Service, Harry had applied himself only twice. First, briefly, at Penn Law where it hadn't been enough to earn a place on any of the law reviews, but sufficient to put him in the middle of his class. The State of New Hampshire was hardly in the big leagues as far as legal talent was concerned, so even this standing had qualified him for a spot at Cruikshank and Hannah, New Hampshire's biggest, and arguably its best, law firm. There, Harry had put in three years of serious effort, working directly for Zach Hannah, the firm's top litigator. No possibility of sloth there. Seventy hour weeks were the norm and always under the tireless guidance of Zach himself. Harry came first to dread and soon to tire of the wry smile of disappointment from the *wunderkind* of New Hampshire lawyers far more than the tirade of any judge. Then, magically, at age 31, he became a judge himself and was freed forever from both.

People want to think the best of judges. Harry had heard it said a thousand different ways. The clients were greedy, guilty liars and their lawyers, incompetent or insincere or both. But the judge, ah the judge. He was 'patient' or 'wise' or 'don't put up with no nonsense.' People believed this because they wanted to, had to. Zach Hannah had told him as much when he'd first gone on the bench. "Deep inside, below the level of common thought, they know, they just know, if it isn't so, they've gone and entrusted their hopes, their freedom, even their lives, to just one more frivolous myth like democracy, Santa Claus or the Easter Bunny," Zach had said. "Just remember, Harry, just because they think it doesn't make it so." Harry hadn't needed the warning. He already knew he lacked the qualities people thought they saw in judges. He had never been patient or wise and he talked 'nonsense' all the time. Perhaps this was because he had a particularly unfortunate background for developing 'judicial temperament.' As a boy, schoolyard opinion of him had divided evenly between loathing and disdain.

Harry pretended not to care but, like any boy would, he hated that this was so. He relieved his solitary, unloved childhood much more than most, with daydreams. In those he was clever and brave, and usually he wore some kind of uniform.

As a young man caught up in Viet Nam, Harry had found he reacted to gunfire with the same terror that spoiled his tryout with the Hadley Little League, even to the point of just starting to run away when he "fell for freedom," as the Hadley *Argus* put it. Harry's daughters, Leigh and Samantha, were still little girls when his wife, Emma, somehow found the back issue of the *Argus* in which this wonderfully inaccurate account of his short military career had appeared. She made a reprint of the picture of an emaciated Harry in a bemedaled bathrobe, his eyes fixed on a young soldier with an MP armband. The girls helped Emma place it in one of her gilt frames and gave it to Harry as a Christmas present. It was a grave ceremony, for they were convinced as only child-daughters can be that, secretly, their father was very brave indeed. Harry's proof of valor sat in a discreet corner and he never spoke of it. This was not modesty. Life was full of surprises. You never knew when someone from long ago might show up on the doorstep with the real story. That day at the Hawaiian hospital, Harry thought they'd come to arrest him, not give him a medal.

Harry had never advertised his crowded hour. He didn't need to. It was the limp. People asked, he said something appropriately ambiguous, and the story got passed on, usually better than he could make it and always much, much better than reality. A hell of a thing.

The girls had moved away now and Emma seemed much more likely to leave him on his own these days as she had the previous weekend. In fact, the day-dreaming man in the black robe had spent the past three nights alone, wandering the rooms in a now far too large house, and for the first time in years he had picked up the picture. At least he hadn't had to face Emma while the shock of Ephne's re-appearance was still fresh. Or worse. What was it Ephne had said? "Maybe I could drop in for dinner, say seven?"

◆△◆

THE SMILE THAT came so quickly over the face of the presiding judge of the Hadley County Court seemed to come from nowhere.

It couldn't have anything to do with the case going on before him. The late Monday morning sunlight slanted through the windows of the nearly empty courtroom onto sentencing proceedings in *State of New Hampshire v. Marjorie Tuttle*. Nothing funny about that. From time to time the judge had shifted his foam cushion an inch this way or that to take up some of the weight from his aching left buttock, the site of his old war wound as everybody knew, but that wasn't likely to bring on the rueful grin or the slight shake of the head that came with it.

Harry prided himself on being able—usually—to daydream and still keep track of what was going on in the courtroom. However, amidst reflections on disasters both recent and past, he had completely lost the thread of the argument the young public defender was making on behalf of Margie Tuttle, a recently convicted shoplifter. Margie was also a stealer of credit cards, connoisseur of a surprising variety of illegal substances, and a frequent visitor to his court.

"Margie ..." he heard the name as his attention wandered back, was now "... *dealing* with her *challenges* as a drug abuser and a single mom, Your Honor. Margie has held her new home-care worker's job for six weeks. While she did have a little backsliding, its true, her last two drug screens were negative and she is willing to continue to face these challenges and very much wants to resume visitation with her son, to be a real mom again for Travis." *Dealing, issues, challenges, single mom.* For the thousandth time Harry vowed painful revenge on whoever it was that first counseled young lawyers to call clients by their first names and refer to them as 'mom' or 'dad' whenever possible.

With disappointment, he fixed his gaze on the speaker, a small woman with frizzed reddish hair who had assisted at Marjorie's trial two months earlier. Harry had known two types of redheads. Rarely, they were beautiful, like his wife, Emma. The rest looked like this public defender, a 'P.D.' as they were called: pug-nosed, pale, freckled and small featured. Still, this one was already a better lawyer than the senior P.D. she had assisted. And though she had acquired the unhappy habit of calling guilty strangers by their first name, her language hadn't yet made the full descent to where crimes were 'issues' and sins merely cause to 'reach out.' There was hope. She hadn't used 'impact' or 'interfaced' even once.

The tiny P.D. had a small audience to work with in the largely empty room. Harry's bailiff, Russell, sat in his chair to the right of the jury box. One elderly woman, an aunt and apparently Margie's sole supporter, sat in the first of the six rows of seats reserved for spectators. Two City of Hadley cops, there on another case, lounged on seats across the aisle. A stenographer clicked away just below the judge's bench. At a table opposite the defendant, seeming to fill a space made for three people, sat the Hadley County Prosecutor, 'T.J.' Carr.

T.J.—Timothy Joseph—Carr was a large man who hadn't buttoned the top button of a shirt in living memory. His frequent tantrums were legend and the tiny public defender kept a wary inventory of his mood. T.J.'s hair, what he had left, was also red though his sprouted from his head in irregular tufts. He had it trimmed into an approximation of a crew-cut from time to time, but it was now weeks past due. His shoulders sloped into almost simian arms which hung to his knees. One arm was now cocked, as if levered, a finger busy in one ear. When he removed the finger he examined what he had recovered then flicked it onto the floor.

Harry winced, but inwardly. T.J. and Harry had a complicated relationship, made worse by Harry's testimony in an ethics complaint against Carr three years earlier. Suppression of evidence. Some men could have forgiven Harry for that. After all, the reprimand T.J. got from the Bar Discipline Office had doubled his majority in the next Hadley County election. "*T.J. Carr* - he goes the extra mile for *us!*" But even Harry had been surprised at how even Carr's friends had drawn back from him, returning only when he escaped with a reprimand. T.J. would never forgive, or forget. Harry turned his gaze back to the defendant.

Margie Tuttle had grown heavier in the two years since Harry last convicted her. This morning she appeared at the defense table in a roomy aqua-colored sweatshirt. Pink script extolled the virtues of "Old Orchard Beach, Maine." This cheerful garment came down to the middle of two sizable thighs, both wrapped in grey tights that quickly tapered into much smaller calves. These in turn disappeared into high-cut military style black shoes topped by frilled white ankle socks. It was quite a costume, even for Hadley County. Harry assumed Margie had stolen the sweatshirt.

Margie wore the discouraged but resilient look most defendants put on at sentencing. In the movies, villains faced the music right after trial. In real life, the ceremony of passing sentence came weeks later. And a good thing for defendants, too. By then the subject had changed from crime to the sad, dirty little stories that are most felons' lives. Sometimes these rose—or sunk—to tragedy. Not often, and not today, but Margie had always been game. She rewarded each of the P.D.'s platitudes with nods of confirmation and approval. Her own tightly curled hair bounced in emphasis as she alternated between nods and wary upward glances at Harry. "Your Honor," the P.D. waited for the smiling judge's attention to fall back on her, "there is, well, one additional thing that I think the court should consider." She looked down at the report on the table in front of her, then pushed it away squaring herself. She made a becoming gesture, darting her eyes off to eleven o'clock and took a breath. "I know this is going to sound technical, but, well, I think the court should consider its impact anyway." Harry frowned. She had finally said 'impact.'

"Go on," he said.

She breathed in again, committed.

"These items were valued by Appliance-Land at $308.98 at the time of the theft, but, well, there was a twenty-percent-off sale in effect that day. The value, or at least the sale price would have been $247.80, bringing their value below $250 and reducing this to a violation level offense. The, er, impact of the offense should be con..."

He frowned again. "This wasn't raised at trial."

"No," she said, ignoring the second expression of displeasure. Oh, she was a better lawyer than her boss. She would have argued that as a lesser-included offense at trial and Margie might have ended up with a fine only—which of course she would never pay—and finished up with, at worst, a minor probation violation. The young woman's look down at the pushed-aside report said everything about the short, tense, lost argument over tactics.

It was then that the door at the back of the courtroom opened and a well made young man in the uniform of a New Hampshire state police sergeant came in, his mud-colored boots leaving small pellets on the floor. He whispered first to Russell, who placed a paternal hand on the man's shoulder, listening. The gesture reminded Harry that the sergeant was Russell's nephew. Russell turned his face to Harry, raising his brows in inquiry. Seeing the judge nod once, the sergeant moved up to the prosecutor's table to place a note by T.J.'s left hand.

T.J. ostentatiously ignored the note. He let everyone else—the judge, Margie, her public defender, the stenographer, even Russell with his knowledge of all things stare at it stupidly, catching each other out in their momentary neglect of the fate of Margie Tuttle. Everyone had heard about what they found on Green Mountain earlier that morning and Hadley County was still small enough for an unexplained death to make them gape.

"Mr. Carr?" Harry asked, interrupting the P.D. with a raised hand, "All set?" T.J. waved at the unread note while he continued to ignore its bearer.

"Fine, Your Honor." T.J. was one of the dwindling number of practicing lawyers who had known Harry before he was a judge and even before their trouble had never felt the need for flamboyant deference. There was a noticeable gap between the first word and the second two. He made no effort to stand when he spoke, something the woman from the public defender's office would never have dared. Then, his point made, T.J. looked up at the policeman and dismissed him with a circular nod that said both 'go away' and 'sit over there' toward the front row of empty seats.

The young P.D. returned to her argument about the value of the things Margie stole, but she had lost her enthusiasm. When she finally sat down, it didn't look good for her client. T.J. was beaming.

"We have nothing to add to the pre-sentence report, Your Honor." Carr said, just as she finished, rubbing it in.

The P.D. looked back and forth between T.J. and the judge, torn between embarrassment and irritation. Harry nodded to her to sit down and pretended to re-read and reflect further on the pre-sentence report. He already knew that Margie's virtues, if she ever had any, lived mostly in the realm of intention, as ephemeral as Harry's own. Margie Tuttle had been a fourteen-year-old juvenile runaway when he first saw her. Behind the heavy eye shadow and the wispy hair-in-the-face coiffure then in fashion, she had been pretty in a back-seat-of-the-car kind of way. That was when she stole the cash register out of the Cumberland Farm convenience store where she had an early morning job cleaning the floors and ran away with her twenty-year-old boyfriend to Boston with the $380 proceeds. She made it on the run just long enough for him to get her pregnant and get himself five years for statutory rape. Harry had placed her in foster care and given her the standard lecture on the dangers of drugs and unprotected sex. T.J.'s recommendation now was two years in the state penitentiary, one year suspended. All in all, a fair sentence. But Harry remembered how once she had flashed a spark of hope from those over-painted fourteen-year-old eyes.

He looked down at her. On sale or not, a year was a long time for a Taiwanese CD player and two computer disks. Margie had been around, but never to the penitentiary.

"Ms. Tuttle, would you stand please?" She swallowed and made nervous movements with her hands. If the tights had pockets, she'd have put them there.

"You have been found guilty of two counts of theft. Each is punishable by no less than one nor more than three years in the state penitentiary. These are your eighth and ninth convictions and it is apparent from this pre-sentence report that you are a frequent violator of other state and federal drug laws."

Margie cast a worried look at the now resigned, stone-faced P.D. who wore the look of someone who had bet the farm against the mortgage and just turned over a four. They had tried the case together but Margie would do the time alone. Neither moved, but the distance between them grew. Margie took a breath and reddened. Her mouth began to form a word. The P.D., to her everlasting credit, gave Margie's arm a stroke of consolation.

"You neglect yourself. You neglect your children. Your life is an ever tightening spiral of indulgence and excuse." Harry paused to let the cruelty of the language penetrate. "You are an unskillful thief." At that—in spite of herself—Margie made a small smile. For an instant, at the edges of her eyes, she was fourteen again, and she'd escaped eighteen months in jail.

"Your counsel tells me, however, that I'm wrong. She has faith in you. She makes imaginative and ingenious arguments in your defense. She is young and still has hope while I, well ..." Harry couldn't very well say how he'd lost faith in everything but his own fallibility, so he gave her another long silence. "I suppose I could be wrong."

"I sentence you to two years' confinement." Harry paused again to let the bad news sink in. "I will, however, suspend eighteen of those months provided you are of good behavior..." He went through the formulaic language for each count. If she behaved at all she would be out in four months, and like nearly all thieves, Margie always behaved well in jail. "... to be served in the Hadley County house of correction..." Then as a special gift to that fourteen-year-old, he added "...concurrent with vacated suspensions in cases 00-917 and 00-918. Report for confinement January 10th."

T.J. was counting on having Margie out of the local malls for at least a year. But Harry liked the business about the sale price and Margie had made that little smile.

Harry could see Russell turn his head from side to side. Thus was justice done in Hadley County.

T.J. made a small hole with his mouth, stared for a moment at a spot about midway up the bench and appeared to levitate from his chair. "Excuse me, was that 'concurrent,' Your Honor?" His long arms seemed to get up after he did. He looked for a moment like a gorilla robbed of his banana.

"Yes, concurrent, Mr. Carr."

T.J. took another breath and his neck swelled to fill even the unbuttoned collar. He further loosened his purplish tie. Then, apparently thinking better of the bellow they all expected, he subsided back into the chair, a man with more serious things to deal with in life than a recidivist shoplifter and a feckless judge. But his scalp stayed pink underneath the overgrown crewcut and he replaced papers with careful emphasis into his upright oversized lawyer's briefcase.

Margie had turned wide-eyed to her public defender. Harry heard her say "Christmas" as part of a question. Then, as the lawyer nodded, she began to weep gratitude to the young P.D. The lawyer patted her shoulder and risked a quizzical glance. Judge Harry Warren nearly always followed sentence recommendations, had for years. Then, whatever the P.D. thought, she showed she was savvy enough to pull Margie away from the table and start her toward the door. After a surprise win, she knew to get out of the courtroom before the judge came to his senses.

"Anything further, Counsel?" Harry asked unnecessarily to the now retreating lawyer. He was ashamed at this play for gratitude, but not much.

"No, no Your Honor." She turned back briefly and rewarded him with a shy, grateful smile, her eyes bright with this uncommon, small victory. For a moment the cheap clothes, the scuffed shoes with the worn-down heels, the pallor of too many long days with hopeless cases like Margie, the life Harry had expected for himself, seemed to fall away. "Interesting point about the sale price," he called out, making sure she would win the argument back in the office. But now T.J. was on his feet again.

"Mr. Carr?"

"We'll just keep our eye on the tightening spiral, Judge." T.J. gave a surprisingly good imitation of how Harry pronounced 'tightening.' "Toitning," he said and gave Harry his sunniest smile. A nervous, treacherous, titter of laughter came from the P.D. Was there no loyalty? Even Russell winced at how Harry walked into that one. Of course then, in his last days of innocence, Harry had no thought for how dangerous it might be to offend T.J. Carr.

"All rise!" Russell called out, and Harry turned to the door behind him.

HARRY PULLED UP his robe as he walked alone down the quiet hall. The robe had just been purchased and was at least six inches too long. He could hear his own footsteps on the damp floor. By afternoon, when motions had been heard and all but protracted hearings were finished, transcribing stenographers and ringing telephones would fill the hall with sound. Mornings were for hearings and getting ready. Quiet work. No doubt this was why Lionel Whitcomb, the head custodian, had chosen now to mop the terrazzo floor.

"Morning, Lionel," Harry said.

"Mornin." Lionel glanced reproachfully at the newly wetted and shining surface that Harry would have to cross to reach his office.

Harry hesitated, but saw he had no choice and proceeded to the last of three doors sporting matching brass plaques. This read "Chambers of Judge Warren, Presiding Judge." As he turned, he could see faint footprints on the wet part of the floor and heard a sound midway between a grunt and a sigh from the janitor as he flopped his mop against the floor.

Grace's office was a room anyone would recognize who spent time in the principal's office thirty years ago. Three beige plaster walls were traced with dark stained oak trim, the fourth dominated by institution-sized windows heavy with mullions. An ancient silver-painted radiator clanked to life as he walked in, a prelude to a coming surge of excessive, metallic smelling, steam heat. Flourescent lights had been attached to the ten-foot ceiling in the 1950s, just high enough to make them impossible to maintain. The custom of Lionel and his staff was to let most bulbs go dim and burn out before making wholesale replacements. Harry's first complaint about that custom had first taught him that Lionel worked for "the county, not the court."

The wall space between the two windows held a pair of formally mounted photographs of Harry with two governors. One picture, black-and-white, showed a youthful, thinner version of Harry the day he was first sworn in, sideburns just a touch too long, hand raised, Emma looking on. The second was in color and showed him, again observed by Emma, but as he was now—heavier, with shorter hair gone to gray. Emma looked the same in each picture. So did the two Governors Reese, a father and son as it happened, with a remarkable family resemblance, photographed at about the same stage of their lives. The governor's office, where both pictures were taken was more a museum than an office and was also unchanged. The world, it seemed, had remained the same while Harry Warren turned old.

"Anything new, Grace?" As he spoke, Harry picked up a stack of junk mail and began sorting through it.

"At my age nothing is new," she answered, cupping the mouthpiece of the phone in her hand. She turned her head to speak into it "...well, let me see about the objection ... uh huh ..., I will, ... uh huh ... good bye." Her voice rose with a saccharine happiness not reflected on her face. When she set the receiver down, her perfectly painted nails lingered momentarily. "Shithead," she announced to the silent telephone. "Cruikshank and Hannah," she said. "Arrogant little prick." Her voice dropped a full octave revealing all seven of her decades.

Grace adjusted her green plaid jacket, replaced her glasses back on her nose and made a burlesque of a smile showing teeth far too old ever to be white again. "Or am I forgetting your alumni status?" She gestured toward the phone. "One of Zach Hannah's boys, just like you when the world was young."

"Long ago, Grace. Long, long ago," Harry said and began to drop form letters into a wastebasket.

"Well, he ought to send them to charm school. They are being a real pain in the ass about the Martin sisters' case. By the way, Miss Smarty Pants has done a nice job on you ... again."

"Grace." Harry's eyes narrowed and he went back to close the still open door.

"...and wishes an audience at your convenience, my lord."

Grace knew as well as he did that Judge Amanda Stevens, his fellow county court judge, had still not forgiven him for being named supervising judge instead of her. Grace grew up Irish and knew a thing or two about grudges. She was equal to any contest. But Harry wasn't and 'smarty pants' was an epithet arcane enough to put its source beyond denial in the little world of the Hadley County Court. "Grace, please," he said in his best 'I'm above all this' tone.

She shook her head as she handed him some opened mail, two pink phone message slips and a file, *New Hampshire Hospital v. Dickson*. "You don't know what I'm talking about, do you?"

"Haven't the faintest."

"She wants to"—here she paused meaningfully—"explain the Dickson case, I assume you saw the Channel 8 truck pull up."

He shook his head no and went to the window. There was a white truck with a dish antenna. "TV 8–Action News."

"Film at eleven," Grace said.

Misunderstanding, Harry shook his head. This was not modesty. His talent for TV justice was nil, with past performances ranging from mumbling indecision to rambling incoherence. It had been years since film of Harry Warren had appeared anywhere. Film was Amanda's province.

After all, the public Amanda was St. Gaudens' young woman on the silver dollar, yellow hair carefully gathered, posture straight, penetrating blue eyes level, who spoke firmly in complete paragraphs. She imposed sentences that were reassuringly harsh and her praise of jurors' 'courage' after almost any conviction was benedictory.

What was there to explain? Before Harry could ask, the phone rang again. While Grace took the call, Harry walked with the telephone slips and the file into his own adjoining office.

The Friday before, Harry had denied a motion to televise argument in the Dickson medical malpractice case. It was the kind of lawsuit the public couldn't get enough of: a perfectly routine knee replacement, until they replaced the wrong knee. There, in his handwriting, the words "Motion Denied" appeared just above his signature on the "Motion of Windsor Broadcasting, Inc. d/b/a TV-8 Action News." But beneath it, Grace had marked a document with a post-it note decorated with a single exclamation point. Harry turned the page.

When he did, he found a "Motion to Intervene and Emergency Motion to Reconsider" date-stamped 3:47 p.m. the previous Friday afternoon. It was filed on behalf of TV-8 and the News & Observer. Motions to reconsider were supposed to be—were always—routed to the judge who made the decision in the first place, never sent to another judge. Harry remembered how, still recovering from Ephne's sudden re-appearance, he had left the courthouse the past Friday, even earlier than usual, a short time after three p.m. And there was Amanda Stevens' recognizable schoolgirl-perfect handwriting filling the margin.

> *In view of the authorities cited in the Emergency Motion not earlier brought to the attention of the Presiding Judge, and that Judge being temporarily unavailable, the Court is persuaded that the underlying order should be and, accordingly, is VACATED.*

Overruled by his own associate judge! "Temporarily unavailable." Nice. Even if it was true. Amanda must have put this handwriting in the margin at about the same time that Harry, twenty miles away, was putting a substantial quantity of old scotch over some new ice cubes. Well, this was turning into a hell of a morning.

The door came open and Russell Chase's six-foot-five-inch frame leaned around the door into the room. "Channel 5 just rolled in," he said. A Boston station. Just what Harry needed. Their eyes met, Russell taking in the smaller man's frustration.

"Well, Judge, at least you won't have the suppression hearing to worry about. Gregg'll be running back and forth to Green Mountain all day. That fatal up there, shotgun wound."

"Shotgun?" Harry said, adding, "Anyone local?"

"Nope, no one seems to know who she is."

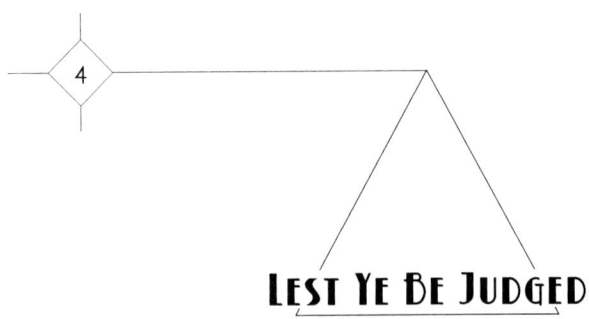

4
Lest Ye Be Judged

As he waited for her arrival Harry tried to prepare himself for the force of nature that was Amanda Stevens.

Her appointment two years earlier to the county court at the laughably early age of thirty-two had made her New Hampshire's youngest county judge since, well, since Harry. But unlike him, Amanda's appointment hadn't coincided with a sudden flush of campaign funds from a distant state. She was a frequent lecturer at Bar functions and the author of regular articles for the State Bar Journal, a publication Harry seldom read and for which he had never written. A former law clerk at the State Supreme Court, she was openly talked of as a future justice. Her work on Bar committees was tireless and effective. Her fine features graced the newspapers and radiated from television screens.

So superior was she that a year earlier, "The Capitol Insider," a regular unsigned column in *The New Hampshire News & Observer* had dismissed as ludicrous the rumor that Harry Warren might get the newly vacant supervising judge's job. Even a weakling like the younger Governor Reese, whose chances for re-election looked dim, would never make the 'perverse' decision to pass over the "talented and well regarded Judge Stevens" for someone like Harry Warren, "near the end of an undistinguished judicial career with little to recommend him but a plummy accent and a fortunate background."

"Fortunate background." Wouldn't his in-laws, the Llewellyns, have had a laugh at that. Still, not a bad turn of phrase for the "Insider." Happily for Harry, the writer showed the same disdain for the younger Governor Reese. "Governor Fils," he called him. Again, not bad, but like most clever remarks it backfired. Piqued by the insult, the scion nominated Harry the day after his election defeat and applied himself with previously unsuspected energy to Harry's speedy confirmation, by two votes. If Governor 'Fils' had devoted half as much energy to something worthwhile, he might have kept his own job.

Harry didn't weep for Amanda. He believed a little disappointment in youth was good preparation for the bigger ones to come. Say, that thin envelope with the crest of Yale University in his mail box at the Devon School, or the fat sergeant telling him what 'APO San Francisco' meant on his first set of orders. Sure, she should have got the job but, after twenty years, Harry was tired of circuit riding with its long drives and nights in distant motels. Moreover, the appointment had cost his father-in-law twenty-five thousand dollars sifted with careful illegality into a failed political campaign. And there was that column.

In her brief life Amanda Stevens had known few such disappointments so this one had left her unable to bring a smile to that beautiful face for weeks. But time passed and her flashes of impatience had subsided. The dazzling smile returned. Why not? She knew the tables would turn. When her moment came, of course, Harry knew to expect no mercy, so it was important he not need any.

AMANDA GAVE RUSSELL her warmest greeting as he held the door open for her. She was a tall woman and four-inch heels and abundant hair made her taller. Her teeth were a glistening testimonial to the supremacy of American orthodontia. Almost eye to eye with this beautiful girl, even Russell's face softened for a moment. Turning to Harry she took in the presence of the malpractice case file and his lack of enthusiasm with a single glance. She motioned to the sideboard.

"Coffee, Harry? Russell makes the best coffee."

Harry misinterpreted this as a command and even started up out of his chair toward the sideboard before Amanda took him by the arm and showed those gleaming teeth again, the gums just visible. She leaned a portion of the substantial Stevens bosom into his side. "No, no, let me do it. I always feel like it's a party when I use these things." She went over to the tray while he subsided. Almost unnoticed, the clerk of court, an Amanda ally, had sidled in behind her and stood in silence chewing on his fingernails. With his receding chin and protruding lips, he looked like an unhappy trout who, inexplicably, had chosen to grow a mustache. Russell closed the door and left them alone.

Watching Amanda, gnawing all the while, and without fully withdrawing his hand, the clerk said in an 'oh by the way' tone, "We're going to have to postpone that suppression on the Tillinghast case, Judge. All the deputies are up on Green Mountain. There's a fatal up there... A woman," he added. When Harry didn't respond, he fell silent and gave the finger a rest.

"Oh, sure, whatever you say," Harry's voice trailed off.

Amanda came back to the desk, put the demitasse down in front of her, and sat down. She carried herself with the assurance that any beautiful woman has with two men who are not. True, the tiny spoon rattled slightly in the saucer, and her smile was about three lumen too bright, but no one could doubt the *froideur* of her *sang*.

As was customary for him, Harry had silently rehearsed reaming out the both of them. *"Look, bitch. You and your shifty-ass friend have gone too far."* A little eloquent manliness. Given his limitations, what he actually said was:

"Uh, these TV trucks. Something going on?"

The clerk swallowed. If he thought Harry wasn't going to make him bring the bad news, he was mistaken.

"Probably the Dickson case." The clerk leaned forward to reach for the file, but Harry picked it up before he could, gathering a breath of courage from the man's discomfort.

"TV for a discovery hearing? I wrapped that up last week, didn't I?" Harry pretended to fumble with the file wondering if he could muster a convincing 'Oh, what's this?' if one of them didn't wilt first. Amanda glanced between the two men, her impossibly blue eyes bright, guileless, waiting.

"Well, Judge, it isn't exactly closed," the Clerk announced at last.

Harry pretended then to find Amanda's handwritten order and turned the paper sideways to follow the precise rounded letters up the margin. "No, it isn't," he said. "In fact, I appear to have been overruled."

Amanda made a sort of giggle. "Of course not. Actually, don't blame the staff, Harry. It was my idea." She sipped. "God, this is good coffee."

Harry leaned back in his chair and waited. The silence deepened. It could only be seconds before Amanda would begin praising his china or necktie.

Instead she said with almost friendly intimacy, "Well it was Friday and you were gone." With that, she reached across and pulled the file out of his hand.

"Yes, see." She curled the page over, pretended to read, and handed it back. "It was four o'clock, four-oh-eight."

"They were going to take it up." The clerk returned to his finger. He meant the news people would have made an immediate appeal to the Supreme Court.

Amanda leaned back. "We couldn't very well tell them the Chief Judge had knocked off early." She made a conspiratorial giggle as if to say 'No, no, don't thank me, it was nothing.' She made no move to give the file back. She leaned forward and said, "They would have won, Harry. *Adkins* and *S.A.D. 79* are both on point."

Amanda was reminding him that she could speak in the lawyer's shorthand of recent court decisions, a fluency which always put the less conscientious, like Harry, at an instant disadvantage. "*S.A.D. 79*, yes of course ..." he said. He knew S.A.D. meant "School Administrative District," but he had no idea what had brought District 79 into court or whether it won or lost when it got there. Amanda did, and he knew he was about to lose another argument.

The silence rose up again. Amanda suddenly was all business. "Harry, if I've upset you, please say so. It just seemed like the best thing to do at the time."

She regarded him with rounded eyes. In the direct sunshine Harry wondered if anyone past twenty had more perfect skin, although there were just the beginnings of parallel lines descending from each side of her mouth. A small oval scar he hadn't noticed before was visible on her forehead. Chicken pox probably, and he comforted himself imagining Amanda with a pustule. She took another sip and Harry expected a new encomium on Russell's brewing skills.

"Well, I...," he began.

"Look Harry, if you like, I can just say you've recused yourself. It's not like we really disagree, now that you've had a chance to think about it." Amanda the problem-solver. Brisk, no nonsense, now. People to see, things to do.

Harry could now see red blood on the clerk's finger. "Yeah, some unexpected conflict. Avoiding the appearance of impropriety. That sort of thing." The clerk's words came just fast enough for Harry to know the two of them had already agreed on what to say.

"And I can fit it into my docket," Amanda offered. Her voice dropped. "I know how you feel about television."

Game set and match. Once the cameras were let in, they would stay in for the whole case.

"Okay." Harry said at last into the renewed silence. "But next time... Well, let's not have a next time."

"Sure, Judge. Sorry," the clerk said, relieved, not pretending to mean it. Past it now. Safe.

"You call me, right?"

"Of course, absolutely."

The clock began to chime the third quarter hour.

"Good Lord, look at the time," Amanda said making a grimace and checking her own wristwatch. She had never once let loose of the file. "I better get cracking." It was her only false note of the morning. She'd succeeded in putting herself in another high-profile case, just like she'd planned, and had more than enough time to come up with a better word than "cracking." But how could she know Harry would cave in so quickly?

Amanda stood, raised her eyebrows as if to say, 'are we done here?'

until the other judge nodded without speaking or changing expression. Amanda had been a good trial lawyer. She knew better than to hang around after she won the argument. With a parting smile she was out the door, her acolyte right behind her.

After they had left, Russell returned to catch the judge staring out the window. He pointed his head with those all-seeing eyes into the room. "Get you anything, Judge?"

"No, Russell. Thank you." Russell seemed about to say something, but he only nodded. Then Harry was alone.

◆Δ◆

BACK IN CHAMBERS after an afternoon of routine bail hearings, Harry found Grace with her coat already on.

"What you do with Fogarty?" she asked, referring to one of the defendants.

"Five thousand dollars personal recognizance."

"Sissy."

Well, he'd proved that already.

She picked up a collection of files held together by a substantial rubber band.

"Here's your homework. Remember, you've got to read the orders and listen to the depositions in the Martin case."

"Mmm." Harry took the file.

"No. Listen, this is a Zach Hannah case. He must have fifty requests for factual findings in there. If you don't do the homework you're going to look like an idiot at the hearing."

Harry wondered if any other judge's secretary spoke this way. But Grace had seen him put in extra effort on Zach's cases for years, still seeking approval from his old boss. He watched as Grace knotted a scarf under her chin. When she finished, she said, "You ready for Friday? Emma's big day?"

"Ready as I'll ever be. You know how it is with Emma. All I need to do is show up showered and shaved." That Friday would be the annual benefit dinner for the Crowninshield Museum, an event planned, arranged and managed by his wife, Emma Warren.

"See that you do. Will you be in on Friday?"

"Probably not." Harry pretended to shrink from Grace's disapproval.

"Well Miss Sm ..., Judge Stevens, is chairing a three-day conference over in Vermont. You'll have to be available for search warrants, all weekend."

Harry scowled.

"I mean it," she said, quietly serious. "Don't you know she's keeping a book on you?" Grace nodded in the direction of Amanda's chambers.

Harry put a hand on her shoulder to show that he understood.

"Of course that won't keep her away from Emma's dinner. That little snot-nose reporter from the *News & Observer* is taking her to that."

"Good night, Grace." Harry remembered seeing the reporter coming out of Amanda Steven's chambers. So *that* was who wrote the column.

"Good night m'lord."

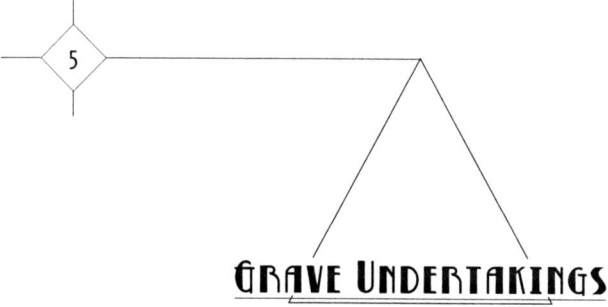

5 GRAVE UNDERTAKINGS

By November, night comes early in New Hampshire. At six p.m. it was nearly dark, and the reflected light that gleamed off the undertaker's almost perfectly bald head was wholly artificial. The bright sodium white of a street light caught the pink rounded top of his skull at a shallow downward angle causing the pea-sized mole there to cast a small shadow. The still-blinking red and white lights of the bright red emergency truck deepened the lines in his forehead and raised highlights on the bridge of his nose. The stutter of blue strobe lights from West Harbor's only police cruiser added a sinister shading to the lower half of his face, and especially the rounded soft area between his small mouth and knotted necktie where most men have a chin.

As Hadley County's least popular mortician, Lester Long, had to supplement a precarious income by serving as deputy county coroner. For two hundred fifty dollars a corpse, it was his duty to provide assistance at autopsies and it was to these preparing rooms that many of the demonstrably dead were first taken when the cause of that death was found "indeterminate," which in Hadley County meant "suspicious." A gunshot wound, perhaps, or something prominent struck in the chest. The undertaker was a serious man. Everyone called the man "Digger Long" but not to his face. Looking at him it was hard to believe he was ever young.

Of the sizeable collection of state troopers, sheriff's deputies and local police that had gathered on the neat square of asphalt that served as the funeral home parking lot, half were in blue uniforms of varying hues and designs and the rest in drab olive, though one sported a bright red coat. They were gathered between the emergency truck and the windowless one story flat-roofed addition sprawled out from the main structure, three stories of elaborate carpentry, including a mansard roof and, improbably, a widow's walk. The premises were noteworthy on the otherwise shabby and declining street for that precise and perfect maintenance that everywhere proclaims the undertaker. For those who might not have made this deduction, a white oval sign was set on a small patch of lawn, its black letters spelling out *Long's Funeral Home*. A blue-clad man was slumped against it, away from the others, as befitted a chief of police.

When a gurney emerged from the rear doors of the truck, the cops gathered around it and made its small covered burden hard to see from passing cars that slowed the traffic on West Harbor's Main Street.

The remains of the woman who Oscar Leighton had discovered were now encased in a heavy black rubberized bag. She had stiffened into sitting position at the base of the tree. After much picture taking back on the mountain, the policemen and hunters had man-handled her back up to the logging road and from there down to the rescue truck in the back of a jeep. The thing in the bag had swung and lurched back and forth between the two men who rode with it. They steadied the load but touched it as seldom as possible.

There had been strong language on the mountain when the chief had tried to lay claim to the case. 'Chief' was a somewhat elevated title since he was one of only three West Harbor policemen, if you didn't count the college kids who directed traffic and gave out occasional parking tickets during the summer. The prospects of an investigation supervised by him were obvious to all. Fortunately, since West Harbor's year round population was less than two thousand, the state police could assert their jurisdiction and this is what the new sergeant, Gregg Leavitt did. Confronted with the bland half smiles of the others, the chief had subsided into grudging silence if not surrender.

Gregg had driven to the courthouse and tried to get T.J. Carr, the county attorney, to sort all this out earlier that day but had found him tied up in sentencing a shoplifter and later storming around his office shouting about the 'panty waist' judge and how they needed a real judge in Hadley County and 'don't bother me about the damn West Harbor Chief.' So nothing had really been settled.

Gregg knew the county attorney would be at the funeral home soon and expect a report. It wouldn't be much. The woman wasn't a local. None of the local boys knew her. In fact, no one had any idea who she was. Gregg had grown up in Hadley, a small city, but a city nevertheless, whose thirty thousand people assured some level of anonymity. His two years on the job in the western part of the county with its small lakefront towns had taught him that in these towns everyone—everyone—was known, even the people from away. No one had recognized her so far, so it was safe to assume she was a stranger to the area.

Her clothes were too good and sure not the kind of clothes you'd wear for a walk in the woods. She hadn't been raped, or if she had, someone had dressed her very neat and careful afterward. She didn't have a wallet or purse on her, so she might have been robbed. But if she was, why was she still wearing jewelry? She had a hook-on holster on the waistband of her slacks for a telephone or a beeper, but it was empty. The one shoe she still had was low and brown, almost a slipper. On the sole, just forward of the heel, the name *Ferragamo* could still be seen. The thin sole had started to separate from the soft brown leather upper. A short search at the scene for the missing shoe had turned up nothing. The West Harbor Chief's suggestion that she might be from the Lake Wasoka Club had seemed promising, but a call to the club manager turned up nothing. Only two of the houses there were still occupied this late in the year and no one was missing from either.

The woman's hands were scratched and her face was marked, but it was hard to tell what had been done before death and what had been done afterwards by the birds. Hands and head, Gregg knew, were now encased in clear plastic bags.

Her white cotton blouse could have been a boy's shirt. The front was brown, almost black, with dried blood as were the top of her fitted wool pants. The size and pattern of the multiple holes in the shirt showed she'd been shot with bird shot. No hunting accident, this was deer season. Bird hunting was three weeks past, and bad as she looked, she hadn't been out there more than a few days.

The ring he'd pulled from her closed hand was now in a separate evidence bag. He'd put it in the body bag with the woman and wanted to be there when it was removed.

◆Δ◆

THE HIDDEN PASSENGER was pushed through the garage past an aged but still glistening hearse toward specially adapted doors which jerked open automatically. Behind the doors was a room filled with the stuff of nightmares. Steel tables, elevated trays with hoses, drains and unfamiliar plumbing designed for only one purpose known to all lay all around them. A second gurney at the far end of the room was piled high with what might have been laundry, but probably wasn't. The smell of formaldehyde was heavy in the air. The gurney came to rest against the first stainless steel table with loud metallic clank. Gregg heard himself take a sharp breath at this. The undertaker smiled for the first time.

An interior door on the opposite wall of the room opened with a squeal of hinges needing oil and Gregg turned to see the white-haired pathologist from Hadley Regional Hospital come into the room wearing a large olive-toned rubber apron which he was tying behind him as he walked. The police all knew him from the scenes of a hundred accidents and house fires, and the occasional killing. He was accurate, impressive and implacable. He suffered fools not at all.

"All right, if you please." The doctor and the undertaker opened the body bag and hefted the surprisingly light woman onto the table. A small evidence bag remained. The doctor looked up at Gregg.

"A ring," Gregg said softly. "She wasn't wearing it. She was holding it," he added. The group shuffled closer to hear.

"Okay, okay, everybody out except those that have to stay," the doctor said to the crowd of policemen as he set the evidence bag on a nearby counter. If they had any mind to defy him, that sentiment evaporated when T.J. Carr came through the same door the doctor had just used. As the County Attorney, T.J. was definitely one of those who could stay. In fact, he was required to be present to view the bodies in all suspicious deaths. But T.J. would have come and stayed anyway. He had paid his way through Boston College working nights and weekends at a Roxbury funeral home. He had seen and smelled and touched all the forms of death. The paraphernalia of rendering it presentable bothered him not at all.

The doctor put on gauntlet length rubber gloves and a plastic face guard like a welder's mask. The funeral director did the same. The Doctor emptied his tools out onto a smaller table and plugged the cord of a circular knife into an overhead outlet. He tested it with a sudden loud "whrrr." He placed a camera on a work counter next to the ring and set a small tape recorder down, spoke into it, played it back and, satisfied, left it running. T.J. held the woman's shoulders up while the undertaker removed the clear plastic bag from over her head. As he did so, an amber comb dropped out and her straw-colored hair fell girlishly away, the way it would have if she were getting up from the table.

Slowly, the doctor, undertaker and lawyer undressed the body which, in the warmth of the van, had begun to lose some of its rigor. With the warmth the smell began, not strong, but unmistakable. The doctor spoke continuously toward the microphone of his tape recorder throughout. "Female subject ... thirty-eight kilograms with a four-centimeter half moon pattern of contusions beneath her right breast: both breasts have been enhanced..." He stopped from time to time to take his own pictures of the hands, the pattern of small holes in her abdomen and several of her teeth as Lester Long obligingly pulled her jaw open and her cheeks back to reveal her bridgework. T.J. occasionally murmured to the doctor, peered at her abdomen, and was heard to say distinctly, "bird shot." A cake of beeswax was put far into her mouth and the jaw pushed closed and opened again, the wax removed with a sticky sucking sound.

The doctor had the undertaker hold the ring next to the woman's right hand, next to a narrow indentation at the base of her pinkie finger, and snapped a picture. Her fingernails were then scraped, clipped and bagged. Then she was quickly and expertly fingerprinted by the bald man as he hummed some unidentifiable tune.

An hour and a half of cutting, picture taking and the sounds of the pathologist's and undertaker's equipment, now whirring, now suctioning, again reduced the population of the room. Gregg had left first, feeling his empty stomach rebel. He was grateful the chief had lasted only five minutes more, departing only as the woman's large bowel was displaced with a prolonged damp flatulent sound, revealing slight but discernible movement inside. The chief had time to hear a Latin name for a parasite, a colony of which had reached "one half centimeter in length" before the door closed behind him.

As the last policeman left, the doctor winked at T.J. Even the undertaker indulged himself with another flicker of a smile as he re-bagged the woman's hands.

By leaving, the police missed the only expression of surprise to come from the white-haired doctor. It came when he turned her over. He let out a short, low whistle and pointed at three small perforations in the purple flesh of her lower left back. In one of these a pellet still lay close enough to the surface to see. The Doctor removed this one with a pair of tweezers and placed it in a separate bag.

"This woman was shot twice, Mr. Carr," he announced. "You agree?"

"Never knew a bullet to chase someone around," T.J. said. "Dig... ah, Lester, please make sure that nothin' falls out of that coat."

When they finished, the woman lay flat at last, naked, her abdomen loosely stitched back together a distinct half-moon pattern of small discolored holes running from her navel to the first of the prominent ribs. She was pale, almost parchment colored, except for her buttocks and the backs of her legs which remained liverish from accumulated blood. The doctor and lawyer leaned back against the other table, indifferent to its covered burden, and watched as the undertaker methodically began to wash the tools of his trade. "I can't understand it, T.J.," the doctor said, leaning forward to gesture toward her abdomen. "Th' shot group is too small for so little penetration. She's been shot with a shotgun and the spread of the pellets is no more than two, three inches." He held his hands that far apart. "That would indicate a discharge within ten feet at the most." The doctor then settled back against the table. He moved something underneath the sheets to make a better spot to lean on.

"Ten feet, maybe twelve," T.J. said simply. He had seen a dozen shotgun wounds in his tenure as county attorney. Accidental shootings, self-inflicted, a murder and two attempted murders. Usually, shotgun wounds were ugly cases that left large parts of the anatomy shot into pulp or just missing. Far-off shots were seldom serious, because the spread of pellets was more than a foot across, and the penetrating power of the shot dissipated quickly with distance.

"But these pellets penetrated no more than a couple of inches into the abdomen. If she hadn't been so thin, t'wouldn't've killed her," the doctor said.

T.J. considered this. "She did die of the gunshot though?"

"That, an' blood loss. Unlucky for her that tear in the mesenteric artery. Even with that, if she'd lain still, she might still 'a' lived."

T.J. shook his head dismissively. "More likely just long enough to get shot again."

The doctor shrugged and leaned back. He pointed to her feet. "There's a sprain in that ankle," he said poking at one ankle visibly swollen half again the size of the other. "From th' swellin' and th' looks o' the sole she run quite a distance with the two wounds. Then she must have felt faint. Blood loss. Just sat down, probably just thought she'd rest a while." The doctor sighed. "She died slow, but it's homicide no doubt," he said.

T.J. was an experienced prosecutor and knew the value of an unequivocal entry on the death certificate.

"Cause?" he repeated.

"Shock, exsanguination, traumatic gunshot wound to the abdomen," the doctor said with a trace of impatience. He pulled off his gloves and lifted the upraised mask off his head. Pink grooves appeared on either side of his damp forehead. He then wrote what he'd just said on a green form.

"Well thanks, Doc," T.J. said reading the entry over the doctor's shoulder.

"Are you content, Mr. Long?" The doctor turned to the undertaker, his deputy, who nodded formally, dried his hands and countersigned the green sheet of paper with the pen given him, before giving the paper to the prosecutor.

The doctor walked back to the door dropping the apron and gloves into a bin. "She'll need to be X-rayed," he said. "You'll take her to the state laboratory tonight then?"

"Of course," said the undertaker in a tone that suggested he needed no reminder.

Without anything further in the way of goodbyes the doctor left the way he had come.

"Here, let me give you a hand," T.J. said companionably to the undertaker who knew T.J. as a fellow craftsman. T.J. wanted to make amends for his earlier slip. The two began preparing the woman for the trip in the undertaker's second-best hearse, the Chevrolet, to the state forensic laboratory in Concord.

GREGG AND THE OTHERS were gathered at the still open garage door in the twilight, their camaraderie partly restored by the shared failure to stay through the ordeal indoors. There was even time for speculation on the state of Oscar Leighton's "peckah" and the probable impact this would have on Mrs. Leighton's evenings. With the right retellings, that tale could be made ready to follow Oscar for the rest of his life.

For a quarter hour, they heard rushes of water from a hose and the snapping metallic sounds of equipment being put away, some one-sided bantering conversation punctuated by the County Attorney's too-loud laughter, and finally the long cello-like sound of a heavy plastic zipper being fastened. Still, even though they knew he was coming, everyone jumped again when the automatic doors jerked opened in their halting, preternatural way, and T.J. emerged. Proud of his unflappability in the face of the unthinkable, T.J. walked over to the chief, the only one still smoking, who stood over a collection of stamped out butts.

"Give me one of those, will yeh, Chief?"

T.J. fingered the proffered cigarette appreciatively and bent over the man's cupped hand to receive a struck match. He stepped back, inhaled deeply and exhaled a cloud of smoke into the chill twilight.

"You know," he said with a satisfied grin, "Doc better be careful in there or he's gonna lose that girl."

Gregg Leavitt remembered the woman, laid open on the table, her insides gleaming in the harsh light and his stomach gave a final involuntary heave that would not be denied. He ducked and ran in a half crouch to the edge of the parking lot and vomited onto the manicured grass. The others laughed appreciatively, grateful for T.J.'s remark and already beginning to savor the times they would repeat and embellish this new story and the effect it had on the young sergeant.

"*Then y' know what T.J. said,*" they would say to appreciative anticipatory laughter.

"*Fuckin' T.J.,*" their listeners would agree as they waited for the line they'd hear a hundred or more times. "*They're gonna lose that girl.*"

But they fell silent as Gregg finished and exchanged glances, waiting for T.J. to say something more cruel and memorable.

"Don't be too hard on him," T.J. said with uncharacteristic softness. "I'm going to need all you boys tomorrow." Then more softly he said, "Chief, no more B.S. about who's runnin' this case right?"

"Well..."

"Don't screw with me, please. I've had a long day." T.J. draped his long arm around the shoulders of the crestfallen chief. "Chief," he began, his smile wide.

The chief made a noise between "Uh?" and "Yah?"

"Thank you for this cigarette."

T.J. then walked over to Gregg, pulling the green piece of paper from his shirt pocket as he did.

◆Δ◆

It was 7:45 and full dark when Gregg Leavitt finally pulled the Ford Crown Victoria police cruiser into his driveway immediately behind his wife, Angela's, parked powder blue van. Coming to a stop, he saw a stain of rust on the van, just above the exhaust pipe. Less than three years old, another year of payments, and rusting already. Leaves blew in a circular eddy of wind between the open garage and the corner of their ranch-style house.

The van's rear window proclaimed *"We Support Our State Police."* Gregg wouldn't have mounted the sticker, but Angela liked it. Angela liked everything about the police. She liked the shop talk of 'perps' and 'vics.' She used the statute numbers for crimes as verbs or nouns. To Angela a drunk driver was a '547' and a repeat offender a '547-A.' A man didn't beat his wife, he '641'ed' her. Just last week Gregg heard her ask his dispatcher, "C'n you NCIC a 547 OJ, or does it have to be a 547-A?" She meant, "Does your computer terminal score a hit on first time drunk drivers from other jurisdictions or does it only catch the repeat offenders?"

At first he thought this was cute, like everything else about the little school teacher with the turned up nose who looked so good in her summer-job EMT uniform. They'd met at Hampton Beach where all the young troopers picked up overtime—and whatever else that came along. Angela was part of that small but loyal minority of girls who liked the cops. And girls who liked cops liked troopers best of all. He enjoyed the challenging way Angela had tagged him out when they'd played softball, the way she didn't talk dirty like the waitress he'd been dating. He liked the shine of her hair and the soap and water smell to her. Angela kept her mouth shut and knew to listen quietly when shop talk was going on. The other guys liked her too. She was too good to be true. At first.

When Gregg married Angela, he'd been the envy of the barracks. This was a girl who knew the score, the older men said. "No pissin' and moanin' over you out pulling double shifts on holidays." Even after they were married, six months pregnant and still flirting harmlessly with the older troopers, she fit right in, happy with the life, happy with him.

But slowly, lovingly, Angela acquired more and more of the terminology and used it with more and more assurance. Right after the baby was born the sticker had appeared. Now the troopers, even his Uncle Russell, retired from the Hadley Police and working as a bailiff at the county court, kidded him about it.

Gregg pushed through the side door, directly into the kitchen and surprised his daughter, Erin, at play with an empty milk carton. She drew herself up to her full two and a half feet and waddled over to him, arms out, smiling, a plume of yellow snot hanging from one nostril. Erin's high color signaled a fever and Gregg resigned himself to yet another cold. It would be the third or fourth that year. He'd lost count.

"Hi Erin-bee," he said, raising her to his shoulder taking in the combined smells of cough medicine, sour milk barf and urine. A trickle of moisture traced the inside of one leg of her snap-away pants. Well, after getting sick on Lester Long's lawn he supposed he didn't smell like roses. "Dadee," she said softly, moving a finger toward her nostril. Gregg got a napkin from the counter and wiped her face. She squirmed but submitted. Then, exhausted, she laid her warm head on his shoulder.

Angela, came into the kitchen preceded by an enormous belly over which a jersey knit shirt proclaimed "I should have danced all night." Gregg threw the napkin in the trash. Angela kissed him, retrieving Erin, who protested momentarily before subsiding onto Angela's newly capacious breasts. Erin's legs settled on either side of the protuberant mound that contained her brother to be, as mother and child sat at the kitchen table.

"Anything more on that 615 on Green Mountain?" Angela asked.

Gregg knew he had let her habit go on far too long to say anything about it now, at least not while Angela was pregnant, so he just said "Nope," and opened the refrigerator. He took a can of beer, popped the top and had a long swallow. Then he said, "We sent the prints down to Washington."

Angela knew that the computers there contained fingerprints for most of the country and that there was a fair chance they'd reveal the identity of the mystery woman, eventually. "What will that take? 24 hours?"

"I don't know, it could take a week. All we can do is wait." Then, Gregg said, to fill the silence, "She might not be American." He put the beer down and made to reach for his daughter.

"She's got a cold, I'll hold her." Angela said warning him, now too late, away from Erin. "Strange, no one's come forward. No 345?" She used the form number, not the statute, for a missing person report.

"Tell me about it," Gregg said. "Strange she's got no ID. Strange she's been shot, twice. Strange she's sitting under a tree up in the middle of east goddamn nowhere," he said with sudden vehemence that surprised him.

Angela frowned and glanced at Erin. "You're starting to sound like T.J. Carr."

"Him I've had enough of," Gregg said, taking a second long swallow.

"Then don't talk like him."

"Sorry."

"In front of Erin," she added unnecessarily. Erin, her thumb now deep in her mouth moved only her eyes in her father's direction, conscious a rebuke had been delivered, but unsure whether to sympathize or join in.

A longer silence followed. Gregg stretched and drank his beer while Angela rocked the child. Each looked into a space before them. Gregg tried to think how to restart the conversation. He supposed Angela did too.

"You hear anything?" Angela asked at last, returning to the subject that was uppermost in their minds, one that had nothing to do with the '615.'

"No, Angela." He raised the can to his lips but stopped.

"Doesn't the process have an end? It's been more than a month since the interview," she said.

Like it was his fault. "Twenty-seven goddamn days," he said. He took a long swallow of beer as Angela arched her eyebrows at him and scowled again. He started to say 'Perhaps I could give it a number,' but thought better of it. He gazed around the kitchen. Two of Erin's scrawled pictures were held on the refrigerator door with magnets. The sink was half filled with dishes. The faint numbing of a single beer settled over him.

He knew he had no right to criticize Angela. She had as much riding on this as he did. It was their ticket out of Hadley, back to Concord, the state capital. If he screwed this case up she would pay the same price.

They had been in this house for three years now and it was starting to look permanent. The first couple of years with Angela teaching, it seemed like they had plenty of money. Then the baby came. Angela stopped working, but the car payment, the mortgage, the credit card balances that seemed to creep up month after month, they went on. Angela couldn't go back to teaching until next September. And then, there would be day care.

The 'interview' Angela spoke of was for chief of the governor's security detail. Promotion to lieutenant, and most of all, a move to the center of things: regular meetings with the Attorney General, being first-named by people who mattered. Royalty. The visibility would leap-frog Gregg into the upper echelons of the department in one jump. But his interview had been four weeks ago tomorrow. He thought it had gone well, but then he'd heard there had been other interviews. He'd played and replayed the questions and answers over and over in his head. The governor, oddly different from how she looked and sounded on television, reminded him of his favorite teacher in grammar school. She shook hands like a man. She let her chief of staff ask the preliminary questions before taking over the questions for herself. The chief of staff, a pale little man who needed a shave, had taken notes and gave Gregg nothing but a skeptical smile and a wet handshake when the interview was over. Since then, silence.

The wall phone rang and Angela looked at him.

He shook his head from side to side. The last thing he needed now was to go out to pull some drunk off his girlfriend, especially with the better part of a beer in him.

Angela waddled to the phone. "Six-thirty, it's probably mother." She meant his mother and her voice was not enthusiastic.

"Hello," she said into the receiver. She listened for an interval, then said, "Just a moment please. I think he's driving up." She put her hand over the mouthpiece and said, "Speak of the devil."

"My mother?"

Angela scowled. "No, T.J."

She handed the phone toward him. Resigned, he got up and took it. They both knew that T.J. Carr would keep calling until he got an answer. Gregg crumpled the can.

"Hello?"

"You got the area search laid on?"

"Uh huh, we'll meet at the barracks at six-thirty and drive up the back of the mountain at first light."

"How many people you got?"

"Thirty, counting the trainees."

T.J. fell silent on the phone.

"Is there anything...." Gregg started to say.

"You okay? You gonna be okay?"

"What..."

"Cause if you aren't, let me know. All I got to do is call Capital Crimes and they'll send a team."

Gregg didn't like what that would do to his chances with the governor. Word would spread and one or another of the other applicants would pass on to that little prick chief of staff that he'd been "pulled off" a major case.

"No, no... ah, we're fine."

"You're sure kid? No hard feelings."

"No, I'd..." Gregg breathed deeply. "I'd really like to keep going on this."

"The governor doesn't have to know."

Gregg could hear the cruel smile in T.J.'s voice. It was the same tone he'd used when he said 'he's gonna lose that girl.'

"Uh huh," he said hearing a waver in his own. Angela, sensing something, looked at him with alarm. He turned toward the wall. "Is there anything else?" He wanted to sound firm.

"Relax, relax," T.J. said. Just find me something, will ya? We'll talk about it tomorrow."

Hanging up the phone, Gregg turned to Angela. "T.J. knows about the governor."

"Damn it," Angela said, her lips compressed.

"Dm" said Erin.

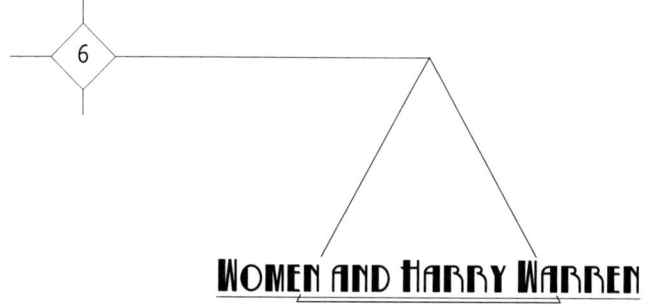

6

WOMEN AND HARRY WARREN

That same evening Harry Warren was savoring his wine while he considered how women had always played a much larger role in his life than men ever had. First there was his mother, Barbara Warren, the poet. Close companions through most of his childhood in Hadley, New Hampshire, Barbara and Harry had been forced together to contend with the impossible mood swings of his remote and alcoholic father in the zero-sum game of family intimacy. His father's death in an automobile accident, more ambiguous than tragic, had occurred just as this behavior was becoming unbearable and just as Barbara began to achieve prominence as a poet. Prominence was perhaps too strong a word. Having abandoned rhyme, no American poet had been widely celebrated for a generation. Still, although Barbara hadn't published anything for years, not since *Aisle of Sorrows*, new acquaintances would occasionally ask Harry when they met: "Any relation to Barbara Warren? The poet?" But that was outside of Hadley. In Harry's home town, the real question was whether his father had killed himself.

Perhaps as a reaction to his own unhappy childhood, Harry had become closer than most fathers are to his own two daughters, Leigh and Samantha, now grown women in their twenties. This was not easy. They were Llewellyns after all, Philadelphia Llewellyns at that. Life's rough edges had been regularly smoothed away for them, though even they experienced occasional disappointment. As Llewellyns, losing at anything was rare and particularly painful. At times like that, they turned to their father. Within the family no one knew how to lose better than Harry.

But of course the real mainstay of his daughters' lives, and his, was *their* mother, Emma Warren: Emma *Llewellyn* Warren, Harry's wife of nearly thirty years, whose candle-lit profile was now less than a yard away.

Subdued by his disappointing day in court, Harry was content to spend a late dinner observing as Emma alternately listened and spoke with that level of self-assurance and casual cruelty that only sisters can share. On this night the sister in question was Olivia 'Livy' Llewellyn, who was bringing the exiled Emma up to date on their old Philadelphia friends. The two hadn't been together since a family wedding the previous spring and a second bottle of wine had them laughing and saying things that, while profoundly felt, would never find voice outside the family.

Both women now set reading glasses on their classic profiles to cut their food, the frames resting at the same spot on the straight bridge of each sister's nose. They held their forks at the same angle and the motion each made from plate to lips was identical, a habit they'd acquired as girls from the same nanny. To Harry at the head of the table, they looked like two actors pantomiming a reflection. When listening, Emma's face acquired vertical lines of concentration about the eyes and mouth, an expression Harry recognized from the times she cleaned a painting, repaired a table leg, or ran her fingers over a gouge in a Georgian high-boy—whenever serious business was at hand: like, who was up or down, in or out, in the Llewellyns' tiny, gorgeous world.

Livy Llewellyn had two reasons for this rare visit to New Hampshire. The first was to arrange for an interview for her son, Carter, at the Devon School, Harry's alma matter. The second was to help her sister with the upcoming benefactors' dinner for the Crowninshield Collection in Windsor, New Hampshire's small but well-regarded art museum. Emma, as chairman of its board of directors, was responsible for the annual fête. Emma, confident and kind with children and animals, generous if distant with employees, competitive but scrupulous at any sport—where she always excelled—Emma succeeded at everything. Despite this, Emma hated being the focus of attention and particularly hated speaking in public. She would have to endure both at this year's dinner.

Harry had never understood how Emma had become so competent on the one hand and so self-conscious on the other. She certainly got no guidance from her distant, preoccupied father, L.L. Llewellyn. He spent her childhood multiplying the Llewellyn millions that *his* father left him. As for Emma's mother, Penelope 'Pippi' Newbold Llewellyn, she had seldom been sober enough to give anyone advice, if she had any she wanted to give.

Whatever the cause, Emma's tension had been mounting for weeks and it was up to him to console her. Harry knew that whatever he did as a jurist, his real job was as consort for this beautiful woman he fooled into marrying him when she was young. To disappoint Emma Warren was a dangerous thing. Emma's cold anger of an hour earlier had reminded him just how dangerous, though then it was directed at her sister.

"I just can't believe Livy. She puts Carter on a plane to Philadelphia and proceeds to go to the Burgoyne with this, this *guy* and calls me as soon as I got back because he's *dumped* her there. I literally had to run down and fetch her from the parking lot." The Burgoyne was an old motel widely known as a place that catered to short if meaningful relationships.

"He dumped her there?"

"She *says* he had to get back... oh, yah, here's the good part, he's an advisor at Devon. Screwing one of Carter's teachers after a school visit! I just don't...uhh!" Emma threw up her hands.

Hearing this, Harry's first thought was that his rather dim nephew, Carter Belanguer, only offspring of Livy and her polo-playing second husband, Eduardo, would be grateful for the assurance of at least one passing grade, no matter how it was earned, but it was not the moment to share this insight with Emma. Nor was it the time to remind her of her sister's reputation.

Emma Warren. Good, decent, honest, and—despite her exasperated expression—still beautiful Emma. She would never understand her older sister. Though both sisters shared the same well-scrubbed, fresh-from-the-playing-field looks and belonged to the same Alpha sorority, an institution known for well brought up daughters of successful fathers, 'Livy' Llewellyn had never played the part. In fact, she had been famously promiscuous at Penn, the college all three attended. Harry had known Livy in those days. More accurately, he had known of her. He knew she had slept with four members of his fraternity and perhaps more in just the two years their college careers overlapped, something Emma would never have done. But Livy was five years older than Emma and had graduated before Emma arrived.

Livy hadn't changed, would never change, would certainly never measure up to Emma's cheerfully absolute standards. But then, relations between sisters are things of permanence. One didn't discard a sister. Husbands were something different.

"Warren, you're staring," Livy said. Her tone reminded Harry that she cared for him now no more than when they were undergraduates—Harry had never enjoyed her favors. She never had, never would, approve her sister's curious choice of a husband.

"I've got Penn's most beautiful Alphas sitting at my table. Of course I'm staring." Harry hoped that the mention of the sorority would soften his sister-in-law's disapproval, if only for a moment.

"Oh, nice try Warren," Livy said, but threw him something like a smile. It was true, they were still beautiful, and he had them to himself.

Then Livy changed the subject. "How old were you when you went to Devon, Harry?"

"Sixteen. I was there from sixteen to eighteen," Harry said.

"Do you think Carter will like it? He's fourteen, but a jock, like Emma." There was a certain reverse logic to this, so Harry nodded. He was never a jock, and his two years at the Devon School had not been happy. Harry pretended to pour the last drops from the now empty bottle, a silent plea for more. This met with Emma's equally silent disapproval, but she went to the kitchen for more.

OLIVIA LEANED BACK and stared into the fireplace where three logs were burning. She was a slightly more delicate and, truth be told, more striking version of Emma. When Harry first caught sight of her on Locust Walk thirty years earlier, Livy had the same reddish gold hair her younger sister still wore. However, Livy had since adopted the carefully simple waves of mixed yellow and grey that come from twice a month visits to hairdressers with names like Roger or Karl.

Dangerously, he remembered how Ephne had called her own treatment 'three-color rich-girl's hair,' and how once, in an unguarded moment, Harry had told her she looked exactly like his sister-in-law from behind. Ephne hadn't minded. She enjoyed any successful imposture, especially her own.

And there could never be any doubt that Livy Llewellyn was a 'rich girl.' She and Emma had been born to riches beyond the dreams of avarice. It would have struck neither of them as strange or even noteworthy that the table at which they sat had cost more than the State of New Hampshire paid Harry for a year of judging. No more than it would have occurred to either to ask Harry the size of his salary or care what it was. Though they postured at self-sufficiency early in their marriage, the Warrens really lived off Emma's money. Harry had come to think of his salary as a sort of allowance.

Like most people without money, Harry had silently contented himself in youth with the folklore that the Livy Llewellyns of this world would one day get their comeuppance. In this, as in so many other things, he couldn't have been more wrong. In middle age, Livy had retained her looks, and in the little world of horses and horse people, her reputation as a rider was favorable and wide. Her three marriages may have been failures but no one had humiliated her with either their, or her, infidelities. There was even a strange equivalence between Livy's horses and Emma's work at the Crowninshield. Both activities were considered suitably decorative by the hard, successful people who could indulge in either.

"So, how did you get Tee ... excuse me, 'Ted' Ingersoll to speak at Emma's dinner?" Livy's voice intruded into his thoughts.

Harry knew that Livy was not overly impressed with the prospect. Like Harry, she had known Tee, or 'Ted' Ingersoll as the nation now knew him, before he was famous.

"I didn't. Someone on the board called him."

"I'll bet Emma was thrilled with that." Emma, Livy knew, disliked Tee Ingersoll very much indeed.

"She was able to contain her joy."

"Harry, you roomed with him, right?"

"Freshman year."

"What a pair." Livy was smiling broadly at him now. She could always do this to him, bring him back to what it was like to stand on the edges of a party in a borrowed dinner jacket, nervously fingering the pasteboard invitation in his pocket, wondering if someone was going to ask him to leave.

"We got along very well," Harry said.

"I never saw you two together."

"He was in St. Mike's by the time you got to Penn. I was in Phi Psi." Harry tried to bring them back to the present. "He'll be a big draw. I know its not your thing, Livy, but he's the biggest thing on PBS these days."

"And to think," Livy said, "back then we had to listen to him for free."

EMMA RETURNED FROM the kitchen then, followed by a young woman, bottle in hand. She poured for Emma and got only a little more in the glass than on the table. This seemed to discourage her so she set the bottle down and left. She was a good cook, but there were some things even Emma hadn't been able to teach her. Emma raised her eyebrows as she left and Livy shrugged back. Despite the exchange of glances, the two said nothing further. There were some subjects best not discussed within hearing of the help, or poor relations.

But when she received the bottle from Emma, Livy turned boisterous and convivial. "Hey, what about Blondie the judge."

Emma explained: "Olivia saw Amanda on TV this afternoon."

"Sure. Emma sent me to my room, so I watched the local news. I don't know, Emma. She looked pretty hot to me." Olivia ogled Harry over her glass. "You know what they say, 'Big hair, big time.'" She laughed softly, taking in his wordless discomfort as she took a long drink. He had never thought of Amanda's hair that way.

"You think her hair is—big?"

"Well ... elaborate," Olivia said at last. Livy and Emma then giggled together in a deep-throated conspiratorial way. One sister might be a tramp and the other a paragon, but these differences shrunk to nothing in the face of a poor grooming choice. Livy curled one leg underneath her and pushed back her chair and leered. She liked to get under Harry's skin.

"I thought you were doing that case," Emma said.

He shook his head 'no,' then recklessly asked, "Did I get any calls?"

"No," Emma said, "I told you." Then, "You were expecting someone?"

"Ah, no."

"I told you, when I got home the answering machine was filled. Policemen leaving messages, and that prosecutor, D.J."

"T.J.," Harry said.

"Okay, him, the big ugly one. Honestly Harry, I don't know why you installed the thing if you're never going to answer it."

Harry was befuddled enough now to forget, to get himself into trouble, so he shook his head again to say 'no' and settled into silence, deciding to let the Llewellyn sisters get back to their talk about old friends. They had been lonely for one another and were happy in their talk and memories. Soft firelight dappled the room and gleamed back from the surface of a two hundred-year-old table onto the faces of these two, still striking, women.

"My darlings," he said. "I'm off to bed."

IN THE DARKNESS Harry came awake as Emma slid into the bed beside him. She molded herself against his back and, wordlessly, he took her hand.

"I'm sorry I woke you," she whispered.

"What time..."

"After one. Livy caught her second wind. She's got a new fella."

"You don't mean..."

After a pause Emma yawned and said, "No, someone in Florida. Wellington." Harry made a 'mmmh' sound of gentle disapproval at the mention of the town where Livy kept her horses.

"Another horse guy," Emma said.

Harry pretended to pull the covers over his eyes. The break-up with Eduardo had been a trauma for them all.

"Harry?"

"Mmmh?"

"I don't know, it's just that I don't tell you often enough how important you are. I couldn't stand to live like Livy. All her men, and her men with all their women."

Emma yawned again. "I just know you're always there for me." The words came out as part of a sigh and she tightened her hold and fell silent, her breathing becoming regular, then deeper. Harry heard it all, eyes opening as she spoke. Well, he had got away with it. That was close to innocence, surely.

◆△◆

INFIDELITY NEVER PLAYED much of a part in either of the two marriages important to Harry Warren. For all of his parents' unhappiness with each other, there was never a hint that either of them had sought solace elsewhere, and their antagonisms had been so freely expressed it was unlikely he wouldn't have heard about adultery if it had occurred. Years later, his mother Barbara affirmed her own virtue. "Never, darling. Not once. Your father was quite dashing in England. By the time we got to Hadley, well, he wasn't dashing any more, but no one else was even remotely interesting. It was not a stern test of virtue."

Emma stirred beside him, shifting on to her back. Gently, she began to snore.

In the first twenty years after Harry's vows, he had slept with one and only one woman. In the early days, at least, Emma had been an enthusiastic lover and she remained a considerate one. She was so obviously too good for him, that the prospect of looking for something else simply didn't come up. Not that Harry had that many opportunities, but he didn't look for them either. So much of virtue is simple inertia. In adultery as in so many things, a man had to make his own luck.

Harry told himself he would have remained faithful, even up to this moment next to his softly snoring wife, if only he hadn't been dragooned into the twenty-third annual National Judicial Conference on the Unified Expert Evidence Code (non-medical) being held that year in Atlantic City. He'd resisted, he claimed prior commitments, he feigned illness, but it did no good. Ordered to go to the conference, Harry found himself spending a gray, rain-swept Thursday afternoon in March with fifty other judges in a conference room of an Atlantic City Hotel that looked—*tried* to look—like a large bordello, listening to a presentation: *Codifying Qualification of Expert Witnesses: A National Solution.*

Harry slid out a back door at the first break to see what the surrounding city had to offer. That March day, it wasn't much. No one at Penn ever went that far north on the shore in the days before gambling, so he knew almost nothing about Atlantic City. An hour's walk through the raw ocean air left him shuddering and taught him only that the streets really were the same as the ones in Monopoly. There was nothing to do but return to duty. If it had been ten degrees warmer in Atlantic city that afternoon, Harry never would have met Ephne Newsome.

Harry knew, slightly, two judges from Maine, both earnest and conscientious men who looked as though a 'national solution' to witness qualification would be the answer to their fondest prayers. They sat at the front of the hall attentively taking notes. As he took a seat next to them, Harry saw that a new panel was now on stage.

"*An expert,*" Zach Hannah, always said, "*is a guy with a suit, a briefcase and shined shoes who's more than fifty miles from home.*" Not a bad summary and at least as good as New Hampshire's common law standard: "*A person whose professional, vocational or occupational training, knowledge and experience, is likely to assist a fact-finder of ordinary understanding to resolve a factual dispute.*" Well.

This panel's mission was to discuss whether some kind of National Registry would help establish 'unified criteria' for who was and who wasn't an expert on autographs and handwriting. Utter foolishness, of course. The real definition of 'expert' in Harry's court, and everyone else's, was whoever the judge wanted to listen to. He could always find a reason.

On stage were the obligatory clever Brit, and two older law professors with bad comb-overs and numerous degrees from down-market mid-western law schools. There was also a small, boyish but well-tended blonde woman in a pale blue suit.

The young woman in blue was herself an 'expert' on 'maker's marks' and 'artifact authentication.' She limited her comments to signed furniture or paintings. Harry knew a little about this sort of thing from Emma, but this woman was a pro. She had testified recently, apparently to great effect, in an antiques fraud case that a clutch of judges from New Jersey and Pennsylvania kept referring to in their questions. Her resume blurb showed that she had graduated from Penn State, had a Boston University MFA and belonged to something called the American Society of Antiquarians and Authenticators. She had that Alpha look, almost. Her hair was cut and colored to look like she just left field hockey practice. Still, she had an edge to her voice that Emma never would have shown and didn't hesitate to contradict the others when they got into her area. Harry saw with interest that she worked for Wharton Biddle, the big Philadelphia law firm that the Llewellyns used. Her name was Ephne Newsome.

During the second afternoon break she stood and yawned. When she stretched she didn't look quite so boyish. Harry was appreciating this when she caught him watching in mid-stretch. She smiled and shrugged, and Harry made a smile of apology in return, the old judge flirting with the pretty girl.

There was a cocktail reception at five, free drinks in a plastic glass. Bored to numbness by the book he'd brought, Harry wandered down to the reception to find the usual crowd of judges, law clerks and spouses. It was still mostly judges' wives in those days, though the occasional judicial husband was even then beginning to appear. The two law professors from that afternoon were enjoying their moment in the sun with that year's crop of judges assigned to 'host' the Conference. Later, the professors would author the inevitable Draft Report that would become a footnote-laden, unreadable article in the *Drake Law Review* or the *Minnesota Law Journal*. This prospect had rendered them giddy with heavy gaiety.

Harry saw the guys from Maine and had decided to invite himself to dinner with them when a voice said, "Judge Warren?"

He turned to see the yellow-haired field hockey player from that afternoon. He hadn't worn his name tag and looked down at his vest pocket. "Guilty," he said, and smiled foolishly, pleased like any middle-aged guy would be when a younger woman shows a little interest.

She gave an obligatory turn of the lips, almost a smile, but no more than that. Up close her effect was different from the stage. She looked tired, the patches of skin under her dark blue, almost purple eyes were shadowed with fatigue. There was the faint heaviness of tobacco smoke about her, and the beginnings of vertical lines were etched in her face. For all this she was a very good-looking woman, past first bloom, but enjoying a second season. A piece of lace intersected with the beginning of cleavage between the lapels of the suit. The hair and suit were Alpha but not the blouse. She held one hip slightly forward. Just the faintest breath of sex.

"I was curious, are you any relation to Emma Warren?" she asked.

"My bride," Harry said. He felt a frisson of disappointment. Role change, the worthy spouse—out of the running for this one.

"I thought I'd take a chance," she said. "Such a great story. That business with the Corots in the basement of that little museum you have, the Crown-and-something?"

"The Crowninshield," he said, "and one is still only 'attributed' to Corot."

"Oh they're real," she said, being bumped just then by a fat, white-haired judge used to having people step aside for him. She glared at him momentarily, the way a child would. Then, as if she hadn't been interrupted, she asked, "Tell me, did she know right away?" She referred to Emma's find of a cache of unattributed impressionist paintings in the museum vaults.

He decided then, for strangers, they were standing much too close together. It was the only way they could hear one another over the babble of the crowd, but his reluctance to move away had little to do with that. "I think so. You seem to know all about Emma," he said.

"No, just the paintings. Everyone's dream, you know, to turn over a dusty frame and find a Vermeer."

'Not exactly that," Harry said.

"Oh, two Corots will do."

"They certainly did wonders for the Crowninshield."

"I'll bet."

She looked around then, as if for someone else, and Harry expected her to tell him then how nice it had been to meet him and then head back into the crowd. What she said was, "Buy a girl a drink?"

"Why sure." But she hadn't meant it as a question and was already turning away to walk out of the function room. They settled in a dark lounge where, since they charged for drinks, privacy was assured.

In his adult life Harry had been spared the regular company of drunken female companions. Emma never misbehaved. Ephne Newsome was a different matter altogether. She drank a great deal and did so quickly, almost hungrily.

As she did, she became talkative, and in short order he learned that she had been adopted and had still been at BU, unable to find a decent job in the art business, when the story of Emma's find had come out. For Ephne Newsome, Emma Warren's find was high adventure, but of course she had never had a moment like that. Ephne had gone back to Pennsylvania to work at a variety of jobs in Philadelphia before she'd finally been taken on as a paralegal at Wharton Biddle. At first, she arranged authentications for them. Later, she started doing them herself.

"The hell of it is that you can do just so much. Test the wood, get a spectrograph of the paint. X-rays. Cross-check the provenance. But eventually you have to guess." She moved ice around her glass with a finger.

"And of course you always say just that from the witness stand."

She smiled and winked as she played with her drink.

"So, tell me Judge. What brought you to Penn?"

"Wholly attributable to the short-sightedness of the Yale Admissions Office." Harry was keeping up with her and said this with an expansive gesture that almost knocked his glass over. He didn't remember telling her he had gone to Penn.

"I would have liked Penn," she said.

"Why didn't you go?"

"Money. Money and the idea of commuting into town from West Chester every day. No, the idea of commuting back each night." West Chester. Her Alpha appearance, then, as he had guessed, came later.

Dinner turned into successive dishes of nuts and even a couple of cigarettes, a guilty pleasure he hadn't indulged in in years.

Like everyone who grew up around Philadelphia, Ephne Newsome had heard of the Llewellyns and like everyone who had worked at Wharton Biddle, the Philadelphia law firm that catered most of all to the city's old families, she knew more about them than most.

"So Harry"—'Judge' had disappeared with the third martini—"what made you decide to practice up in zip code ee-yi-ee-yi–oh?" And now she gave him the full benefit of the violet eyes. She sucked out a pimento, then nibbled around the edges of the flesh of the olive. One of her incisors was slightly offset, but her teeth were bright white for a smoker.

"I knew I could never make it in a place like Wharton Biddle," Harry said, looking again at the bit of lace.

"C'mon, you went to Penn Law." She bent forward and reached for some almonds revealing more lace. Then she said "And..." giving him a conspiratorial smile.

"The son-in-law factor," Harry said.

"In the tradition of all good Philadelphia lawyers, a little nepotism never hurts."

"True, but you never lose your amateur status," Harry said. "There are some things in-laws aren't supposed to know and I wasn't, I'm not, not strenuous enough to carve out a practice area."

"What a nice word for lazy." She returned to her last olive.

"Oh yeah. All the vices. I smoke too," Harry reached again for her pack of Parliaments.

"I don't want to lead you astray." She struck a match and let him hold her wrist while he took a light. He felt her pulse under his thumb. They shared a look then but pretended they hadn't.

Then she said, "No, I do understand you wanting to go back to New Hampshire. It's beautiful there. I went to camp on Lake Wasoka."

"I can see Lake Wasoka from my house." Harry coughed, still unused to the smoke. "What camp?"

"Camp Abenaki. It's Indian for 'Philadelphia in the Pines.'"

They laughed together, too loud at this tiredest of Philadelphia jokes.

"My oldest daughter went there, before it closed. Same joke. My wife too." He noticed he had said 'my wife,' not 'Emma'.

"And no doubt to St. Agatha's," Ephne said. "Llewellyn Hall, Llewellyn Lodge."

"No, Emma went to Miss Porters but her sister Livy went to St. Agatha's. You seem to know a lot about these places, Ephne."

"You're right, Harry," —she gave his name an ironic emphasis in response to his first use of hers— "I was at St. Agatha's for a year. When you lose something, when it's taken away from you, you remember every crack and crevice." She began to play with a small signet ring on the small finger of her right hand. "You ever lose anything, you'll remember it too." She put the glass up to her lips and drained it. She waved at the waiter, got his attention, then asked Harry with her eyes if he wanted another. "Sure," he said. She made a small circle over the glasses.

"Sorry," she said turning back to Harry, "No more speeches."

They left the bar an hour and three drinks later. The sensible thing to do was to leave her at the elevator door, the old guy, past it, no hard feelings, no confrontation. Of course by this time, Harry was well past sensible.

Unsteady, they leaned briefly against one another as they walked into the elevator. After riding to her floor Harry walked her down the hall to her room. She said nothing after they left the elevator, just went to her room, opened the door with a card and without looking behind her and walked in. The door began to swing close.

Then Harry put his hand out. He walked in and let the door bang shut behind him. She still didn't speak, just took off her earrings and then the jacket of her suit which she tossed on one of two large beds, giving him a lopsided smile as she did so.

Then she walked over to him and they stood hip to hip for a moment. She put her hands behind his neck and moved against him. They kissed.

"I guess you *have* decided," she said.

Harry later told himself he hadn't gone looking for this. Sober, he might have let the door swing closed, or held it just long enough to say "Well, goodnight, Miss Newsome." But of course he wanted her, or someone like her, and had for a long time.

In bed she could not have been less like Emma. She was small, insistent and quick in her movements and they fell apart in their excitement twice before he grabbed her to steady her as much as anything else while he pushed to a gasping, solitary finish.

Spent, Harry began to roll off but she turned him all the way over and put him back inside her. While she moved she inflicted a series of pinches and scratches, her ribs showing as she rubbed and strained. She bit, then tickled, always moving this way, then that. When Harry began to recover some initiative, she teased and taunted him.

"C'mon, c'mon," she said in an insistent, imperative tone, letting him know he was going to have to do better than that.

Drunk as he was, Harry thought he had risen rather well to the occasion already and didn't take to suggestions to the contrary. Her frank insistence was a challenge and he began to assert himself. But she was well beyond submission by then.

The next ten minutes were as close as Harry had ever come to having a fight with a woman. It started with fending off her hands, or more accurately, trying to. He found that only by grasping a wrist or elbow could he get any respite. She didn't like being restrained and jerked free one moment laughing, the next almost angry. They shoved and writhed with each other with selfish intensity, each giving only seconds of satisfaction before pushing to the top of the other. The kisses they exchanged now were more like bites. In the half light he could see she had blood on her chin, hers or his, he didn't know—or care. Their breathing became heavy and regular, but more from effort than anything that could be called passion. They fought on, their hoarse panting punctuated by involuntary cries of surprised sensation.

Finally, she got her way long enough for her breathing to change into a series of deep groans that were part response, part announcement.

"*Uhh, uhhh... Oh... Uhh.*" She relaxed enough at this for Harry to turn her over and have his own selfish moment of noisy affirmation. Whatever else, this was his alone. He didn't need, didn't seek, the approval of any Llewellyn. The girl received these last exertions with less energy, but willingly, like a winning runner welcoming the also-ran across the finish line.

Harry collapsed on her and lay damp and gasping until she pushed him up by the shoulders. If she wanted to go on he knew he was now beyond trying. But her need had changed by then and she only smiled shyly and said, "Truce?"

"Truce," he agreed.

If that had been the extent of his sin, a sordid, drunken twenty minutes of rough sex with a stranger, it might have come to nothing. But they fell asleep then. At some point they awoke in the dark, loved again, and slept some more. By morning what they did was much gentler, something like love.

After this, they lay on their backs. Wordlessly, she lit and shared her last cigarette. Grey light was coming through a crevice in the curtains. Perspiration stood in tiny droplets on either side of her nose.

She inhaled deeply, blowing a plume up in the air only after holding it in for maximum effect.

"You going..." She cleared her throat and laughed at herself. "God, I sound like Barry White." She cleared it once more and tried again. "You going to more classes?" But her voice remained in full contralto.

Harry tried not to laugh. She pushed him. "Oh, now its funny," she said.

"Well you can't be that, ah, vocal, and expect to sound like Buttercup."

"You weren't exactly quiet," she said taking back the cigarette.

"People will say we're in love."

She grew silent at this and took another drag. "You want any more of this?" she asked. Harry misunderstood, but then saw she meant the cigarette. He shook his head and she crushed the remains of the cigarette out in the tiny hotel ashtray.

"Well?" she said at last.

"Well??"

"Well, whaddaya thinkin?" She tried to hide her concern behind the Philly streetwalker enunciation.

"I think the people in the next room have renewed their faith in the myth of the simultaneous orgasm."

"Only if they can't count." She smiled happily, but seemed almost immediately saddened.

"I don't know what to think," Harry said to the ceiling, letting her know he was willing to talk seriously.

They turned and looked at each other for what seemed a long time, then leaned toward one another only brushing their swollen lips.

"You can go," she said then, eyes steady. "Just go. You know that, don't you?"

"No. I know I can't do that."

The violet eyes blinked and acquired a shine. "You too?" she said. "I was sure you were smarter than that."

"Yah. Me too," he said.

◆△◆

AFFAIR, AN OLD-FASHIONED word. In later years, when he thought of it, Harry knew he had an affair with Ephne Newsome. It consisted of that night, the next, and the day between. Then there were two other weekends and the promise of a third. There were ten, perhaps a dozen telephone calls and one letter from her to him. Perhaps a hundred hours in one another's company—a hundred and twenty at most. They made love no more than a dozen times.

"When did you know?" she asked during their next meeting.

"For sure? For sure, when you saw the mimes on the boardwalk. You clapped your hands and did a little skip step." This conversation took place three weeks later over dinner at Cornflowers, a white clapboard Connecticut inn with a half dozen dependent bungalows. The night and part of the next day were still ahead of them.

In the dim light of the mostly empty dining room she seemed to gain color. "And you?" he asked.

"Oh that's easy. Right after the second fuck." She was buttering a roll as she said this but looked up and then around. A woman three tables away stared back frankly. Ephne hunched her shoulders in mock alarm, then broke into a smile as she whispered, "Sorry, that came out louder than I meant. You should see your face."

"It's just that I thought the first one was pretty good."

She chewed her piece of roll, set the remainder down and leaned forward. "Oh, it was fine, but in a 'race-to-the-finish-line' kind of way."

"Funny, I thought of it the same way."

"Which, I won if I remember correctly," Ephne said finishing the small roll with a single bite, smiling as she chewed.

After dinner came she returned to her subject. "No, it was the second time. You were so gentle. I never had anyone call me 'my darling.' Well, not just then."

Harry took her hand. "Love then."

"You bet."

It was during those hundred or so hours that Harry told her everything. Barbara, his father, Devon and Penn, and Zach and Tee, even the Army.

"You *roomed* with Ted Ingersoll?" She called him by the stage name. "Is he really that smooth?"

"He was the same at seventeen as he is today. A little thinner, we all called him 'Tee.'"

She turned thoughtful. "So I guess those stories about him…"

The sharpness in his voice surprised him. "Look Ephne, Tee's off limits. You'll meet him one day and make up your own mind." There was a short spasm of shame as he said this, what had he ever done for

Tee that gave him the right to get starchy over his reputation?

Later, in their bungalow, Ephne became the only person to hear the accurate version of his brief ignoble combat service.

"Well I don't see why you're so ashamed of it," she said, inspecting the ruined buttock. "It's not like you ran away."

"But that's just it. I was trying to. Hell, I'd *started* to when I got this."

"Well all soldiers go through that *Red Badge of Courage* thing, don't they?"

"I hope not, but it makes you wonder how many men get medals just for having a slow reaction time."

"Well, I'm here to tell you you're marked 'paid-in-full,'" she said tapping the great hollow scar with each of the last three words.

Their third weekend took place at a dreary B&B outside Albany. By then Harry had begun to fear that Emma might suspect something and his preoccupation hung over him like a cape. Ephne, too, seemed to come with her own concerns. It was early spring by then, between daffodils and tulips, it should have been beautiful. But the weather matched their mood. It rained and rained. It never stopped.

She had had a row with her mother.

"My adoptive mother, really." They sat on an empty covered porch in their coats, watching the rain. Harry was silently reprising the deceitful phone call he'd made to Emma an hour earlier and hadn't been following Ephne's own train of thought.

"I don't know," she went on. "I can never please her. She's resentful if I succeed and just devastated if I fail."

Remembering Barbara's gentle pessimism at his own prospects, Harry said, "But your mother cares doesn't she? That's the main thing."

Ephne went to the porch railing and put her hand out to catch the water dripping down. "We're so different. There's always this, this *thing* between us, and it just gets worse. You don't know what it's like, being adopted, knowing there's this other family, this other life out there, the life you might have had."

"You can change your life," he said. "You don't have to take the one they give you. I know a little about that."

She turned, the cold had brought circles of color to her cheeks. She wore jeans over very small boots. Her brown suede jacket hung to just above her hips, a white woolen turtleneck cinched at the waist where a wide brown belt showed off her figure.

"Yes, I guess you do." She looked down while he absorbed her use of the second person. "But it's different for you. You made yourself a new life and now you're deciding if you still want it. You think I don't know that?" He started to protest but she put her hands up. "We're not going to talk about it," she said, "not now."

She turned and put her hand out to catch more rain, then shivered and wiped it on the back of her thigh. She was right, talking wouldn't help.

Still facing away from him, she returned to her first subject. "But you see, mine was stolen from me." She played with her pinkie finger and the small signet ring he had seen in the bar. "Stolen. I know that my family, my real family is out there, somewhere, somewhere close and, goddamn it, I'm going to find them." She said this with too much vehemence for Harry to respond. But when she turned back to him, he was surprised to see she was smiling. Her voice dropped a full octave. "Are you just going to sit there or are we going to bed?"

"Aren't you going to tell me about the ring?"

"Soon," she said and pulled at his arm.

But loss was much on her mind—that night and the next morning. Ephne usually announced her verdict on their exertions with a mixture of triumph and amusement, but her near sobs the next morning ruled out any post-coital banter.

Instead, he told her about the Endicott case. The story of the lost grandson seemed to prompt her to take up the story of her own family. "You know I almost found them."

"Them?"

"My family. My real family."

"What happened?" Harry turned to her. Her eyes were on the far wall of the room. When she didn't answer he nudged her with his unshaven chin.

"Oh sorry, It was at Camp Abenaki, my third year. God, I was so happy there."

She sat up in the bed. "I was supposed to finish my swimming test, the written part in the main lodge, the Llewellyn Lodge. I got there early and was sitting on the hall bench like a good little girl. The door was open and I heard the camp director, talking to the swimming instructor. I wasn't snooping. It was just voices, you know. Two short-haired ladies with whistles around their necks talking camp business until I heard my name. Then it was like my ears grew. The director said, '*Well. You're not surprised, are you? We know who else was a good swimmer don't we?*'

"By then I realized they were talking about me, me and someone else. Then the instructor said, '*So it is true?*'

"'*Of course it is. She was a junior counselor here when you started wasn't she.*'

"'*We all hated her.*'

"'*Of course you did.*'

"Then the two of them went quiet for about a minute. I could hear them breathing, but they didn't speak. I could hear the floor boards squeak. The whole camp knew about them, of course. They couldn't keep their hands off each other. Then I heard the instructor say, '*Everyone said she was your favorite ever.*'

"'*How can you say that?*'

"I sat there on the bench, Harry, scared to death. I knew they were talking about me and this other, other person. Should I go? They'd hear me and there'd be hell to pay. So I just held my breath. I could hear soft brushing sounds like clothes rubbing together. Then the director made a sound like clearing her throat and said, '*It's remarkable. They do look alike... They even swim alike.*'"

Harry smiled at Ephne's ability to mimic the Philadelphia grande dame voice, but she wasn't trying to amuse.

"I must have moved on the bench then, because they stopped talking. Then there were footsteps and the director poked her head around the door. I pretended to be reading the Red Cross manual."

"'*Oh, Ephne dear,*' she said. '*Right on time.*' The look she gave me, Harry. I just knew they were talking about me." She turned to him as she said this.

Harry gestured with both hands. "So.... they were talking, about your natural mother, you think they knew who she was?"

"Well you know how it is. You married a Llewellyn. You know how Philadelphia, old Philadelphia, is. Just a small town, and you don't get much more old Philadelphia than Camp Abenaki and St. Agatha's." She held up her hand to show the signet ring. "You see, they even paid for it. Camp, even school—until they took them away. But if you're not part of the small town, you don't know, do you... know the things everyone else knows."

Sunday noon, when it was time to leave the Inn, she held Harry close and hard as they stood between their two cars. The rain had finally stopped. When she released him her eyes were shining and her nose was red.

"Love you," he said.

"Oh I know, I know." She put her head against him looking sideways. "Call me 'darling' Harry, please."

"Darling," he said.

Then, stiffening and brightening she adjusted his lapel. "Okay, 'nuff of that. Till June."

"June," Harry said closing her car door for her and, with a wave, she drove away into a brightening sky.

◆△◆

In the darkness Emma shifted again. "*I know you're always there for me.*" Harry wondered. When Emma found out, which would she consider the most shameful: the way he had taken up with Ephne or the way he had let her go? But she hadn't found out. He was safe. Surely.

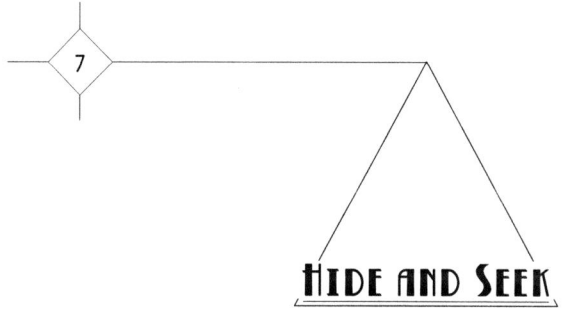

7 HIDE AND SEEK

Russell Chase had always liked the Mill Falls Café. He liked the smell of coffee and bacon, the way the worn tops of the black formica tables shone briefly when wiped clean with a wet cloth. He liked the welcoming five a.m. glow of yellow light in the midst of the dark city best of all. Old men needed less sleep.

The City of Hadley had at least three other diners but Russell had been loyal to the "Falls" through four owners, five if you counted the time the present owner, Marcel LaChance, tried to sell it to his good-for-nothing nephew. Russell almost looked for another place then, and the desertion would have been forgivable. The place got dirty and twice Russell's home fries came out of the kitchen with a little ketchup already on them. The nephew lasted six months then ran off to Florida with a seventeen-year-old waitress and stuck his uncle with a half year of bills.

When Marcel showed up back behind the counter in his apron he should have come in for serious teasing, but one look at the old man's face took the fun out of that, so everyone pretended nothing had happened. Besides, it was good to have Marcel back. The dishes shone again, the coffee was fresh and hot, and a man knew the food on his plate was there for the first time. Marcel wasn't a friendly man but he always had a word or two for each of the twenty or so men who got breakfast there most days. Not that the "Falls" was ever a place for long conversation.

There were regulars who traded daily nods of greeting with Russell even though they had not actually spoken for years.

Like most Tuesdays, Russell nursed his second cup of black coffee in his usual booth. He looked at this watch, five-thirty. *Usually here by now*, he thought, even as he frowned at his own impatience. He liked his nephew's company. He liked the feeling of passing something on.

When his brother-in-law had died—poor man, nine weeks short of retirement—Gregg had been nineteen. With no son of his own, Russell had tried to fill in. Not pushing it, a day fishing, a few football games at Plymouth State where Gregg played special teams and third string halfback, quite a come-down after his days at Hadley High. At first the boy had kept him at arms length. It was only when the state police brought Gregg back to Troop H, the Hadley County Barracks, that the two began their Tuesday mornings at the Falls.

The counter waitress called over to him. "Russell, you havin' eggs this mornin'?" The girl couldn't have been more than twenty, too young to call him 'Russell,' but she was the kind to take advantage. He could see it in her soft smile and hard eyes. Skinny little thing when she'd come to work a year back, but filling out now, nicely up top and only a little too much in the behind. Russell wondered what Marcel LaChance's nephew was doing now.

"We'll give it a minute," he said. He knew his impatience was mostly curiosity over that new murder case that Gregg was handling. His friend, Conservation Officer Omer Gingras, had called him about it the night before.

"Real strange this one, Russell," the man said.

"You see her?"

"Oh yah, sitting up against a beech tree like she'd just stopped to take a nap," Omer said.

"Who found her?"

"Bunch of West Harbor boys. Those hillbillies dint shoot her though." Russell shared a laugh with him. "Don't shoot nothing without horns or feathers, them. Don't miss much either."

"I heard."

"Chief caused a little ruckus."

Russell smiled at the thought of Gregg and the West Harbor Chief. He knew the man. Even a small town like West Harbor ought to do better than that. Twenty years earlier he had applied for a job on the Hadley Police Department. Already overweight, dumb as a brick and mean. Chief? Jesus!

"Didn't get himself in any trouble?" Russell had asked, knowing that Gregg had a temper.

"No. No. Just smooth, the way he can be. Nice boy. He got the chief under control. Too bad he got sick at the funeral home, though."

The bell over the café door sounded. The counter girl elevated her chest perceptibly and announced, "Bout time, Sergeant." She drew out the title to emphasize that she was not impressed but willing to discuss it. "Russell's about to starve to death. He's been snappin' at me all morning."

Russell limited any protest to a silent stare and pointed to his cup. Gregg slid onto the seat opposite.

When they had their breakfasts on the table, Russell's eggs and bacon opposite Gregg's bowl of what looked to Russell like library paste and bark mulch, the older man wiped his mouth with his napkin and signaled defeat in their weekly bouts of reticence.

"You had a busy day."

"Mmm." Gregg spooned some sugar onto the bowl of paste.

"Get an I.D. yet?"

"Nope. Sent the prints down to the FBI, but that'll be a while."

Russell looked up. "No one gone missin'?"

"No. That's just it. She doesn't seem to have any connection at all with anyone local."

"Think somebody local shot her?"

"That's another problem, we've got nothing to go on. Shotgun, so no ballistics." Gregg leaned forward as he said this, softly so not to carry to the other tables.

"Gotta be a boyfriend," Russell said breaking a yolk and mopping it with toast.

"Lab says no recent sex."

"Girlfriend then. Nine times out of ten, killin' ends up bein' about sex."

"Mmm."

The two then sat in silence for five full minutes. Russell worried a space between two molars with a tooth pick.

Finally Gregg asked, "What does Omer think?"

Russell savored the moment. He had always favored this boy over his thirteen other nieces and nephews. He had been an easy boy to like. Nice looking as a baby. Good at sports, polite to adults and strangers. Smart enough, but not cocky. But, times like this, Russell knew why he loved him. There was no criticism in the question, no resentment that Russell's old friend from Conservation Department, Omer Gingras, might have tried an idea out on Russell before he risked his dignity with the new sergeant from the state police. "*What does Omer think?*" The question told Russell that his nephew would ask him what *he* thought in his own time. In the meantime, what did Omer think?

Of course Omer had his own ideas.

"Strange to say, Russell," Omer had turned thoughtful on the phone. "But she was shot twice. Took one head on, bird shot, but it didn't kill her, not right off. The other was in the back, not much to it, four or five pellets. Edge-of-scatter wound from the look of it. More what you'd expect from a hunter's low shot. But that belly wound was a tight circle, no accident. Meant to kill."

"She was wounded front and *back*?"

"Yah, yah, and the front wound, small group like that, had to be from close up. Funny, you know. At that distance you expect a big hole, not a bunch of shallow pellet wounds."

Russell wiped the remaining yolk with a corner of toast, chewed for a moment, then he said, "Omer thinks something slowed the pellets down."

"Say again?"

"Omer says bird shot makes either a real serious hole with not much scatter or a bunch of superficial wounds far apart. This lady showed superficial wounds but a tight shot group." As he spoke, Russell moved his hands together in front of him making a diminishing 'O' with the index finger and thumb of his right hand.

The two finished their breakfast with the question of what and why still hanging in the air between them. Gregg signaled for a check.

"Carr behaving?" Russell asked. He knew T.J. Carr from his days on the Hadley police force. He didn't like him.

"'Course not." Gregg smiled at his uncle to show him that he had things under control. "He's mean as a snake, but like you said, he's persistent."

"Yah," said Russell. "So's a toothache."

Russell leaned forward. "How 'bout the other thing?" He said it softly without inflection and Gregg knew his uncle was asking about his interview with the governor. Even though it meant a move to Concord, Russell had urged him to pursue it. Gregg was not going to be happy just being a local cop. Already, the strain was beginning to show. The way he looked back at that waitress, for instance.

"Nothing yet," Gregg said.

"Women," Russell said.

"Carr threw it up to me yesterday."

"So he knows too?"

"Oh yah. Made it real obvious, said he'd switch the case to Capital Crimes."

"He would. Look, don't let him push you. Case like this, things come up. Lawyer cuts corners, people expect it. Carr got away with a slap on the wrist couple of years back. Voters think he's a law-and-order man 'cause his heart's in the right place. Lawyer's supposed to be cute. You do it, it's your ass."

"I know, Uncle Russ, I hear things too."

The waitress strutted over and gave them their checks. She pretended to flirt with Russell but the show was for Gregg and Russell didn't like the way Gregg smiled back. This girl didn't need any encouragement. Nothing but trouble there.

Each man put his money on a separate check. The young man slid out of the booth in a single motion. The uncle pushed off using the table top.

"You doin' a search this morning?" Russell asked this holding the door and ushering the younger man ahead of him.

Gregg looked at his watch, "Yah, start in 'bout an hour, first light."

◆△◆

The sector search began as soon as Sgt. Gregg Leavitt, now officially the "OIC" officer in charge, decided it was light enough to see. The weather had turned damp and almost warm. Gregg didn't need a forecast to know rain would begin late morning and their chances of picking up any remaining trace evidence of the woman's path would wash away with it.

He had been given enough people to cover a rectangular swath one hundred fifty feet wide. Thirty strong, twenty-six men and four women were ferried up in the dark over the same logging road Oscar Leighton had traveled the day before. At first light, Omer Gingras had guided them down the mountain to just above the tree where the woman was found.

Gregg stayed with a pair of technical men from the state laboratory, whose job was to fix the location of any evidence the team found, collect it, and establish a chain of custody for court.

Gregg arranged the team members at intervals of five feet with the outside men marking their progress every hundred feet with flags of bright orange tape. They turned and backtracked a parallel course back to the tree where they had found her. All were wearing bright yellow-green plastic vests emblazoned with the word POLICE. The smaller stature of the four women cadets made them appear child-like in the oversized garments, as though they were only pretending to be policemen.

The techs had been in the business too long to even think of interfering with the OIC, even one young enough to be either man's son. They would get no credit for good suggestions and full blame for any bad one, so they positioned themselves behind "Sergeant" Leavitt once the search started and did little but nod.

On the third outward pass the left-most man found blood traces and a recently broken branch on the ground. Using the GPS locator Gregg plotted a path from the tree where they'd found the woman to the coordinates of the branch. He breathed a sigh of relief and drew a line with a grease pencil on the plastic covered West Harbor Town tax map. One tech took pictures while the other cut the branch off and bagged it. Gregg ordered five searchers from the right side of the party to move over to the left before starting again. Adjusting their vector they covered another fifty yards and found more blood. They marked this next find, plotted it and established a new vector. In this way they proceeded down the mountain following the blood trail where they could, reestablishing a sector search when they couldn't.

To supervise properly, Gregg found he had to move back and forth, up and down the steep slope, and by ten a.m. he was light-headed with fatigue. He knew the story of his puking in the parking lot had already made the rounds and was dangerously close to joining Oscar Leighton's wounded "peckah" in the evolving tale of the case. Gregg froze to silence any attempt to include him in the humor and supervised the team with monosyllabic rigor. He was particularly concerned that the technicians not go back to headquarters with any tale of incompetence or humiliation. If they did, the state police team from Capital Crimes might show up after all to take over for the young sergeant in over his head.

But by eleven thirty a.m., he had reason to hope. The searchers' four hours of effort had yielded seven more blood signs over less than a mile of progress, and with each new dot on his map Gregg felt his energy and confidence return. The route they plotted, turning this way, then that, was what Gregg thought it would be, the irregular but gradually semi-circular route of someone running uphill for her life, most likely in the dark. In rough country most people tended, as this woman had, to bear to the left because when they came to an obstruction, all things being equal, they kept their dominant hand up and turned away from what they couldn't see. Since most people were right-handed, they veered left. Back-tracking now, this trail kept turning to the right.

After a dismal morning of blackening clouds and dropping temperatures, noon found them in sight of the lakeshore. A soft cold mix of rain and tiny pellets of snow began to fall, tapping softly on the dead leaves. The path Gregg had drawn on his board had now turned almost perpendicular to the West Wasoka Road which ran behind summer homes built along the lakeshore. "That's it," Gregg thought, "we've found all we're gonna." He was about to send them the last hundred yards down to the road when a woman's cry went up from the clutch of female cadets, her voice suddenly thin and child-like with excitement.

"Sergeant, we got a shoe down here!"

Gregg and the two technicians made their way to a knot of four women and two men standing in a respectful semicircle. Gregg could see it was the match to the small shoe he had seen on her the day before: brown, thin soled, almost a slipper. The two headquarters men photographed and bagged it. One tech gave Gregg a one-sided smile and, looking up into the falling precipitation, said, "Good thing you hustled us out here when you did." The other said 'uhn' and nodded between clicks and flashes of the camera.

When the techs had what they wanted, the team set out again with more urgency now as the pellets of snow turned to rain. Almost immediately, just above the slope cut for West Wasoka Road, they found two bent-over saplings in a grove of young miniature hemlocks, one with a green branch half broken. A matt of leaves on the ground below looked sticky with congealed blood, now rapidly being wetted by the rain.

Turning his attention to the road now, Gregg sent two parties of five on detours so they could inspect the upperside of the pavement without disturbing evidence of where she may have left it.

"Go down a quarter mile then work your way back on the road," he said. "Try to find where she came in."

Within ten minutes the easterly party found a dislodged stone lying in the drainage swale and two breaks in the moss that lined the slope cut. One tech snapped his camera while the other laid down a short twelve-inch ruler to provide a scale. The wind rose and turned colder still, changing the rain back to sleet. Gregg sighed and placed his last dot on the map. They unfolded sheets of plastic and laid them over the hemlocks and the dislodged rock to preserve what was there.

With the whole team finally on pavement, Gregg began a second sweep along the opposite, downhill side of the road. They worked a mile in either direction in the now steady rain. Driveways rose up to this side of the road at regular intervals running from the just visible roof lines of large, now deserted, summer houses. The police turned wide-eyed at these buildings, most of them Adirondack-style homes with extensive stonework and well-tended landscaping. At one house they found and rousted a three-man work crew, supposedly there for end-of-the-season yard work. In fact, they were sharing a six-pack in the cab of their truck. Surprised to see police, the three mouthed off, and since they had the engine running to keep heat in the cab, one of the local cops confiscated the three remaining beers and wanted to charge them with DUI. Gregg just shook his head 'no' and sent the workers back to their truck where they smoked and watched, still on the clock, resentful of the unopened beers sitting up on the side of the road.

The only other living person they encountered was Margie Tuttle.

Margie had come out of a house as big as the others, but this house was dark and anything but well tended. Only a thin plume of smoke coming from one chimney and an old Subaru parked in the driveway suggested anyone was there. Margie had just liberated a bottle of vodka, three-quarters full, from her employers' liquor cabinet and tucked it under the passenger seat of her rusty car. It was one of the two smoke breaks she was allowed each morning. Proud that she had turned the old bitches' rule against smoking in the house against them, Margie's behind was still high in the air when three guys wearing bright yellow vests with POLICE on them came out from the trees all around her. Terrified at seeing so many policemen at the instant her theft was complete, Margie yelped in surprise and despair. She cursed her rotten luck, but had sense enough to slam the car door. Her eyes darted between the car and the officers.

"I been to court just yesterday," she said, and then, she burst into tears. The policemen hadn't seen the bottle and misunderstood her reaction. They were all apologies. Two of them knew her, but it still took a few minutes for them to calm her down.

"It's okay, Margie," one said. "We ain't lookin' for you." Margie, regathering hope, glanced from one nodding head to the other. Relief washed through her, the tears still fresh on her face. Almost at once this turned into rage at their mocking smiles and she shouted, "You should know better. Scared the shit outta me. I might-a peed my pants." She stomped back to the house letting the screen door slap back on their laughter behind her.

"She's a pissah, ain't she! Ole Margie!"
A voice could be heard calling from inside the dark house.
"Miss Tuttle? Miss Tuttle?"
"Yah, yah, I hear you," Margie said before the other door closed behind her.

◆△◆

ONE O'CLOCK CAME and Gregg was standing with the final six wet but grateful members of the search team as they huddled under the roof of a rich man's shed and waited for the school bus to bring this final group back to the barracks. They were grateful because overtime vouchers were always welcome this time of the year. A full day, too, since it was now past noon. For some of the cadets, this was their first real police work and it seemed to embolden them, veterans now, to talk to Gregg as they waited.

"Hey Sarge, what do you think one of these places would cost?"

Gregg looked around at the manicured grass and the tennis court before he answered.

"More than you make, rookie." The two shared a rueful smile.

Gregg relaxed and listened to tiny rhythmic waves lap against a short stretch of sandy shore. The cadets and young officers wondered aloud at where the money must have come from. He wondered too, but kept it to himself. How could anyone make this much money? Two, maybe three million for a house like this and open only eight, maybe ten weeks a year. He didn't know any better than these kids did. The difference was, he knew he never would.

◆△◆

IT WAS ALMOST THREE o'clock before Gregg joined the two technicians, their clothes all still steaming with damp and sweat, for their meeting with T.J. at his courthouse office. The techs were focused on T.J., slouched back in his swivel chair, one foot up on his littered desk, while he consumed a mid-sized bag of potato chips. A pale stripe of white, hairless calf showed between the tops of T.J.'s fallen ankle-length black socks and the hem of his gray trousers. Unlike the techs, Gregg had had to make sure the cadets had transportation, to countersign their pay vouchers, and check his regular duty messages: a bad accident on the North South Road, a wifebeating in the Pine Hollow trailer park, a car in the water over by North Harbor... but all T.J. cared about, he was late.

"Bout time Leavitt," T.J. said.

Gregg was too tired to respond so he simply began his briefing on the search, punctuating the narrative with pictures of the site of each dot on the now rain-stained and wrinkled map. T.J. showed some interest in the shoe, interrupting his chewing and swallowing long enough to hold the plastic bag up to the light, but nothing else interrupted his steady destruction of the chips. When these were finished, his chair squeaked in complaint as he reached for a plastic bottle of Pepsi which he sucked emphatically dry.

Finishing this, T.J. pitched forward, crumpled up the empty bag, and threw it at his waste basket. He missed, shrugged and licked his fingers. Gregg paused midway through his presentation but, like the other two, pretended not to notice. The technicians had seen Carr before. Gregg had been warned by the former troop commander when he began this tour. "Carr is a mean bastard, but he won't hang you out. Can be cute about evidence, but for a lawyer he ain't so bad." So far only the first half of the description had proved out. Uncle Russell had been more succinct. "Oh, he's fair, all right. He's a prick to everyone."

The two headquarters men took in Gregg's hesitation and exchanged knowing glances before one of them retrieved the chip bag and dropped it in the basket.

"I figure she was shot either up on the road or in one of these houses below the road and ran up into the woods to get away." Gregg said. "We don't have evidence yet that points to any particular house, not enough to get a warrant." The two headquarters men nodded together at this, pursing their lips in agreement. Gregg sat down in his chair waiting for the county attorney to tell him what he wanted next.

"Well, she wasn't taking a nature walk," T.J. began, pausing to stifle another belch. "She's out there in the woods in November with her little ballet slippers on, so she had to come out of somewhere. A car?" He pointed his chin at the technicians who shrugged, then nodded in unison. "Possible," one said.

"I like one of those houses," Gregg interrupted pointing at the outlines of summer houses drawn on the map. He emphasized the word 'one.' It was important they go carefully on this. If they went into a house without a good warrant they could lose any evidence they found there, blow the case with an illegal search.

"Yah, I suppose," T.J. said, tracing the GPS route of the signs found by the tracking team. He gestured to the last of the pictures. "You think she hid in those bushes, huh?"

The techs consulted their own clipboards. "She bled out pretty good," one said. "It's just up from the road. Must've been there a while before somethin' started her up again."

T.J. thought for a moment and studied the map. "She'd have run further than that at first if she'd just jumped out of a car." He picked at his teeth with a paper clip. "She at that spot for long?" he pointed to the picture.

"From the amount of blood, it looks that way," Gregg began. He looked at the man with the clipboard who nodded in confirmation. "We're still confirming that it was hers, but it stands to reason…"

"I don't give a damn about reason, Sergeant Leavitt," Carr said, emphasizing the rank. "Make sure you get the blood ID'd. He looked at the technicians. "You got enough for DNA?"

"Its enough," one said. The other added, "It'll take two days for the tests to come back. We can exclude her in about an hour, but after two days the lab can get us something definitive. Depends on contamination." He cocked his head at Carr. "It's hers though."

"Fingerprints?" T.J. asked.

The two techs scowled at each other as if to say 'On what?'

"Well this is just great," Carr said. "I've had a dead lady on my hands for thirty hours now, shot twice, and we still don't even know who the hell she is."

The three watched T.J. think for a while, and finger the map of lots in front of him. "Leavitt, you get an up-to-date list of names and addresses on these houses. Get names and addresses for everyone—owners, handymen, family members. Start with the handymen. They love to gossip about their rich bosses. Put those coffee drinking tough guys who work for you on it and give the speeders and drunk drivers a break for a day or two. Show her picture around. We can't search yet, but we can ask questions. Anyone talks back, you let me know right away." The map showed the roadway and lot lines together with outlines of the houses on each lot. For parts of the lakeshore, the pattern of recent development and subdivision into ever smaller lots could be seen from the landmarks. But in this two-mile section of West Harbor, known to the locals as 'The Gold Coast,' most houses were still set on large lots.

Gregg made a note but didn't respond.

"You saw how she was dressed ... undressed, too." T.J. grinned at Gregg suddenly in a confiding but unfriendly way. "You must remember," he said softly. One of the techs snorted. So that story would get down to headquarters as soon as they got back. Yes, Carr was a prick, Gregg thought, staring back, not returning the smile.

"I think Leavitt's right," T.J. said. She came out of one of these places," T.J. said, then looking up at the ceiling. "She was running away from someone pissed off enough to carry a shotgun and stupid enough to load it with bird shot. If she'd just jumped out of a car she'd have made more distance away from the road than that before she stopped." His finger rested on the map at the spot marking where they'd found the blood.

"We've got to go slow on these," Gregg said, indicating the houses.

"Sure, sure," T.J. said. "By the numbers. No entry without permission. Someone turns you down, we'll see about a warrant. I don't have a motive. I don't have a weapon. The last thing I need now is a bum search."

"We figured you might feel that way," one of the techs said, but softly to show that they did lots of murders. They didn't need instruction, or a tantrum, from a rural D.A.

"All right, to start, I want you to check from here," T.J. pushed a large finger against a square depicted on the map, "to here." He pointed to a second square only ten inches away on the map but almost two miles on the ground.

Gregg counted out twenty-seven shorefront lots with houses on them between the two lots Carr had pointed to. Gregg saw that the area corresponded almost precisely to where Gregg had sent the teams that morning. Well, no one had said Carr was stupid.

"You find me which house she came out of and dollars to donuts we'll find our weapon," Carr said.

"I'll be sure to remember," Gregg said evenly.

T.J. gave him a long look, then said, "Okay." He pointed at Gregg's map. "You did okay." In this softer tone, he said, "Just get me names and addresses for these owners."

Assuming this was dismissal, Gregg began to gather up his materials, so he wasn't looking at T.J. when he heard him say, "You don't want to screw this up, Leavitt. The governor's got a lot of other young studs she can use to hold her umbrella when it rains."

Gregg felt the blood rise and with it the impulse to lash out. He could see that the two headquarters' men were watching, with that careful silence that showed that they already knew about his job interview, but also that they knew how out of bounds T.J. was. So, it was all over headquarters as well.

"Say, 'd you guys hear the one about rodeo sex?" T.J. began, and the two techs winked and leaned back over their chairs, relaxing again. 'That T.J.,' their looks seemed to say as Gregg left.

Ignoring Gregg's departure, T.J. put both elbows back on the desk, a man used to overstepping bounds. The other two leaned forward grinning with anticipation.

"What you do is go home tonight and get your old lady in the mood, ya know?" T.J. chuckled. "Then you take her from behind, titty in each hand." T.J. put his hands out palm up in front of him. "And just as you're goin' for glory, you lean forward and whisper your secretary's name in her ear..." The techs had already started laughing. T.J. leered at them.

"Then you see if you can hang on for ten seconds."

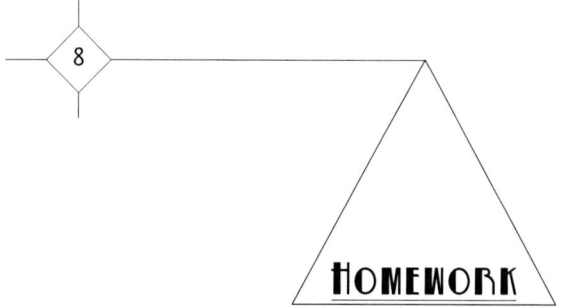

8 HOMEWORK

"Writing days," days free from courtroom work, were suppose to lead to more learned decisions from county court judges. For Harry Warren, they meant at least twice a month he didn't have to make the twenty mile trip to Hadley County. Ordinarily, Harry's devotion to duty being what it was, the files Grace gave him to 'write' on remained undisturbed. There was always something better to do at Langdon House. But this Tuesday he worked. Perhaps because the morning turned gray and rainy and Emma had cleared off his writing table while she took respite in her studio from the Crowninshield dinner preparations. Or maybe it was the urgency of Grace's worries about Amanda. *"Don't you know she's keeping a book on you?"* Whatever the reason, mid morning found Harry actually opening the Order on Appeal for *In Re Martin* from the Hadley County probate court that Grace had packed up for him the day before.

This particular appeal had been sitting in the county court long enough to grow a foot thick and was supplemented by two videotape cassettes. With Emma's music playing in the background, Harry approached the fate of Eleanor and Louisa Martin with feelings of unaccustomed virtue.

Harry already knew the Martin sisters and like everyone else in the Lake Wasoka Club, he had watched the steady deterioration of their summer house, directly across West Harbor Bay from the Club's swimming beach, for the past ten years. The Martins had let their own membership lapse some time ago and in recent years came to the club only rarely. When Harry had last seen them, their appearance was a shock. With lipstick clumsily applied and clothes askew in unexpected ways, the unmarried sisters hadn't held up much better than the house.

Harry took it for granted that the two sisters had simply gotten old and neglectful. They were so old-time Philadelphia, it wasn't possible they were truly broke. But the papers in front of him confirmed that the Martins were worse than broke. They had kept the wolf from the door only by selling off pieces of their lakefront property and finally by mortgaging what was left. Of course, that didn't mean they had felt obliged to actually make payments on the mortgage. They were Martins after all.

Louisa Martin, the older sister, had sized up Harry shortly after he and Emma had married and moved back to New Hampshire. Emma, the daughter of one of the club's oldest families, had married a boy from Hadley, and some members, like Louisa, seemed to regard Harry as a joke made in poor taste, even if he had gone to Penn.

"From Hadley, I hear," Louisa said to Harry when they were left alone together after being introduced. "You must find this all rather strange." She gestured across the square of turf where couples in white were bowling.

"Well, a little." Harry believed he had put just the right mix of deference and sensitivity in his response so he was surprised when she ostentatiously surveyed his costume for the day: blue blazer, Devon tie, Nantucket reds, and exposed ankles.

Then she said, "But you're a quick learner. Anyone can see that." She moved away then to take her turn on the pitch and may not have heard Harry mutter 'bitch.' Or maybe she did. Harry had to admit she was right, he was a quick *learner*, but her tone informed him he hadn't, wouldn't ever learn enough.

◆△◆

EMMA APPEARED in the doorway to her studio. She bent over to kiss the top of his head.

"Harry, you have the most unpleasant smile on your face." He looked up at her. Emma's hair was tied back and she wore her favorite canvas smock. She turned and tilted her head slightly, five minutes on a clock face, a question.

"If you stand by the river long enough, the body of your enemy will come floating by," he said.

Emma scowled and shrugged. She didn't like it when he riddled, but she would like it less if he told her what he was thinking so he asked, "You all set for the dinner?"

"Uh huh. I'm just poking around this morning. No more decisions." She kissed his forehead. "Just saying hello." Emma went back to her studio and he turned back to the file.

The Martin sisters had successfully resisted the bank's efforts to foreclose for more than a year and a half now, largely because of the skill of their lawyer, Zach Hannah. But even Zach appeared to be running out of options, his task complicated by the sisters' apparent refusal to sell up or file for bankruptcy.

The probate court order, Cruikshank and Hannah's memoranda on the firm's distinctive cream colored stationary, and two much shorter and clumsier replies from the bank's lawyers, had been prepared in three revealingly different styles. The bank's brief was written in the exasperated tones of one who has been out-lawyered too long. 'Goddammit' seemed to be its fundamental premise. Summarized in one sentence, it said, 'These arrogant old bitches took our money and won't pay it back.' Unhappily, it was filled with enough 'clearly, thens' and 'it follows, therefores' and 'obviouslies' to droop the eyelids of someone with a better attention span than Harry Warren.

Zach Hannah's pleadings for the sisters were typical of him: polite, thorough, gentle—just a little surprised the bank was so rude, so unyielding. A transcript and video tape of Louisa Martin's deposition was referred to throughout and both were there for Harry to review. But Harry knew Zach, so he turned to the probate court order which, freed from the need to argue the case, explained it much better.

HADLEY COUNTY PROBATE COURT

ORDER

The Defendants LOUISA MARTIN and ELEANOR MARTIN are unmarried sisters, eighty-two and eighty years of age respectively, who now live in a deteriorating, heavily mortgaged but still valuable lakefront house at Martin's Point on Lake Wasoka in West Harbor in this County (hereinafter the "Martin's Point property"). The sisters are the sole beneficiaries of the title holder, the MARTIN FAMILY RESIDUARY TRUST, a Pennsylvania revocable trust established by their late father and mother, HEATHERINGTON MARTIN and MARGARET MARTIN in 1954. The MARTIN parents were Grantors, beneficiaries and trustees of this lengthy and detailed Revocable Trust. MARGARET MARTIN died in 1972. Upon Mr. MARTIN's death as a widower in 1976, the Trust became irrevocable and the Defendant, LOUISA MARTIN, became successor Trustee pursuant to its terms. Neither sister has ever married, borne children or adopted, and since each is well past child-bearing age, they are the only vested beneficiaries.

The Trust assets were once considerable, including marketable securities with 1954 values of more than $1 million, real estate in Haverford and Philadelphia, Pennsylvania and the Martin's Point property, then a 30-acre Lake Wasoka Estate with more than two thousand feet of lake frontage and a fifteen room summer "cottage."

Harry smiled at this. The probate judge was right. Before subdividing it into house lots, it had truly been an estate, but that was not a word the Martins would have used. Tee Ingersoll had taught him that only people who had never lived in one spoke of 'estates.' These were the same people who put 'cottage' in quotation marks.

The assets of the Trust have now been reduced in size dramatically by distribution and sale. The securities have been liquidated. The Pennsylvania real estate was sold long ago as was more than

> eighty percent of the Martin's Point property. The Trust's only asset of substance is the remaining parcel of lake-front land at Martin's Point, the partially winterized "cottage," and the contents of this structure. The contents have been appraised at a nominal value.

Harry chewed the base of his pen. So the Martins had been broke for years. He calculated back to that evening when Louisa had insulted him at the club. Even then.

> All parties agree that the fair market value of even this remnant of the Trust estate now has a value in excess of $2 million. It is encumbered by three mortgages, all facially correct and duly recorded at the Hadley County Registry of Deeds. Each is held as security for one of three notes payable to the Hadley County Trust Company (the Bank). The aggregate indebtedness secured by these mortgages is found to be $658,768.97 as of the date of this order with per diem interest charges of $141.71 thereafter.
>
> All three notes are substantially in arrears and in default under their terms. The Bank has brought an action for foreclosure in the Hadley County Court which has been held in abeyance pending the outcome of this proceeding.

Harry scanned the thinner judicial foreclosure file that Grace had secured with a thick rubber band. The mortgages were properly signed and recorded. The probate judge's values looked about right so he didn't bother with the real estate or personal property appraisals. Harry went back to the Order.

> The question put to this Court is whether the notes and mortgages were executed properly and therefore enforceable against the Trust assets under the terms of the mortgage. An action for declaratory relief brought on behalf of Louisa Martin against the Bank has been consolidated with the foreclosure proceeding and a third action brought against LOUISA by her sister ELEANOR seeking both to remove LOUISA as Trustee of the Trust and appoint ELEANOR as LOUISA's Guardian. In this action ELEA-

> NOR also seeks an order from this Court declaring that LOUISA lacked the authority to encumber Trust assets without first obtaining formal reformation of the Trust.
>
> The Bank responds that ELEANOR is barred from raising such an objection now because she actually benefitted from the funds raised from these mortgage loans and was physically present at at least two of the three mortgage transactions. Further complicating these proceedings is the more recent creation of the MARTIN FAMILY IRREVOCABLE CHARITABLE REMAINDER TRUST, the ultimate beneficiary of the original Trust.

Harry made a sound like 'hah.' Good old Zach. By forming a new entity, the charitable remainder trust, he'd created an 'innocent' party to challenge the banks. Harry rifled through the subfile containing the trusts. The original trust was prepared in Philadelphia by Wharton & Biddle, lawyers for the Martins—lawyers for the Llewellyns, for that matter. The charitable remainder trust was prepared by Cruikshank and Hannah, and of course, there it was: "Zachary Hannah, Trustee." With appeals, no matter what Harry or any other judge ordered, Zach had created a cats cradle of issues here to keep the Martin sisters at Martin's Point for another two years.

> The Court, having taken a view of the Lake Wasoka property, considered the evidence of Bank officials, expert testimony and having had the opportunity to observe the demeanor of LOUISA and ELEANOR MARTIN, concludes by a preponderance of the evidence that at the time she signed the first two mortgages, LOUISA was competent to understand the nature of these transactions. She demonstrated this both to Bank counsel and Bank officers during two lengthy closings wherein she insisted, successfully, in negotiating changes to both Notes.
>
> The Court was persuaded that LOUISA is not now competent to make binding decisions of a financial nature and would be 'incompetent' to consent to a mortgage transaction today. While it is a closer question, the Court concludes that she was also not

> competent to execute the third mortgage. There is no likelihood that foreclosure of either of the first two mortgages would generate a deficiency.

"Deficiency." Harry recalled the Martins cruising into the club docks in their gleaming twenties-era Gar-Wood mahogany runabout, so immune from cares like this.

> The Court reviewed expert reports, viewed a video-taped deposition and conducted a personal interview of Louisa Martin. She was found episodically delusional and disoriented as to time and place. She is disqualified therefore to act as co-Trustee of the Martin Family Trust. The Court was not persuaded that her disability pre-dated the creation of the Charitable Remainder Trust.

Harry decided it was time to look at the tapes so he took one over to the VCR. This deposition had been offered as an exhibit by Zach.

Like all taped depositions there was much time spent on set up, time to see the wreck of what had once been Louisa Martin. The camera ranged this way and that but kept being drawn to the ravaged face framed by a mane of disordered grey hair against a pile of pillows in an enormous bed. She was apparently well enough physically most days, but on this day was in bed with the flu.

Harry found himself staring.

"Jesus," he said.

Eleanor Martin, the younger sister, scuttled in and out of the picture, a smaller, softer version of Louisa. Once the questioning got started, she tried to help with documents, efforts which Louisa rewarded with eye-rolls and exasperated sighs. Eleanor eventually had her hand lightly slapped for her troubles. Eleanor was wearing the same large therapeutic shoes which she wore to court, but the walker she appeared to need in court was nowhere to be seen. Well, that was Zach too.

Harry knew what was coming. The 'Hannah treatment.' "Sincerity," Zach used to say to them, raising his glass during the Friday night drinking sessions to which Harry and the other young Cruikshank lawyers adjourned in Zach's office, "Sincerity is the key. Once you learn to fake that, there's nothing you can't do." They all laughed, but though he worked with Zach for three years, Harry could never really tell whether the counterfeit or the real thing was on display. The nature of the case didn't matter. Zach put in the same effort for an indigent car thief as he did for the firm's biggest clients. Despite his irreverence, most of the time he *was* sincere and the cause was worthy. That was how he got away with the times they weren't. That and hard work.

Zach was never surprised by a statute or precedent. He knew how to announce positions with a half wonder that seemed to invite everyone to share in the revelation that the law was on his side after all. "Actually ..." he would say—it was his favorite word—as if he had started with the opposite point of view but found, quite fortunately, "the case law doesn't allow for this kind of contract." Or tort theory, or indictment, or will, or whatever. If Zach was relying on a particularly uncertain point, the revelation would be punctuated by soft rueful chuckles, as if to say, "Imagine that." When needed, he could inject a note of soft menace. If only the other side had bothered to do the kind of careful inquiry he had done, well, we wouldn't have to be taking up everyone's valuable time, would we, with all this unpleasant speculation.

Harry watched the neatly barbered Hannah head rotate gently from side to side on the screen. Zach had been head boy at the Devon School. His expression showed disappointment—and just a little surprise—at the bank lawyer's irritation. It was the same expression that Head Prefect Zach Hannah would have given a Devon freshman arriving late to lunch.

Harry had seen one unwary opponent after another succumb to Zach's offer of warm collegial spirit. Win or lose, the opponent was, after all, contesting an interesting point of law as an equal with Zach Hannah—Zach Hannah! At first they were all friends, but if the opposition proved difficult, things changed. A note of weary impatience, a mixture of incredulity and disappointment would leak into Zach's voice. The bag of tricks would come out. A favorite was to pretend to consult with an associate as if to inquire, "Have we missed something?" Once he had snatched Harry's notes, studied them and turned toward him as if to consult. Very convincing, except Harry had seen he was holding them upside down and all he whispered to Harry was, "Do you believe this asshole?" Harry realized later his surprised expression was just the one Zach wanted the judge to see from across the room.

Every member of the New Hampshire Bar seemed to have a warm, if faintly rueful, 'Zach' story like that. He was regularly held up to be the model for the rest of them. Big city smarts and toughness tempered with gentlemanly candor and consideration. Straight about substance, slightly and lovably bent about tactics.

On the video tape Zach's latest crop of acolytes basked beside him in the makeshift studio that had been made of Louisa Martin's bedroom. A young woman with a computer sat with Zach on a sort of wide two-person chair. As the camera scanned back and forth to catch the questions, the objections and even Louisa's impossible interjections, the centerpiece remained Zach Hannah's profile with its unvaryingly polite, interested and attentive gaze. He was closer in age to the woman in the bed than anyone else in the room, but could easily have been taken for her son.

Then suddenly there was the face of Smitty: Averill 'Smitty' Smith, Zach's longtime driver, investigator and general factotum.

Harry's path hardly ever crossed Smitty's anymore. Smitty seldom went into courtrooms and would have preferred thumbscrews to coming to Harry's. He looked shrunken, slightly desiccated in the bright light used to make the video tape. The camera paused on Smitty. Annoyed, he scowled and leaned out of the picture. His capacity for hatred came back with all its vehemence.

The bank's lawyer kept trying to get an answer out of Louisa—any answer. As he parried Zach's patient, endless objections, he took on the look of a Pleistocene sloth who had just strayed into the tar pit.

Q. *Let's look at what we've marked as Exhibit 2, Ms. Martin.*

A. *You look at it all you want.*

Q. *Well, yes, thank you, but I'd like you to look at it if you would?*

A. **(After extended pause)** *Well I'm looking. Aren't you going to ask questions. I thought you had come tramping into my bedroom to...*

MR. HANNAH. *Louisa.*

Now Harry saw why Zach wanted him to see the video. Not to show Louisa scoring off the hapless and easily flustered bank lawyers, as she must have thought at the time, but to reveal Louisa Martin as she had become, Mrs. Haversham without the charm. Who wouldn't hesitate to foreclose on an old mad woman, so fallen in the world?

After twenty minutes of outbursts from his client, Zach was sure he had had enough.

The WITNESS. *You must be one of those matchbook lawyers. (Laughter) That's what father used to say, matchbook diploma.*

Mr. HANNAH. *Louisa, please. Maybe we can take a break.*

At this the screen went blue. With the TV silent, the gently repetitive notes of a Vivaldi canon floated into the room from Emma's studio. Harry stretched, turning as he did so. Emma was in the doorway again.

"You want me to close this Harry?" She gestured to the pocket double doors. He could see she had been applying gold leaf to a frame because flecks now glittered on her hands and the sweet aroma of the special glue she used now filled both rooms. Baroque music seemed to go with gold leaf. Unspoken between them was Harry's suspicion that what had brought her into the room was the sound of Zach Hannah's voice.

Like everyone in the office, Harry had been in awe of Zach when they had worked together. Awe always comes with a touch of jealousy, and it didn't help to learn that Emma had felt the same. Of course then it had seemed Harry too would get his place in the sun. Now ...

"Only if you want to," he said answering with as much neutrality as he could muster. As if on cue, the screen came live again with a close-up of Louisa Martin.

"My God, that's Louisa Martin." Emma advanced on the screen, her eyes widening.

"You remember her?"

"Of course. She used to play tennis with Mummy. They have that place across the bay in West Harbor. She looks awful."

"She won't own that place much longer I'm afraid." The sound of the deposition came back just as Emma's music player switched to soft jazz. In spite of herself, Emma said, "Zach up to his old tricks?"

Harry shrugged and they watched together.

> Mr. HANNAH. *Let the record show that we've reconvened and that the witness feels she has a better understanding of the question.*
>
> By Mr. WALKER. Q. *Okay, Ms. Martin. Is that your signature or not?*
>
> Mr. HANNAH. *You're referring to Exhibit 2?*
>
> Mr. WALKER. *Yes, Exhibit 2.*
>
> Ms. Martin: A. *What?*
>
> Q. *Is that your signature?*
>
> A. *It might be. I don't know.*

Louisa Martin laughed at this. No one joined her.

> Q. *Well, you remember whether or not you signed this mortgage don't you?*
>
> Mr. HANNAH. *Objection as to form. You may answer.*

While Louisa gave her combative answers, Emma moved closer to the screen. The video cameraman continued to pan back and forth across the bedroom repeatedly scanning Zach's profile. A sound off-camera caused the camera man to turn to another corner of the room.

"Oh for God sakes, is that Smitty? He still works for Zach?" Emma, kind to almost everyone, had always made an exception for Smitty.

"Uh, huh."

"God, I dislike that man."

"Well, *actually* ..." Emma gave Harry a smile for his use of Zach's favorite word "... Smitty qualifies for a handicap plate, so Zach uses him as a driver." Emma scowled, but shook her head indulgently and turned her attention back to the screen, dropping her glasses from the top of her head.

"Harry, can you run it back?" Emma asked suddenly, and moved closer to the monitor. Reluctantly, Harry tried to reverse the tape, but only succeeded in making it go faster. After two tries Emma gently took the remote from him and moved the video to the spot she wanted. She muted the tape and ran one section backward and forward. In trying to focus on each lawyer as questions were asked the camera bounced from place to place in the room. Finally, Emma froze the tape and moved close to the screen. The frame showed Zach's female associate, a woman with abundant hair and long legs, in the middle of the picture.

"Zach still has good taste," Harry said. They both knew Zach's reputation with women.

Emma ignored him and squinted at the screen. She let out a soft whistle. "Probably a reproduction," she said, more to herself than to Harry. As she ran the tape back, paused as the camera moved from Zach to the bank's lawyer and finally froze it on what looked like a new shot of the woman's legs and briefcase.

"The legs are right," Emma said.

Harry smiled. "That's my line, isn't it?"

But she was interested in something else. "Don't you see the tracery on the cabriole?" She pointed to a spot on the screen without looking away, forgetting that Harry didn't know what a "cabriole" was. "And the matching medallions," she said.

"Emma, what the hell are you talking about?"

"The settee." A 'settee.' Only Emma would know it was a settee. She resumed playing the tape backwards and forwards. She seemed to forget Harry altogether.

"Emma?" He suffered as any man would who has surrendered command of television controls to a woman.

"Sorry, but look at this," she said at last. She motioned and Harry got up and came closer to the screen.

"See, four matching cabriole legs, three-toed with matching sun bursts. Here, you can see one just under Zach's leg when he leans forward and here's another just behind the tall girl with the laptop."

"Very interesting, darling. Fascinating. Shall I order a garage sale?"

"Some garage sale," she said turning her serious school girl frown on him. "Sotheby's more likely."

"Emma, the Martin girls can't even pay their mortgage. The contents, except for some pictures, are appraised at next to nothing. What are you talking about? Sotheby's!" He pushed the folder containing the unread appraisals toward her. Emma thumbed through it and put it back. "Well, the lady seems to know her business, about the silver anyway." She put the appraisal back but squinted again at the screen.

"Hang on," she said. She paused the tape and went back to her studio. A drawer opened and closed and she came back with a looseleaf binder holding old yellowed pages, each clad in its own plastic envelope. She sat down cross-legged in front of the monitor and pulled out two pages to compare with the grainy image on the screen.

"Couldn't be," she said at last. "Still, it looks too old to be a reproduction."

Harry saw the loose-leaf had a typewritten label legend on its front.

TAC
1763 Sketchbook

"I know you're going to let me in on this eventually," Harry said, but Emma was still looking back and forth from the screen.

She replied more to herself than to him. "The settee looks late Georgian. You can see that it's almost an exact replica of Figure 67, here." Figure 67 was a yellowing black and white photograph of what looked to be a stripped wooden chair frame.

"Okay. I know there's a significance here."

"Well if it's real ... Philadelphia made, probably Colonial." Emma looked up at him over her glasses. "Don't you see Harry, only a few families could afford furniture like that in the 1760's. People like the Chews, the Cadwaladers, the Shippens."

"Or the Llewellyns?"

"I think we were still stealing English sheep along with your relatives. No, Mummy's people, not us."

"So it's valuable, then?" he asked, changing the subject back to the screen. "If it's real. How valuable?"

"Harry, if it's what it looks like, it would be priceless."

"C'mon Emma, it's an old bench. Hell, it's ripped."

"Settee. And the fabric doesn't matter. Last April a side chair—a side chair with two repairs," she held up two fingers, "—and a questionable provenance—went for a million-two."

Harry had no illusions about his own aesthetic judgment. He understood nothing about the fine points of cabriole legs and matching medallions, but a million dollars always commanded his full attention and respect.

"Emma, you can tell that from comparing it to that old drawing?"

"No. You'd have to check the joinery, test the glue, see if it still has any maker's marks. But the pattern looks right out of the 1763 Sketchbook. I can't be sure but the medallions look carved, not applied, and the nineteenth century copies were more delicate than this." She pointed to the screen. "Nobody did faithful reproductions like that until recently." Then more to herself than to him, "The Martins never seemed to me the kind of people who would buy reproductions."

"Whose sketchbook?" Harry asked.

At this Emma simply turned to the plastic encased front piece.

Sketches & Patterns For The Convenient Design & Easy Manufacture Of Chests, Tables & Chairs.

Thos. A. Chippendale Co.

"Not the ..."

"Old Tom himself." Emma stuck her chin out. "All the Philadelphia makers used these sketches. But don't bet on it. These things are usually false alarms."

She turned off the machine. "Some time today, you want to check your dinner jacket, please? Last year you couldn't find your studs. I don't want to be looking for them on Friday."

Emma went back into her studio. Over her shoulder she called out, "Let me know if any of those pieces turn out to be real. We're thinking of doing a Colonial room at the Crowninshield."

Harry snorted. Zach would never miss anything as obvious as that.

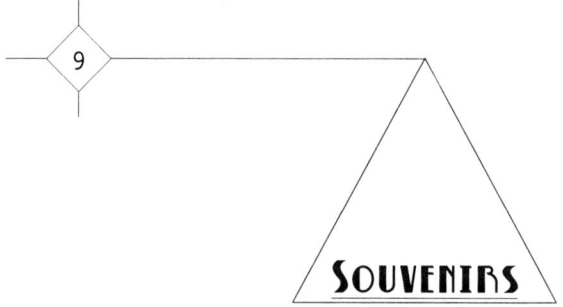

9 — SOUVENIRS

A yellow taxi jerked to a halt in the street in front of the LaGuardia terminal. The door flew open even as Gregg was raising his hand to signal for one of six already waiting at the curb. The driver had cut in front of the others and two men were shouting out of their windows at Gregg in languages other than English. Not sure of what to do, Gregg hesitated, shrugged an apology at the shouting men and got in the yellow car. That driver wore an elaborate salmon-colored head scarf, the hair on his cheeks pulled up into the fabric. Discordant singing by a high-voiced girl filled the cab, like Brittany Spears with a head cold, backed up by sitars and bells. The cab smelled of food that might have been a possibility for dinner, but nothing you'd eat at ten in the morning, even in New York. Already regretting his choice of cabs, Gregg gave the driver the East 78th Street address the New Hampshire medical examiner's office had faxed to him. The man pushed the handle of the meter down and a pulse of clicks began running up the fare at an alarming rate.

Gregg had been to New York City only twice before. The first time was a school trip: Statue of Liberty, Empire State Building, U.N., Radio City Music Hall. Shortly after he joined the state police he'd come again, that time to share escort duty with a fat state prison guard. They'd had to bring a paroled Honduran drug dealer back to New Hampshire for shooting another Honduran drug dealer on the second day of his release. Gregg and the guard took custody of the fugitive after Gregg had wasted two hours in a waiting room with the guard, talking, the way men do when they don't know each other but don't know anyone else.

"D'jou see this?" the guard had asked, handing his paperwork to Gregg face-up. "Guy's name is Jesus," the guard said, pronouncing it "Jeezis," and nodding toward a shackled man at last coming toward them from the cells.

"Heh-soos," Gregg corrected him, but keeping his eyes friendly as if to say 'I get it,' trying to be nice.

"Huh?"

"They pronounce it 'Heh-soos.'"

"Yeah, well, but no shit, look at this. Guy's name is Jeezis and the guy he kil't is Jeezis." The guard's shapeless middle shook with soundless mirth. Gregg hadn't joined in. Seeing this, the guard turned dissatisfied and said, "Course, it don't sound so strange th' way you say it."

THE CAB PULLED UP to a whitish building with its street number written in gold over the entrance. A tall, ruddy, white-haired man in a bright green uniform stood very straight in front of a pair of glass doors at the edge of the sidewalk. He was talking to two other men but watching the street. One of the other two men was black and the second looked Spanish. They each wore the heavy-soled black shoes by which all policemen recognize one of their own. Both wore tan colored top coats. Each was nursing a paper cup of coffee. The Spanish man wore a small hat, the black man was bareheaded.

Gregg paid the driver, careful to get a receipt, and as he walked up to them, he consulted the fax again. 'Ruiz' was the man he was looking for. Gregg was in civilian clothes, but he could tell from the way they turned to him they already knew who he was. He found himself looking up at the building with the involuntary reflex of the countryman in the city. This would be the tallest building in New Hampshire, but here it looked small among the buildings around it. Gregg and the doorman were each almost a head taller than the two New York cops. Their eyes met for that fraction of a second that tall men share in the presence of the short.

"Detective Ruiz?" Gregg began, facing the Spanish man, but it was the black man who shifted the coffee to his left hand and extended his right.

"I'm Ruiz, Sergeant Ruiz," he said shaking hard.

"Gregg Leavitt," Gregg said, feeling his cheeks redden, "New Hampshire State Police, Sergeant Leavitt," he added.

"Applebaum," the Spanish-looking cop said with a wave, turning away before Gregg could answer.

Before Gregg could decide if he should introduce himself to the doorman as well, the uniformed man turned away and led them through a small lobby behind the glass doors. He opened an elevator with a key on a ring that hung under his long green coat. Close up the doorman didn't look as good as he had from the cab. The ruddy complexion that contrasted so well with his white hair and grey-blue eyes was made up of numerous broken and swollen capillaries. The eyes were red-rimmed. There was a tremor in his hand.

"Miss Newsome's in 804," he said simply, speaking for the first time as he got in with them. Four was pronounced "fo-wah." The door closed. They faced forward and rode in silence to the eighth of twenty-four floors. The sweet smell of aftershave and something else filled the small space. Gregg and the two New York cops got out and waited for the doorman to show them which way to go and followed him down a beige-colored corridor to a plain metal door painted dull brown with a peep hole just below the number "804." He rang the bell.

"She ain't home, General," Applebaum said, and smirked at his partner. Ruiz only rocked on the balls of his feet.

The doorman waited, ignoring the remark, as much to annoy them as anything. Then, when a sufficient interval had passed, the man took a different key off the ring with a shaking hand and handed it past Applebaum to Ruiz. Ruiz took it, turned the key, opened the door and walked in. Applebaum motioned Gregg to precede him with mock formality. The doorman hovered in the hallway.

"Okay Captain, we got it now," Applebaum said, demoting him with a smile.

The doorman hesitated in the open doorway. Ruiz nodded confirmation then gestured with his chin that the doorman could go. As he did this Ruiz lowered the lids of his eyes and made a small smile to show that it was okay and that he had to put up with Applebaum too.

The doorman said, "Just drop that off..." He pointed at the key still in the door, "at the front desk." Gregg was still trying to square the man's appearance with a voice like Archie Bunker's as the door closed behind him.

Applebaum sat down on an upholstered chair. He pushed his hat to the back of his head. "Okay Sheriff, so what brings you down to the big city from Maybury?"

Gregg stared at him, surprised at his flash of hostility. Applebaum just stared back.

"Don't mind him," Ruiz said.

"Yeah 'don't mind me,'" Applebaum mimicked. "Just start lookin' for the stuff us dumb-ass New York cops can't find."

"Sam, shut the fuck up," Ruiz said. Applebaum only smiled back at him.

"Look, this wasn't my idea," Gregg began. He was thinking of the profane end of the conversation he had endured that morning in Carr's office. But these guys didn't know that.

◆△◆

THE MEDICAL EXAMINER'S OFFICE had scored a major coup. The afternoon before, starting with only the serial number off a breast implant, the assistant medical examiner had worked her way through the manufacturer's sales and legal departments until she learned the company was being sued over their implants. Given the number, the plaintiffs' law firm had given her name and address of the recipient in a matter-of-fact way.

At the same time that was going on, the car Gregg's men pulled out of Lake Wasoka turned out to be a rental taken two days earlier from the Windsor Airport Alamo agency.

When Gregg saw the information on the faxed copy of the rental agreement, he called T.J.

"We've got something that may be related to the West Harbor Jane Doe," Gregg said, when he had T.J. on the line.

"Did you?" T.J. seemed to be laughing.

"Uh huh, rental car, leased Saturday morning to a woman, early forties, New York address."

"Let me see if I can guess," T.J. said, "Newsome, Ephne, age 41." He read the same New York address Gregg got off the car rental agreement.

"Uh huh," Gregg said, "that's her."

"That's her," T.J. mimicked. "Tell me something, Sergeant, with a whole barracks full of state police, why do I have to learn this from some registered nurse in the M.E.'s office?"

Gregg made a discouraged sound into the telephone as the tantrum mounted.

"Goddammit, this is my case," Carr said. "Our case," he added in a softer voice. "Our case, and I'm goddamned if the M.E. is gonna go around telling everyone how she solved our case."

Before Gregg could ask him how he would stop that, T.J. said, "I told 'em no press release and the Attorney General's Office is backing me up. We want the perp to get comfortable thinkin' we still don't know who she is. That'll keep them quiet in Concord. Tell the papers we're lookin' for next of kin." Gregg thought putting the name out would help, not the other way around, but he knew better than to contradict Carr when he was like this.

"And you, you get your ass down to New York. Next thing, NYPD will be claiming they broke the case."

◆△◆

THE APARTMENT WHERE Applebaum had made himself at home wasn't at all what Gregg had expected; nothing more than one good-sized room with a bathroom and a kind of an ell for a kitchen. So small.

There was an oversized fawn-colored couch that could be pulled out into a bed. A small triangle of white sheet showed between a pillow and arm. Gregg could picture the dead woman leaving in a hurry, confident she would tuck the sheet away before anyone but her would see it. A drop-leaf dining room table stood against the opposite wall with two pull-up chairs next to it. Two others flanked the one window. Like the table, their wood was smooth, reddish brown, polished to a soft warm shine.

A mahogany writing desk with a bookcase above it, old, like the table, sat in the corner, very fancy for this little place. Water-stained prints in black and gilt frames covered most of the available wall space behind the couch and two flanking end tables, and there was a large faded oriental on the floor with two gray upholstered chairs drawn up in front of it, one occupied by Applebaum who had pulled a copy of the Daily News from his pocket and began reading.

A silver-framed color photograph on the desk showed two women with a background of blue water and a picture-postcard mountain rising behind them. One woman was short, boyish, smiling confidently at the camera, a red bandana kerchief over her hair. The other woman was taller, homely, masculine. Both were dressed in very short skirts, a style from fifteen years before. The girl with the bandana, her eyes intact, was Ephne Newsome. She appeared to be laughing at something the photographer had said. Her hair had been darker, shorter then. She had been good-looking, but a little flat-chested. The implants had done her some good. From its profile, Gregg recognized the mountain in the picture as Green Mountain, making the water almost certainly Lake Wasoka. There was a small crack in the glass at a lower corner of the frame.

The apartment looked like the woman propped up against the far away beech tree. Small, a little worn down, but confident, still trying, assertive in the way her challenging smile came from the picture. Gregg remembered how she'd looked at Long's Funeral Home and shuddered.

"Take what you need," Ruiz said gesturing at the picture in Gregg's hand, apparently taking Gregg's pause as indecision. "We'll log it all in down at the precinct."

Gregg set the picture aside and began with the desk drawers.

Fifteen minutes revealed that Ephne Newsome subscribed to *Architectural Digest* and *Southern Living*. She had a balance due of $4,805.68

on one Visa card and $3,204.57 on another. She was an alumna of and contributor to both Penn State and Boston University. Household bills for several months past were held together with rubber bands with notations of the dates and amounts paid. She paid $1,300 a month rent and made monthly payments of between $250 and $350 to something called The Brandywine Home for a woman named Carol Newsome. Verizon statements showed that she had a cell phone somewhere. The area code for New Hampshire appeared on the numbers of a half dozen calls.

There was no address book and no computer in the apartment, but a printer, a surge protector and an empty space on the desk surface asserted the existence of a laptop somewhere. Gregg wrote down the New Hampshire numbers from the phone bill in his notebook.

He found a file labeled 'MARTIN-FINANCIAL,' which revealed two credit memos from Cruikshank and Hannah, the big Windsor, New Hampshire law firm. Three of the numbers from the phone bill matched the office number of the law firm printed on the memos. One memo confirmed a '$5,000 payment for appraisal services and trial prep. Hadley County Prob. Court, on account.' The other said, 'Retainer, $2,500, Martin Estate.' There was no covering correspondence. Now he was getting somewhere. He smiled at Applebaum but got no response. He made a pile on one of the chairs for Ruiz.

But after the bills and phone numbers, Gregg found no further connection with New Hampshire or West Harbor. In fact there was little in the desk or the one closet or the side table that served as a night stand that told him much more about Ephne Newsome than what Ruiz could have found. Gregg went through her bureau, her underwear, the pockets of clothes hanging in the closet. Nothing. Neatness was never a help in an investigation.

He pulled open a series of keyhole drawers at the back of the desk. They were mostly empty but in one he found two yellowish paycheck stubs, nearly a year old, from Bernano's Gallery, with a Park Avenue, New York address. Her gross pay on the stubs was $1,850 per week. The lady made nearly a hundred grand a year, he thought, nearly twice as much as he did, and still lived in a tiny place like this. He pursed his lips and looked up from the check stub to see the two New York cops regarding him.

"Either of you guys know this place, Bernano's?" Gregg asked, displaying the check stubs.

Applebaum reached over and took the slip of paper, dropped his hand and chin in unison and looked up at Gregg. "Sure, shop there all the time." Applebaum gave Gregg a hard New York smile.

Ruiz took the slip from Applebaum. "About ten blocks from here. Over on Park. Antiques, pictures, Persian rugs, that sort of thing."

"You take me over there?"

"Sure." Ruiz looked at Applebaum. "Sam take this other stuff back to the station and get it faxed up to cow country." He pointed at the list of numbers on the phone bill. "603? That your area code?" he asked.

"Yeah" said Gregg.

"Maybe your lucky day," Ruiz said. He riffled through the credit memos. "Looks like she was doin' some work for this law firm. Probably what brought her up there."

Gregg tried to make the kind of face appropriate to a detective. "Maybe," he said.

◆△◆

BERNANOS WAS A SHOP with two sidewalk level showcase windows and a recessed door between. One window display contained a desk and small table on an oversized oriental rug folded back against the wall to show its color and design. A drop-leaf dining table with a half dozen small chairs and hunting prints on the wall was in the other. Gregg guessed he knew where Ephne Newsome got her furniture.

The inside of the shop was stuffed with the same kind of things as in the window, but not displayed to the same advantage. The musty smell of old upholstery had almost, but not quite, disappeared beneath the scent of furniture polish. Music played softly from unseen speakers somewhere in the empty shop. There was just enough light to see. In this place it was always evening.

A small, thin man with a full head of steel-grey hair all cut the same length, just long enough to lay down flat, came out of the back of the store to greet them. He didn't seem to like what he saw. His posture was alert, youthful, but up close his tanned skin showed the lines and falling facial muscles of a man nearer seventy than sixty. The man appeared to be alone in the store.

"May I help you?" he asked, giving them an up and down look. His tone made it clear he didn't think he could.

"We'd like to speak with the manager," Gregg said, when Ruiz remained silent.

"I'm the owner of this shop," the man said. "Michael Bernard."

Gregg deferred to Ruiz who pulled out his wallet and flashed his card and shield, and said without further ceremony, "NYPD and New Hampshire Police are doing an investigation into the whereabouts of a Miss Ephne Newsome. You acquainted with Ephne Newsome, Mr. Bernard?"

"I am, or at least I was," the man said. Gregg's eyes met Ruiz's. Both noted the use of the past tense. "But I haven't seen her for some time, about six months."

Ruiz didn't respond, waiting, trusting the older man would fill in the silence. After a substantial pause it became apparent he wasn't going to.

"Well, she work here?" Ruiz said at last.

"She used to," Bernard answered, standing very still. Then he turned and started toward the back of the shop, expecting Gregg and Ruiz to follow. They did.

Following him, Gregg saw that Bernard carried himself very straight, but held one arm in front of him, as if carrying an unseen tray. The arm swayed from side to side as he walked. His feet splayed outward, almost at right angles making his stride jerky, almost clumsy. Like the doorman, he was best seen at rest and from a distance. They came to a door marked 'OFFICE' which Bernard opened and held open for them.

The small room was as dirty as the show room had been immaculate. Boxes and papers were piled on very available horizontal surface. An unwashed window revealed an obscured view of a brick wall. A door completely blocked by stacked chairs and cartons was marked 'EXIT.'

Bernard pulled papers off two fragile looking chairs which he set before a desk with some formality before motioning to the two of them to sit down. He didn't sit, however, choosing to lean against the front edge of the desk, carefully hitching his unwrinkled trousers as he did so. Gregg sat down, then regretted it seeing that Ruiz was still standing behind his chair, leaning over the back.

"Don't push on that please," Bernard said.

"Old, huh?" Ruiz said. "Valuable?"

"Old? Yes, about 200 years old. It's priced at $15,000 if you're interested. I can probably get it for you for twelve." Bernard smiled as Ruiz straightened up, looking down to confirm he hadn't broken anything.

Ruiz said, "No shit, fifteen thou for a chair?" He inspected it doubtfully. "This chair?"

"Uh-huh," said Bernard. "But you're not here for chairs. You were talking about Ephne Newsome."

"Yeh, I was," said Ruiz, but then only waited. Gregg liked the way Ruiz tried to let the story come from the man, who at last seemed willing to speak.

"She worked for us for four years."

"You own the place Mr., ah…"

"Bernard, Michael." He repeated with studied patience.

"So you must have kno… you know Miss Newsome pretty well, huh?" Ruiz caught Gregg's slip and Gregg saw that Bernard had as well. The old man's eyes widened for only a moment before he said, "I suppose so. I couldn't say we were close. She worked her regular shifts, was polite to the clients." Bernard inspected his cuff. "She had a very good eye."

Not any more, Gregg thought.

"When was the last time you saw her?" Ruiz asked.

"About two months ago, at an auction, Parke Bernet. Not to speak to, of course."

"Of course?" Ruiz said.

"I can't say we parted happily." Bernard shifted his weight putting both hands on top of the desk behind him as he leaned back onto it.

"Fired, or she quit?" Ruiz asked.

"Oh, I guess you could say she quit." He looked at the two, considering, then said with impatience. "Look, I don't know what this is all about, but Miss Newsome cut the shop out of a private sale of a very valuable highboy in a most unethical way. She never tried to deny it. She knew when she did it that I'd find out, of course. You always do in this business. When I confronted her she just said, 'Well that's that then' and left."

"Cut you out?"

"It's part of our business to buy as well as sell, uh officer ...?"

"Sergeant, Detective Sergeant Ruiz."

"...Sergeant. We inspect, authenticate when we can, and either purchase directly or on consignment. This particular piece was museum quality. Undamaged, original finish, good provenance. She simply arranged a direct sale to one of our more substantial and more unscrupulous clients and took God knows what as a commission for herself."

"Must of made you pretty mad," Ruiz said.

"Oh 'mad' doesn't begin to cover it," Bernard said. We didn't just lose the sale, we lost one of our best clients." Bernard's voice was rueful, weary.

"Why the client?" Ruiz asked.

"Even billionaires are embarrassed to do business with people they've cheated out of small sums of money. I'll be frank. If the gentleman walked in here tomorrow, I'd greet him with open arms and not a word said. But, of course, he'd be uncomfortable. Believe me, Sergeant, when you have the resources this particular gentlemen has, you have long since ceased to endure discomfort. We'll never see him again."

Gregg spoke up. "You know what she's been doing since she left?"

Bernard gave him a skeptical look, then said, "Freelancing. She has a few clients, does some buying, does some appraisals. She's testified in lawsuits." The man turned his attention to Gregg. "And you are...?"

Bernard looked inquiringly as Gregg produced his own identification, imitating the way Ruiz had done it. Bernard looked at it wearily, then showing sudden interest, he said "Ah, New Hampshire, God's country. I envy you." He handed back the identification. "Is it Officer Leavitt?"

"Trooper," Gregg said, deciding not to make an issue of his rank.

"Trooper. Marvelous. Trooper." He showed the beginning of a smile.

Gregg looked at the older man levelly. Long enough. Bernard cleared his throat then and returned to his story.

"Yes, Ephne had a good eye, particularly for the colonial pieces. She was interested in it, you see. Not just the furniture, but everything that went with it. Who had owned it, how it got passed down, what houses it had been in, who was related to whom. She was very good at establishing provenance."

"Provenance?" Gregg asked hearing the word for a second time.

"The origin of the piece. Sometimes if you're lucky you can establish a chain of ownership right back to the maker. Ephne was tireless and, well, fascinated by the hand-to-hand part of it. What house it had been in, sometimes even which rooms. And the people, well she just knew who was whom. Remarkable."

"What does that have to do with furniture?" Ruiz said. "A chair's a chair." He looked down at the chair in front of him. "Or so I always thought."

"Sergeant, a good provenance can double or triple the value. If it can be traced to a famous owner, well the sky's the limit. George Washington once made a gift of three identical field desks to Lee, Hamilton and Lafayette. There are at least twenty known pieces by the same cabinet maker, identical, most in better condition, but they won't fetch a tenth of the price."

"You know of any customers she might have had up in New Hampshire?" Gregg asked him.

"No. The Boston market is all tied up with local shops, and north of that, well..." He opened his palms in front of him and looked sadly at Gregg. "Beautiful country. You have a few rustic pieces, but furniture?" He brought his hands down. "Well, we can't have everything."

"Any family, boyfriends, girlfriends?" Ruiz asked, making Bernard turn his attention back to him.

"Ephne?" He considered for a moment. "A mother outside of Philadelphia. Boyfriend? Many, I think. But no one close. Ephne Newsome was—it is 'was' isn't it?" Bernard looked at Gregg and then at Ruiz who only shrugged. "Thought so. Always thought that girl would come to a bad end, even wished it from time to time. What was I saying? Ah, Ephne was not popular with other women."

Bernard then moved around to behind the desk.

"For someone so comfortable in the past, Ephne Newsome was quite vague about where she herself was from. Somewhere outside of Philadelphia." He opened his hands in front of him. "She knew New York and Charleston, Salem and Boston, Newport, of course, but she knew all about Philadelphia."

"But nothing that would connect her with New Hampshire?"

Bernard turned back to Gregg. "Not that I know of. She had done some appraising before coming here. As I said, she did a few turns as an expert witness, some connoisseurship. She was very sure of herself, too sure. But frankly, uh, Trooper, the country pieces from your part of the world weren't in Ephne's line, or mine."

"She worked here four years," Ruiz said. "Before that?"

"She'd worked in Philadelphia for, let me see…" he looked up at the ceiling thinking. "Wharton and … Wharton & Biddle."

"An antique store?" Gregg asked.

"Ah…" the man laughed. "Oh, that is good," he said. "No, a law firm… 'Antique store,' that's too good. Wouldn't they love to hear that." The man chuckled then gave Gregg a look of patient disappointment.

Gregg decided he didn't like Mr. Bernard. "So she came to you from this law firm?"

"No, she was a curator for a time at the New York Historical Society before coming here. I recollect there was some excitement when she left them as well. You'll have to ask them what it was." He looked down at his nails. "I know I wish I had."

"You didn't have any, ah, social relationship … with her?" Ruiz asked.

Bernard made a small sound of exasperation. "My romantic interests, when I still have them, lie in other areas, Sergeant. He glanced at a thin gold wrist watch, then back up. He adopted a friendlier tone. "It was nice of you to ask. Thought I'd save you the time."

Gregg asked, "Did she wear a ring?"

"Oh yes. What an interesting question. A gold signet pinky ring. Very exclusive. Said she'd attended St. Agatha's. She was quite proud of that, our Ephne. Don't think she graduated, though. How did she die?"

"Someone shot her," Gregg said.

"In your 'part of the world,' as you put it?"

"Yes."

The old man shot his cuffs and straightened. "Are we finished?"

The two policemen nodded. Ruiz regarded the chair for a final time, shook his head and looked up with a smile.

Bernard went to the door and opened it. "Odd," he said. "I thought I'd be happy to hear of Ephne's misfortune but, strangely, I find I'm not."

The man seemed to want to talk as they went back through the store so Gregg favored him with an inquisitive look.

"She was so, curious," Bernard said, taking time to find the right word. "You see, she believed in these things, not just in what they'd bring at sale. She thought they meant something. It was almost as if, if she could just possess them, just for a little while, something in them would rub off on her."

They stopped abruptly and Bernard made a short chopping gesture with his hand. "There was something about New Hampshire. A camp! A girls camp. Lake Wa– something or other. I remember she was acquainted with the niece of a client who had been there with her. We had quite a good sale out of that."

"Lake Wasoka?"

But Bernard wasn't sure. "Could be." He shook his head in doubt.

"Remember the name of the camp?"

"No, no." The man pursed his lips and shook his head.

When they reached the front of the store Gregg was surprised to have the old man offer him his hand, even more surprised to see that Bernard's eyes shone in the reflected lights from the street.

"I was fond of her, you know. At first."

◆Δ◆

AT THE PRECINCT station house Gregg made arrangements to get Ephne Newsome's mail forwarded as well as copies of any bank statements.

"Christmas is coming up. Everyone gets lots of stuff at Christmas," Gregg said.

Ruiz looked at him sadly. "You don't spend a lot of time in New York, do you?"

Applebaum, still aggrieved at something, shouted loudly into a telephone, then hung it up, grinning. He leaned back in a battered metal chair putting his hands behind his head. Gregg thought that he and Carr could have had a contest.

"Well, Huck, you're in luck." Applebaum said. "The next phone bill comes out tomorrow and covers everything up to midnight Sunday."

"Uh huh."

Applebaum sneered at the quizzical look Gregg gave him. "So I don't have to get no fuckin' court order to get the dead lady's phone records, Huck. I just go over there tomorrow and pull the envelope out of the mail box. Like I said, you're in luck." Applebaum sighed in contentment as he crossed his hands behind his head.

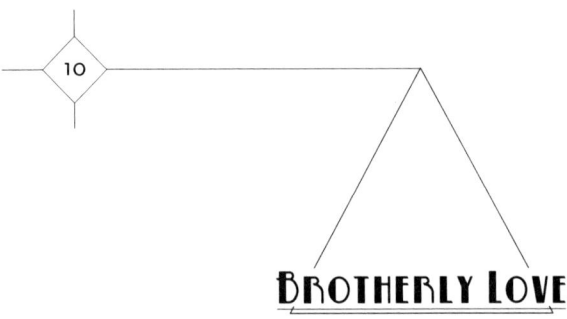

10
Brotherly Love

Thursday morning Harry arose in the gray half light, Emma next to him, snoring in her soft questioning way. He tried to go quietly, but she mumbled, "Make sure Abigail gets out, okay?" Placing one hand on the warm place in the bed he had just left, he brushed the hair from her forehead and brushed it with his lips. She smiled without opening her eyes and pantomimed a kiss.

Stepping around Abigail, impatient after a night of continence, Harry started a pot of coffee before going to the front door to gather up the *News & Observer* and *Boston Globe* from the driveway. Abigail pushed by him and peed on the grass beyond. It was still damp, an unseasonably warm morning for November. More rain coming. When the dog had finished she pushed by him again. Back in the kitchen, brown liquid gurgled into a glass decanter. The dog yawned and the man read.

It hadn't been such a bad week. There had been some unpleasantness in Lionel Whitcomb's divorce that finished with Lionel firing his lawyer amidst much courtroom shouting, but Harry's humiliation of Monday had barely left a foot-print. A paragraph in *The Capitol Insider* wondered rhetorically whether 'changes are in store up in Hadley County' or if the 'old boy network' would hold the line despite the 'judicial floundering' that was 'starting to cause concern.' 'Old boy network' seemed pretty shopworn shorthand for how Harry Warren was still holding back the ever-so-deserving Amanda Stevens. The author and Amanda had to be talking daily to have a column ready for the paper this quickly. But no names were used. She wasn't that confident. Yet. Harry sighed as he read. He could picture the smirk the young News & Observer reporter would give him when next they met. Harry made a dismissive sneer, practicing how he would pretend not to notice. He knew with a few weeks of conscientious effort that this would blow over.

The story that had led the *News & Observer* on Tuesday was the mysterious killing, almost certainly a murder, of a still unidentified woman found dead on Green Mountain in 'the upscale summer resort of West Harbor,' revisited in a front page box in the *Boston Globe*.

MYSTERY KILLING RAISES NEW QUESTIONS

The body of a woman discovered by local hunters Monday morning in the forest above West Harbor, a fashionable summer resort town on the shore of Lake Wasoka in New Hampshire, remained unidentified last evening.

Cause of death had not been established by State officials but knowledgeable sources close to the investigation confirmed that the victim had suffered at least one gunshot wound.

Controversial Hadley County Prosecutor T.J. Carr declined to speculate last evening on any aspect of the case other than to say he was "confident" that the New Hampshire State Police who are heading the investigation in conjunction with his office would lead to a speedy resolution.

> Eighteen months ago Carr was sharply criticized by the New Hampshire Supreme Court in connection with the prosecution of a homeless man for...

Harry smiled at his luck. Who would remember his foul-ups with both a murder and T.J.'s past sins to read about?

He put on a fleece and brought his coffee and the papers outdoors to the patio. Settling himself on a metal chair, he turned to the jump page in the Globe. He started to read but got no further than "Carr has released no information on the victim's identity." He put the paper down and let the coffee and morning air work into his system. Abigail moved about between the remnants of outdoor furniture sniffing deeply in the moist air.

The White Mountains, the highest already tipped with early snow, were spread out as if in miniature. They framed a round valley shaped like a dinner plate. The outlines of Lake Winnipesaukee and Squam Lake were just visible in the middle distance with Lake Wasoka in the foreground.

To his left Harry could pick out the almost perfect pyramid of Mount LeFarge, the one they climbed every Devon Headmaster's Day. To the right, out of sight at the base of the eastern slope of the mountains, was Hadley, his mill town childhood home. Though unseen, Harry could calculate precisely where Hadley was because he could just see the beginning of a pass—a 'notch' in New Hampshire—that cut through the mountains there. As a boy he had had a distant view of the other side of that same notch from the bedroom of the house where he grew up. Directly to his front, at the far end of Lake Wasoka, were the outlines of the Wasoka Club golf course. Three chapters of his life, so different, so distant, but captured in a single glance.

RETURNING TO THE *Globe,* Harry had just returned to the rest of the story about the unknown woman when a door opened behind him. It was Livy, pulling her sweater around her. Abigail raised her head, rose and frisked behind this new source of approval and affection. Most people found this view of the New Hampshire mountains spectacular, but Livy only frowned disapproval.

"Cold enough?" Harry said in greeting.

"I don't know how you stand it here," she said, adding "all winter." She took just long enough to convey her real meaning. Warm as it was for New Hampshire, it would have been a cool morning for Philadelphia. "You look contented," Livy said, sitting down. "Oooh, this chair's made of ice!" She jumped back up.

"Not so bad," Harry said. He gestured at the view, but took in Langdon House with a gesture which suggested it could pass muster even for a Llewellyn.

"Yah, Berchtesgarden without the uniforms. I'm freezing my gonads off."

"That I would have to see."

"The Lake freezes, doesn't it?" she said, ignoring him. Absently, she scratched the top of Abigail's head. "When we were kids we didn't believe it. We thought you townies made it up to impress us." Livy folded her arms beneath her breasts the way women do when they're cold.

"Two feet thick," Harry said, "some years." Then, "You're up early."

"Emma wants me to pick up some things in Boston. It's only one more day, by the way, for the dinner." She looked at him levelly. Their eyes met as they weighed the prospect of another seventy-two hours of one another's company.

"How does she seem to you?" Harry asked.

"Scared shitless, like always. Does she really have to give a speech?"

"An introduction, Livy, is not a speech."

"To Emma, telling the time of day to more than three people at once is a speech." It was just cold enough to see Livy's breath. She shivered again. "I don't know about you but I'm freezing my ... ass off." She walked off briskly, then stopped at the edge of the patio while she eyed him over her shoulder. She wasn't finished. "C'mon Warren, walk me around this spread. Show me what it is that Emma finds so great about it." When he didn't follow, she turned and added, "We have to talk."

There was an unexpected note of sincerity in her voice, so he caught up to her halfway down one of two stone stairways. A single balustrade traced the outside curve of each to a second terraced level below.

"Well, there is the view," Harry said, filling in the silence.

"Uh huh, that's the Club, isn't it?" She pointed toward the distant outlines of the Wasoka Club golf course.

"Yes."

She smiled at something and continued down a second smaller set of stairs cut simply into the side of the terracing. These ended at the edge of a fenced off swimming pool, now covered for the winter. She put her elbows on the top of the fence.

"This has worked out pretty well for you, hasn't it?" She gestured with her hand but didn't face him.

"Pretty well?"

"Come off it, Warren. Don't pretend to be stupid. You're a long way from where you came from and no one knows that better than you."

Harry regarded her with a sideways look, but he wasn't going to admit she'd read his mind. "No, I actually came from right over there." Harry pointed at the notch. "Not far at all."

"Not that kind of far. You know what I mean. Don't be clever. This isn't Penn where you can get by making fun of people."

Of course he knew, and so did she. This wasn't his house and not just because they still called it by the name of the long dead shoe-shop baron who built it. It was Emma's house, bought by one of Emma's trusts and maintained by another, both efficiently managed by trust officers at Wharton & Biddle, where the Llewellyns kept a score of lawyers employed.

Livy leaned over the top of the fence. She didn't see him flush but she knew she'd struck a nerve. It was one thing to be a kept man and another to be called one.

"You really think a school like Devon will be all right for Carter?" It was a sincere question and her change in tone seemed intended to change the subject back to neutral ground. No one would have claimed that Devon was a fashionable school or even a good one, as most of the fashionable schools later became.

"I assumed that wasn't your first choice."

"Well, he hasn't exactly covered himself with glory at Fay."

"Good athlete. He'll be fine there." At fourteen, Carter could already beat Harry at golf, which didn't mean much. He could beat his eighty-two-year-old grandfather as well, which did.

"I didn't know what else to do," she said.

"You look at any other..?"

"Oh, like he's another Samantha." Livy's reference was to his second daughter Sam's effortless progress through Deerfield and Princeton.

Harry shrugged. They were all in awe of Samantha.

Sam had always been an enigma to Harry. Her older sister, Leigh, he understood. He and Leigh shared the same dark, androgynous features. Leigh had followed him to Devon and later to Penn. Conscientious, loyal, practical, Leigh had been everything one could imagine in a daughter—until Samantha came along. But the little sister had all the gifts. Taller than her mother and sister, she was a better athlete and even more beautiful. At fifteen, Samantha Warren's follow-through at the Club driving range was turning twenty middle-aged heads at a time. Where Leigh worked for success, Samantha floated. But Samantha had the Llewellyn toughness as well, underneath. She dismissed the thought of Devon with a shrug and gave up competitive skiing with a smile. They had all been surprised at that, assuming she would go to Dartmouth where she could still compete. Harry hadn't minded. His skiing days were long behind him, but Emma, who spent days freezing on ski trails, had let her daughter know that in any future sports ventures, she was on her own. Most unhappy though was Zach Hannah who had stood in for Harry at so many of those races. It wasn't like Zach to get flustered the way he had, but that was Samantha, careless of everyone.

Livy turned around and set the small of her back against the fence. "Warren you're day-dreaming. Look I couldn't have him growing up in Palm Beach. Eduardo would have him going to all those parties before he starts to shave."

"Mmmh," Harry said.

"What did you mean by that?"

"Nothing. Just Mmmh."

"Don't patronize me Warren. You haven't come that far."

Harry held her gaze long enough to show that he felt the cruelty of the remark, then turned toward the house to emphasize that he didn't have to take it. It was true, of course. Livy hadn't spoken in anger or sarcasm, but there was a limit, even for him. He heard her footsteps as she followed him back into the shadow of the house.

When she caught up to him, Livy seemed to understand, perhaps even regret, her words. "Look, Harry," she started. Then she seemed to reconsider. "Oh, forget it. Let's go in, I *am* cold."

As they started up the steps Livy let herself be jostled by Abigail and patted her head in return. Then she said, "You two *are* all right, aren't you?"

Harry tripped on a step. "Of course. Of course we're all right."

"Okay. Sure."

"What? Look, Livy, if you've got something to say, please say it. I think we've covered the subject of my upward mobility."

"No, honestly, I don't. It's just, well, you two seem different. I can't put my finger on it. Does she spend many weekends at the summer house?"

Harry felt his eyebrows rise, but said nothing. He detoured onto the patio to retrieve his newspapers but also to hide his confusion. He was sure Emma had told him she was staying in Boston the past weekend—meeting with the caterer, auditioning the quartet—but he wasn't going to share the deception with his sister-in-law.

Livy waited at the door and faced him. "Look, I don't know. Hell I'm a three-time loser, so who am I to say." She looked down then added, "I never understood you two. In the beginning, I figured Emma felt sorry for you because you were the only guy who really did get his ass shot off in Vietnam. Then I guessed I had to be wrong. Now I'm not so sure."

How like Livy to talk about him, to talk *to* him like he was one of her horses.

"Look, Emma and I are fine."

"Uh huh. Well, just don't let that halo of yours slip, Warren. If it does, you'll find Emma's little doll house won't be the happiest place on earth."

Safely in the kitchen, Livy folded herself onto a ladder-back chair at the breakfast table. She looped one arm through the back while she drew her knees up and together.

"You could have got another guy you know," she said softly without further ceremony. Harry had lost his train of thought and it was a moment before he realized she was back talking about the Museum dinner.

"*I* didn't get anybody. The Museum wanted a name, someone to bring people out," Harry said, adding "I told you Tee Ingersoll wasn't my idea."

"But naturally your old playmate gets elected." Livy said as if he hadn't spoken.

"Tee was a roommate, Livy, not a playmate." He felt warmth come to his face, for the third time. It had begun as such a quiet morning. Then, "It's not like you don't know him. He was my best man for Christ-sake."

"Look, I don't know and I don't care what did or didn't happen between you two at dear old Penn. But I do know that Emma's got to get up in front of a couple hundred of your nearest and dearest and remind anyone who didn't already know that her husband long ago had a short but meaningful relationship with America's most popular faggo...." She stopped at the sound of Emma's footsteps on the tiles of the kitchen floor. Interrupted, Livy scowled and pretended to drink from her cup.

Emma came into the kitchen wearing slippers and a quilted robe. Her hair was pulled back, her eyes still puffed with sleep. She gave them the suspicious, disapproving look one gives to those who have fallen silent at her approach, unfooled by the wet noises they made with their coffee.

Emma kissed them in turn and, stopping by Livy, she made the beginning of a yawn. "You two fighting again?"

"No, Harry just found out I'm staying till Sunday. He expressed his joy."

"Livy's worried about your introduction," Harry said, earning a widening of the eyes from his sister-in-law. He was going to say something flip about their being "all right," but something in Livy's remembered tone warned him away.

Emma said nothing. She bit onto her lower lip, cast a quick sideways look at Harry, and went to the sink to fill a kettle, her slippers slapping softly on the floor.

"Tea?" Emma asked as she tore open a packet holding a single bag.

"Yeah," said Livy. "This coffee Harry made tastes like shi..."

"I'll have Grace type up all Tee's biographical stuff," Harry said to Emma, interrupting. "You don't have to read it, if ..."

"Of course I do." Emma spoke quickly, sharply. "I'm the chairman. If I don't it'll be a wink and 'you know why Emma Warren wouldn't make the presentation, don't you?'" She waved her hand to cut off Livy as she took in a sisterly breath. "I said I'd do it. I'll do it. But I don't want to spend the next two days talking about it. You like green tea, right Livy?"

Emma was opening drawers and closing them with punctuating precision while Livy and Harry exchanged 'See what you started?' looks. Livy pushed her cup of coffee away.

"It's nearly eight," Emma said, finally finding the tea she was looking for. "Don't you have court? Didn't you say the clerk was starting to take attendance?."

"You're right, I'm off," Harry said. "Picking a jury today."

"Harry Warren swinging a gavel and Tee Ingersoll on television," Livy said. "Only in America..."

She flashed the remembered killer smile. He knew it was as much the physiognomy of Livy's features as anything else, something to do with a narrowing of the eyes. He had seen the same arrangement of features when she expressed genuine pleasure to others at family gatherings, but to Harry it always said, "What are you doing here?"

◆Δ◆

As he drove north on Route 16 to Hadley County, Harry pondered Livy's question. *'You two are okay, aren't you?'* Perhaps he hadn't managed things as well as he thought recently, but then Tee always seemed to bring the worst out of Emma.

Even before Tee's metamorphosis into 'Ted' Ingersoll, the producer and star of *Profiles*, Harry knew he would never really understand his old roommate, now the only famous person he knew. He and 'Ted' Ingersoll now had little in common except memories, but Harry and 'Tee' Ingersoll had lacked even that when they'd met thirty years before. Emma, Livy and Tee, on the other hand, had grown up in that little world of old Philadelphia families that Ephne described as a 'small town.'

That Tee and Harry had met at all was only because freshman roommate parings at Penn were intended to throw together complete strangers. Harry could have just as easily been matched with a Polish linebacker from Johnstown or a Jewish pre-med from Rockville Center. But he drew Theodore Cadwalader Ingersoll, III. Harry came to realize Tee would have never so much as spoken to him otherwise, but thrown together, Tee 'took him up.' It was the kind of thing Tee said, in those days.

At first, 'Theodore Ingersoll, III' was a wraith, an unlikely name stuck upon the door above his whose bearer never appeared. For a week the bed opposite his lay empty. Then Harry came back from class one day to find stacks of record albums, pictures, an expensive stereo and an old oriental rug. Still no Ingersoll. Another week passed.

Harry gained minor celebrity from this. None of the rest of the boys on the floor had known each other before Penn except Morty Appel and Cary Hymerling, two bespectacled sixteen-year-olds from Bronx Science who had the room across the hall and who, because of their youth, had special dispensation to room together. But Harry was the only freshman with a bona fide ghost for a roommate.

"We think you made him up," Hymerling said early that second week. He leaned against the open door of Harry's room, eyeing the pile of things on the other bed.

"I thought so myself before that stuff arrived."

"You imagine actually having a name like that?" Behind his glasses Cary's face sloped from all sides to the end of an enormous nose. In repose his face settled into a natural smile giving him the look of an amused mouse. He traced the card with a finger.

"Hymerling a common name?" Harry asked.

"You got something against Jews?" Cary's smile remained pleasant enough but he had a point. Anti-Semitism was still new to Harry. Before Penn he didn't know anyone named Appel or Hymerling. Anti-Semitism was no more than a curiosity, something he read about in books, a vaguely shameful, silly sentiment held and practiced in exotic ways by vulgar people. It probably would have prospered in Hadley or Devon, too, but there simply weren't any Jews to be jealous of. In Hadley, they tormented French Canadians.

"Naw, just Catholics," Harry said, and he and Cary looked at each other across a space both great and small. Cary held his eye for a full second before nodding down to Harry, lying on a bare mattress below him.

"Warren, we've been here ten days. Don't you have any sheets?" Cary wasn't a bad guy. He said this as if he would give Harry some if he asked.

"Sheets are bourgeois."

Cary blinked. "Cool," he said. Then, as though that was settled, "You goin' to dinner?"

"Sure."

Cary, Morty and Harry hadn't learned yet that Penn, for all its progressive pretensions, was still contentedly medieval in practice, with a student body carved right down the middle. There were Christian fraternities and Jewish ones. Jews dominated the intellectual life of the campus, except the campus humor magazine and the all-male musical review, Masque and Whig. Christians dominated sports, except fencing. The separation was both muted and firm.

In class and around the campus, people remained civil, even friendly. But once inside the clubs and fraternities with the doors safely closed, the jibes, the exchanged assurances that there were people 'not like us,' were allowed voice along with knowing smiles, raised eyebrows and the occasional act of heart-stopping cruelty. No one at Penn would go up to Morty Appel and actually call him a "Kike" or try to beat him up, but good luck to him if he tried for an editorial spot on the *Penn Anecdote* or a place in the Masque and Whig chorus line. If he showed up for rush night at Phi Psi or DKE or St. Mike's across the street, he would face nothing worse than a polite lack of interest. He would come and go and never hear himself dismissed as one of the 'chosen,' Penn's gentler, crueler epithet for Jews. Similar treatment awaited Harry at the editorial office of the *Daily Pennsylvanian* or at ZBT and SAM. Where Christians were known as WSGs—for 'World's Stupidest Goy.' There were exactly twelve black male undergraduates that year and four of them were on the basketball team, so the starkness of the religious divide was as yet unsoftened by complaints of racial bigotry.

Unlike Harry, Morty and Cary already seemed to know all about sides and which one life had put them on. It seemed much on their minds. Harry felt he was being tested. Perhaps they hoped his bohemian pretensions and naivete might prove the rule and not the exception, and as Barbara Warren's son, Harry had enough verbal virtuosity to hold his own at first. Pleasantly surprised at his responses, they nevertheless knew in their hearts he would soon enough reveal the inescapable twin attributes of the goyim—stupidity and bigotry. They were right. Harry's complicity in Penn's original sin, to which he was to succumb fully, waited only for Tee Ingersoll.

It was in the third week that Theodore "Call me Tee" Ingersoll, III, was finally made flesh. Harry was reading a Harold Robbins book enjoying a moderate hard-on and listening to a Buddy Holly album. Both the record and the machine playing it were Ingersoll's.

The bearer of the impressive name announced himself as "Tee" Ingersoll. He had a plume of brown hair that drooped across his forehead. Only through frequent shakes of his head could he keep the hair from his eyes. Harry later learned they had called him 'Teedie' at Lawrenceville but he came to Penn determined to be known as 'Tee.' He wore loafers with no socks. A tiny bow-tie barely crossed the frayed collar of his pink shirt.

"Well you made yourself right at home," the stranger said, picking up, then dropping the empty album cover on his bed.

"Sorry," Harry said, getting up. "You want me to turn it off?"

"Naw, just ragging you." He turned the volume down, but not off.

"I was beginning to wonder if you existed. I'm Harry Warren."

"Tee Ingersoll," he said again. "Just got down from Maine. Got my uncle's boat from Northeast Harbor to Damirascotta. Took longer than we thought. Daddy's really pissed." He repeated the shake of his head.

Arriving so late, he needed his class schedule explained to him, and the roommates found they had two lectures in common.

"You smart?" Tee asked.

"Who knows."

"I am. About the things that matter. Lazy though. Bottom of my class at Lawrenceville." He seemed proud of this, but his expression turned skeptical. "You can't be that great yourself if you're here," he added.

As Tee said this, Morty put his head through the door. "Warren, you comin' to dinner?" He stared at Tee, his eyes artificially enlarged behind his glasses.

Tee looked at Morty carefully.

"You Ingersoll?" Morty asked. "Really, no shit?"

"Uh huh," Tee said. He didn't ask Morty's name. Neither made any move to shake hands.

"You comin' too?" Morty said at last into the silence.

"I suppose so," Tee said.

Their talk at that night's meal at the Houston Hall commons lacked its accustomed frivolity. Cary tried to bring Tee into the conversation but Tee only played with his food and looked around. When Morty or Cary said something calculated to get him talking, his usual response was "Really?" But the way he said it had nothing of a question in it. It was more like, "How remarkable." Finally after many long silences Tee waved to a group at another table. They were dressed the way he was and two of them had the same problem with hair in their eyes. When one of them waved back, Tee left, saying "See ya fellas." After he'd been at the other table long enough to finish a sentence, a loud burst of laughter came from their direction.

"Well, Warren, the fuckin' guy lives," Morty said, seemingly indifferent.

"You think so?" Cary said, and shook his head. He seemed unconvinced.

"He does lack a certain—warmth," Morty said.

Harry saw they were both watching him. "Hey give me a break, will ya?" Harry said. "I just met the guy."

When the three left, they passed the other table. Tee, very relaxed now with a group none of whom, Harry was willing to bet, were named Morty or Cary, called out. "Warren, Harry, come meet Tom Adams."

He hadn't asked Morty or Cary, and Harry hesitated.

Then Morty, always the wisest and most pessimistic of them, said, "We'll catch you later." Harry went over to the group and, with this, joined in the larger sin. Within days he had shed his socks, and innocence.

Tee Ingersoll never ate with Morty and Cary again, and after a week's time, neither did Harry. Cary stopped poking his head in the door and Morty's watchful smile became thinner. In the months and years that followed, the three continued to greet each other with the false gentle gaiety of strangers even as the occasions became more infrequent. Morty and Cary had been right after all.

Tee became Harry's friend, but not right away, perhaps because Tee realized that his fascination with the world he loved was slightly indecent, best savored in silence and then only with others who knew how to enjoy it. Somebody once told Tee that a 'gentleman' was someone who reveals his prejudices only to those who share them, an anecdote he repeated to Harry. But as the weeks went by Tee seemed unable to help himself. Few true lovers can resist a willing audience. He shared his insights slowly at first, as if testing. Would Harry ever learn to appreciate the secrets he had learned from Tee and, should he do so, would he, too, love them? Keep them?

And what secrets they were. Tee Ingersoll knew clubs and schools like a dowager. He went into microscopic detail on the difference between Brooks Brothers and J Press shirts. He was an apostle for the virtues of Daks trousers and Peel shoes. He sailed large boats and seemed astonished that Harry didn't know the difference between a yawl and a ketch. He knew exactly where a man could get the right shade of red pants on

Nantucket. He rode. He played squash. He never did succeed in explaining to Harry the difference between the people one found at the Merion Cricket Club and those at the Philadelphia Cricket Club, but he believed, passionately, that it was profound. He could deduce an astonishing amount of information about other undergraduates just from the shoes and socks they wore or, almost as importantly, didn't wear. Occasionally, showing off, he would confirm his conclusions with a seemingly innocent inquiry of a passerby that always left Harry a wide-eyed Watson to his Holmes, amazed at the accuracy of his deductions.

People often commented now on the verbal quickness of 'Ted' Ingersoll, the irreverent host of *Profiles*. Harry wondered what they would have said if they'd seen him at eighteen. One thing was certain, his boast of intelligence at their first meeting wasn't hollow, he wasn't stupid.

Usage was everything to him. People were 'rich' not 'wealthy.' Something was 'cheap' never 'reasonable.' One wore a 'dinner jacket,' never a 'tuxedo.' There was a very small portion of the world that was not 'unattractive,' the only people worth knowing—who called their parents 'mummy' or 'daddy' not 'my dad' or 'my mom.' "Trust me, Warren," he said. "My cousin, Professor Rush says 'that possessive pronoun marks the most visible fault line in American life.'"

And Tee knew how to speak to 'servants' —Harry's word, not his. At his own home outside of Wilmington, an elderly black man, addressed as 'Devereaux' even by Tee's fourteen-year-old sister, seemed less an employee than a distant cousin taken in from misfortune. A younger, enormously fat, black woman who went by the diminutive of Sarry, enjoyed the status of an aunt who just happened to enjoy cooking and ironing the Ingersolls' clothes.

At the homes of friends, Tee seemed to know already the names of the 'people' who worked there. He treated them all like respected tradesmen, as if he had just bought the top coat from the man he handed it to and both were satisfied with the transaction. In later life, Harry came to know plenty of men with decades of experience and a lot more money than Tee Ingersoll ever had, some of them astonishing snobs, but he never met anyone with the mastery of the inconsequential that

Tee Ingersoll had at eighteen. Emma's complaints that Harry let himself be bullied by the ser..., that is to say, the "people" who worked at Langdon House, whose names he could never seem to remember, were fully justified. The worse they were at their job, the more ingratiating Harry became. Tee could have predicted it. "It's dysfunctional, Warren, always. Whenever the unworthy employ the indifferent."

But Tee—the things he knew. He couldn't decline a french verb, but he could order dinner. He could barely manage a 'D' in American history but he knew every family tree in Philadelphia. He knew, perfectly, how to be a nineteenth century gentlemen. Unfortunately, there didn't seem to be much call for that late in the twentieth.

Naturally, he considered even Penn's relaxed academic requirements an imposition so he quickly solicited Harry's help with U.S. History and Intro to English Literature. Harry wrote book reports for him extolling the virtues of *Absalom, Absalom,* and *Portrait of a Lady* earning him what he claimed were his only As at Penn, outside of Prof Rush's courses. The English instructor had particularly liked 'his' analysis of the social strata of Yocknopatapha County. The Sutpens would have pushed their way into the Philadelphia Cricket Club, while Col. Sartoris would have belonged to Merion. Tee had liked it too. "When you put it that way, Warren, Faulkner begins to make sense." It was evidently as a reward for this that Tee, having weaned Harry safely from the world of Morty and Cary, determined he might as well confirm Harry's passport into his.

Tee signaled this with a beige paste-board invitation. "Free booze, pretty girls. A part of town refreshingly different from this one." He gestured toward their open window and, on cue, the sound of a horn and the squeal of tires came up from Spruce Street below. He scaled the invitation across the room.

Harry caught it, looked at his name, and handed it back. "This doesn't seem like your sort of thing at all," he said. "It says 'informal.'"

"Warren, Warren, Warren ..." Tee held the invitation to the base of his nose and gazed at Harry over its edge. Then vertical lines appeared on his forehead and he sighed, "You don't know, do you."

"Know what?"

"What 'informal' means."

"Of course I know what 'informal' means." Harry spoke with just enough asperity to reveal a complete absence of certainty.

"Mmmm?"

"Sport coat, no tie," Harry said, closing the subject.

Tee was silent but shook his head slowly back and forth.

"All right, a tie."

"This is beyond belief." Tee fell backwards on his bed.

"Look Teedie, Tee, this some kind of trick question?"

"Warren, informal means black tie," he said to the ceiling.

"You mean a tuxedo?"

Tee sat up quickly. "Warren, we have to understand one another," he said.

It was Harry's turn to sigh. Another disquisition.

"No, Harry, this is serious. It is never, *never* a 'tuxedo.' It's 'black tie,' 'dinner jacket' if absolutely necessary, but never, ever 'tuxedo.'" He spoke with unaffected gravity. "Tuxedo is a small, very pleasant town in New York. It is never an article of clothing." Now, thirty years later, that same tone of didactic urgency— '*You must understand this*'—jumped off a million TV screens with every episode of *Profiles*, PBS's most widely watched show as 'Ted' Ingersoll, as he had come to be known, explained just what a Los Angeles teen gang leader could, and could not, say if he wanted to survive.

But then Harry had said, "Well so what? I don't own a tu...dinner jacket so we don't have to worry about it."

"Thought so, which is why you and I are on our way to Germantown Avenue right now."

By dark Harry was inspecting a collection of mostly black clothing from the Chestnut Hill Thrift Shop in varying states of disrepair spread over his now sheeted bed.

"I really have to wear these shoes?" He held up a pair of scuffed, cracked patent leather pumps with grosgrain bows. They looked suitable for a very large six-year-old girl.

"Warren, I'd've bought them myself if they fit. Did anyone ever tell you you have very small feet for a man? I promise you, they're perfect."

◆△◆

HARRY LATER LEARNED the fundamental purpose of 'coming out parties' in the only sociology text he ever read. "How Elites Parcel Out the Virgins" was the chapter title in the textbook for a course taught by it's author, Dr. J. Lippincott Rush, Tee's distant cousin, entitled *The Rise and Rule of American Elites*. This was also the course title for "Sociology 250," though everyone at Penn called Dr. Rush's course "Dinner at Eight." An anomaly among the serious minded scholars, Prof Rush had actually gone to Penn himself and still frequented undergraduate campus activities, gorgeously dressed beneath his perfectly barbered steel-colored hair. His lecture style matched his looks.

"*Any elite wishing to perpetuate its, ah, prerogatives in a settled social order has the fundamental, indeed the foundational task of parceling out the, ah, virgins.*" He had given the lecture a thousand times and waited with perfect timing for the hundred or so students to stop groaning before proceeding.

"*The heavy lifting is done in modified convents, the girls boarding schools where the virgins are assembled, graded and prepared. Anomalies of speech and dress are ruthlessly suppressed, primarily through ridicule and peer criticism. All this is preparation for being ceremonially, ah, exposed for inspection. These affairs are known as 'coming out' parties.*"

But when Harry took the course, Tee had already instructed him. "Not 'debutante parties,' Harry, 'coming out parties,' and never, "deb parties,' never."

Thus instructed, Harry joined Tee clad in his discarded finery at a number of these fetes outside the city, stumbling back into the quadrangle at six a.m. on Saturday and Sunday mornings, stared at by the studious and industrious. By then Harry's hair had grown and he too was finding it hard to keep it out of his eyes.

Tee's tutelage also proved enough to get Harry entree into the half dozen old-line fraternities that sat clustered at the center of Penn's campus.

"Phi Psi is the place for you, Warren," Tee announced after the first week to fraternity rush. As usual Tee's eye for nuance was precise. It *was* the place for Harry, but on the occasion when Tee first said it, he was really telling him that St. Michael's, the house they had just left, was not.

But Tee was right about Phi Psi. On the surface it was similar to its more staid and dignified neighbors. However, Harry soon learned that in addition to the sons of mere millionaires it counted members like Mike Amatore, youngest son of the head of one of the Five Families, who spent most of the past year being attended by two young men with elaborate haircuts who never seemed to take their coats off. There was also Jack McCarthy whose parents' very public divorce had almost overshadowed his father's decision to move an AFL team from Chicago to California. Later there was Tommy Shields, a standout P.G. quarterback at Mercersburg who never quite hit his stride at Penn. And soon there was Harry Warren, the son of Barbara Warren, the poet, who wrote the book for two Masque and Whig shows and those stupid verses for the *Anecdote*.

Phi Psi consistently earned the lowest grade point average on campus and was the place where girls like Emma and even Livy Llewellyn went to show they were daring. It provided Harry with the majority of his adult friends for more than thirty years. Whatever else was wrong with it, Phi Psi was the only place he was ever fully, unqualifiedly, even ceremonially, accepted.

Morty never could see it. As seniors, shortly before graduation, he and Harry had lunch. "One tweed is pretty much like another, Warren." He didn't know how wrong he was, or how right.

Harry tried to explain to Morty that while hedonism had begun as temptation from the drudgery of study, it had become something more akin to a job, and he'd simply gotten better at it.

"So what you're saying, Warren, is that you pissed away your college education so you'd know what tie to wear?"

Whatever the wisdom of Harry's choice, Tee Ingersoll knew from the first that "St. Mike's," the most stolid of the older fraternities, was the only place for him. It had some Greek letter affiliation as well, but everyone referred to it by the diminutive of some Greek saint who had died theatrically some centuries before. Most members of the Locust Street fraternities affected a certain louche disdain for the rest of Penn, but the people in St. Mike's were the ones who really meant it. Tee might be able to palm Harry off at a deb... coming out party, or two, but no such favor could be expected over something serious like St. Mike's. For they took it very seriously indeed.

At the end of freshman year, during Rush Week, the fraternities held themselves open for the twenty to twenty-five new members each one recruited each year. True to Tee's prediction, Harry got his Phi Psi key to the house the first evening.

Tee, however, returned to their room tight-lipped. Excited as Harry was, it didn't occur to him that Tee might not have been invited. The St. Mike's were so tight and formal, Harry assumed that there must be some secrecy involved.

When Tee returned the next night, however, he was white-faced. With some alarm Harry saw he was close to tears.

"You mean they didn't..."

"No. I'm sure it's that fucking Tony Rhoades. Blackballed. Wouldn't say anything to my face." Tee's voice caught. Harry didn't know what to say so he went out in the hall. Morty and a couple of the more resolute independents remained mocking but not unfriendly. "Warren. C'mon, no shit. Do you tweeds really piss on each other?" He seemed ready to taunt Tee as well but Harry headed him off.

Early on the morning of the fourth and last day of Rush, two long-faced St. Mike's came to their room. They greeted Harry with pleasant and cheerful handshakes. "Phi Psi! Well, good for you Warren. Great guys. Good man." What they meant was 'Get lost,' and there was an awkward moment before Harry took the hint and left.

By then rumor had spread down the hall. "What's going on with Ingersoll?" Morty looked up from his desk as Harry leaned on his open door.

"I'm not sure."

"He's not with you, at 'high five,' or whatever you call that place?"

"No, and it's ..." Harry stopped as Morty's eyelids drooped. Morty, at least, knew it wasn't something they could talk about. They all still smoked in those days and that's what they did then.

That morning became a series of phone calls. Sons to fathers. Fathers to other fathers and fathers back to sons again. Another St. Mike's deputation appeared that afternoon. Harry knew by then to clear out early and heard only some of what went on. There were raised voices. At one point Tee emerged, went to the bathroom and was sick. Harry was grateful for two afternoon classes which, contrary to his growing custom, he actually attended.

Tee departed at seven for the final night of Rush like a man going to execution. The Phi Psi's were still vying with the Dekes for three freshman lacrosse players and at the Phi Psi house there was loud rejoicing that night when two of the three took keys. It gave Harry the chance to forget Tee's troubles as he and his new 'brothers' gloated and peeped through the windows at the more somber goings on down the street.

On this last night of Rush the houses were permitted to serve alcohol openly, though the Phi Psi's had been doing it covertly since the beginning, so Harry and two other of his newly minted brothers were contentedly swallowing beer back in the dormitory by ten. They were bantering the way semi-strangers do when the door opened and there was Tee. He tossed the hair from his eyes with his familiar hauteur, "Well, you boys seem to be enjoying yourselves." At last the glint of a St. Mike's cross had found its place on his lapel.

◆△◆

IN THE DISTANCE the Hadley County courthouse came into view. Harry eased his silver car into his parking spot and got out to face the new day. He hadn't thought about Tee and his early troubles with St. Mike's for years. At his tenth class reunion Harry had recounted an expurgated account of Tee's brush with rejection to another Phi Psi.

"Can you imagine your father calling anyone about getting you into Phi Psi or any of your friends calling their father?"

"Nope."

"Or have the guy even listen if he did."

"Well, I guess he'd listen if it was Mike Amatore's father."

SMOKE AND MIRRORS

Gregg heard his own involuntary groan as T.J. worried the cellophane off a pack of Pall Mall Lites. Gregg's mouth was dry and he yawned. The last flight from New York to Windsor hadn't landed until after midnight.

T.J.'s was the last public office in Hadley County where smoking was still allowed and the odor of stale smoke hung heavy enough in the air to make every breath an act of penance for a non-smoker. Gregg dreaded the first sharp smelling cloud he knew was coming. But then T.J. was in the penance business

Carr's foot was back on his desk atop the photocopies Gregg had brought back from New York. The top sheet was already wrinkled and had a small tear. Carr leaned backward in his chair toward an easel holding pictures of the victim, the search map, and a list of landowners by home address, most of them out of state.

T.J. had been silent for exactly five minutes. Gregg knew this because he had started to speak but Carr had waved him silent saying, "I'm thinking" at 9:37. It was now 9:42. Gregg calculated how much further Carr would have to lean back to fall over. He suppressed a giddy wish to lift the feet and spill the man onto the floor.

Gregg had to admit this investigation was a novel experience. In truth, he had never really 'solved' a crime. Four years as a trooper had taught him how to collect evidence, establish times, chains of custody, document warrants and take statements. But it had always been after they knew what had happened and who had done it. The typical suspect had either already confessed or bragged to a girlfriend. When he dumped her, she paid him back. Sometimes he did something even dumber like sell a stolen VCR to one of his loser friends who always seemed to have the loyalty of snakes.

Not that the job of backing up the case wasn't important. The girlfriends were always retracting their statements, especially if they were pregnant. The loser friends had lied so much, they were disasters at trial, unable to remember which story they'd told last. And who wouldn't think better of a confession after a week in the county lock-up?

So Gregg had concentrated on making good arrests, on learning to gather the evidence, to document it, hand-to-hand, from the scene of the crime to the moment the prosecutor handed it to him on the witness stand. A trooper who didn't get his evidence excluded was a good cop, a guy to be depended on. So far, no one could say he'd ruined a case. But to actually solve a crime, and a murder at that, was the sort of thing to move him to the head of the line at the governor's office.

And they hadn't solved this one yet. Any one of a million people could have killed that woman up on Green Mountain.

Calls to the billionaire client that Michael Bernard had complained about had been diverted to a team of impatient New York lawyers who gave them absolutely zero. Without denying or confirming anything about the past dealings between their client and Ms. Newsome, they did confirm that the client had been on a boat off the coast of New Zealand for nearly a month. No, he didn't know anything about Ephne Newsome except that she'd authenticated one highboy that may or may not be in his Greenwich house. He may, or may not have actually met her in person and no, he wasn't coming back any time soon. Jesus! Three days since they found her and all he'd been able to learn was her name, that she lived in New York where a sissy antique dealer didn't like her very much. That and she had some connection with New Hampshire's biggest law firm, Cruikshank and Hannah.

They had the bird shot pellets, front and back. Two shots, confirmed now. Credit card records were on the way. But time was ticking away and he was stuck in this dirty little office with this madman. It hadn't helped that Carr still refused to release the woman's name. The *News & Observer* reporter made it clear he didn't buy their 'notifying next of kin' story, but hadn't pushed it either. The story had disappeared from the front pages.

Gregg had begun this morning saying he wanted to go down to Windsor and find out who it was that Ephne Newsome knew at the Cruikshank law firm.

"No, no, no. For Chrissakes, if you do that, everyone will have their story ready. When we *know* who it is, that's when we question them. What's the matter with you?"

Carr finally got the box of cigarettes open, extracted one and put it between his teeth. Then with some difficulty he pulled a lighter out of his pants pocket and almost knocked over a cold-looking, half-full styrofoam cup of coffee. The scum of congealed cream shivered on the top of the brown liquid, but the cup didn't fall and unfortunately neither did Carr. Instead, T.J. lit the cigarette with an expert flourish as he swung his feet off his desk. He blew out smoke as gravity brought his chair back to level. Gregg felt his throat contract with the asthmatic reaction of the non-smoker.

"Okay," said Carr. "We got a forty-one-year-old lady who gets her tits done in New York. She knows about antiques, providences, that shit."

"Provenances," Gregg said.

"Yea, provenances. She's been in New York six, seven years. She makes a decent living but she decides she wants a little more. Six months ago she shafts her boss and skims a little off a deal. Cuts him out of..." He looked down at Gregg's report. "...forty thousand dollars, back in May."

"Uh huh."

"But you don't like the antique dealer for this?"

"No. Not enough money. Too far away." Gregg looked at his watch.

"So what brings her up here to the Granite State?"

The question was rhetorical—it was Cruikshank and Hannah—so Gregg said nothing. Another cloud of smoke emitted from T.J. and

Gregg coughed softly, fighting the constriction of his throat in the hot, close air of the room. Carr shot him a look. "Mmm," he said. "Forgot, you don't smoke." He stabbed the cigarette out. "Sorry."

Mildly surprised at this sudden act of consideration, Gregg decided to risk an opinion. "It figures it had something to do with antiques, her being here. The bill says 'appraisal.'"

Before Carr answered his secretary pushed open the door behind Gregg. "T.J.," she said, "Some guy named Ruiz for Gregg."

"He'll take it here," Carr said. He handed Gregg the handset.

"This is Sergeant Leavitt."

"Hey, Leavitt. You back in God's country, I see." Ruiz imitated Bernard's careful but weary pronunciation perfectly. Gregg smiled at the thought of the old antique dealer.

"Yah, birds and trees, 'marvelous,'" he said getting into the spirit. "What you got?"

"We just got her phone bill up through October 30th. Ruiz paused. "There's a couple of more numbers with a 603 area code."

Gregg felt a warm flush. "I've got a pen ready."

Ruiz gave him the numbers as he wrote.

"Great, can you fax the bill up here?"

"Sure."

Gregg confirmed the numbers he'd written down.

"Jeez, that's only a couple of digits off from your number," Ruiz said. 'You don't have a lot of numbers up there I guess."

"One, two and many," Gregg said.

"Hey, I didn't mean anything by it."

"I know. You think you can find any calls made after Saturday? We still haven't found the cell phone. Someone took it, might just be dumb enough to use it."

"Oh sure. It'll take a couple of days, but the company'll do it all right. Day after tomorrow at the latest. You let me know, kid, if you need it expedited."

"I will, and thank you. Thanks very much." He hung up the phone. "Two more New Hampshire numbers," Gregg said to T.J. "Fax on the way."

Carr buzzed his secretary. "Stacy, you get a fax in a minute or so from New York? Check'em against the reverse directory. Make me two copies." He clicked off the intercom in the middle of her reply.

When she brought these in, one number was to the Alamo car rental agency at the Windsor airport. The second was a West Harbor number.

"L. and E. Martin, 360 Shore Road, West Harbor," Stacy said, dropping the directory dangerously close to T.J.'s coffee cup which, without being asked, she reached over and picked up. "You're welcome," she said.

Gregg went over to the map. Number 360 was less than five hundred feet away from where the Newsome woman had left the road.

He put his finger on the map. "And, back at her apartment ..." he said, waiting for T.J. to look up, "There was a file in her desk titled 'Martin Estate.' We should get over there," he said, holding his finger on the map. "You want me to go over now?"

"Uh huh. But just ask, don't push," T.J. said. In case Gregg hadn't gotten the point, he added, "They don't want to talk, they don't let you in, just come on back here and we'll get a warrant. You understand?"

FORTY MINUTES LATER, Gregg pulled his cruiser up to the Martin house. Its brown-shingled exterior was moss covered in places where the sun didn't reach through the pines. The windows were dirty and the trim around them, a light cream color once, was flaked and peeling. One large shutter was leaning against the house. Above it a window gaped with a matching shutter still hanging askew on one side, and a dirty shadow of unbleached shingle the same size on the other.

In the driveway a rusting Subaru, once metallic blue, sat inconveniently close to the front door. A sticker on the bumper said "Old Orchard Beach. Playground of Two Nations."

Gregg squeezed around the car, climbed the steps and adjusted his hat. He knocked.

Two women's voices came from inside, one obviously instructing the other. Then footsteps. The door opened.

Margie Tuttle told her boyfriend later that night, "*Geez, when I saw him, I nearly peed my pants. I seen nothin but cops this week.*"

"*You been stealin' again Margie?*"

"*Naw. Well, nuthin you'd expect a 'statie' to show up about. Him in that big fuckin' hat. But geez you nevah know, do ya.*"

In actuality, when she first saw him, she had just stood there looking at Gregg, her jaw working silently, on a couple of sticks of Dentyne. She wore a man's blue work shirt loose over the same tights she had worn to court three days before.

"Ms. Martin?" Gregg said, thinking he had seen the woman before.

"No" Margie said, the first flush of fear passing.

"Can I see Ms. Martin, please."

"Which one?"

"The owner of the house," he said.

"Lemme see."

She left the door ajar but didn't ask him in. Gregg heard more voices and then the woman in the blue shirt returned with a smaller, older, untidy woman with gray bangs that covered half her forehead. It was an old fashioned cut, the way a younger woman would have worn it a long time ago.

"Okay, okay," she was saying, before she looked out from the doorway. She sheltered her eyes from the morning light. Gregg heard the first woman say "...trooper..." but couldn't make out the rest.

"Yes. Thank you Marjorie," the page boy said, dismissing her.

"It's Margie," said the woman in tights as she shuffled away into the shadows. Gregg was sure he remembered her from somewhere.

"Now I don't know what you're doing here young man, but you can send any papers down to Mr. Hannah's office. I thought that's what he told you to do."

She had a weary, superior tone. Her accent told him she was not from New Hampshire. Gregg disliked her instantly, but he remembered what Carr had said. "Papers?" he asked as politely as he could.

"Well, writs or suits or motions, or whatever you people call those things. Honestly, I'd think you had better things to do with your time."

She brushed her hair back from her face with its multiple lines. She wore a pair of matching sweaters, both light brown, and a heavy looking brown tweed skirt. There was a stain on the jersey and a moth hole in the cardigan. She fit in with the house. She was wearing enormous shoes.

"Ah, that is, no, no Ma'am, I'm not here to serve you with anything. I'm Sergeant Gregg Leavitt, State Police." When she didn't respond, he added, 'I'm not with the Sheriff's office."

She blinked a couple of times. "You're not here for the bank?"

"No, Ma'am."

Expecting to be asked in now, Gregg gave her his best recruiting poster smile.

"Well, okay, good," the woman said. "You don't have to stand there grinning like an idiot young man, what is it that you want?"

Gregg squared himself and adjusted his hat. He stared at the old bitch and allowed his smile to tighten. He could see his reflection in a mirror hung on the wall behind her. He thought he looked tough enough, but she stared right back.

"Do you know a woman named Ephne Newsome?" he asked.

"Why?"

"This is a police investigation Mrs. Martin. If you could just…"

"It's *Miss* Martin, Mr. Level…"

'Leavitt, Ma'am, L-E-A-V-I-T-T. Sergeant Leavitt."

"You spell very nicely. But I don't have to speak to you, do I?" She smiled, girlish now, but sly, confident she had him in the wrong.

"Well, no Ma'am." Gregg couldn't remember disliking anyone quite so much on short acquaintance.

"Don't I get to have my lawyer with me?" She asked this almost musically, taunting him.

"Well, if you think you need …"

"That's for me to decide, isn't it?" she said interrupting.

"Of course, if you want…"

"Well, you just call Mr. Hannah down in Windsor. He'll make the necessary arrangements. Good day."

Gregg started to say something further but the door closed firmly on him.

He adjusted his hat, his eyes working, the beginning of a smile.

Mr. Hannah. Cruikshank and Hannah. That wasn't much, but it was something.

◆△◆

"Let me see if I've got this straight, Leavitt. You're telling me that the old bitches wouldn't even let you in? 'Talk to my lawyer' she says?" T.J. was half standing behind the counsel table in courtroom number two, his voice rose and Gregg was aware of the lawyers at the back of the courtroom grinning at each other and gesturing toward them. Old T.J., chewing up the ass of another young cop.

"Mr. Hannah, she said." Gregg half whispered the name.

"Hannah. Zach Hannah. Zach Hannah himself?"

"She didn't give a first name. She said he was in Windsor."

"That's Zach Hannah," Carr said, subsiding into his chair. "There's only one." At the front of the courtroom a stenographer was adjusting herself at her keyboard. Deputies just brought in a skin-headed youth in an orange jump suit. One of the lawyers who was grinning at T.J. left the others to go up to the boy who tried to shake hands with the manacles still on.

"Go back to the office, see if you can get Hannah on the phone," T.J. said. "Maybe you can use your considerable persuasive powers to get *him* to talk to you."

"All rise," cried the bailiff as Judge Stevens came through the door behind the bench. "The county court for Hadley County is now in session, the Honorable Amanda Stevens presiding." Gregg stood at attention until the judge was settled, then left. He kept his face neutral as he passed a knot of lawyers who shook their heads in sympathy.

Mr. Hannah, Gregg found, was in, but 'in conference' according to the second of the two secretaries Gregg was shuttled to. "Was there any message?"

"Just tell him we're trying to interview his client, a Miss Martin. Yes, today if possible. A homicide investigation. No that's Sergeant Leavitt … two Ts. Yes, yes please, as soon as possible."

Gregg sat back in the chair in a column of afternoon light thick with glittering motes. Now he couldn't even get the lawyer on the phone. That would mean another chewing-out from T.J.

The outer door burst open and T.J. marched in. Gregg braced himself as he saw Carr stop at his secretary's desk to drop some papers. She was on a call but nodded to him with her hand over the mouthpiece. She hung up and the phone rang almost immediately. Carr came into his office.

"Well?" he asked.

Before Gregg could answer the secretary yelled, "Sergeant Leavitt, Mr. Hannah on three."

Carr paused, then pursed his lips as if to acknowledge that Gregg had done something right at last. "I'll take this one," he said.

Punching the button, T.J. yelled into the phone "Zach, you old bastard, how are yuh?" There was a pause. Then he said, "Oh, okay, yah, fine." He looked up, annoyed. "They're getting Mr. Hannah now," he said in falsetto.

"Hi Zach, yah T.J. Carr. How are you?" T.J. nodded and smiled as he spoke. "Look, Zach, I got Sergeant Leavitt here. He's the officer in charge. Let me put you on the speaker."

Carr pushed a button and hung up the phone. "Zach?" he shouted.

"Still here, T.J.," said the voice from the speaker.

"Say hello to Gregg Leavitt, Sergeant Gregg Leavitt," Carr said.

"Sergeant, how are you?" The voice was reassuring, friendly.

"Fine sir. Thank you for getting back so soon."

"Well now, what can I do for you?"

Carr shouted back, "Who's this Eleanor Martin you won't let talk to us, Zach?"

"T.J., please." The voice made a soft two syllable chuckle. "First I've heard of it."

"Yeh, well she gave Leavitt here a full ration of B.S. this morning. Says you told her to."

Gregg's eyes widened. She had said no such thing, but T.J. only winked at him.

"T.J., T.J.," said the voice from the speaker, "I do represent two ladies named Martin in a trust interpretation case. What brings the state police to their door?"

"This isn't any will case, Zach. We got a homicide up here and, turns out the victim made phone calls to your office and to your client's phone."

The voice came back over the speaker surprised, confiding, helpful.

"Whoa, Jesus, homicide, Eleanor Martin?" Now the voice laughed ruefully. "Believe me T.J., you don't know how incongruous those words sound in the same sentence. You know we don't do much criminal work down here."

T.J. pursued his lips. "Someone named Ephne Newsome involved in this trust case?" Carr pronounced it "Eefnee."

"Who?" said the voice. Gregg heard the man's confidence, his assurance, disappear.

Carr repeated his pronunciation of the name. "Ephne," Gregg added, pronouncing it correctly.

"Ephne," the voice responded, "Lord, homi ... Ephne Newsome?"

"You know her?" Carr raised his eyebrows at Gregg.

'Yes, sure. We hired her to appraise some of the Martins' property, some paintings, family silver, you know." Then, "You're sure this is the same person. Small woman, forty-something, blonde, pretty?"

"Not so pretty when I saw her," Carr said. He winked again at Gregg.

"Sweet Jesus," the voice said. "I talked to her last Thursday." He trailed off. "Can you tell me any more about it?" the voice asked.

"Just that we found her up on Green Mountain Monday morning."

The voice spoke, but not to them. "Of course, the Green Mountain lady." Then, "You mean ... you don't think Eleanor Martin may have something to do with ... that?" The tone conveyed dismissal of the very thought.

"Dunno. Won't know 'til we talk to her, will we. The victim wasn't found so far away from the Martin's place. There's another Martin isn't there?"

"Yes, Louisa. A sister." The voice trailed off, as if thinking.

"Look, T.J.," the voice resumed, now confiding, intimate. "Let me talk to them. They're a bit brittle, if you know what I mean, and pretty worked up about this estate litigation. Scared of anybody in a uniform. Let me see if I can smooth the way. But T.J., I'm sure they don't know anything at all about this."

"We need to move on this," T.J. said. "It's going on three days now."

"Of course. The Martin case isn't one I've spent a lot of time on personally, ah, lately. We have a couple of associates working on it. You need to talk with any of our people about, ah, Miss Newsome?"

"Sure do, but we'd like to start with the old ladies now. And we'd like to look at the house."

"Of course, of course. Just give me a chance to talk with them first."

"Yah, sure Zach. Get back, okay?"

"Sure. I'll call right now."

The phone went dead with neither man saying goodbye and T.J. pushed the button to terminate the speaker.

"Well, what do you know. Zach Hannah," Carr said.

"Seems okay." Gregg gestured toward the phone. His usual dealings with lawyers were mostly insinuating accusatory affairs.

"You just got a little taste of the 'Hannah treatment,'" T.J. said to Gregg. "Next thing ya know he'll have you drivin' down to his office so you can talk to her there. Have you pickin' up coffee for him on the way. You heard of Cruikshank and Hannah?"

"Yah. They do some assigned defense cases. The younger guys. Full of themselves. Pains in the ass." Gregg said.

"Believe me, you don't know what 'pain in the ass' means until you get on the wrong side of Zach Hannah," Carr said. "One minute you're talking, all buddies, you know, 'all friends, all in this together.' That kind of thing. Next minute, you look down and your pants are missing. That man on the phone would have been your Congressman, probably your Senator, if he'd bothered to get a hunting license."

"Hunting license?"

"Long story," T.J. said.

Gregg smiled.

"How 'bout those other num...."

Before he could finish, Stacy shouted, "T.J., Mr. Hannah again."

T.J. yelled back. "Well, is it him or some secretary on the line?"

Carr's secretary appeared in the door almost instantly. She was dressed like always in a shabby skirt and turtleneck shirt. Gregg had heard she was the only one who could talk back to Carr.

"That's about the tenth time you've shouted at me today," she said. Red-faced, she stared at Carr levelly until he looked down.

When Carr didn't respond she said, "It's his damn secretary." She gave Gregg a "What are you staring at?" glance before turning back to T.J. who raised one hand in apology and picked up the phone with the other.

"Yah, hi, thank you." Carr rolled his eyes toward where Stacy had been. "Hey Zach, what's the good word?" Gregg watched T.J.'s expression turn from unaccustomed contrition, to disbelief, and finally back to the familiar, barely contained rage he was used to.

"You're kidding, right? Really? No.. no, no, no ... look ... well you work on it, okay? Tomorrow? Okay, I think it'll keep till then. No, no more than that. Hey, I wouldn't do this for everybody. Yah, sure. Yah. Goodbye."

"Jesus, Mary and goddamn Joseph" T.J. said, hanging up.

"He didn't give us the okay?"

"No. He claims the one you met won't listen to him and her sister's a fruitcake. He says we can talk to them but only with him there." T.J. breathed heavily in frustration but subsided. He made a tent with his fingers leaned his chin onto it, eyes closed. "Why all the song and dance?"

Carr rose then and went to the door. "Stacy, my beloved, could you give me a few minutes of your time?"

"Uh huh."

"There's a pending case in the probate court. *In Re Martin*, Eleanor Martin. Cruikshank office. I want a copy of the file pleadings, transcript, everything."

◆Δ◆

THE NEXT MORNING a dark green Lincoln pulled into a handicap parking space just below where T.J. Carr had stationed himself on the courthouse steps five minutes before. The highest button on T.J.'s shirt front was undone and his pants and jacket were undeniably parts of different suits. He watched as a man in a much trimmer gray suit unfolded himself from the back door of the green car. The man made a short wave at T.J. before he reached back inside to retrieve a briefcase. He had a brief conversation with the driver, a hard-faced man who nodded back.

T.J. sucked on his half-smoked Marlboro and moved his head from side to side. Leave it to Zach Hannah to hire a crippled driver. A two-fer if there ever was one: get credit for hiring the handicapped and a guaranteed parking space wherever you went. The passenger closed the door and T.J. returned Zach's wave with what he hoped was the good humor appropriate from one pillar of the bar to another. At the same time he ignored one of the veteran P.D.s from the Hadley office who approached from the step below him.

"Say, T.J., you see my discovery motion in ..."

'Yah, later," T.J. said as he walked down past the defense attorney to take Zach Hannah's proffered hand. The two then turned and walked together into the courthouse, the deputies waving them around the metal detectors past a line of people emptying their pockets into plastic trays.

When they got to his inner office, T.J. swung the door closed and pulled two large files off one of the three chairs, leaving the others fully burdened, and motioned to Hannah to sit down. The visitor could see an easel behind T.J.'s desk but it was turned away from them, toward the wall.

"Still got that dog-robber Smitty working for you, I see."

"Been driving for me twenty-five years," Zach Hannah said. "I fire him once a week but he refuses to go." The two men then allowed each other thirty seconds to break the silence. T.J. gave up first.

"So Zach, how'd you meet this cute little thing in the first place?" T.J. pushed a particularly gruesome photo—he'd picked it out for just this moment—of Ephne Newsome across the desk to Hannah. The other man half rose to accept the picture, but when he looked down his mouth fell open. T.J. saw him try to hide the shudder.

"Jesus, T.J." Zach fell back into the chair, leaving the picture where it was, his eyes reproaching the smiling county attorney.

"C'mon Zach, it's not your sister," T.J. said. "I didn't know you were so sensitive." He perched one buttock on the corner of his desk.

"Okay. You made your point," Zach said, his voice declining to a sigh.

"And what point would that be?" T.J. leaned forward.

"You tell me. It's your party."

"Okay, just so we're clear. There aren't any ambiguities here. No fraternity boy who went a little too far with one of the town girls." T.J. paused.

"Jesus, T.J., I thought that was behind us," the lawyer said. Some years before Hannah had taken a rare criminal defense case and defended the son of the chief of surgery at the Windsor Hospital against charges he had raped and beaten a Hadley girl. With photographs of a black eye, split lip and good rape kit results, T.J. was sure he had a slam dunk case. Then the calls started. The presiding justice, the Attorney General, even Hadley's female police chief. Felony rape turned into misdemeanor assault. The Hannah treatment.

"Uh huh," T.J. nodded. "This is a murder. No way to dress it up like it's something else. If one of your clients, one of those Martin women, had anything to do with this, I'm gonna find out, and we're going to do something about it."

"Now wait a min..." Hannah shifted forward.

"That's fine. That's fine," T.J. said, interrupting him. "I understand, that's okay, I don't need a lecture on attorney-client privilege, but let's get to it, shall we? This is murder, not rape, and no chief judge around to help out behind the scenes."

"Rape? You still on that?" The look of mystification made T.J. suspect for a moment that the other man had forgot but then Hannah added, "C'mon T.J., that girl's legs were further apart than Sharon Stone's. Actually, I think we got that about right."

T.J. reddened, remembering the humiliating plea. "She was sixteen years old, sixteen," Carr said. "Her old man fills up my car every Monday mornin'. He cleans the windshield and looks straight at me the whole time. He doesn't say a word, but his eyes say the same thing every time. 'Probation, two lousy years probation. That's the best you could get for my little girl.'" Hannah's expression didn't really change but his steady gaze asked the silent question. "So, why'd you settle?"

T.J. felt he had lost a round, but an early one. "Okay, Zach. You're right. Maybe she was a tramp. She is now for sure." He poked the picture with his finger. "But this is different. This lady is going to be as dead tomorrow as she is today. Someone has to answer for it and everything is pointing toward 360 Shore Road, so let's leave the holier-than-thou Cruikshank and Hannah bullshit at the door."

Hannah watched the other man's anger rise and pass. After the silence had hung between them, he said "Okay. You got that out of your system. Fair warning. But what is it you think I can do with my two elderly spinsters? You really think they had anything to do with *that*?" He gestured toward the top of the desk.

T.J. gave a short dismissive wave, "What am I suppose to think?" The redness drained from his face. T.J. had expected more push back, even a short speech on the duty to vigorously defend one's client, another touch of the famous 'Hannah treatment.' When it didn't come, he cleared his throat and said in a much softer voice, "I mean, what's the problem with those Martin ladies givin' us permission to search? Just to clear the air." As he looked into the other man's eyes, T.J. thought he saw a flicker of concern.

"Well, T.J., I'll go over it with them in detail. There may not be a problem at all. I'm going over there when we finish here," Hannah said. "You tell me what two refugees from the Main Line are going to think about a foul mouth Irish prosecutor poking through their linen drawers. A certain reluctance perhaps? But who knows?"

"All right, you got a point. Blessed be the peacemakers. But I've lost a day here. When you goin over?"

"Right away. Promise." Hannah held up his right hand.

"Okay, okay. Now, what do *you* know about this lady?" T.J. asked tapping the picture again. Again T.J. felt the other man shrink. There was no movement. The eyes remained steady, but ...

"Not much. She's been ... she *was* retained to appraise some pictures and see if anything else in the house had value. She's ... damn, I keep putting her in the present tense... She *knew* a number of dealers. She was supposed to meet someone from our office on Saturday, pick up four pictures and see if she could help the Martins sell them. You do know the ladies in question are broke?"

"I heard. That was a pretty tough order the probate court gave you."

"Ah, you read the probate file. Okay, so you know we were engaged to try to stop a foreclosure. We've held it off for a year. We may be able to buy them a little more time." The lawyer shrugged. "Who knows? The two ladies are a handful but they're harmless. You know, once you get beyond the society nonsense, they're actually rather vulnerable. Eleanor's a retired school teacher, boarding school. She might as well have been a nun, poor health and completely impractical. Louisa's healthy enough but belongs in a nursing home." He tapped the side of his head.

T.J. retreated behind his desk.

"So you guys hired her, the Newsome woman? Cruikshank, not the Martins themselves? She's not someone they knew? The connection was through your office?"

Hannah crossed his legs and settled back into the chair. "Yah. She came highly recommended and she came cheap. Said she used to come up to New Hampshire summers when she was a kid, so she was happy to make the trip. The bank's lawyers had her on the deposition schedule for December." Zach reached into his briefcase and pulled out a manila file folder. "Here's her CV and here's a copy of the expert report she'd done for us. Never had a chance to sign it." He put the documents on the desk over the picture.

"She any good?" T.J. pulled the file off the desk.

"Oh excellent. You'll see from her report. Decisive, no B.S., nice long list of comparables."

T.J. frowned down at the report. He opened to a copy of a charcoal drawing. "Looks like two homos sizing each other up," he said.

"That was elegantly put," Zach Hannah said, but smiled just unevenly enough to convey complete agreement. Then he leaned forward, studied the page and said, "You know, they do at that." The two shared a short unpleasant laugh. Then Zach Hannah said, "Ephne, Ms. Newsome, she said they may be the real deal. And she knew her business. She ah …"

There was a silence then. T.J. waited for the man across from him to finish his sentence, finish his thought. He waited.

"Say, why don't you put those away," Zach Hannah said. T.J. reached for the drawings, uncovering the photograph as he did.

"That too," Hannah said.

T.J. didn't look up right away. There was something in Hannah's tone. This was going to be good. Still he waited. He retrieved the photograph and put it and the drawings upside down on the desk surface. When he thought he'd made Zach Hannah, the great Zach Hannah, squirm enough, he raised his eyes to the man in the chair.

The man gave a sort of shrug and made a rueful smile. He inclined his head slightly to the right. "We, ah, Ephne Newsome and I …"

"Jesus, Zach, at your age," T.J. said, laughing softly. But he was too good a prosecutor to let Hannah off with an ambiguity. When Hannah didn't respond he said, "What were you saying Zach?"

Hannah seemed to sag. "We, ah she and I were, ah, intimate," he said.

"You had sex with her, intercourse?"

"Yes."

"Well that doesn't fall under attorney-client privilege," T.J. said, trying to make a joke of it. When Hannah didn't respond he rose up and stretched. "Am I supposed to read you your rights now? You gonna confess or something?"

"I thought I had. Fornication is still a misdemeanor, even in Hadley County." Hannah's voice had recovered.

"You know what I mean," T.J. said. "I gotta ask. A lovers' quarrel thing goin' on?"

"Actually, no. It wasn't that way. And no, it didn't have anything to do with..." The lawyer looked at the desk and gestured toward the edge of the woman's photograph. "... with that. But I know you, T.J. You'd find out eventually. Thought I'd save you the time."

"Okay, just so we're straight. You know what you're telling me has to go in the file? If there's a trial, it'll come out."

"Of course, but there was nothing much to it," Hannah said. "She was a good expert and good looking, ah, before. She assessed all the pictures on the walls and picked through the attic. Efficient, good at her job. I liked her. We got back to the office late. A pretty woman leans against you after a long day like that, hell, I saw my chance and I took it. We got it on a few times after that. To be honest, I was kind of hoping to see her last ... An associate in the office was supposed to take a meeting with her at the Martins on Saturday. She was going to call, afterwards, but she never showed. I assumed she'd had to get back to New York." He held his hands palms up in front of him. "I never made the connection until you called."

"Saturday? We got her coming up on the shuttle on Friday," T.J. said. "M.E. puts the time of death some time Friday night, Saturday morning."

Zach put his hands up. "Well, I don't know about Friday. We weren't expecting her until Saturday."

"I'm not gonna shit you. This could get nasty, Zach. I heard you were separated from ..." T.J. turned a wrist over to show he couldn't remember the name of Zach Hannah's third wife.

"Suzanne," Zach said. "And it's worse than that, Suzanne and I are getting divorced. Hearing in January, Sussex Family Court."

There was a pause while T.J. considered his situation. Revenge was appropriate. He'd earned it. It wasn't just the humiliation of the fraternity date rape. Zach Hannah had sat on the discipline panel that heard the complaint against him.

But to be owed a favor by Zach Hannah was something else again.

"This probably doesn't *need* to come out," T.J. said, after he'd thought for a while. "Need your statement, where you were Friday to Monday, but we can wait, see how the evidence comes in."

Zach responded, "Well, I appreciate that. Like you said, this is too serious to screw around with. If it comes out, it does. Post separation sex doesn't amount to much in a divorce these days 'specially when you get to be my age. But let's be clear, I'm not asking you for anything, and you're not offering. This is nothing to risk a career over."

The words were casual, dismissive, but the look in the other man's eyes was not. T.J. knew this was as close as Zach would come to asking. He gave him a non-answer.

"I appreciate the candor, Zach. I really do. If it's nothing, and I believe you, it would only be a distraction. Slow down our investigation is all. But once we get focused on someone, if they decide to go to trial, you know this'll have to be disclosed to defense counsel. I don't need another adventure with exculpatory evidence, as you well know."

Hannah hadn't forgotten the complaint. "Look, that has nothing..."

"I know, I know. Nothing to do with this. I'm not saying it does. But don't talk propriety to me, okay? Every time one of you pilgrims starts to talk ethics, I feel like I'm about to get kicked in the ass."

"T.J., you only got a warning. What'd you ex...?"

"A censure. But hey, am I complaining? Just remember I'm not going down that road again. If we catch a guy and he wants a trial, everything goes in the file."

"Fair enough," Hannah said, acknowledging that this was all the assurance he would get. For a moment the two men regarded different walls of the office. Finally, Hannah clapped his knees gently and said, "So?" as he started to rise. He didn't like T.J.'s look. He'd seen this volcano erupt before.

"Keep in touch, ah, as soon as you've met with your clients," T.J. said, offering his hand over the desk. The two shook hands and exchanged a short stare.

"I'll talk to them. I"ll call you. "

But T.J. held his hand. "Competency?" T.J. asked, "A real issue?"

Hannah smiled and nodded. "You *did* read the file. Yah, for real, the older one, Louisa. The younger one's okay, though. You know, you may want to get a warrant anyway to cover yourself."

"Belt and suspenders," T.J. said. "But I'll give you today. Better for them if they cooperate."

The two nodded in agreement with one another and T.J. let go of Hannah's hand. As he went through the door, Hannah gave him a final look to convey gratitude but said nothing further.

When he had gone, T.J. picked up the woman's picture, then dropped it again. "Oh darlin' how the mighty have fallen," he said softly.

He could hear Stacy's footsteps enter into her office just beyond his door. There was a sound of something being dropped on the floor. Her computer whined to life. He heard a desk drawer open and close. "Stacy?"

"Yes boss?" She came to the door.

"Find Leavitt. I need his typed statement on the lady's New York apartment and all this stuff about the phone.

"He's probably back at the barracks, boss."

"Well tell him I need him over here, and line up Judge Stevens for a warrant."

T.J. had finished half a cigarette and was staring with vacant contentment into the middle distance when Stacy came back in. "No luck on Leavitt, he's got escort duty tonight down in Windsor. I tried to line up Judge Stevens but she's over to Vermont running a conference. That's why Judge Mix is here today. Loretta says she'll be back in Windsor tonight for some dinner but she'll be going straight back. You want I should ask Grace for Judge Warren?"

T.J. scowled, the way he did whenever Harry Warren's name came up. Stacy took this as assent. T.J. turned the easel back around. He fingered the map Levitt had given him. The Martin house was only five hundred feet away from where she went into the woods.

Well, Judge Warren would have to do.

"I checked with Grace," Stacy called to him five minutes later.

"She said he would see you at his house tomorrow if it can't wait till Monday."

"Sure, sure. That's fine. Hannah says he'll try to talk sense to his clients, but that means 'no.' We'll need a warrant. Just make sure Leavitt knows to be here first thing tomorrow."

"Me too?" Stacy had made her way back to his office as he spoke.

"What do you think?"

As they were speaking, the heavyset form of Lionel Whitcomb appeared in the doorway behind Stacy. She jumped.

"Jesus, Lionel, couldn't you knock or something."

"You want the trash picked up or not?" Lionel's face and eyes were red. He was carrying a large plastic trash bag.

"It's okay, Lionel. Here." T.J. went over and handed his wastebasket to the man.

"You need to let folks know you're there, that's all," Stacy added.

"Mmm" the man said and handed the basket back. He gave Stacy an unfriendly smile but said nothing more as he left.

When he was gone Stacy saw T.J. laughing soundlessly at her and said, "Oh, sure. Fine for you," she said. "That guy's breath is strong enough to straighten my hair."

"Ah, he'll be okay once he gets through his divorce," T.J. said. Everyone in the courthouse had heard the details of the Whitcomb divorce.

"Just the same," Stacy said. "He creeps me out."

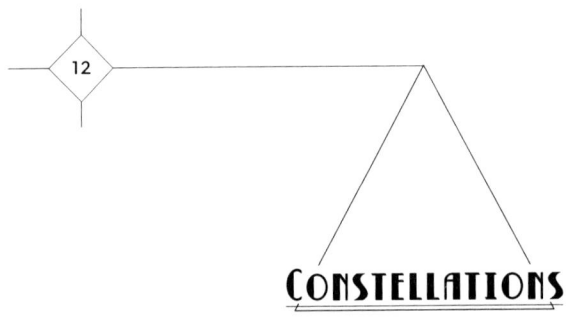

12 CONSTELLATIONS

Livy's tanned shoulders made an un-November-like contrast to the white tape trim to her navy gown. Her ash-blonde hair was gathered just off her ears by a simple black ribbon held with a gold clasp. A large-linked chain necklace gleamed golden from her neck. Seated on the edge of a chair, her chin sunk onto one hand as she studied a program for the Crowninshield dinner, she looked ten years younger than Harry knew her to be. A short dark whiskey was on the table before her.

Looking up at him over the tops of her glasses, she said, "Warren, you clean up pretty good." She removed the glasses and snapped them into a small purse.

Harry gave her a small bow, pleased with how proud Tee Ingersoll would be later that night of his continuing mastery of 'informal' attire. But Livy frowned, and wordlessly rose to snatch away his pocket handkerchief. Leaning a knee against his, she refolded and replaced it, the points just peaking over the pocket's edge.

"It's a hankie, not a fucking flag," she said, showing Harry her teeth from less than a foot away. Satisfied with his confusion, she remained close to him for a second longer than she had to before giving the pocket a finishing pat. "Men always look better in black tie," she said. "Even you."

"You do know how to send a man out with confidence."

She regarded Harry for a moment longer and apparently deciding he wasn't going to retreat, turned and went back to her glass. "I can't believe Lew is cutting this thing. He can be such a shit."

Harry said "Uhmm," as neutrally as he could and went over to the fireplace to absorb some heat on his backside. The failings of the brother and the decline of the father were not topics where Harry's opinion, indeed, his notice, had ever been welcomed. Livy was only showing irritation. She was not inviting discussion.

The rise of Lloyd, IV—Lew—to a level of parity with his father in the family enterprises had only recently become an accepted fact of life. Since Lew was reasonably astute and seemed to be making the family more money than any of the rest of them could make for themselves, this had never become a matter of serious controversy. Who else would they have? Harry? One of Livy's unsuitable husbands? So, Lew it was.

But, lately, Lew had taken to exercising the prerogatives of a great man, too busy now to hide his good-natured indifference to the activities of his nonproductive sisters. A dinner in New Hampshire, even one at the Crowninshield, had not proved enough to lure him or the latest Mrs. Llewellyn up from Philadelphia, though it was an easy trip on a Llewellyn company airplane that could have them up and back on the same night. Emma had received the news of Lew's desertion with a chirp of brittle cheer meant to convey both understanding and resignation. It had fooled neither Livy or Harry into underestimating her disappointment. Yes, Lew was a shit.

Still, the family would make a good enough showing with both Livy and the patriarch, L.L. Llewellyn, in presence. On the last occasion L.L. came, more than half a million dollars had passed into the Crowninshield's coffers. Even the apologetic note from Lew had arrived with a check for ten thousand dollars. It was safe to assume that this year's Crowninshield dinner would not pass without additional compensations.

Harry had just dropped ice into a glass of his own when Emma walked in. Her dress was a green version of Livy's but somehow simpler, with squared-off shoulder straps. She had less tan, more freckles than her sister and her hair remained the color she was born with. She had few occasions to dress like this in New Hampshire.

"Beautiful, darling," Harry said. She had worn green the night he met her and it was still his favorite color for her.

Emma, still adjusting an earring as she walked, gave him only a sideways glance. "Just one, Harry, okay?"

He nodded silent submission but continued to pour for somewhat longer than first intended. 'One' meant one, but not necessarily a small one.

"It's a long night and I don't want you yawning... Livy, can you snap this?" Emma presented her back to her sister who, glasses again low on her nose, began adjustments to the back of the dress.

In the distance a phone rang.

A woman in a grey uniform appeared from the dining room. "Call for you, Judge. It's Mrs. Carroll." Harry frowned and looked at his watch. six p.m. Grace wouldn't call him if it wasn't trouble.

"Fresh disasters?" he said into the phone.

"Maybe. T.J. Carr just called. Says he needs a search warrant before noon tomorrow."

"Can't it wait till Monday?"

"No, so he says, and Miss... Judge Stevens is running that conference in Vermont. She'll be at the dinner tonight, but she's going right back."

Harry groaned.

"Look boss, it's just a warrant. You don't need T.J. on your case right now. He'll come to your house."

"Okay, okay, eleven o'clock."

When he returned to the living room he heard Livy say, "Daddy called. He's driving down from the club with Edgar."

"God, they won't get back till midnight."

"You know Daddy."

They spoke with the mixture of fatalism and awe that daughters reserve for fathers. For them, at least, paternal faults were only to be endured, not corrected. Like the weather.

"You canceled the car?" Emma asked.

"Hell, no. Now Harry and I can party." Livy came over to drape her arm over Harry's shoulder.

"Like old times," Emma said. Since Harry belonged to the fairly select group of Penn undergraduates who had not slept with her sister, he felt no guilt from Emma's pretended suspicions.

Livy, however, had standards. "Oh Christ Emma, I was never *that* hard up," she rolled her eyes and moved away. As she did, Harry saw she had put on slightly too much eye makeup. Poor Livy, she wasn't going to be the hot young matron for much longer. Headlights played through the window.

"God, you really had the car come *here*?" Emma looked from Livy to Harry.

Livy shrugged. It was fruitless to explain to her sister that Emma couldn't act like a Llewellyn in New Hampshire. The cars and planes, the people waiting discreetly in hallways to eliminate, or at least smooth, the indignities of everyday life, had to be kept better hidden than in Philadelphia.

Emma went to the window and peered. "Oh good. A van," she said.

"I could'a got a 'leh-meux,' hon." Livy said in perfect South-Philly.

"Livy..." Emma closed the subject with a short hand gesture of dismissal.

Livy recovered quickly. "This is a fucking cash bar I suppose. God, I hate charity do's. This is for you Emma. I hope you got a lot of money on you Warren."

Harry patted his breast pocket in confirmation.

Livy looked in her purse anyway, then snapped the purse shut. "Anyway, Emma, good pick on the dress. You're still hot."

◆Δ◆

As they were driven to the front door of the newly scrubbed and flood-lit museum, now alive with arriving people, Harry remembered how different it had looked on his first visit.

Then, the Crowninshield lay crumbling, dirty and empty except for its collection of mediocre paintings, mostly landscapes in the White

Mountain or Hudson River Valley School tradition. The museum had just turned insolvent and was under orders from the New Hampshire Office of Public Charities to itemize and inventory its assets for distribution. Harry, as a new man in the Cruikshank office, was assigned to complete the legal paperwork. The size of this job came home to him when he was shown through the gloomy galleries with the elderly curator, a small grey woman full of memories.

Convinced that the drudgery of going through the piles in the Crowinshield cellars would actually be a pleasure for Emma, Harry suggested that she might help. After some initial reluctance, Zach Hannah had said to go ahead.

Though she had some talent as a painter, Emma's real gift was seeing art, not making it. She delighted in technique and knew the ebbs and flows of the schools and traditions. Her special interest was something called the 'Barbizon School' and other early impressionists. Just out of her teens, she could already attribute and date the works of dozens of painters at a glance. It shouldn't have been a surprise. She had grown up in a house that was almost a museum itself, and effortlessly earned straight A's at Penn in art history before dropping out. She had even begun a small business for herself, cleaning and restoring. Till then, she had found only tiny jobs, commissions intended to keep her, and her checkbook, coming back to the antique shops that used her services. But her persistence and child-like fascination with winkling beauty out of decay kept her busy and contented. No restoration was drudgery for Emma. Her enthusiasm sometimes made her forget his ignorance.

"Harry, do you see this overpaint? See how he changed the position of the hand. Feel. See? Now go up to the eyebrow." She took his hand. *"Feel it? He changed the whole composition!"*

At times like that it was impossible not to love Emma, but also to be a little frightened of her as well. Of course Harry could never "see" what she pointed out and certainly didn't feel it. Worse, Harry was always getting Manet confused with Monet and couldn't tell a Picasso from a Brach. But he did know a thing or two about how things could be made to appear other than they really, or at least originally, were. As good as

Emma was at seeing beneath the surface of these canvases, when would she get to the underside of his?

Emma had found small treasures at the Crowninshield her very first day: Four Champneys, one of which now hung in his chambers, and a Quing Dynasty tea set, apparently in its original crate. Then she identified two chairs as Portsmouth Chippendale, and a Seymour writing desk, unfortunately with some repairs. Taken together, their value was enough to put the museum back in the black.

Harry remembered the unframed Champney canvas Emma had brought home to show him. He fingered the frayed side of a picture of the White Mountains. "Ten thousand dollars? You're sure? For this?"

Emma shrugged. "I've never understood the White Mountain School myself, but it will get at least that much, easy, once I restore it."

It was two days later that Emma opened the bin that held things put there by the founder's widow. That evening, reticent and preoccupied, Emma retreated to her studio with a new rectangular bundle wrapped in brown paper. Strange shadows cast by her black light mixed with the sounds of atonal jazz in her studio. Harry knew better than to interrupt her at times like this and went up to their bedroom alone. He awoke in an empty bed.

"*Emma, it's three o'clock in the morning.*" Harry found her now no longer in her studio but at his desk making notes from an untidy pile of art books open before her. He picked up one with the title, *Les ReFusées*. It had rich color plates, but was in French. Harry put it down with a shrug.

"*Couldn't sleep. I'm just so afraid I'll look like such a fool.*"

"*About what? What are...*"

"*The pictures, the pictures I found today.*" She pointed over her shoulder to her studio. "*Those pictures.*"

Three sat on a semi-circle of easels in the half lit studio.

"*What are you worried about? It's not like you painted them?*"

"*No, but I'm scared. I certainly can't sleep.*"

The title of the book she was reading, *Barbizon and Beyond*, was at least in English.

"Boning up? You look like you're cramming for an exam."

"Well, that's just about right. You know the old joke, 'Corot painted five hundred pictures, only seven hundred of which were sold in America.'"

"Who's Corot?"

◆△◆

EMMA NEEDN'T HAVE worried. Three days later, experts at the Gardiner Museum gave astonished confirmation that there was indeed at least one Corot and a Millet among the canvases Emma brought down to Boston for them to see. It was all: *"And when, Mrs. Llew ... ah Warren, can we come to Windsor to see the others?"*

Their trip to Windsor confirmed another Corot and two Boudins from the remaining canvases interred by Deborah Crowninshield, widow of the museum's benefactor, a half century before. The Crowninshield was now more than solvent. It was rich.

"It's logical, Harry. Deborah Crowninshield was a country girl. She liked these rough looking portraits of country life, heavy hard-working peasant girls like herself. But everybody told her they weren't any good. She hung the paintings in her bedroom, and since they weren't attributed, no one gave them a second look when she died."

Lucky? Yes, but it was Emma who found them. Emma, who unlike Deborah Crowninshield's executors, bothered to read the neatly tied bundles of Deborah Crowninshield's correspondence, mostly filled with petty disputes with local tradesmen but also with receipts and acknowledgments from small time Parisian and Lyonnais dealers confirming just when and where she bought each canvas.

The discoveries made Emma Warren—always "Emma Llewellyn Warren"—briefly famous. In art, as in other things, Harry learned that celebrity begot celebrity and money generated more money. With the millions these discoveries added to the value of the museum collection, all thought of closing the Crowninshield ceased. And, more importantly, Emma became interested. Donations flowed in, helped along now with matching gifts from the Llewellyn Trusts. L.L. could deny Emma little and for a few years a considerable portion of Llewellyn charitable giving found its way to New Hampshire. There were long faces in the development offices at Miss Porter's and Penn. Penn Charter and the Philadelphia Symphony suffered. Even Princeton may have noticed.

Emma was elected to an expanded Crowninshield Board of Directors shortly after the first check cleared. With the help of new staff members and some strategic loans from the Philadelphia Museum, the Crowninshield initiated a series of respectable shows that generated articles in the *Globe* and *Inquirer*. And more gifts.

The fame proved transient. There were no further discoveries. Emma's real expertise, after all, was in antique furniture, not painting, and she was quick to acknowledge her coup as a fluke. But even though out of the papers for decades now, her power at the Museum had become total.

TONIGHT THE CROWNINSHIELD'S main hall showed how far she had taken it from bankruptcy. It glowed golden with candles. A string quartet played Bach and Vivaldi variations and filled the big atrium room with the soft, fat music of viola and cello.

Livy was right. Almost any man looked better in black tie than in the things he'd choose for himself. This was certainly true of the New Hampshire men gathered there. Their wives and girlfriends, left to wider choices, achieved more disparate results. Mostly worse.

Not all, however. On this night a few of New Hampshire's finest were striking indeed, and none more so than the Honorable Amanda Stevens. Her pale blue dress hung from one shoulder leaving the other to rise with surprising delicacy above the substantial Stevens bosom. She had gathered a sprinkling of black-tied admirers into the penumbra of that abundant yellow hair. She even smiled and gave a small wave to Harry, one old friend to another. This he returned while still a sufficient distance away to spare them the pain of actual conversation. Waiters wandered among the guests with trays of wine glasses. The two doorways were each manned by a pair of solid, well-barbered New Hampshire state policemen in green dress uniforms.

Emma plunged into earnest conversation with the museum director, alternately nodding and shaking her head over sheets of much edited paper even before she got her coat off. Harry watched Livy measure one of the troopers with an appraising eye. Then catching sight of Amanda, she said, 'There's Judge Goldilocks, your pal, Harry."

Harry scowled and to punish him Livy said very clearly, "Good choice on the dress. With a figure like that you don't need to show cleavage." Heads turned toward them.

"Thank you for that," Harry said into Livy's smile.

"Believe me, it was nothing." Just then Amanda threw her head back and laughed, the men around her joining in.

A waiter proffered a tray of glasses of white wine and Harry started to take one for his sister-in-law.

"No thanks to the Chateau New Hampshire, Warren. You *could* get me a real drink."

"All right, Livy, you win," he said. "Scotch?" He left her standing by herself before she could answer.

As he moved across the room, Harry could see that all the local worthies were present. The present governor was there as well as two of her predecessors, including Harry's benefactor, the man she'd defeated just two years earlier. New Hampshire's senior senator worked the crowd with heavy good humor while he and the governor, a likely future opponent, each measured the reactions the other received as they circled each other around the room. Professional photographers took candids and posed group shots.

◆△◆

WINDSOR AND NEW HAMPSHIRE were too small, too poor, to nurture anything that Professor Rush, would have called a social elite. He would have concluded there were insufficient quantities of rich virgins to be protected. Harry agreed but had come to feel that 'Prof,' growing up rich himself, never understood the real allure of entitlement any more than Tee Ingersoll did. The real charm of the parties that Tee had brought him to when they were at Penn wasn't their opulence. It was the fact that no one had to earn the right to be there. The golden children were present simply because they were asked. They had done nothing to deserve it. Privilege was much prettier than merit, especially to the unprivileged.

Despite this evening's meritocractic foundations, Harry decided it remained a good show. Zach Hannah, having sponsored a table, was manning his station. Standing next to him Harry saw their old Devon headmaster, known to all Devon boys as 'the Head.' He was more stooped, thinner but still resplendent in the dog collar and violet front of an Episcopal priest and substantial enough to overtop the man he was speaking with. Leaning forward, the old man showed that mix of authority and rectitude only a man who was both cleric and headmaster could possess. Zach turned aside to motion someone into the conversation and Harry could see that the Head's still substantial form was hiding none other than his father-in-law, Lloyd 'L.L.' Llewellyn, from whom the Head would soon be extracting a spare million or two for Devon. Harry detoured and came up behind them.

Lloyd, feeling Harry's hand on his shoulder, half turned to see who it was. "Harry," he said, only slightly disappointed.

"Mr. L." Father and son-in-law had settled on this greeting a decade into Harry's marriage after both reached the silent conclusion that there would never be sufficient excuse for Harry to call him 'Lloyd.' 'Mr. Llewellyn' would have left Harry too obviously distinct from the 'Lloyd' even distant Llewellyn cousins were permitted, along with the more acceptable, however transitory, spouses of his other children. 'L.L.' like 'Ted' Ingersoll, was too much a thing of the public domain. The single initial was a compromise that satisfied them both.

"Another Devon boy. We're all so pleased about Carter," Lloyd Llewellyn said, turning back to the old Headmaster.

The Head held his giant hand out to Harry. "Mr. Warren," he said, warm and beaming, the look of a man already debating between neo-Gothic and Tudor revival for the new Llewellyn Science Laboratory. 'Mr. Warren' was what the man had always called him at school. Only the favored few, like Zach Hannah, were called by their first name, and they and only they were permitted to call the Head 'Head' to his face. Even now.

"A Devon reunion, Head," Harry said past the Head's fading smile as he took the big hand. Harry knew that their headmaster had despised him almost as much as he loved Zach. Only the prospect of Llewellyn millions had brought him here tonight.

Zach Hannah, of course, knew exactly what had happened. He moved his head slightly side to side as he in turn greeted Harry. "Harry," he said. "You'll never learn," was what he meant.

But Zach's discretion was unnecessary. The two old men had already turned back to barter, Lloyd to lobby for his least promising grandchild, and the Head for his dream of laboratories and computers, without ever mentioning either. Zach fixed Harry with a wider, more familiar, crooked smile.

"That was deftly done," he said, just softly enough so he wouldn't be heard over the surrounding din.

"Surely I'm permitted at least that," Harry said. Then, noting an unfamiliar pallor and what appeared to be a wince when Zach took his hand. "You okay, Zach?"

"Touch of the flu," Zach said again. "How are you?"

Harry looked across the room at the radiant Amanda. Her escort was the *News & Observer* reporter he suspected. He gave an involuntary shake of his head.

"Oh, c'mon," Zach said, misinterpreting. "I'm fine." Then, "Emma's in the pink." He changed the subject with a gesture toward her in the midst of a half dozen well-wishers. "Family? Girls?"

By "girls" Harry knew he really meant Samantha, Zach's favorite. Zach, still a legend at the Devon School when Harry went there, had nearly made the Olympic ski team before a knee injury took him out of the top tier. He had helped Samantha almost to the top of the very narrow pyramid of Eastern skiing, not easy to do from Deerfield. When she went to Princeton, not Dartmouth, he had shown an uncharacteristic flush of temper. "I suppose the Llewellyns will get their way in this like everything else," he had snapped. He hadn't said a word when Leigh had decided to go to Penn, even though she had skied for Devon.

"Girls are fine," Harry said. "Leigh's at Brown Brothers. Sam's doing boat building in Maine."

"Boat building," Zach said, shaking his head. Then, still the head boy running interference for a clumsy underclassman, he said, "Now get the fuck out of here and let the Head raise some money."

"All right, but not all night. We don't want to burn Lloyd out." Harry remembered all those Devon mornings with the Head shouting out the liturgy from the back of the chapel.

"I believe in one God."

"I'll shut him down in a few minutes." Zach gave Harry the gentlest shove. "The things I do for you, Warren."

He could and he would. Zach had been one of the Head's beloved. He remained one of the favored handful for whom the Head would do anything.

Negotiating past round tables heavy with flowers and hotel china, Harry saw that Livy's and Emma's efforts had not been in vain. Silver frames held announcements of who was paying for the tables and with whom the luke-warm tournedos and the wit and wisdom of Ted Ingersoll would be enjoyed.

There were tables for bankers—New Hampshire's three state-wide banks each had one. At least three other tables had been bought by other, lesser law firms from Manchester and Concord. There were tables for realtors and one made up exclusively of doctors. Two of Windsor's new dotcom tycoons had established competing constellations of acolytes at opposite ends of the room. Their respective wives stole glances at one another, each with the hard alert look of first wives of rich and powerful men, men whom they had married when they were young and not yet rich.

Having procured two clear plastic cups of brown liquid for Livy, Harry wondered what Tee would say about the enormous silk flower on the shoulder strap of the older and harder of the dotcom wives. Not watching where he was going, Harry bounced off a solid form and felt cold liquid on his hands. He looked up to complain only to find the gaze of Russell's nephew, the young policeman. Harry tried his brightest smile while his memory refreshed.

"Ah Officer, uh… Sergeant, Leavitt… uh, Gregg. Surprised to see you here," he said. "*Inane enough*," Harry thought. The man was obviously on duty.

Gregg Leavitt looked down to see if anything had spilled on him. There were drops on the toe of one highly polished boot and several others which had caught on the sharply creased twill of his trousers. He brushed his pants, then regarded Harry before saying softly, "Security detail, Judge. Excuse me?" He nodded toward another cop at the entrance by way of explanation.

"Oh, of course, of course."

"Took you long enough," Livy said a moment later as she took the plastic glass from him and downed half before inspecting it. "You think you could have found a smaller one?" Moments later Harry was off to purchase two more.

"Ten-fifty," a thin, pinch-faced woman wearing a man's dinner jacket said from behind the bar. Harry looked back at her dumbly, then realized she was saying this for the second time.

"Yes?"

"Ten-fifty… that'll be ten dollars and fifty cents please … look, I'm kinda busy here."

"Yah, sure, sorry. Uh, keep it." He gave her a twenty.

She stuffed the change in a plastic glass on the bar. "You come back again," she called out. Whoever said you can't buy love didn't understand the uses of over-tipping.

The dinner by then had hit critical mass, the moment right after the arrival of the last guests and just before the delivery of the third drink. The string section was still at it but no one could hear them now. Everyone's conversation had risen a number of decibels and there were outbreaks of mostly feminine hilarity against the background din. There was much waving and air kissing. The false heartiness had become heartier and more false. A success.

A stir in the crowd announced Tee's arrival. Despite the presence of three past and present governors, a senator and at least three billionaires, no one else in the room generated anything like the energy of Ted Ingersoll. Each of the others had his or her followers, even some admirers, but people did not break off conversations to crowd near them. Tee made his way across the room a few steps at a time responding to the greetings of people he didn't know with the identical direct gaze and handshake. People eddied and leaned toward him. An exchange of a sincere sentence or two with one couple ended with vigorous nodding all around. He confided a smile and laughter on another. One woman put her hand to her throat after Tee turned away from her. Her husband, the man Harry's daughters and five thousand other teenagers knew as "Chicklets" Ciccarone, New Hampshire's leading orthodontist, beamed like a man newly satisfied that his two-hundred-dollars-a-plate had been well spent after all.

The museum director, a slight, short balding man intercepted Tee and delivered him to Emma just as Harry completed his second mission for Livy. His wife and best friend embraced affably enough, considering. Emma offered a cheek before making unnecessary introductions to the people standing nearby, her best Miss Porter's manners on full display.

Tee looked up then from over the bald head of the director. Seeing Harry, his fixed smile softened with recognition. He detached himself from the others, took one hand and lay the other on Harry's shoulder, but Emma spoke first.

"Harry, where have you been?" Emma looked directly at his glass.

"I couldn't let Livy die of thirst. She was about to have an attack of sobriety." Dutch courage was better than no courage at all.

Emma only turned Tee to follow her toward the first of the competing courts' computer wizards. "Go rescue Daddy," she said pointing her chin at a distracted Lloyd Llewellyn, now with Livy but still receiving the full attention of the Devon School's best fundraiser. "And don't get Livy drunk." Tee looked back, shrugged, made a sad smile as Emma guided him. He was 'Ted' Ingersoll again.

◆Δ◆

'Ted' ingersoll followed Emma Warren as she led him from group to group. A veteran of dozens, hundreds, of dinners, he knew that he was expected to give a quantum of face time to the big givers and he also knew that the pretense of intimacy, properly acted out, was worth more than gold. He recognized, but couldn't identify, a couple two tables away. He had even given the woman an answering smile, and remembered they had given a bundle to PBS that spring.

As Emma disengaged him from a group of local bankers Tee leaned close to her ear.

"Next table: Wilshire?"

Emma didn't change expression, but let him get just in front of her before she said softly, "Wechsler, Jack and Eadie."

"Eadie..." Tee said a moment later as he exchanged air kisses with the woman temporarily flattening a puff of fabric apparently intended to replicate a flower. "... and Jack." It was the full two hands and the meaningful look into the eyes for Jack. The Wechslers were new and, in Boston or Philadelphia, just one more rich couple. But New Hampshire was home so Tee allowed himself to be displayed to their appropriately awed clutch of retainers in the glow of the Wechslers' obvious intimacy with fame. They had paid for it after all.

Emma gave Tee a precisely appropriate interval with each benefactor. After one minute with the bankers, five with the Wechslers, as she leaned into the conversation laughing at their unfunny jokes, her hand inside his elbow gently propelled him away.

At the next table, a particularly beautiful blonde woman in a pale blue dress turned to meet his gaze with a smiling challenge. Now *there* was an invitation, Tee thought. Ah, but how could she know?

"Ted, this is Judge Amanda Stevens."

"Judge ... Stevens." The surprise was genuine. The woman didn't look thirty years old.

"For my sins," she said, and introduced a slight young man with a cowlick and a newspaper connection, *News* and something.

"Of which there were few, I'm sure," Tee said, still watching her as he turned to take the man's hand.

"None I regret," she said.

Tee turned back from the man. "Sin without shame? And you a judge?" She blushed with pleasure. The Concord law firm sponsoring Amanda's table had only earned a minute, and as soon as introductions were over Emma was leading him away. Tee looked up. Oh hell. There was the Senator he had to cultivate.

"The Senator?" he whispered into Emma's ear.

"Blaine," she said her lips not moving, "Arthur."

◆△◆

"Few people truly deserve the label 'Renaissance Man,' but if one person in America does today, that man is Ted Ingersoll."

Emma read her remarks with schoolgirl precision softened by periodic shy smiles. Harry knew the word 'luminous' was almost as overworked as 'heroic,' but it fit Emma at the microphone. Her voice was confident, confiding and at once somehow vulnerable. Hearing her, one would think she did this everyday. People always seemed to like Emma, to want her to succeed. If they saw the tremor in her hand as she turned the pages of her little speech, they would have wanted it even more.

"An entertainer, a writer, and a connoisseur of the first rank, Ted Ingersoll has brought art into millions of homes across the world. More recently he has turned the nation into a new kind of canvas through the medium of television. There, for our pleasure and to our benefit, he paints astonishing portraits of American lives and, through these, American life."

She paused for polite applause and made a shy smile.

"Who better then, to help us celebrate the restoration of our own little corner of America, our own special treasures collected here, than the man who introduced millions to the Uffizi, the Louvre and the Prado? Please join me in a warm New Hampshire welcome for Ted Ingersoll."

She said this last without looking at her notes and welcomed Tee into the applause as everyone stood. Livy caught Harry's eye from the table where she sat next to her father and made a 'who knew?' expression with her eyebrows.

Emma accepted Tee's ritual embrace amid the noise, then sat down and exhaled heavily.

"You wrote that?" Harry asked, meaning it as a compliment, realizing too late that it wasn't.

"Not everyone from the Main Line is as dumb as you think," Emma said primly. The room quieted, then turned to give studied attention to Tee 'Ted' Ingersoll who, for the thousandth time, began to speak to a room full of strangers.

Chastened, Harry confirmed that L.L. was still at his table with Zach, the Head and one of the Governors Reese. Livy sat next to her father. It was easy to see from her relaxed, almost slouching posture that it was a good thing her little sister had done the talking.

"Thank you for that undeserved introduction, Emma," Tee began. "You know when I come to gatherings as distinguished as this I find that people say wonderful things. Some are pardonable exaggerations. Some are outright lies. I'm here to tell you that while I appreciate the exaggerations greatly, I really love the lies most of all."

Ordinarily, Gregg didn't mind security details. He needed the double overtime pay and when he'd signed up for this one it had looked like a welcome chance to show the governor what he could do.

But the Crowninshield dinner had been laid on long before the investigation, before T.J. had begun to take up his every waking moment. Exhausted, he had donned his dress greens that afternoon and fortified himself with Angela's coffee. More importantly, he stepped in the bathroom to take a trio of the small green capsules out from a bottle he'd saved from a drug arrest a year earlier. He hadn't found much need for them since leaving highway patrol duty, so the first pill gave him a palpable rush, a slight tingling in the fingers and then a cleansing onset of focus and clarity as it took hold.

With all the tuxedos and long dresses, tonight was different from the political dinners and rock concerts he was used to. It was a small group, the guest list totaled two hundred sixty-eight. Three skinny girls and an Asian sawed on violins and a cello in one corner. Careful to get himself noticed by the governor when she arrived, Gregg was rewarded by being called by name and with a touch on the sleeve. But that had been a half hour ago and—maybe he imagined it—her aide hadn't seemed to want to meet Gregg's eye.

Now his mouth had turned dry and the weariness was starting to leak back in. Gregg fingered the two remaining capsules in his pocket. He stood at the far end of the room by the door to the small service kitchen where caterers clattered dishes and cursed each other in several languages. He motioned to some Hispanic men to keep it down, but still smiled with as much enthusiasm as he could muster. They returned the smile and pretended to quiet down.

The man speaking got a big laugh just then and Gregg took this opportunity to move along the side of the room to the entrance doors. Here, one of the new troopers was trying to make time with a tight-assed little waitress who was taking pains to stick her behind out and puff up her front as she pretended to solicit drink orders. He had to put a stop to this. Gregg checked to see if he was being watched. The governor, still clapping, smiled broadly toward the podium. Her aide, the man he expected would make the decision, looked at his watch.

Gregg saw the little judge, his uncle's judge, at the head table.

"*Uh Officer, uh, Leavitt ...uh Gregg.*" The judge had given him the kind of smile a drunk gives right after hearing the words, "license and registration please."

Gregg remembered his feelings of sudden rage at the man as he looked down to see if he had marred the spit-shine on the toe of his boot. Must have been the pill. He had to be careful, not overreact.

"*Surprised to see you here,*" the judge said.

"*Security detail, Judge.*" Gregg wondered again what it was Uncle Russell saw in this guy. Well, that judge didn't matter, not with this governor.

Gregg reached the rookie trooper.

"Arsenault, get laid on your own time." The trooper's smile of greeting disappeared and he straightened to attention as if he'd been struck. The girl heard this and gave Gregg an 'oh please' look before she stalked away. Gregg then turned and stood next to Arsenault and the two, now a matched set, stared impassively over the crowd. Cameras flashed toward the podium and another appreciative collective cry came from the audience followed by applause. The first pill was definitely losing its punch now. Gregg kept himself square-shouldered to match the newly rigid Arsenault a minute longer. Then, deciding he had punished the man enough, he leaned close so that their caps almost touched. "Time enough for a little of that later, eh?"

The trooper accepted the unexpected gesture of forgiveness and complicity with a smile. "Sure, Sarge."

Gregg surveyed the tables. One lady, a nice looking blonde in a navy blue dress, made eye contact. She was stuck with an old guy, old enough to be her father. Gregg left Arsenault and strode over to the service door exchanging a second glance with the blonde who dropped her eyes and showed some teeth before turning back to speak with her white-haired companion. As she did, she moved her shoulders and traced an ear with one hand. When she checked to see if he liked what he saw, Gregg smiled.

THE DINNER BROKE UP quickly. Tee's speech had been a great success but Harry knew there were no after-parties for the middle aged. Emma said her public thanks to the noises of scraping furniture and immediately descended to bestow serial two-handed goodbye handshakes and air kisses. The quartet, audible again, played Brahms to the emptying room. Emma eventually moved to preside at the door with Zach and two other directors, thanking people as they left.

Harry had only a moment with Tee.

"Great speech, for a St. Mike."

He returned a facsimile of the look they'd exchanged in their doorway more than thirty years before. "You still remember, Warren."

They shook hands.

"Don't you ever come to Philadelphia anymore?"

"Not enough."

"Well call, will you?" Tee looked at Emma, busy, laughing. "She's really pretty good at this Warren. Make sure you tell her so." Then he went into the night. "Call me," he yelled back.

L.L. was being helped into his coat by his driver, Edgar, who had appeared, as always, without needing to be summoned.

"Ah. Well, Harry, great to see you." Lloyd took his hand, dropped it just as quickly, and turned back to interrupt and kiss Emma, just disengaging from a admirer. "Good night darling. Great speech. You should go into politics. You'd be at least as good as that poor thing I had dinner with." He shook his head, then left with Edgar. When they reached a big SUV directly opposite the steps up to the museum, Edgar opened the door for him. While Emma waved at her father, Harry wondered if L.L. Llewellyn had ever gotten a parking ticket.

Her father gone, Emma went back in the building and thanked the quartet. After that she went to the kitchen to thank the caterers, and in between she embraced a few stragglers, all the things Harry knew he wouldn't have thought to do. When at last she joined him at the door and pulled her coat around her, they were almost alone. She looked around. "Where's Livy?" she asked.

◆Δ◆

GREGG FOLDED HIS HANDS behind his head on the pillow. He decided he had every reason to be pleased with himself. He had the perfect cover story for Angela: a drunken VIP that he and Arsenault had to drive home. Contributor to the governor, all very dark, very secret. Arsenault would back him up because he did pick up the tough little waitress and needed a story for his own wife. No, it couldn't have worked out any better.

He yawned, thought of his daughter, Erin, frowned, and pushed her out of his mind. That was the second pill wearing off. Everything always felt so right going up and so wrong when you started back down. Well, it wasn't like he made a habit of this. It was almost two years since that curly haired girl doing advance work for the Vice Presidential candidate almost broke his dick off. He hadn't dared go near Angela until the scratches had healed. This one hadn't scratched, but she did everything else.

Gregg smiled.

Everything. She picked the motel, paid for the room, handed him a rubber and with no preliminaries gave him a ride to remember. He stretched and yawned again. Definitely wearing off.

She lay face down next to him, her ribs faintly visible at her sides. There was a small shadow of a bathing suit tan line across her round bottom which had felt surprisingly muscular in his hands just an hour before. Her blue dress lay across a chair opposite the bed. Parts of his green and gray uniform lay in a trail on the floor from the door to the bed. He snorted and turned his eyes to the ceiling, remembering.

"Uh... ohh," she said when he entered her. "That's better."

Now that was a hell of a thing to say and the way she said it got them both laughing, but not for long. They got right to it and were going pretty good, he thought, when she slowed him. "Wait, shh, wait," she whispered. When he paused in some confusion she said, "You don't mind do you?" With that she turned him over, settling herself on him in one practiced motion. Her pale hair hung around her face in the shadows.

"You don't mind do you?" she said again, taking his hands with hers. "Ladies first?"

And 'first' she was. Her hands moved to his shoulders going alternately limp and rigid while she made noises of satisfaction interrupted by surprised gasps when he thrust back against her until she finished with a tremble and a noise deep in her throat.

She took a moment to catch her breath, putting a finger to his lips while her own panting subsided. Then she rolled off but pulled on his shoulder to take him back on top of her. She gave his balls a squeeze and said, "Bet you can do that too, if you try." And of course he could, especially with her hard ass in his hands still flexing in rhythm with his own.

Gregg considered the sleeping form beside him. He looked over at the illuminated clock. Three thirty-five a.m. He followed the line of her hip to where the sheet fell across it. Well, he'd wasted at least one good fuck by falling asleep, pill or no pill, but he knew there was no time now.

He went to wake the woman but hesitated, not sure how to do it since he didn't know her name. Three thirty-six a.m. He was stretching it. It would be nearly five before he got back to Hadley.

He cupped a hand around her shoulder and kneaded it gently.

"Mmmm," she said, looking up through her hair where it fell in front of her eye. "Well, well, well. Colonel, this is a pleasant surprise. I always like a man with stamina." Her hand reached for his crotch.

"Well, ah...." Here Gregg would have called her by name but had to stop. He glanced toward the clock.

She raised herself on one elbow, blinked and tried to focus on the lighted dial as well. She squinted. "Shit," she said and raised herself to a sitting position.

"Way late, Colonel," she said swinging her legs over the side of the bed.

"Well, me too, I guess," he said, suddenly disappointed now that leaving was her idea. He lay watching her move about the room, finding pieces of underwear and putting them on. Then he said, "I'm only a sergeant."

She was into her panties and had just put herself into a small half brassiere as he said this. She smiled and came around the bed with her slip in her hands and put his head against the embroidered fabric elevating her breasts. She was silent for a moment and held his head against her. Then she stepped back and pulled the slip over her head, blowing the hair away from her eyes after she done so. Smoothing the slip, she said "Well, you were a fucking General last night. I promise you that."

She picked up one of his boots and threw it onto the bed. "C'mon, we've got to move," she said.

"It'll just take a minute," he said.

"Oh sure, a minute. It took you a fucking hour to get them off," she said.

"Where do you live?" he asked when they were outside, walking to the van.

"Far, far away." She smiled and shook her head from side to side. He felt his dick twitch. The two regarded each other. She seemed to read his mind. "Hey, I'd love to, but I really do have to go."

"What I mean is, do you want a ride?"

"Oh, I need a ride," she said.

In the harsh light of the lighted sign that read "General Bourgoyne Inn" her face looked more angular than he remembered. He had guessed forty at the museum, but that was in candlelight. In the neon he could see she was older than that.

Grateful now that he had taken the van and not the cruiser—he got mileage when he used his own vehicle—Gregg held the door for her. As she got in she said, "Do you know where Great Falls Road is?" Gregg remembered it, off the North-South Road to Hadley. He walked around the van. Behind the window in the Inn's office across the parking lot a bald man faced them as he stretched and yawned.

Gregg was about to get in himself but saw Arsenault's car was still parked two spaces down. He went to the door of Arsenault's room and knocked. If he didn't get home at about the same time as Gregg it wouldn't be much of an alibi. There was no answer to the knock so he put his ear to the door and heard why. Well, no alibi is perfect, and some things even a sergeant shouldn't interrupt. He went back to the van and started off toward the perimeter road north of Windsor. He had never worked the area around the city and wasn't familiar with the roads.

"There's a Target store," she said. "We took a right at the Target store, so you can hang a left there."

Gregg knew the store and turned at the intersection as instructed, "Great Falls Road."

She recognized the road. "It's a couple of miles on the right. Just a break in the trees, so take it easy," she said.

They drove in silence. He looked over at her. She had her head back against the seat. In the car she looked young again.

'Up here," she said, gesturing to a gravel drive.

"You live up here, uh..." Gregg gave the gravel road a dubious look.

The woman turned on the seat and looked at him with a smile of incredulity. "Shit, you don't know my name, do you, General."

"Well, no." He stared straight ahead. "I don't think you told me."

After they made the turn she said, "God, I am a tramp."

"Awwh," Gregg started to say something, but the sound he made came out higher then he wanted. He cleared his throat.

"Hey, it's okay." She laughed, a deep laugh for a woman. The headlights played on two stone posts, some kind of letter in a metal plaque, 'L.' The lights of a large house appeared as they came out of the trees.

"You, ah, you live here?" Gregg gestured at the front of the big building. "What is this, a condominium?"

"No. Visiting," she said, ignoring his second question. They came to a stop. Then she said, "I don't suppose you know whose house this is do you?"

"No," he said. Then, "This is a house, huh?"

"Well, I don't suppose you have any more interest in telling anybody about tonight than I do," she said, and gestured toward the groove in his finger where his wedding ring usually sat.

He put the van in neutral, switched off the ignition and went to open his door, but she reached across him and put her hand over his to take it from the handle. "Don't get out," she said. Then she kissed him, one hand behind his neck. Their tongues met and after some moments he felt her other hand on his crotch. He returned the kiss and tried to reach into her dress, but she pulled away.

"Ohh, I'm gonna miss you, General," she said, giving a final short strategic squeeze that made him jump. Then quickly her steps were making crunching sounds in the gravel leaving him to pull her door closed. She paused at the front of the house, looked back and made a shy wave, smiling under her tousled hair. Then she opened the door and disappeared inside. Further down a row of windows at the other end of the big house, a light came on. Gregg started the engine and eased the van into gear. By the time he was through the stone pillars he couldn't decide whether he felt relief or regret to be away. He slipped his wedding ring back on.

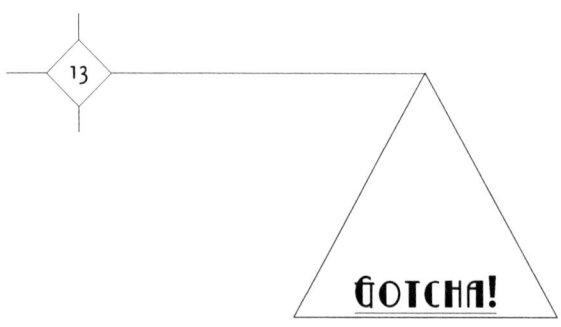

13 GOTCHA!

"Turn up here," Carr said, and Gregg found himself on the same gravel road he'd left eight hours before. Miserably, he confirmed a growing fear he'd had since they turned off Route 202. This was the same place! Jesus. He glanced over at Carr. Their eyes met, but Carr's mischievous smile was born of other things.

What T.J. said was "This'd be a lot better if we could find Judge Stevens."

"I thought she was tough on warrants," Gregg said.

"Not tough, Leavitt, thorough, and right now we need thorough. With Zach Hannah involved in this, anything goes wrong with this warrant, and the case goes up for grabs."

Gregg didn't like Carr's tone. It wasn't his fault that Judge Stevens had gone back to Vermont.

The morning had started well enough as Gregg summarized what they knew for the affidavit. They now knew what Ephne Newsome was doing in New Hampshire. They agreed that people don't kill each other over "highboys," even the old man from the antique store, but they knew now she'd been at the Martins' house. They were getting close. Gregg couldn't see either of the two woman he'd met at the door to the deteriorating lake house as a shooter but now they had probable cause to search the house. They could get a warrant now, a good thing because that lawyer, Hannah, hadn't been any help at all.

"Sorry, T.J.," his voice had said on the speaker phone. "All I can give you is Eleanor, Louisa—the Martins—their home-care lady, Margie something, and me of course. We're all available for questions, but I can't get the girls to consent to a search."

"You're still sure you don't want to confess yourself? T.J. barked back at the speaker phone.

"Hey, anything to help out, but I'll need some details to make it convincing."

"You can't help us out at all?" T.J. said, turning serious. It would take hours to get a warrant. Judge Warren had the weekend duty and he lived all the way down near Windsor.

"If I think of something..."

"Yah, yah, okay. Thanks." T.J. pushed the button and disconnected him. "For nothing," he said to the dead phone.

So for two hours and three drafts T.J. walked him through the affidavit. Gregg had the kind of shakes that only uppers left behind. His mouth tasted like pet food and he kept slipping into the half light that comes just before sleep. He used his last pill to stay awake for the drive down to Windsor.

The drive from the Hadley County courthouse took a half hour and at first T.J. filled it with anecdotes of old cases and campaigns, but as they got closer he turned thoughtful.

"You know that Judge Warren was a Hadley boy?"

"No, I didn't," Gregg said. "You don't think of him as ..."

"Yep. His old man killed himself. Probably tough on Warren. Explains a lot."

Gregg gave the man a sideways glance.

"His mother's a poet, I guess, and she moved them down to Boston right afterward. I suppose that's where he picked up the snotty way he speaks. You ever hear anyone in Hadley talk like that?"

T.J. was quiet for a while but picked up again as if in mid-sentence. "Don't get me wrong. I don't like the guy. He's not the kind of guy you can count on, not someone like your Uncle Russell, for instance."

Gregg's surprise must have shown because T.J. laughed then and said, "Oh, I know Russell can't stand me, thinks I'm a prick. Well, I *am* a prick.

I'm willing to live that way. My old man was a mailman. Everybody loved him. Everybody called him by his first name, even kids. 'Good ole Tim Carr' they used to say and then give that smile, you know the one, the one that says they're better than you. Well no one smiles like that at me."

Gregg decided the best response to this was to keep his eyes on the road.

But T.J. wasn't finished. "Look, I'm mouthing off. It's just, ah, well, you seem a lot like Russell. Even though he doesn't like me, he never screwed me, never acted like he was better. Guys like Harry Warren, Zach Hannah, they're okay when it suits them, but they smile like they did to my old man. You do 'em a favor and they say 'thank you' but, time comes to pay the favor back, they don't know you from Adam."

◆Δ◆

AND NOW HERE HE WAS, back at the two stone posts, each inset with bronze plates bearing that unhappily familiar scrolled 'L.'

"This is Judge Warren's place?" Gregg asked, "This place?"

T.J. only grunted and nodded.

"Jesus," Gregg said, as they came out of the trees. The lawns were wet with frost or dew depending on where the shadows fell. Two of the house's four chimneys sprouted thin plumes of white smoke into the morning air. It was the same place as last night but it looked even bigger in the daylight.

T.J. seemed amused at his reaction.

"Hey, you knew our good Judge Warren was loaded. He made it the old-fashioned way. He married it."

"Yah, I heard he had money, sure, but..." Gregg gestured over the steering wheel at the expanse of the house, glad of the excuse for confusion.

Carr had no way to know as Gregg parked the car that he was trying to think of what to say to his friend from the night before. "Just remember to keep your pinkie finger up," Carr said, sticking his little finger crookedly up in the air.

Gregg got out, suddenly happy he was dressed in civvies. Somehow, being humiliated in his uniform would make it worse. 'General' she had called him.

Carr held the warrant file in his teeth as he pulled on a blue windbreaker with a New England Patriot's logo. There was a smell of wood smoke. Inside the house a dog barked. With his luck the blonde would be there to greet him. 'Hello, General, long time no see.'

Instead, just as they reached the front door, it was opened by Judge Warren. It occurred to Gregg that he couldn't remember seeing this man before without a tie, usually a stupid little bow tie that always seemed crooked. The judge seemed even smaller in corduroys and sweater.

"Morning, morning, T.J.," Judge Warren said, shaking the county attorney's hand. Then, "Gregg, isn't it?" and he took Gregg's as well. He restrained a golden retriever who alternately nuzzled him and tried to break away. Succeeding, she buried her nose in Gregg's crotch.

"Abigail!" the judge said, adding. "She doesn't bite."

"Not yet," Gregg said, and patted the dog who kept her nose firmly between his legs. She turned to survey T.J.'s crotch momentarily, made a dismissive sniff, and returned to Gregg.

"Why don't we go into the library," the judge said. Without waiting for an answer he turned to walk ahead of them toward an arched entry at the end of a long hall. For a moment he remembered what T.J. had said about the way these people smiled.

T.J. mouthed the word 'library' to him and raised his small finger as they followed the judge down the hall. Its pale green walls were hung with pictures of birds. As they walked, Gregg looked through a double doorway that opened onto a large room, more like the lobby of a hotel. Floor to ceiling windows on the far wall gave a distant view of Lake Wasoka and mountains. Then Gregg's stomach lurched. Halfway down the room the woman with yellow hair sat studying a magazine as she drank from a mug of coffee. They passed the doorway before she looked up.

"Right through here," the judge said. He stopped at the arch at the end of the hall and ushered them through.

The dog shouldered past T.J. and Gregg to get into the room before them. She ran to a dog pillow in front of the fire place, sat down and faced them, tail going. Behind her a low fire made soft burning noises.

Well, it was a library all right. The high-ceilinged room was filled with books. Most of the wall space was bookcases, room for a couple of thousand books at least. There had to be another twenty or so in piles on a big table that sat in the middle of the room and a half dozen more on a desk beyond, sharing space with what looked like legal briefs.

The judge motioned them to sit together on a leather couch while he took a matching chair opposite. The judge didn't close the door, but Gregg took the inside seat and, with T.J. between him and the doorway, was fairly confident he couldn't be seen from the hall. Though the judge's limp had been barely noticeable as they walked, Gregg saw how he took both arms of the chair and lowered himself carefully down. The judge's shirt collar was frayed under his green sweater. As always, he wore his glasses around his neck on a string, like a school teacher or—he smiled at the thought in spite of himself—a librarian.

The judge crossed his legs, lifting one over the other with his hands. He wore a pair of carpet slippers, dark but with something embroidered on the top. Behind the judge, Gregg could see the opening to a second room of similar size. A work bench, a sink, and an easel were visible. The easel was covered with a paint-stained cloth. There was a faint smell of turpentine.

T.J. set his folder on the table between them and got out the affidavits, Gregg's and the medical examiner's. The judge reached into the neck of his sweater and pulled out the thick black fountain pen that was his trademark. He unscrewed it, then smiled at them, waiting. "So, what've you fellas got?" he asked.

"Well, Judge," T.J. said, opening his file, "We finally got a break in that Green Mountain case." T.J. handed the affidavit to Gregg who signed it in front of the judge and ceremonially raised his right hand as he gave it to him to read.

The judge took the papers, smiled at Gregg and said, "Under penalty of perjury, et cetera?"

Gregg instinctively began to stand to attention but he looked up to find himself face-to-face with an auburn-haired woman. She could have been the same woman—she wasn't—but his throat had tightened so much he pretended to cough, to cover his confusion.

"I'm sorry," she said, seeming to draw back at Gregg's look, "I'm interrupting."

But even Carr stood then and said, "Oh no, ah, Emma. Nice to see you again. This is Sergeant Levitt."

At this she came all the way into the room, showed them her perfect teeth and said, "Thought you might use some coffee." Crossing to Carr she said, "T.J., please sit, sit." She didn't shake his hand, she just took it for a second. Then she turned to Gregg and extended hers to him. "Hi, I'm Emma Warren." Must be a sister. This must be the good girl. He'd met the other one.

"Mrs. Warren," he said.

"Coffee would be great, darling," the judge said.

"Let me get something out of the studio," she said, and went into the room beyond.

Gregg concentrated on moving his eyes away from her retreating form. Sisters for sure.

"Fine, fine," the judge said, motioning Gregg and T.J. to sit back down. As soon as he took the packet of papers and pictures, T.J. began to speak.

"We've kept the identity secret. The lady's name is Ephne Newsome, Judge," T.J. said, pronouncing 'Ephne' correctly now and with emphasis on the first syllable. "You can see from the post mortem pictures, she's been shot, bird shot wounds. We can put her at the Louisa and Eleanor Martin property, West Harbor. It's down the mountain about a mile and a half from where we found her. We've tried to interview the Martins. They've been evasive, uncooperative. They're represented by Zach Hannah. You know Zach, he tried to get us permission he says, but," T.J. held his hands out, palms facing. "We'd just as soon have a warrant in case they don't change their minds."

Just as T.J. finished, Mrs. Warren reappeared and made toward the hall carrying what looked like a small brush.

"I'll just be a minute," she said. Then, "Are you alright darling?"

The judge had opened his mouth then as if he was about to say something, but seemed to think better of it. Then he fumbled with his glasses and dropped the pen as he did.

Gregg reached down for the pen, seeing how the small blotch of dark blue ink it made seemed to disappear into the pattern of the Persian rug where it had fallen.

"Ah, fine. Fine," the judge said to his wife.

As she left, Carr continued, "Daylight search. Material evidence, weapons, blood, the usual. It's all in the affidavit."

The judge took the pen back from Gregg. He started to speak but only swallowed. He read the affidavit and then looked back at the pictures. As he did his foot began to move rhythmically up and down. Then, as if he seemed to think that his foot was swinging too much, he stopped, then picked the leg up again with his hands and put it on the floor.

The judge cleared his throat, then cleared it again and began to initial each page on the coffee table between them. Gregg could see the judge was turning the pages much too fast to be really reading. By the time he got to the lab report, he had stopped even pretending to read. Gregg looked over at T.J. and saw that T.J. and the dog were looking at the judge the same way. Both had become still, alert.

Then the judge turned back to the pictures yet again. He inspected them one at a time. Turning over one, he made a small noise, like a man who just cut himself shaving. He looked up then. "Pretty, ah, gruesome," he said. His voice wavered.

He started to speak again. "Ah, fellows..."

But he was interrupted by the sound of dishes being carried down the hall as Mrs. Warren returned with a tray.

After she set it down, T.J. and Gregg mumbled their 'thank yous' as she half filled their cups and she smiled in return. "That's milk, that's cream," she pointed at two pitchers in turn. "Well, I'm going to get a little work done." She started toward the other room, then stopped.

"Unless you need me to..." She was facing her husband and made a finger-walking motion at him, asking him if he wanted her to leave. Again the hundred-watt smile.

"Ah, oh, no, darling. Thanks, thanks." The judge motioned for T.J. and Gregg to help themselves, and they did.

"Well, ahem, a, a daylight search?" the judge asked.

Gregg nodded and heard T.J. make an 'umm' sound of assent just as the judge dropped his pen again. The dog got up from her pillow then and stationed herself in front of the judge. She made a soft series of whimpers and tried to lick his hand.

The judge picked up the pen himself this time and said, "Of course, you must be used to this." He smiled at them reflexively, apologetically. Then he screwed the pen's cap on, pushed himself up from his chair and went over to the desk where he exchanged it for a felt-tipped pen. Gregg gave Carr a questioning look over his cup. Carr just shook his head 'no,' warning him to stay silent.

When the judge came back to his chair, Gregg could see a shine on his forehead. When he sat, his dog began a little dance. T.J.'s eyes took on a lazy, almost sleepy look.

From the other room, soft piano music began playing. There was the sound of water in a sink and then a woman humming.

The judge turned to complete the warrant. He seemed to have an easier time working with the felt tip, finally handing the signature page to Gregg, initialed but not signed in one of the places clearly indicated on the form. Could it be he didn't know where to sign?

Gregg handed it back. "Uh, Judge..." The man looked down and back at him quickly, as if startled, then signed where Gregg pointed.

"Of course. Of course," he said.

Handing the last papers back, the judge got up all at once, lurching slightly as he did so. "Uh, can you fellas excuse me a minute?" He gave them a ghost of a smile. "Too much coffee," he said by explanation and left the room quickly, his limp more noticeable. He hadn't touched his cup.

GREGG HEARD A SECOND feminine voice from down the hall and decided it would be good to put some more distance between him and the doorway. He rose from the couch and pretended to look around the room. He fingered the spines of books. These varied from matched sets of Mark Twain, Dickens and Washington Irving to more recent biographies, novels and histories. Most still wore their bright dust jackets and about half of them were wrinkled just enough to show use.

T.J. didn't move from the couch.

"Guy must read a lot," Gregg said over his shoulder, but softly enough so Mrs. Warren couldn't hear from the next room. On a corner table he saw what looked to be a framed newspaper story. He bent over and read the yellowing newsprint.

"Here's how he got that limp," he said quietly to the still silent T.J.

Then T.J. got up, yawned and stretched. Gregg saw T.J. wasn't looking for conversation so he turned to a small section of wall not taken up with books. There was a black and white group photo of about forty young men dressed in the style of thirty years before. The judge's diplomas hung atop one another in a second space. Devon School and two from the University of Pennsylvania.

"Huh," Gregg said, returning the framed newspaper article to the table. It was the judge all right, but still hard to imagine this guy in the army. They heard the sound of distant plumbing recently engaged, then footsteps as the judge came back toward the room. They were both back on the couch when the judge returned.

"Uh, Judge," Gregg said, handing the warrant back to him with his finger on the line requiring the judge to set times for the search. The man looked back at him dumbly. There were water spots on his shirt collar. Then he stared down at the paper where Gregg still pointed to the empty box. "'Daylight search' will be fine, Judge." Gregg again put his finger on the page.

"Oh, of course, sure, sorry," the judge said. He sat back down, almost falling. He tried to smile, but his face seemed to fall back from the effort. He scrawled the required words at the bottom. Gregg took the packet back and went through it. He hadn't really been sworn, and he wondered if this was important enough to mention. T.J. remained still and silent. A long time for T.J.

"Well, fellas. That do it?" The judge stood, almost jumped up on his good leg, then staggered. Gregg saw him put the plastic pen in his pants pocket without capping it.

"Sure, Judge," T.J. said. "Thank you for seeing us." He said this softly, almost warmly, then nodded Gregg toward the hallway. Before leaving, T.J. leaned through the opening to the other room and said "Thanks, Emma."

"Anytime, T.J.," she said, coming to the doorway. "A pleasure, Sergeant Leavitt. Hope you get your man." The voice was the same. *"I'm going to miss you General."*

"Yes Ma'am," Gregg said, feeling unaccountably foolish.

The dog stopped her pacing around the judge and looked at Gregg, her tail lowered, still now. Her claws clicked on the floor as she followed them down the hallway in silence.

That was when the blonde woman emerged from the big room. "Hey, Em?" she was calling just as she turned into the hall, heading past them but not five steps away. "Oh, sorry. Didn't see you fellas." Then to the judge, "Sorry, Harry."

"It's okay, Livy, we're, ah, just finishing," the judge said.

She gave Gregg, then T.J. in turn the same perfunctory imitation smile.

"Hi," she said and moved around them, shoulders hunched. She'd looked right at him, through him.

"We appreciate your seeing us, Judge," T.J. said, when they reached the door.

"Of course, anytime, anytime." The judge held the door with his hip, and the hand he gave each of them as they left was damp. Gregg felt that moment of displeasure that a damp palm, recently emerged from a bathroom, will always produce.

"Well goodbye, Judge," T.J. said, once they had stepped outside. "Thanks aga..." but the door had already closed. T.J. reddened then but when he turned to look at Gregg over the car, his smile had returned. They got in, their closing doors making a single sound.

"Drive," Carr said motioning with his hand. "Drive... let's get out of here."

Gregg started the car and instantly put it in gear, leaving a small trough in the loose pebbly drive.

"I don't get it," Gregg said, as they passed between the stone posts. "He always like that?"

"Like what?" T.J. was putting his seat back to stretch out.

"You know. First it's: 'Glad to see yah,' butter wouldn't melt in his mouth, then all at once it's like he has a hot poker up his ass."

"Naw, Harry Warren's not moody."

"Well, what do you call that?" Gregg motioned behind him.

"That?" T.J. smiled and folded his hands on his paunch. "That was scared."

"Of what, the pictures? Jeez, he's had to see worse than that. My uncle says…" Gregg paused and looked both ways before turning left onto the highway. He had to lean back to see around Carr's head.

"Who knows?" Carr said. "But, Leavitt, I've known Harry Warren for more than twenty years, and that's the first, the only time, I've seen him write with anything except that goddamn fountain pen."

When they reached the highway T.J. seemed to relax. "I think our little friend just stepped in shit and I don't want him changin' his mind while there's still time to clean it off."

"The judge?"

"No, the tooth fairy. There's something funny here. You know he used to work for Zach Hannah. We'll know more once you toss the Martin house."

T.J. held the papers against his belly and closed his eyes. Then after they'd driven for a while he said, "You know, I didn't know Judge Warren went to Penn State," Gregg said. "Doesn't seem like his kind of school."

"It's not. He went to Penn, no 'State.'"

"Uh huh," Gregg said, not understanding.

"Ivy League," T.J. said.

"Yah?"

"Well, sort of," T.J. added, "Like Harry Warren."

Fifteen minutes later, they were halfway back to Hadley County. T.J. began to snore softly. Gregg had never seen anyone look more contented.

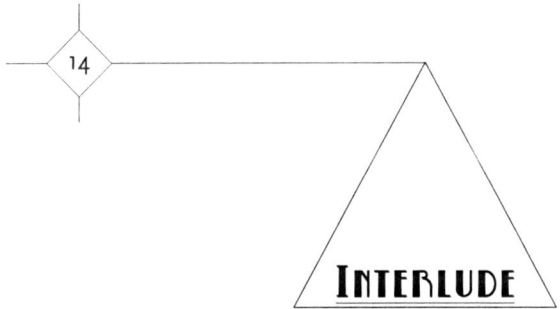

14
INTERLUDE

Harry preferred analysis to action. By three o'clock that afternoon, still no closer to doing anything about his predicament, he at least had satisfied himself as to why he was where he was. Surely this was payment for sins, and for sins committed with eyes wide open.

For his graduation thesis, Harry had chosen the title "Castes and Classes: Barriers to Social Mobility in 20th Century America." Even the Harry of those days would have agreed this was a precious and pretentious title coming as it did in the turmoil of the civil rights revolution so soon after the death of Dr. King. Professor Rush, however, had been delighted with it, and seemed unusually pleased when Harry asked him to be his thesis advisor. Attendance at Prof's lectures had declined. 'Dinner at Eight' had lost its cachet. The '60s had become the '70s and affirmative action brought hundreds of new black students to Penn every year. There was no longer room for benign anachronisms like T. Lippincott Rush. The previous term Prof had been the target of a student 'sit-in,' and that spring there was even talk of dropping his courses from the curriculum.

Prof seemed to forget his problems as he steered Harry through collections of letters, old society columns, long forgotten works of popular fiction, wedding announcements and obituaries. One section of Harry's finished product was titled "Ambitious Love." After explaining that a woman could storm the gates to society through and only through a fortunate marriage, he turned to the probable fate of men with aspirations.

> For men, however, the coin is reversed. While a woman may seduce and scheme her way into a fortunate marriage, and even be seen to do so, once she succeeds, she is forgiven everything. Her vulgarity will be reborn as 'energy' and her ignorance of tribal custom proclaimed 'informality.' Since she now bears an exalted name, she need produce only one male child to cement her status against any indiscretion short of opening a bawdy house; except in New York, where even that is permitted.
>
> Unhappily, if a man fails at matrimonial ascent it means certain and lasting derision; to succeed means this as well, but sharpened now by the pangs of envy. Nor are children much help to fathers. A cadet branch is better than bastardy, but only a little. For a man to indulge in overtly ambitious love he must either (a) make a large fortune, (b) shoot down a Von Richtofen or (c) reconstruct the legend of his past to make it seem he hasn't "succeeded" at all, which is to say, lie a lot. It is rare, and what's worse, hard, to make a fortune before thirty, and there is lately a dearth of Hun Foemen worthy of the steel of young men with matrimonial objectives. No, reinvention of one's past is much the preferred means to assure a young man's rise. South of Baltimore, it is the only means.

Prof had recommended an 'A' for his finished work but one of Harry's other two advisors had labeled it "a glib confection of unfortunate epigrams" while the other nodded. Harry was content that two PhDs would feel obliged to insult him though he felt the 'B' they gave him was unjust. He had, after all, placed a colon in the title.

Five years after that, with the Army, three surgeries and two sober years of law school behind him, it might be said that Harry had matured, though he would have admitted to anyone that, mostly, he was just tired. The Penn Law School faculty was made of sterner stuff than their Arts and Sciences brethren and Harry knew better than to advance any "Castes and Classes" sentiments there. But while he kept his head down, he hadn't forgotten the few life lessons that he *did* learn as an undergraduate. Nor had he forgotten how poor a prospect he was for winning the heart of someone like the nineteen-year-old Emma Llewellyn.

Years later Emma summarized the early moments of their romance: "Of course I'd picked you out already. You were older, almost a lawyer. Roger called you 'our war hero.'"

She referred to their chance first meeting at Harry's old fraternity which came about only because of the misbehavior of Emma's date, Roger Adams. Like Emma, a nineteen-year-old sophomore, Roger had some experience with beer, somewhat less with marijuana, but none at all with the two taken together. Emma was already roughing it, being at Phi Psi at all. 'Slumming,' Livy would have called it. So when Roger's incoherent hilarity finished with him passing out, Emma turned to the quiet man with a limp and asked him to walk her home.

Harry actually had an excellent memory of Emma's long ago date. "That was nice of him."

"Yes, Roger was nice. If he knew how to drink, you and I would never have married." But Emma always needed better reasons than fate. After thinking for a short while, she added, "You looked interesting, self-sufficient, happy being by yourself on the edge of a crowd." She said this to suggest she had known even then how it would turn out, had orchestrated it herself. Harry knew, however, that he had merely succeeded in 'Plan C,' the third course of action he had outlined five years earlier.

The decisive moment came early, at the end of their walk back to her fortress-like women's dormitory. They exchanged a chaste kiss, no more than a faint brushing of lips, hers full, dry, textured like the inner skin of a peeled orange.

"Can I call you?" His throat was tight. Emma Llewellyn, then as ever, was far too young, too beautiful, too vibrant for him.

"You'd better," she said, and strode away, rewarding him with a quick, furtive backward look, then a smile when she saw he was still standing, watching her.

◆△◆

THE FOLLOWING WEDNESDAY Emma asked Harry to ride with her out to the 'farm.' Her ostensible purpose was to pick up clothes, but really to show him the old homestead. Nor was he unwilling. He'd fallen hard and, for some reason, so had she. The mysteries of secured transactions under the Uniform Commercial Code were supposed to be revealed to Harry that afternoon. Well, they could keep for another day. They would keep for thirty years.

They were already lovers. They had made love on their second date as was customary in that brief interlude between the Pill and AIDS. He had been clumsy, nervous and then too intimidated to make it up to her. But later she woke him and set about him with strenuous insistence, impatient as if her goal was just beyond reach. In the darkness she made small noises of effort and frustration from back in her throat, then a surprised series of gasps and thrusts before falling onto him, then off, and then to sleep. So now as she drove, Harry's thoughts were still of sweat and laughter, the novelty and equality of early love.

Harry's idea of a 'farm' before that day was a house, a barn, perhaps a few cows, some crops, maybe a tractor. Given that Harry, like everyone else in Philadelphia, had heard the name Llewellyn, he figured a horse or two would probably wander into view. But, for all he had learned from Tee and Prof Rush, Harry was still a Hadley boy, unprepared for what was coming.

Then he saw it. Round Hill Farm sat, appropriately enough, on a small, almost perfectly circular, hill like the top of a green billiard ball just emerged from the surrounding flatter country. White painted fences traced rectangles of five and ten acres in three directions. In one of them a half dozen adult mares accompanied by a like number of colts, about three-quarter size, looked up from the grass to stare.

The house was red brick, half covered with ivy. The predominant impression was of overwhelming, unapologetic size.

They came to a stop in a circular drive at the front of four sandstone columns. It was at times like this that people said stupid things and Harry had learned by then it was best to say nothing.

"Great big place, isn't it," Emma said, helping him up out of the low seat of her car. Harry pulled on the side of the windshield with his free hand. In the distance he heard the "pop pop" rounds of gunfire. Briefly, he turned toward them.

"Does it hurt?" She gestured toward his hip. In the half light of Tuesday morning, when she first had seen his wound, she had gasped. "Oh Harry. My God. What did they do to you?"

But she was used to it now, almost proprietary.

He said, "A little tender, I got bumped around a little last night." Emma made a sound between a snort and a laugh. "You didn't seem to mind," she said as she led him up the steps.

The same double popping sounded again. He looked up. He placed it somewhere beyond the house.

"Skeet," she said, leading him through the front door.

"You'll find, Mr. Warren, that Round Hill is a fine example of its period." She gestured around her and affected the manner of her art history instructor. "McKim, Mead and White, 1910 to 12. You'll agree, Mr. Warren, that it's a faithful, if somewhat overstated, acknowledgment of the Georgian Palladian School."

The two-story entry hall was dominated by a curved, double balustraded stairway that Cecil DeMille would have rejected as excessive. Leaving it, they entered a second, slightly smaller room which was a blur of vivid colors, yellows, reds, blues and greens; of polished wooden tables covered with beautiful things. Lamps, photographs in silver frames, china boxes, vases of flowers, all competing for space on every shining horizontal surface.

Presiding over all this beauty was a painting, a full-length portrait of a red-haired girl-woman who looked like Emma and smiled confidently down on them. Harry stopped and stared back. She had looked right at the painter, her mouth slightly open, her hair giving the impression of arrested motion. The outline of the woman's breast was still alive and real under the ice blue gown. Harry wondered if a shadow of freckles had also stopped just above the aureole. Perhaps she had just turned to answer a foolish question, or maybe it was the look she saved for future viewers and their pornographic musings.

Emma said, "Granny Kaye. Mummy's mother."

"Beautiful," he said.

"I think so," she said, pretending to speak of the picture, not the person in it. "It's a Sargent, one of his last." But she knew what he'd meant.

After a pause, still without looking at him, Emma spoke more softly. "I never knew her like that. She broke her back riding, when she was thirty. I only knew Granny Kaye in a wheel chair."

Harry winced at the appalling vision of the proud, beautiful woman sprawled on the ground just aware that she couldn't feel her legs—those long legs. In the painting, one was thrust forward just enough to show a narrow white slipper, the curve of her thigh suggested by the drape of the gown.

Emma turned back into the silence. Then she shook her head and took his hand with her thumb and two fingers, lifting it slightly.

"Mummy hung it there right after Granny Kaye's funeral. I think I was eight. I didn't cry until then," Emma said. She played with his thumb and looked down.

"Granny Kaye was loud. She was ferocious. She had a whiskey voice and smoked all the time. She was always yelling at us to get back on after we fell off one of her damned horses. She couldn't stand not being able to ride any more so we all had to. That's why she took up shooting. She made us shoot, too. I thought my shoulder would break. She won the Pennsylvania women's trap shooting championship, four times from her chair."

Emma said all this in what seemed like one breath. Harry put his arm around her.

More slowly she said, "Until I saw the painting, you see, I never thought about how much she'd lost. I guess that's why Granny Kaye kept it hidden away all those years. But when I saw it, all I could think of was all the times I'd said under my breath 'I hate you, Granny Kaye! I hate you.'"

The woman in the picture was unfazed by her granddaughter's admission. She continued to regard them with her unchanging air of amused superiority, the unthinkable fall forever safely consigned to the future. "I used to think it was haunted," Emma said, pulling him away from the painting. "That she was looking at me, knowing at last all the things I'd thought about her. When we moved out here from Chestnut Hill I cried and cried, but Mummy insisted."

"Granny Kaye was from the polite side of the family," Emma said leading him out of the room.

"Polite?" he asked.

"The Llewellyns, well, we're rather recent. Granny Kaye was a Shippen and *she* married a Newbold. She had a great-great aunt who screwed Benedict Arnold, married him I think."

It was only the second time Harry had heard Emma use a vulgar term. Her lovemaking was vocal enough and she was frank in her moments of appreciation, but she wasn't theatrically crude like her more famous sister.

"Sleeping with soldiers must run in the family," she said, pushing him now into the next room, the 'Gun room' she called it. This was a mellow pumpkin color, wood-paneled walls hung with old prints of dogs and horses. There were floor-to-ceiling bookcases and green and brown leather chairs clustered around a rough stone fireplace.

Here Emma pushed against him for emphasis and they kissed. Harry began to respond to this when she pushed him away.

"Hold that thought," she said and went through another door. Left alone, he examined the bookcases which held the obligatory matched sets, obviously unread, as well as some recent detective fiction that showed signs of use. The prints were a matched set depicting a foxhunt, start to finish. Very tough on the fox at the end.

Two glass-fronted gun racks held a small arsenal. Harry was trying one of the doors when, in the distance, he heard the sound of someone, Emma, running up a flight of stairs, then the faint sound of women's voices. This would take a while. He sat down.

Then a new sound of footsteps, purposeful and definite, came through the still-open door from Granny Kaye's room. Not Emma, he thought, and looked up in time to see a tall, very good-looking man with reddish brown hair, going gray at the temples, striding toward him. He wore a dark brown sweater and tortoise shell glasses. He was carrying a large double-barreled shotgun.

The transition to abject terror was instant. Harry had no doubt it showed. The approaching man seemed to understand because he smiled and chuckled at the same time.

What he said was, "You're Emma's friend." He held out his free hand. "Loy Llewellyn."

Harry got up slowly to take the hand, reassured to note as he did so that the gun cradled in the man's left arm was broken open. "Uh, Harry Warren, Mr. Llewellyn."

"Nice to meet you, Harry." He shook briefly and firmly, then turned and walked over to one of the cabinets and unlocked it with a key he took from his pocket. He snapped the shotgun together and put it away.

"Unusual name, 'Harry.' Don't think I ever met a 'Harry' before." He said this to the case as he locked it.

"My grandfather's name," Harry said.

"Emma tells me you're at Penn law." Lloyd Llewellyn turned toward him. He was getting Harry to speak the way a man would have a horse or a dog turn this way or that before he named a price.

"Third year," Harry said, nodding. So Emma had spoken to her father about him. She hadn't told Harry about that.

"Like it?" he asked.

"It's fine."

"Beats Vietnam," the man said, smiling. Ah, she hadn't told him very much.

"Oh, it's much better than Vietnam." Harry was glad for the momentary advantage.

Lloyd Llewellyn took this in. Then he said, "I'm sorry. It's a figure of speech, a pleasantry. All the kids seem to use it when you ask them how school is going." He gestured vaguely with his hand.

Harry couldn't think of anything to say to this so he made a small smile which the older man seemed to take for forgiveness.

"So you were there? Already did your year?"

"No, I did thirteen days, thirteen and a wake-up," Harry said.

Lloyd Llewellyn was still holding the key. He looked at it for a moment as if he'd forgotten what it was for then put it back in his pocket. Harry *had* knocked him off stride, but he would know what 'thirteen days' meant. "I was flip," the man said. "I have no right to be, uh, Harry. Did I offend you?"

"No sir," Harry said, "You didn't offend me."

Emma appeared in the doorway then with a small pile of folded clothes over one arm. She crossed over to her father glancing at Harry with raised eyebrows before turning to her first love. They held each other's eyes with the perfect confidence of fathers and daughters.

"You're investigating my beau," she said.

"Not at all," he said. "Though I was just about to ask Harry what a 'wake-up' is."

She turned away from her father. "What *is* a wake-up, Harry?" They both looked at him, their two pair of eyes suddenly identical.

"It's your last day, what they called the last day 'in-country,'" Harry said. "You wake up there but sleep somewhere else, hopefully on a 707 back to the 'world' they call it." He knew this was already too much talk about his brief military career. He knew it was far too soon to mention his medal. In spreading rumors of valor, less was always more, so he put his hands up and made a small half shrug, an all-purpose gesture. No one asked questions after that, except Lloyd Llewellyn, who asked, "'They?' Why do you say 'they'?"

In his nervousness Harry had used the third person. Only candor would do now. "I got shot right after I got there. It didn't seem long enough to think I belonged."

"Harry Warren," Lloyd Llewellyn said then, "you're an interesting man."

◆Δ◆

ON THE WAY BACK to Penn, Emma turned to him at a traffic light and said, "Daddy likes you."

What a day. He'd put her father off balance. He was in control, on top of the world. Harry knew as sure as the light was green that at that moment she loved him, too. In love and loved. Invulnerable. But of course Lloyd Llewellyn hadn't cared for him at all, something that became clear soon enough.

Olivia proved tougher than Emma, more like the grandmother than her little sister. Later Harry would see close up how Livy never shrank from the necessary cruelties that kept the lives of the Llewellyns' separate from, well, the Harry Warrens of this world. So it was when two months later, after Emma accepted him, Olivia was the first family member Emma told. Olivia's response, reported by a tearful Emma, had begun as amused disbelief but, when Emma persisted, her sister moved to insistent rejection. Emma's surprised tears and nineteen-year-old determination allayed Harry's initial fears as she delivered this report, but he remained fatalistic. He had asked her and she had said yes, an improvident decision by a stubborn teenager. He had followed Tee's formula perfectly. He was the son of the widowed poet, Barbara Warren. He had a good record in an unpopular war. Emma knew almost nothing of his father, of Hadley, and of course nothing of the real events of that far-away morning outside Mi Tho, Vietnam. He had lied just enough to make himself acceptable. There was nothing more he could do to make it so. The only question was: Would she stick?

Olivia, however, saw this was a matter requiring action, and serious enough for her to break their sisters' code and tell Daddy.

And so, two days after the first report, Emma returned with more sinister news of a gentler interview. This time the details were not shared, but it had left Emma distracted and distant. That weekend, Emma flew down to the family place in Hobe Sound, "To tell Mummy," she said. The implication was that her father hadn't felt up to it.

◆△◆

"Mummy." Such an innocent word, though innocence, the stupid kind anyway, was not a quality anyone would have associated with Penelope 'Pippi' Llewellyn. For in her, her mother's portrait lived, and one look at Harry had been sufficient. Lloyd Llewellyn may have suspected Harry's impostures, but Pippi Llewellyn had known instantly. Harry knew Emma's trip to Florida would be decisive because 'Mummy' had already gathered all the information she needed when, a month earlier, Harry had returned to Round Hill for a second visit.

Pippi Llewellyn received Harry while seated just beneath the portrait of her mother. Her navy blue dress contrasted with the yellow brocade of the chair. Her hair was teased out in the formal style of the time. It was just slightly too young for her but, good looking as she was, it worked.

"So you're Harry," she said. Her hand came out and for a moment Harry thought he was expected to kiss it.

"Sit, sit," she said, "Lloyd, Harry doesn't have anything to drink. What would you like, Harry? I hope we have it."

'Lloyd' regarded him from in front of the fireplace, his head at his late mother-in-law's slippered feet.

"Thank you," Harry said. "Scotch?"

For the first and last time Lloyd Llewellyn made him a drink. Pippi Llewellyn gestured to a chair opposite her. Harry sat.

"You're from Boston, I hear?"

"Cambridge."

"But you went to Penn, with Livy, right? A change of scenery?"

"The shortsightedness of the Yale admissions office," Harry said. When deprecation was unavoidable, self-deprecation was always best. She rewarded him with a bit of merriment but quickly returned to her inquiry.

"You grew up in Cambridge?"

Lloyd handed Harry a heavy, cut glass tumbler brown with scotch.

"No," Harry began to describe Hadley to her.

"It seems like the town where Loy's father grew up," she said, interrupting. Then, "Lloyd, darling, would you bring me another?" She held her own glass up showing it was empty, summoning her husband again to his unaccustomed duty as bartender. Lloyd hesitated, but took the glass with a smile and again went over to a drinks table. Emma studied the floor.

"Your father died some time ago I understand."

"Ten, no, eleven years ago," Harry said.

"How awful for you. Now was he a writer, too?"

"No. He was a banker."

"In Boston?"

"No, in Hadley. Hadley's more than two hours from Boston." In the back of Harry's mind Tee Ingersoll and even Professor Rush were beginning to mutter 'Too much, Warren. Too much information.'

"It must be interesting, being a banker in a small town. I have to admit that most of Lloyd's banker friends, well I just can't figure out what they do half the time." She inclined her head toward her husband. "Lloyd, Harry's father wasn't a writer, he was a banker, in Hadley up in New Hampshire."

"Yes Pippi, *Mrs.* Warren is the writer. Barbara Warren? Her poems are in the *New Yorker*."

She leaned forward and put her hand on Harry's. "It must be so interesting, having a poet in the family. But when did you leave Hayley?"

"Hadley."

"I *am* sorry, Hadley."

"After my father died, when I was sixteen."

"And your mother just—decided—to be a poet?"

"Well, it was a bit more complicated than that."

It might have been the warmth from the drink that Lloyd Llewellyn gave him or the relief from the tension of a first meeting, but, dangerously, Harry found he had told Pippi Llewellyn even more about the aging mill town where he'd grown up, and just enough about himself. It was stupid of him to hope to find friendship or understanding in this unexpected place, to think he might charm his way into her affections. Anyone less desperate to believe could have seen that she was only pumping him. Twenty minutes was enough. All of the Prof's insights and Tee's careful training fell apart. She was inside the gates, looking around at will, and—who could blame her?—not much liking what she saw.

Harry didn't know the extent of 'Mummy's' alcoholism then. He should have been grateful because, without the half bottle of liquor she consumed in his presence and God knows how much before that, she'd have had him saying much more. Evidently she heard enough because just before they went in to dinner she seemed to lose interest in him. At the table she turned vague and monosyllabic as they ate—she took almost nothing from the two people who offered dishes to them.

Coffee was served in the dining room, and Emma's father was in mid-sentence when, without warning, his wife rose to her feet.

"Please don't stop Loy, I'm just a bit tired." She was beyond waiting for a response from anyone. The pleasantry was merely a reflex and she turned and walked out in the same way she spoke: deliberately, without slur or stumble, carefully touching pieces of furniture as she went. Harry saw a heavy-set black woman awaiting her just outside the dining room.

When she had gone, Emma folded her napkin carefully, the way she must have as a little girl. Her eyes shone and she had bright red patches on each cheek. "Well," she said, forcing a smile. Father and daughter reached out for one another's hand. This was done silently and neither looked at the other.

"Mummy drinks too much," Emma said as they drove back to the city.

It was not for him to agree, so Harry said nothing.

"Sometimes, sometimes... Oh it's all such a waste," she said, and hit the steering wheel with her hand in frustration.

"Emma, it was fine. I enjoyed myself."

"No, you don't understand. It's like you get twenty good minutes a day with Mummy. She's usually sick in the morning and she's, she's just *gone* by dinner time. I mean I spend the whole day just waiting for those twenty minutes when she's herself again."

"But I do." Harry remembered his long dead father.
"Do what?"
"I do understand."

◆△◆

By the time Emma spoke to her father the Llewellyns were gathering at Hobe Sound for the Christmas holidays. Emma flew down, presumably to catch the right twenty minutes with Mummy.

Emma telephoned Harry the first day, twice. She was all brittle cheer and see-you-soon. But on the second day she didn't call at all. On the third day, Harry called for her and a polite voice with a Spanish accent assured him that 'Mees L'ellen' would get the message. When silence persisted through the afternoon of a fourth day, he resigned himself to a new, unfamiliar emptiness that seemed to deepen by the hour.

The evening of that fourth day, a Tuesday, Harry closed one of the campus bars in the company of two other third-year law students. Their bittersweet night of shallow introspection had led the three to the joint conclusion that they had now stretched childhood to its absolute tattered, ragged end. Harry was tempted to talk to them about Emma, but found he couldn't bring himself to say her name. At last, they wished a bored, impatient bartender good night and leaned into the bitter chill wind blowing up Walnut Street.

Harry found the door to his house ajar. He pushed it open. Emma sat on the floor in the dark hallway, knees drawn up, all in blue: mittens, a blue sailor's jacket that no sailor ever wore, a wool watch cap pulled down over her ears. Behind her, on the other side of the wall, the phone in his room was ringing.

Harry stood stupid with cold and beer and surprise. She looked up but didn't get up. Her face was swollen and red in the half light of the hallway.

"It's been ringing off and on for the past two hours." She sniffed wetly. "I'm sure they've guessed I'm here."

The phone rang two more times then stopped. "Must not be good news," Harry said, still not moving.

She took off a mitten and unwound her scarf but still didn't stand so Harry slid down the wall opposite her, their knees almost touching. She took off the other mitten and worried the seam, turning it inside out and back again, building herself up.

Finally she said, "I got a plane in Palm Beach. I didn't tell anyone, I just got a plane."

The phone began again.

"So you see, that's probably about me," she said gesturing with her chin toward the sound.

Good manners would have sent him to the phone to reassure her worried parents, but the verdict was coming, so he waited. He wasn't brave enough to look away.

"I thought you'd *be* here," she said, her words accelerating in a last rush to get them out, "but you were gone." Her voice broke then and her shoulders shook.

Harry shifted over to her side, then held her and rocked her. The phone fell silent.

"Thank God for that," Emma said, sniffling again, then laughed at the sound she made.

"Wrong number," he said.

"You don't know the half of it," she said, and laughed more confidently. "God, you smell like a brewery."

"I was revisiting my roots." He thought for a moment of his father. "Smokes," he explained, naming the bar. Then they each said, "Well ..." at the same time and fell into the same nervous laugh.

"Me first," Harry said. She nodded.

"I thought you were gone," he said. "Oh, you'd come back in a week or so. We wouldn't say anything about it at first, but soon enough we'd have one of those painful talks and I'd do the civilized thing, we'd get together for a while until one day you tell me you're going skiing in Vermont or back to Florida. And soon, I'd see you walking with people I don't know and you talk to them with that smile you have. I can't hear what you say but I can hear you laugh. That laugh that I thought belonged only to me. That only I could bring out of you. All I can hear is just that. And just from the tone, I know, you see, I *know* right then, that you're gone ... Emma Llewellyn, the love of my life, is gone forever."

By then Harry was crying, too, because she brushed his face with a mitten. Not a bad speech, he thought later, drunk as he was. Try saying Emma Llewellyn after ten beers.

"Never," she said. "Never, never, never, never." Her face tasted of salt.

◆△◆

OLIVIA AGREED, OF COURSE, to be matron-of-honor at her only sister's wedding. No gesture or word came from her or any Llewellyn to suggest anything but complete approval. The wedding they staged the following May was a classic Main Line bun-fight, though somewhat asymmetrical, given the diminished representation from the groom's family. From below an altar manned by a dean and a bishop, Harry and Tee Ingersoll, his best man, could see his mother, a few friends, a dozen or so Phi Psi's even a few classmates from law school. Professor Rush helped fill out the side, but his sympathies were clearly with the legions of Philadelphians on the other side of the aisle.

Lloyd Llewellyn treated his mother, Barbara, with elaborate courtesy and even made a smooth and gracious speech at the rehearsal. His theme was that, as a loving father, he could deny his Emma nothing, and that no one would deny her, young as she was, so suitable a choice.

If Harry received these assurances a little blandly, it was only fair to remember that two weeks earlier, fresh from a final in Creditors Rights, he had been summoned downtown from the law school to the gilded offices of Wharton & Biddle, the Llewellyns' lawyers. Lloyd Llewellyn awaited him there with a man his age, introduced as 'Jack' Decker. A second man, 'Bob' Lefkowitz, was no older than Harry.

Lefkowitz shook hands with Lloyd first. "It's Rob, actually, Mr. Llewellyn." Then he turned to Harry, "Mr. Warren." Rob's hand was soft and damp. Wharton & Biddle was regarded as Valhalla by Harry and his classmates at Penn Law. Only members of the Law Review received offers here.

The four shared lunch in the firm's dining room—they had dining rooms then—while Harry watched the two lawyers try to decide where he would stand in the Llewellyn pecking order. Over soup, Jack Decker expressed polite surprise at Harry's plan to return to New Hampshire. "Mighty cold winters up there, Harry," he said. What Decker meant was, "How do you expect to make a living suitable for a Llewellyn daughter?"

Rob Lefkowitz already knew enough to listen and say almost nothing.

Emma had dismissed the meeting as "something to do with the Trusts," so Harry was not entirely unprepared when, as soon as the dessert cart rolled away, Lloyd departed and he found himself left alone with Jack and Rob. With the departure of the great man, all pretense of conversation disappeared. The two lawyers watched Harry finish his coffee in silence. Every time Harry put his cup down, Lefkowitz put his napkin on the table. When Harry picked the cup up, Lefkowitz retrieved the napkin. This happened three times. Decker looked briefly at his watch. When Harry finally finished, they escorted him to a smallish office with arctic air conditioning. There Jack Decker abruptly took his hand.

"Well, congratulations, uh, Harry. Great young lady, Emma. Mavis and I are looking forward to the wedding. Rob will take care of you. Let me know if there are any errors in the documents." His tone showed there was no possibility of that, and he left Harry and Rob Lefkowitz alone.

Despite the temperature of the office, Lefkowitz still managed to sweat and small dark stains dappled his blue shirt. He had the pale soft look of a man who spent his life indoors. His hair had thinned almost to baldness, the way a plant deprived of sunlight loses its leaves.

"We need you to confirm the asset disclosure form, uh, Harry."

"Sure, uh, Rob."

"For the pre-nup."

"Uh huh."

Lefkowitz appraised Harry over the top of a pen he suspended between his two index fingers. "You *have* read it?"

"Mr. Lef... Rob, I have no idea of what you're talking about. No one has shown me anything."

Lefkowitz sighed. "That's what I thought," he said, and put the sheath down out of reach. He picked up his phone and punched some numbers. While he waited for an answer, he saw Harry's look of impatience, shrugged, and pushed the neatly typed agreement back toward him. "You'd better read this."

Then he said into the phone, "Yes, Helene, is Oswald in?—No I need him right away." He waited then, while Harry read.

The document described Harry's educational achievements in glowing terms, confirmed his full understanding of its as yet unseen provisions together with a half dozen tax code sections Harry had never heard of. He saw he was about to "renounce any claim, right or obligation arising in law or equity to any alimony, property settlement, spousal right in probate"—anything at all from the beginning of time—in exchange for Emma's selfless renunciation of all claims to his 1969 Volkswagen and the $571.87 in his PNB checking account. Harry had no idea how they'd learned that. Somehow they also knew the amount of Harry's monthly disability allowance and what he received from the GI bill. Emma's precise, schoolgirl signature already shone in bright blue ink from the last page. While Lefkowitz was busy with the phone, Harry turned with guilty curiosity to Emma's asset disclosure pages. He skipped right down to the bottom, it was seven million something. Harry didn't bother to focus after that.

Lefkowitz's voice changed, became excited and Harry looked up. "Well, damn it, Oswald, he hasn't even seen—I know, I know—but, he's not separately represented—well, okay, sure."

Lefkowitz hung up the phone and said, "Mr. Popp is coming down to see us."

Harry didn't answer. He couldn't stop smiling.

"I'm sorry about this," Lefkowitz said. "I thought you knew, but you don't look exactly unhappy." It didn't seem the time for Harry to say that he had thought it would be a lot less, but the absurdity of it all overtook him and he burst out laughing. To his credit, Lefkowitz laughed too.

At this the door opened abruptly and a bald, alert little man came into the office stopping just next to Harry's chair. He stood on the balls of his feet like a boxer. He was never exactly still.

"I'm Oswald Popp. You boys seem to be having a nice time here." He pointed his brown-black eyes at Lefkowitz first, then Harry. He didn't offer his hand, a man with no interest in even pretending to butter up the latest entry to the Llewellyn clan.

Lefkowitz got serious and cleared his throat.

"As I was saying, Oswald, Mr. Warren hasn't seen the prenuptial agreement and I'm concerned about the knowing-waiver provisions."

"Yah, yah," Popp said. He pointed at the document in Harry's hand. "Well, you just graduated from Penn, ah, Harry. Harry? You need this explained?" He made a smile with half his mouth.

Harry looked from one to the other and said, "If Emma and I are divorced or she dies before I do, I get nothing, right?"

"Not exactly," Lefkowitz said.

But Popp made a quick hand gesture to Lefkowitz. When he turned back to Harry he was grinning the way a man will when someone he didn't like got bad news.

"Bingo on divorce," he said. "But if she predeceases, you receive $150,000 for every year of marriage or part thereof, and a life estate in whatever home you reside in."

Then Lefkowitz added, "She can bequeath property to you, of course, but you waive any forced statutory share." He frowned. "Of course, there are also the trusts." Lefkowitz held his hands up to Popp.

"Look, Warren..., Harry," Popp said, "They really call you Harry?" His mouth worked. Harry suspected he was chewing gum.

"Yah, Harry."

"Harry. Bottom line, you can't make her give you anything. Nada. Takes eighteen pages, but that's what it says. The lady can give you more if she wants, but you can't insist. Clear."

"Okay."

Lefkowitz started to interrupt. "Uh..."

But Popp said, "Okay, okay, good, right. Okay, sign here. Rob, get a notary in here." Almost instantly a grandmotherly woman came in and dropped copies, a heavy seal and some extra pens on Lefkowitz's desk.

When they finished, the bald man just stepped back and regarded Harry. He'd made his kill. Harry couldn't remember disliking anyone more. He clicked the ball point once. "So, do I get to keep the pen?"

Popp's eyes narrowed. He made a soft snort and left without saying goodbye. The elderly lady notary gathered up her seals and pens, then looked from Lefkowitz to Harry. She made a shy smile, the first real sign of friendship Harry had seen that day. Apparently people didn't speak to 'Mr. Popp' that way. But with Popp safely gone, she said, "It's a nice pen, Mr. Warren. I hope you get some use out of it." Then she gathered the papers for copying. Lefkowitz and Harry were alone again, waiting for her to bring back the copies. The spots on Lefkowitz's shirt had grown into dark blue patches.

"I'm sorry about that." He said and waved his hand at the open doorway.

"No big deal," Harry said.

"You gave up a lot of marital rights, Mr. Warren."

Harry was relieved he'd given up on the 'Rob' and 'Harry' business.

"Mr. Lefkowitz, to get marital rights, first you've got to get married."

Lefkowitz was nodding mechanically as Harry spoke. Then he stopped. "Ah," he said.

◆△◆

Harry had no trouble tracking Tee down to ask him to be his best man. They had spoken hardly at all that year, but by then Tee was something of a celebrity in Philadelphia.

"Harry Warren? Lord, is this some kind of joke?"

"No," Harry said, hurt. "No, its not a joke."

After a pause, the old insinuating laugh came through the phone, the one they were starting to hear on the Philadelphia stations. "You don't have some law school buddy, some war-hero pal? How come you have to dig up old Tee?"

"But you're my best friend."

There was a sound like a throat being cleared. "I suppose I am," he said at last, "but I didn't think you thought so." There was a silence.

"You're not very communicative, you know."

"No, but that never meant anything between us."

"Not between us."

"Well?"

"Well, of course. Everyone will be there."

So Tee was there, too. At the age of twenty-six he had almost fully changed into the man he became. His early celebrity on local television had made him easy with the attention of strangers. He had filled out and softened, both in manner and appearance, into the kind of young man that most old men, and all old women, liked right away.

But not all young women, and not Emma Warren.

One picture from the Warrens' wedding album showed Emma and Tee dancing, Emma smiling at someone just out of the picture as Tee looked across at her. To a stranger, Tee's expression was admiring, sympathetic, a younger version of the famous connoisseur pleased with his find. But Harry knew it was also the look a man might give to an expensive painting a friend just bought. He doesn't like it very much, but has better manners than to say so. As for Emma, well, she always knew how to talk to the people she danced with, like all the girls from Mrs. Lewis's dancing class. But she had nothing to say to Tee.

Nevertheless, for the wedding toast, the new Tee was already on full display. 'You know who that is' whispers greeted him when he stood behind the couple.

"I first met Harry Warren when he was fresh from a small, windswept New England penal colony called Devon." He spoke with no trace of the nervousness and hesitation displayed by Harry's Phi Psi friends who had gone before. He accepted the small patter of polite laughter with a quick bow. "He was a diffident little guy who rarely smiled and always seemed to be watching, waiting. Hopeful, but usually disappointed. Naturally, we became friends." More polite laughter. Tee had already learned the trick of speaking loud enough to be heard but softly enough to make people listen and stop their sideways conversations.

"'Harry is looking for something,' I thought. Success, fame, wealth—all the things that recently-imprisoned teenage boys dream of." Pause.

"Well, maybe not *all* the things." More laughter but short, nervous, followed by deeper silence. He had their attention now.

Tee paused and surveyed the three hundred heads.

"But it's clear to me now. Harry was looking for love. More particularly, he was looking for someone to love. And this never changed. In the years since, whenever I'd see Harry I'd think, 'still looking, still watching, still waiting. Like a man on a ship that never quite gets to port.'"

The tent now became quiet indeed. The sound of waiters and dishes made a faint rattle in the middle distance. A poorly tied flap fluttered in a light breeze. At the table opposite, Mrs. Llewellyn put her index finger in a glass and gave it a stir. It was a moment when a young man, even one that old men liked, even a Tee Ingersoll, could say something truly embarrassing.

"But lately, something has come over our Harry. He smiles for no apparent reason. His words trail off in mid-sentence—a terrible handicap in your chosen profession, Warren." Louder laughter, relieved. They knew where he was going now.

"No, it's all quite different. He can see land now. The skyline is coming into view. The voyage was fine but this"—he moved to behind Emma's chair putting his long fingers over the back, pausing—"this is home." Tee took up a glass from the table in a single motion.

"To Harry and his Emma," he cried, over the loud beginnings of applause and vowel sounds of approval.

He turned in the noise to give Emma a ritual kiss. She smiled offering her cheek. "That was very nice," she said and turned away.

Late that evening as the reception wound down, Prof sidled up to him. Prof had been relegated to the occasional graduate seminar by then, saved from dismissal only by tenure, but he still cut an impeccable figure in his summer-weight suit. Prof was also undeniably drunk. Only that could account for his declaration.

"Very clever, Mr. Warren, how you managed all, all this." He spoke softly and gestured at the tent full of people.

"Managed?"

"Mmm. Oh I could see years ago that you knew *how* to do it. But to actually pull it off, well..." Prof broke into a smile but didn't look at him. "I thought you'd be pleased that someone appreciated your thesis."

"Professor Rush, let me get you ..."

"A drink? Oh, don't worry. I'm not going to run amok and spoil things. I'm sincere. I'm on your side. I only wanted to congratulate you on your success. Warn you, too." He looked sideways at Harry then.

"You can't ever relax, you know. Keep your wits about you. People don't like to be fooled. That glorious girl coming toward us won't want to wake up one day and find she's in the middle of a practical joke."

Then Emma was next to them. "Hi Prof. Sorry, I've got to steal Harry for a last dance."

The white-haired man leaned forward and kissed her cheek. "Of course, of course."

As they turned to go, the Prof said, "Good bye." They walked two steps and Harry turned back to hear him add in the same tone, but intended only for Harry, "Good luck."

◆△◆

HARRY REMEMBERED THE WARNING and took reasonable precautions. For instance, he never took Emma or his daughters to Hadley. If Barbara was ever indiscreet enough to mention the old days at a family gathering, Harry knew how to change the subject quickly, smoothly. Even in his early days at Cruikshank and Hannah he avoided cases and persons that involved the town where he'd grown up. As far as Emma and his daughters were concerned, life began in the middle of his senior year at Devon.

Perhaps it was simple exhaustion that led him to Ephne. Had he simply tired of posing, watching; tired of heading off this or that conversation? Yet it was his fear of the sight of Emma's surprised, then slowly comprehending countenance, that had propelled him into the panicked choices of the past day. A "practical joke," but on whom?

He had tried to learn from Zach, a man who always seemed to see life twenty-twenty without a flinch. Whether picking jurors or deciding to move the office to new quarters, divorcing his first wife or admitting defeat in an honorable political campaign, Zach looked bad news in the face, weighed the options and moved ahead. He didn't need a judicial title, a big house or the assurance of excess millions to convince himself of his worth.

Harry knew he needed guidance in those days, but something had always warned Harry away from giving Zach his full confidence. It may have been the edge in his criticism of Harry's work which became sharper the year Zach lost his campaign for Congress. At the time Harry had guessed that Zach's more frequent flashes of impatience were payback for Emma's abrupt departure from that campaign, but even after Zach seemed to forgive Emma's defection, Harry stayed quiet, afraid that Zach would despise him, not so much for his deceptions, but for his weakness in admitting to them.

Besides, although Harry never knew the details, there were stories that Zach had taken up with a new girl during those months. Emma's disapproval was followed by depression that seemed to break only when Samantha was born.

Whatever Zach's impatience with Harry, and however disappointed he was once the campaign was lost, even the financial pressures of putting back together the loose alliance of competing egos that Cruikshank and Hannah contained, had distracted him from insuring Harry's selection to the court. Zach had made the calls and pushed him forward. As much as the Llewellyn millions, it was Zach who had made him a judge.

Zach would know what to do now.

◆△◆

WHEN HARRY REACHED HIM on the office private line, it was four-thirty in the afternoon. Zach came right to the point. He had just spoken to T.J. He was not encouraging.

"Harry. I just heard back from T.J. Carr about that warrant, *your* warrant. Jesus, what were you thinking?"

Harry made a neutral sound into the telephone. "I don't know Zach, I..."

"Look, I know about Ephne and, and you. She told me. Why do you think I filed her preliminary report with our memorandum? Don't tell me. You didn't read the report, did you? Well, shit. I *assumed* you would do at least that and figure out a way out of the case without me having to disclose that the presiding judge had slept with our expert."

"C'mon Zach, I just didn't think. I mean, Emma was right there, I, I ..."

"Look, we shouldn't even be talking about this, not smart." Harry heard him exhale his impatience. Then, as if to himself: "But hell, you've got to get out from under that warrant."

"How can I do that?" Harry could hear the waiver in his own voice.

"I don't know, but this news isn't getting better with age. They're executing it right now."

Harry brightened. T.J. wouldn't have done that if he knew about Harry and Ephne. "So T.J. doesn't ..."

As always, Zach was two steps ahead of him. "... have any idea." Zach finished his sentence. "No, he hasn't asked me directly yet and I haven't volunteered. But, you understand Harry, he asks me the right question ... I've got to answer it. I can't ..."

"No, no, of course."

"I can tell you this much, Harry. He's looking everywhere. Right now he doesn't have a suspect unless you count my clients."

"The Martins?"

"Uh huh. Look, I've got to protect them. You understand. They're mean enough to kill someone, but right now they just don't seem up to it. And, unless you know something I don't, there's no motive."

"How, how did you ... you know..."

"She told me, Harry. Ephne saw your name on the pleadings two weeks ago and blurted it out, seemed pretty upset, about you I mean. Didn't want you to get hurt. Said you broke it off eight, ten years ago, water under the bridge."

Harry made a sound of impatience and regret.

"You're right, none of my business," Zach said, "but you are in deep,

deep shit my friend. You know T.J.'s going to find something, a phone bill, a credit card receipt... That means you'll have two, maybe three days. But T.J.'s going to find out. You understand it's inevitable?"

"I get the picture."

"I wish I could do more," the familiar voice slowed and softened.

But Harry was still thinking, 'no motive.' "That's okay, Zach, I understand," he said.

"T.J.'s not going to be easy, Harry. He's got a grudge against you. Your best bet may be to come clean before this gets any deeper."

"No, I can't do that," Harry said.

"Okay, if I can I'll try to give you a heads up, but Harry, that may not be possible." With wishes of luck, he hung up.

Harry exhaled and set the phone down. Well, that wasn't exactly a solution. Telling T.J. now would get him nowhere. But Zach had given him an idea.

Emma appeared in the doorway, "Who was that?" She nodded at the phone.

Since he wasn't sure how much she'd overheard, Harry said "Oh, that was Zach. We were having a wholly improper conversation about a case."

"All right," she said. "None of my business."

"Say, what time does Livy leave for Philadelphia?"

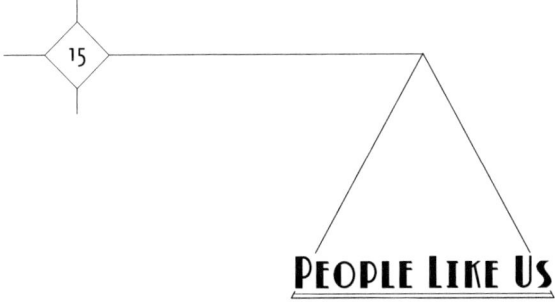

15

PEOPLE LIKE US

The clock in the hall had just struck two when Margie Tuttle opened the front door to two 'staties' in their green uniforms. This time they didn't wait at the doorway, just came through, each filling it in turn as he passed. Margie had been on the receiving end of some searches herself, but after she got over the initial fright that any police uniform brought on, she thought it might be fun to watch how the little old bitch, Eleanor, took it. It was.

Eleanor fluttered up to the first cop, the sergeant, and said, "Mr. Hannah said that you gentlemen wished to inspect the house?"

Margie snorted, 'inspect.' That was rich.

Eleanor stared at her with hard eyes but quickly turned back to the cops.

"Yes Ma'am," the big sergeant said. He removed his hat and laid it on the hall table like he owned the place. He took a pen from his pocket and opened a notebook with a gray metallic cover and began writing. "You are ...?" Margie decided he wasn't as good looking as she'd thought when he was there earlier in the week. He looked pale and he'd missed some spots shaving.

"Eleanor Martin." Margie saw that the old harpie stood very straight when she said this, like they were taking attendance or something.

The cop looked down at his notebook and began to read out loud.

"The New Hampshire State Police have been given full authority to search these premises for material evidence of a suspected crime including, but not limited to, evidence and/or instrumentalities that may have been connected to or shed light upon the homicide investigation now ongoing related to the wrongful death of Ephne Newsome."

"Her again. Well, all right. I guess so." Eleanor's hand went to her throat as she said this. "But Mr. Hannah says we're not to answer any questions."

Gregg nodded. Hannah had conceded the futility of resisting a search but he and T.J. had agreed there would be no questions about Ephne Newsome unless he was present.

Margie had retreated to the next room. *Wrongful death.* She remembered the woman's name. Newsome. The tight-assed little bitch the lawyers brought in to look at the furniture. So that's why she hadn't come back last Saturday.

The second policeman took off his outer coat and began pushing buttons to activate a large camera he carried. A red light glowed from it and it made a series of soft electric sounding chirps.

Then the sergeant handed papers to Eleanor. "Here is our warrant from the Hadley County Court, Ms. Martin, please sign here."

"Margie, Margie," Eleanor called as she ran a pen over the papers. "Please take these gentlemen's coats and then you can get back to the upstairs bath." Eleanor said this in her 'why haven't you done this already' tone of voice but Margie decided not to argue with cops in the vicinity. With cops somehow, no matter what they started with, it always seemed to get back to her. Meanwhile the cops started walking around the ground floor like cops did everywhere, the dining room, the great room. These two seemed to fill the place with their size, their low deep voices, their smell of leather and aftershave. Margie could hear Louisa upstairs calling, "Eleanor, Eleanor." Time for her goddamn pills. She'd be glad when Louisa was up and about again, even if she was crazy.

Margie took the green coats and walked into the great room and dropped them on the first chair she came to. Smiling, she climbed up the stairs to bring the good news of the invasion to Louisa. Halfway up the stairs her smile straightened. She paused at the top. She'd left the

Newsome woman alone with Eleanor and Louisa Friday night. Now she was dead ... well, it was none of her business, besides Margie had deserved that one night out, thinking as how she was about to go to jail.

AN HOUR LATER Margie could still hear them downstairs, drawers opening and closing, the sound of their heavy boots as they went from room to room. Periodically the camera whined and light from the flash threw shadows into the upstairs hallway. Margie mopped the floor of the upstairs bath and scrubbed at the ancient ball-footed tub and sink. Nothing would get the green copper rust off the porous porcelain, and the less said about the plastic shower curtain the better. Only Eleanor used the shower now. The nurse from the VNA did for Louisa. There was a little excitement when one of the cops stepped through a bad board on the porch, Eleanor wondering loudly when they would 'repair the damage.'

'Damage.' Like they were going to find a replacement for the rotten boards around this place!

Margie hung new towels and used a brush on the john. She was windexing the mirror to the medicine cabinet when Eleanor called up for her to come down to the 'sitting room,' as the biddies called it. That was where they kept the liquor. Just like she thought, sooner or later it always came back to her.

Margie walked down the stairs and through the darkened hallway. The place would look a lot better if they'd only pull back the curtains once in a while. She saw then that the four funny looking pictures of naked men that had hung on the wall opposite the bottom of the stairs were gone. Still looking at the wall, she tripped on a frayed hole in one of the hall carpets and turned her ankle. "Ah shit," she said, and was still looking behind her when she stumbled into the sitting room.

Turning to face the three, Margie felt the familiar tightness in her chest that came with getting caught. The liquor cabinet was wide open. The two cops and Eleanor were standing between it and the gun case, talking low.

"Margie," said the sergeant, "You remember when the last time was you dusted in here?" He stepped aside but motioned to the gun case, not the cabinet.

"Jeez, I don't know," Margie said. She felt lighter, the same way she felt the day before, once she'd walked by the security guards at the Walmart with two boxes of Milk Duds under her shirt.

"It was a valuable Purdy," Eleanor said. "My father's." Eleanor moved her hands as if she was washing them. Margie looked past her at the inside of the case and could see that one of the guns that had always been there was gone. Just then the flash went off, making her jump. She treated the cop with the camera to a scowl. She could see a narrow oval of clean wood in the dust on the base of the cabinet.

"I never been in the gun case," Margie said.

Now it was Eleanor's turn to snort. "Certainly not to clean it," she said.

"You know anything about the shotgun that was here?" the sergeant asked, gesturing with his thumb at the empty space.

"Extremely valuable," Eleanor said. "It was a gift from my grandfather." Lady, make up your mind, Margie thought.

But Eleanor and the cops just stared at her.

"Hey, just-a-minute. I din't take no shotgun. I din't even know it was gone, till just now." She looked into three impassive faces. The sergeant closed the case with his pen and peered through the cloudy glass.

"It *is* hard to see," said the one with the camera.

"Not surprising," Eleanor said. "We agree it hasn't been kept very clean." She looked at Margie and added, "Recently."

"'Course, if we had some light in here…" Margie started to say.

The two policemen crisscrossed the top half of the cabinet with yellow tape. The sergeant said, "Don't touch this, please," and looked at them in turn. The other one took another picture of it all taped up.

The sergeant then used the pen to pull open drawers at the bottom of the cabinet. Margie looked in and without thinking took a quick breath that all of them heard. She had looked through the drawers, of course, months ago, but what could she get for a bunch of old ammunition? "Jeez," she said. She'd looked through the drawers a few months before. You never knew when you might find something valuable, something that wouldn't be missed. The neat stacks of boxed ammunition she remembered had been scattered all over the drawer. One box was open and a number of green shotgun shells lay between the boxes. The cops gave Margie the long look again, but didn't say anything else. More tape, more pictures.

Then questions. 'Did she remember the gun? Did it look like the others? When was the last time she saw it?' But for the life of her, Margie thought, who would bother to steal a shotgun like that? And just the one? Dumb thing to do. Getting caught right off was all. Dumb. They ought to give her more credit than that.

LOUISA MARTIN SAT upright on what looked like a kitchen chair drawn up to an ancient makeup table. She wore a beige quilted bathrobe and continued to brush her nearly white hair as Eleanor led Gregg Leavitt into her bedroom. Gregg knew she was pretending not to notice him but she spoiled the effect by following him with her eyes in the three paneled mirror in front of her. These were set so the person at the table could see the result of her handiwork back, front and side. For Gregg, the effect was to be stared at by dozens of eyes.

Gregg turned to Eleanor. "Was Ms. Newsome ever in this room?"

"Yes," said Eleanor. "She was *supposed* to appraise all of our property, even this." Eleanor made a gesture toward some of the dark wooden pieces and a stained and faded chaise lounge. Like the rest of the house, the shades were drawn and two table lamps provided the only light. The air was close and sweet-scented, an old woman's room. Gregg was struck by how different, yet so strangely alike, this house and the Warren house were.

"Supposed?" he repeated the word she'd emphasized.

"Well, she seemed like she had more interest in us than the things. 'Where was this picture taken?' and 'Who left you this chair?' That sort of thing."

The woman in the mirrors made a sound that could have been clearing her throat if it weren't so indignant. This made Eleanor begin to flutter, her eyes darting back and forth between her sister and Gregg. "She was, I guess you'd say, a little *assertive*. Miss Newsome I mean."

The woman at the mirrors gave a soft rolling laugh at this then turned round on her chair. "You mean 'pushy' don't you, Ellie?"

Eleanor's hand was at her throat. "Now Louisa, you remember what Mr. Hannah…"

"Oh damn him. Damn all of you." As she snapped out these words the old woman stood with surprising speed. Then she put down her brush and made an attempt at straightening the robe she wore. Her ankles were swollen and almost maroon above her slippers.

"She was a jumped up nosey little pusher and I don't care who knows it."

The woman walked by them toward her bed, literally brushing her sister aside, her eyes bright and fixed on Gregg beneath her disordered hair. As she walked by she bumped a table covered with framed photographs. In this room, like the rest of the house, there were dozens of pictures of teams, of wedding parties, school girls in uniforms of seventy-five years before. One of these fell over with a clatter and Eleanor rushed to set it back up.

"We've come to this, I see," her sister said after she had settled herself in her bed. "People pawing through our property. First her, now…" she hesitated and gestured with her hand. "Now this gentleman."

"One of papa's guns is gone," Eleanor said then. Her voice fell to a whisper. "Leezie, he has to look in the closet, under the bed."

Louisa Martin rolled her eyes. "Not the first one he's looked under, I'm sure."

Gregg remembered what Carr had said to him that morning, how people had smiled at his father. *"Oh, I'm going to miss you, General."* Now this old bitch who sounded just the same. Then she spoke directly to Gregg for the first time, "Well, go ahead. Go ahead."

Gregg knelt and confirmed there was nothing but an unusually large number of dust balls beneath the mahogany bed frame. As he stood, the old woman laughed at him softly. Feeling his face flush, he went to the closet and pushed the clothing this way and that, more forcefully than he needed.

"Oh dear, we've hurt his feelings," said the old woman.

"Look Ma'am, I'm not enjoying this." Gregg faced the two sisters, now side by side, one crestfallen, the other straight backed and defiant.

"Oh yes you are," Louisa said. "Just like that Miss whoever-she-was. Chatting away about St. Agatha's and Camp Abenaki like she knew us. She made a big show, too, about how 'sorry' she was to be nosing around. She wasn't sorry at all, so don't tell me you're not enjoying yourself."

"Leezie, please."

"Oh, stop it. It's bad enough I have to put up with people like—" she gestured toward Gregg, "*this* in my bedroom." She turned toward her sister. "Do I have to put up with your sniffling too?"

Briefly, Gregg debated whether he should toss her bed. He could justify it. It was conceivable a gun could be hidden there, but the anger subsided.

"Miss Martin," he said to Eleanor, you said there were three more bedrooms?"

Eleanor nodded and headed out the door. Gregg turned, putting his hand to where his hat brim would be if he was still wearing it. "I'm sorry you feel this way, Ma'am."

"Odd, I couldn't care less how *you* feel." The woman said this as a sigh, more to herself than to him.

◆Δ◆

"How long have you worked for the Martins, Mrs. Tuttle?" He kept his voice low. She could tell he didn't want Eleanor to hear what she told them.

"Just four months is all."

"You work here every day?"

"Nope, noon to eight Monday through Thursday one week, Friday through Sunday next. 'Cept last two weeks I been workin' straight through. Justine, used to work the other shift, she got done."

The policeman lowered his voice, turned friendly. T.J. had made it clear to Gregg that his deal with Hannah for no questions was limited to the sisters. "You sound like you're about done yourself."

"Betta believe it. This ain't no picnic. Justine was here nearly a year. Don't know how she stood it so long."

The sergeant was turning out to be okay for a cop. He looked tired and kind of red around the eyes. Margie pulled a strand of hair behind her ear. Nice, but that's when cops were dangerous, when they acted friendly.

"So who worked last weekend?"

"Me, straight through, so's I could get time off for court Monday," Margie lied.

"Court?"

"You don't remember me, do you? You came in all covered with mud…"

A smile of recognition came over his face. "Ah … sure, sorry. So you were here Friday, Saturday and Sunday till eight?"

"Uh huh."

"All day?"

"Yup. Me and the lady from VNA, we get Louisa, the one upstairs, cleaned up at noon. I get 'em supper and leave once she's settled, and I'm off until noon. I come in at noon Saturdays."

"And that's what happened last weekend?"

Margie was careful to look away. "Uh huh, same as always." How could it matter? She was dead now, wasn't she?

"You've seen this woman before?" Gregg held out a photograph of Ephne Newsome.

"Jesus." Margie's head jerked back when she saw the picture. "Well, yah, she came on Friday. Little before lunch. She didn't do much though. Spent most of the time reading papers she got out of the desk in the hall. She left early afternoon but got back at about four, made a call on her cell phone. Supposed to come back next day, too, but she didn't show. Jesus, what happened to her eye…?"

"That was after," the sergeant said, taking the picture back.

The sergeant never asked her about the medicine, and Margie decided that it was reason enough not to say anything. Fridays, like usual, she'd put an extra orange pill in those little cups the VNA nurse made up. The biddies slept like lambs then. She'd have to be more careful now, Margie thought.

◆△◆

STILL DRESSED IN her weekend clothes, jeans and a sweatshirt, Stacy cradled a phone while T.J.'s voice rose up behind her, "I don't care what the clerk says, I want a copy of the whole file." Since she had been good enough to come in and waste a whole Saturday, Gregg thought T.J. could have made an exception and pretended to be human at least to her.

After the drive from the judge's house in Windsor and two hours searching the Martin house, Gregg couldn't wait to get out of there. He resented, no, he guessed he hated the two old women. He even felt sorry for Margie Tuttle. There was something about those damn people. There wasn't much difference between the pleasant Mrs. Warren and the nasty old women, when he thought about it. He'd begun to notice that all of them sounded the same, especially when they pronounced words like 'go' and 'slow' and 'though.' Mrs. Warren was more polite than the Martins, but he'd decided Mrs. Harry Warren and her damn sister were just like the Martins, under the skin.

Stacy had warned Gregg about Carr as soon as he returned. "This has been a hell of a great Saturday afternoon. I hope you've got some good news," she said. "He's been re-reading your notes and it's been 'get me this, get me that' all afternoon. He had me pull the clerk away from his bowling league and he's been botherin' one o' those cops down in New York."

Gregg walked in to find Carr scratching, sighing, and pacing around his office. He didn't seem able to stay in one spot, though he turned still when Gregg told him about the missing shotgun.

"Oh, sweet Jesus, you don't think he'd be stupid enough to keep it? No, no God is never that good to me." T.J. exploded out of the chair, turned fully around and glanced at the ceiling. "Never," he said again.

Stacy dropped two thick files on the desk. One was red and stamped APPEAL-TRUST OF HEATHERINGTON MARTIN—HADLEY COUNTY PROBATE COURT and the other was blue. It was labeled EQUITY —HADLEY COUNTY COURT In Re: Louisa Martin, et al.

"That's only part of the file," she said. "The rest is with Judge Warren. Workin' on pending motions, so the clerk says."

T.J. grunted.

"Clerk also says you take one piece of paper out of either file and it's my job. Oh, and he'll have you disbarred," Stacy made a face. "Which one you want copied first?"

"Uh huh," T.J. said, and instead of answering, handed the probate file to her not looking up. When she'd gone he said softly, "I'm going crazy here." He turned over some pages. "I know the answer's here, but I can't see it." Then, looking up at Gregg, he said, "Sit, sit." Carr put his hand out and Gregg handed him his notes about the Martin house.

Carr read these quickly, seeming to mouth some of the words as he did. "What about these papers Margie Tuttle says the Newsome lady was reading?"

"We checked the desk but didn't find anything there," Gregg said. "I didn't ask the sisters about them because …"

"Yah, yah. You wouldn't want to break a deal with Zach Hannah." His tone let Gregg know that T.J. considered that a disappointment.

Gregg went back to his notes from the Martin house. He saw, with a sinking feeling, that he hadn't gotten a firm time when either Margie Tuttle or Ephne Newsome had left the Martins on Friday. But T.J. was on to something else. "Oh yes, yes," he smoothed the papers. "Listen to this." He read aloud:

> The Court has apprised counsel for the bank of prior acquaintance with the respondents Eleanor Martin and Louisa Martin. The acquaintance was slight and there was never a professional or financial relationship with either. All parties have waived any claim of conflict arising from this as well as from the Court's past professional relationship with Attorney Hannah."

Gregg looked back at a beaming T.J. "So."

"So? ... So!? For Crisssakes, Leavitt," T.J. started ticking off on his fingers. "That's Harry goddamn Warren talking. He knew them, the Martins. You remember him sayin' any of that to us? Jesus, you braindead? You think he'd remember a conflict on a probate appeal and forget it for a murder investigation? AND now we know he has part of their file right there in the room right now."

Gregg blinked. He hadn't noticed.

"Something's damn fishy here." T.J. said this almost as a question and Gregg groaned inwardly. The last thing he wanted was to go for another visit with Judge Warren and the people at Warren's house.

Stacy's head came around the doorway interrupting his despair. "Call for you, Gregg. That New York cop again. Somethin about a phone bill."

T.J. was up on his feet gesturing to the phone.

"Take it. Take it."

"Hello, this is Gregg Leavitt."

Ruiz's voice came over the line, "Hi kid. Don't you know this is Saturday afternoon? You guys got your pants on fire up there?" When Gregg didn't answer, Ruiz said, "We... we went over and got the mail dropped off at her place this morning. I just opened the phone bill. Two more New Hampshire calls."

Gregg put his hand on the mouthpiece. "Two local calls from her cell phone," he said to T.J. who pushed a pad and a pencil toward him.

"Yah, go ahead." He wrote one down, a Thursday call, New York to Windsor, New Hampshire, and pushed the sheet of paper toward T.J.

T.J. looked at it. "Sure, Cruikshank and Hannah. We knew that," T.J. said.

Ruiz then gave Gregg the second number, a call made the previous Friday. Gregg wrote it down and pushed it toward T.J.

"Jesus!" T.J. said when he saw the number.

On the end of the line Ruiz said, "Sounds like good news, kid."

Gregg said, "Could be." T.J.'s eyes were wide.

"Well, that's great. Glad to be of help. I'll fax it up and send the original FedEx. You're on to something, aren't you? You've got that sound."

"That's what it looks like. Hey, I'm sorry about the weekend call. Thanks again."

"Glad to be of help. But look, I come in today but not tomorrow. You make sure that guy Carr knows that?"

"You got it," Gregg said.

◆△◆

AFTER HANGING UP, Gregg looked back down at the second number. "The time coincides with when Margie Tuttle says Newsome made a call from the house," he said.

T.J. tapped the pad he'd written on. "This is the switchboard number for the Hadley County Court. Why do you think she'd be calling that number?" T.J. was thinking out loud, not expecting an answer. He stared at the ceiling, pursed his lips. Finally he called out, "Stacy, see if you can get Zach Hannah for me."

"It's Saturday, boss. He's probably at home."

"I *know* its Saturday. Show me what a great secretary you are."

Then turning back to Gregg, "So what else about the missing gun?"

"Sixteen gauge, double barreled Purdy," Gregg said.

"You think it's the weapon?"

"Figures. It's the only one missing from a set of six. We can put the victim there Friday afternoon. She's got bird shot wounds. We found a drawer with boxes of shells, mostly twenty gauge, but a box of sixteens too. Some twenties were lying loose in the drawer. All bird shot. Cleaning lady says the drawer was neat and the ammo all in boxes last time she saw 'em. The lab is going to do prints tomorrow. They'd do it today but they're working a fatal down in Windsor already."

T.J. made a gesture of frustration. "You'd think we could afford more than one fingerprint team in this goddamn state."

Stacy's voice cut into T.J.'s lament. "I got Mr. Hannah on two. He's in his office." T.J. lifted the receiver and punched his second line.

"You fellas working overtime up there, T.J.?" The tone was pleasant but weary.

"New Hampshire's finest. We never sleep," T.J. said. "What are you doing in the office on a Saturday afternoon, besides charging your clients overtime."

"Don't I wish. No, Saturdays is the only time I can get something done. Damn phone isn't ringing every two minutes."

"You bet, you bet," T.J. said. "Say, we're pretty sure the murder weapon was taken from a gun cabinet in the Martin's house. You know the one?"

"I've seen a cabinet. Bunch of antique guns in there. We inventoried them. You think ..."

"You remember how many?" T.J. asked, interrupting.

"Six, seven. I'll check the inventory if you want, only take a minute."

"Good, thanks. Maybe later. Kinda strange for two old ladies to have an arsenal like that."

"That's what I thought, but they're just for show. Worth quite a bit of money. Belonged to their father. Come to think of it, they did say they used to do some competitive shooting themselves. I don't know much about it. You remember me and guns. But hell, T.J. you can't think..."

"I don't think anything yet. Remember, I coulda had this information three days ago if your ladies had cooperated, so don't start in again about what solid citizens they are."

"Yah, well. Well I'm sorry about that."

"Uh huh. Say, why'd you talk to her on Friday, this Newsome woman?"

"Friday? No, no, I didn't talk to her."

"She called your office."

"She probably talked to one of the associates. Not me. I can check for you."

"She have some reason to call the county court?"

"Cou... She called the court?"

"Yah, kinda unusual, don't you think?"

"I'll say. No T.J., I can't think of any reason at all."

T.J. winked at Gregg and asked, "Anything between her and the Martin sisters other than the case you hired her for?"

"No, not that I know of, why?"

"My young sergeant here says she lives, lived in New York but comes from Philadelphia. That's where these Martin women come from, isn't it?... Uh, huh, I think he said she grew up there ... Worked there for Wharton Biddle, that big Philadelphia law firm. We got old pictures from Newsome's apartment of her with Lake Wasoka in the background. I see from the probate file that Wharton Biddle did some work for your clients. So we've got the law firm, the same home town, the Lake Wasoka tie-in ... that's quite a bit isn't it? And that's all before you exciting people at Cruikshank and Hannah came along."

Gregg raised his eyebrows. Carr had skipped way ahead of him.

"I know she said something about a girls camp first time we went to the Martin house," Hannah said. "She went to camp up here, but when she was just a kid. Twenty-five, thirty years ago. You're right about Wharton Biddle. She worked there, five, maybe six years ago."

"You're sure she had no direct connection with the Martins? She never said anything to you about them, outside your case?"

"Nope. And as for Wharton Biddle, they represent lots of old families down there. What you getting at T.J., if you don't mind my asking?"

"Coincidence," T.J. said. "Too many goddamn coincidences. Her working at their law firm, her coming up here on vacation. Now she turns up dead a mile away from their house and it looks like one of their expensive shotguns killed her."

There was no response.

Gregg could see T.J. reddening as he spoke, and when Hannah didn't seem to be answering T.J.'s voice rose some more.

"That's too ... many ... damn ... coincidences, Zach. You agree?"

"T.J., I don't know what to say, but you may be right about Wharton Biddle. I doubt you'll get much out of them. She was just a para..."

"Yah, yah, And now Harry Warren, my holier-than-thou friend on the county court, issues a warrant and just happens to forget to tell me he might have a conflict in this capital case. You two are thicker than thieves, Hannah. I know you go way back, but goddamnit, this is just too many coincidences."

"Har... he, ah issued a warrant?"

"That's exactly what I was thinking," T.J. said, finishing the other man's thought.

"Yah. He's a hard guy to run down on weekends." Hannah made an attempt to laugh at this. Something in the tone of his voice made T.J. look up.

"Uh huh, like a lot of guys," T.J. said.

"Hey, I've tried to be …"

"Yah, and a big help you've been." The color was leaving T.J.'s face now. Despite the anger in his voice, T.J. winked again at Gregg.

"Look if you don't want our co-oper…"

"No, no, don't get your shorts in a crease, Zach. Look, look, sorry. This is a long, bad day. I flew off the handle. I'll take your word for it. We're gonna need those other shotguns… I'll make sure we take good care of them. And, remember, we're interviewing your ladies next week. Yah … yah… you bet. Okay, thanks. Goodbye."

T.J. set the phone down gently, almost daintily.

"Now *that* was interesting," he said.

"So you think there was more between the Martins and Ephne Newsome, more than this case?" Gregg pointed to the file on the desk.

"I do now."

"But T.J., those old ladies. I saw them. They couldn't…"

"Doesn't take a lot of energy to pull a trigger." T.J. craned around him. "Stacy, you finish making those other calls?"

Stacy brought in her phone diary. "I finally got hold of that woman named in Miss Newsome's will, name of Shubert, works at that law firm, Wharton something. Lives in Philadelphia, seemed pretty upset on the phone about the, ah, deceased." Stacy handed Gregg a typewritten sheet. "Knows a lot about her, too. Mother Carol Newsome, lives in a nursing home outside the city."

As Gregg read, T.J. said, "They can both see you Monday." Then to Stacy, "You make him reservations?"

Gregg turned his head from one to the other. His surprise at how much they'd done in his absence must have shown.

"What? You think we sit around on our asses here?" T.J. said.

Stacy handed Gregg a third sheet with flights and a room reservation. "The nursing home's in a place called Chester, south of the city. You'll have to pick up a car at the airport. Keep the receipts."

T.J. was staring at him, dead serious now. "Philadelphia. That's where the answer is. She might've got shot up here, but the reason is down there."

GREGG GOT UP TO LEAVE, but T.J. still wanted to talk. The minutes ticked by; Stacy left. The outside lights of the empty courthouse clicked on but T.J. meandered back and forth, just a tired, lonely man with nothing to go home to on a Saturday afternoon.

"You never had any dealings with Hannah before, did you?"

"Nope. Heard the name's all."

"Well, when you were a kid, maybe ten or twelve years old, Hannah ran for Congress. He's always been a chaser, so there was some talk about a girlfriend. Looked like he was going to win, anyway, until the other side finds out he's never had a hunting license. Worse, he tries to make a joke out of it and admits he's never even fired a gun." T.J. was shaking his head looking at the ceiling. "And he's supposed to be smart. Christ, he lost by ten thousand votes after that. The sex story was probably right. He got divorced a couple of months after the election, but that isn't what beat him."

By now even T.J. could see Gregg was nodding off.

"Okay, get out of here. You did fine in New York. Philadelphia shouldn't be a problem. While you're down there, I've got some ideas."

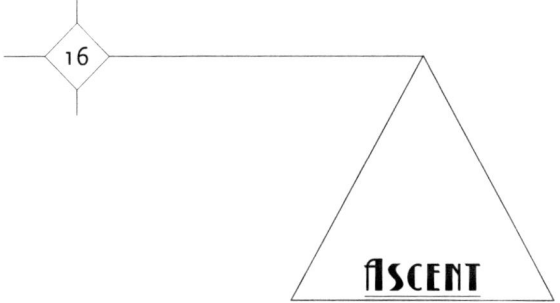

16 ASCENT

It had always been a mystery to Harry Warren that the Llewellyns bothered to stay in one place for any time at all. Not for them, airport lines and check-ins, or narrow seats on overheated planes. Emma's impetuous flight from Palm Beach to Philadelphia was the first time she flew commercial. Once early in their marriage, Harry and Emma had watched a television comedian parody the indignities of airline travel. As Harry laughed, he saw that Emma merely turned curious. She had no idea what the man was talking about.

No, travel *with* Emma, any Llewellyn for that matter, was a different matter altogether. It began with a call to her fathers 'assistant' and, like magic, a Llewellyn plane was scheduled to appear at the appointed hour, not at the main terminal, but an obscure hangar at the far end of Windsor airport. There, a small group of very professional, very deferential people took their things and settled them in a small lounge. Upon request, laconic, minute-by-minute updates of their plane's progress would be given in muted asides. When the plane arrived, distinctive with its navy-blue tail with a silver "L" rising above the rear stabilizer, stairs were brought forth, bags stowed and the four Warrens were escorted onto an empty plane built to carry twenty or so people in an assortment of well-cushioned leather seats arranged more like a clubroom than an airplane. It was not uncommon to be greeted upon boarding by enthusiastic relatives headed to the same destination or, more rarely, by a self-conscious Llewellyn company employee or two who had just checked the rent roll of an office park in Portland or the condition of the roof of the shopping mall in Windsor.

The Llewellyn pilots were all old hands, retired from the airlines and, like all pilots, they favored solid-colored neckties with white shirts of varying levels of translucence woven out of anything but cotton. Friendly, but not their friends, the pilots' bearing made it clear to any passenger that, whoever owned the aircraft, at thirty thousand feet, it was their plane.

◆△◆

THIS SUNDAY AFTERNOON, as she watched the plane power up and pull away, Emma Warren's eyes narrowed and she pursed her lips. It was the expression she would have displayed if asked the value of a Georgian tea service with a minor repair and a piece missing. Harry's moods had ceased to worry her decades before, but the kaleidoscope he had displayed since Saturday morning, capped off by his surprise decision the night before to go to Philadelphia, was something else entirely. Still, she waved to the faces of her husband and sister visible in the plane's small windows as she would any other time.

When the plane was safely aloft she returned to her silver SUV and started home. As she reached the intersection with the airport perimeter road, she had to brake sharply as a blue van sped through. She looked at it resentfully as it went by. "Support your State Police," she said out loud. "Right."

Driving home to their empty house she continued to ponder Harry's sudden decision to go to Philadelphia. "Court business," he had said. She didn't believe him of course. Something had been bothering him since the Dinner. Perhaps she ought to spend less time with the museum, or maybe it was just the effect that damn Tee Ingersoll always had on him.

Then, just as she turned onto their driveway, she remembered he had called Zach. For a moment the woman behind the wheel seemed to stiffen. Her gaze widened and her scalp shifted up from her forehead. Then she settled in her seat and swallowed. No, that couldn't be it.

◆△◆

FOR ALL ITS INDIGNITIES, commercial airlines did provide an interlude of anonymity unavailable on this Gulfstream 7, the smaller of the two current Llewellyn company jets. Livy and Harry found themselves facing the ninety-minute flight to Philadelphia in one another's company, without Emma to intercede.

Once they were airborne, Livy went back to a small galley at the rear of the plane.

"I'm having a Mary. You want one, Warren?" When he didn't answer right away she said, "It's a simple question and you won't find the answer on your wrist watch."

"Okay, sure." He looked up to see she was scowling at him. "It's 1:30," Harry said and turned his palms up in explanation. "You're allowed. I didn't mean it as a rebuke," he added.

"Gatewood never drank before noon and he was the worst lush I ever knew," she said. Gatewood had been Livy's first, worst, but most suitable husband. She busied herself with ice and glasses making noise as she stirred both.

"Except for Mummy, of course," she said handing Harry a Bloody Mary almost pink with vodka. Harry was lost in thought and looked up. "Oh, thanks."

"Mummy was a worse drunk than George, but not half so mean." Livy sat down opposite, hooked one leg underneath her, and seemed to speculate. "Sometimes I think that's why she liked him."

The drink was lethal as it looked. He swallowed and coughed, then said, "She liked Gatewood?"

"Oh Mummy loved George," Livy said. "Right family, right clothes. Deep down she knew he was a shit, but she was comfortable with him." The second swallow was easier but Harry still made a soft gasp. Livy seemed to like that because she saluted him with her glass and said, "Comfortable in a way she never was with Eduardo, or you, for that matter."

Eduardo, Carter's father, was a member of one of those unbeatable polo teams from Argentina, who Livy had met at Wellington. That marriage had lasted barely a year. Gatewood had been around for five, but then Eduardo had left Livy. Gatewood was tossed out.

"Indeed, we were never close," Harry said, speaking of Mrs. Llewellyn, though it could have applied equally well to each of Livy's husbands.

"No," she said. "Not close. You know what she used to call you?" Livy fingered the ice in her drink and that familiar smile reappeared.

"No, but I think I'm about to learn." Harry inserted his half finished glass into a cup-holder built into the chair arm.

"Indeed," Livy mocked him, "you are." She leaned forward. "'Sad sack,' she'd say. 'Emma's stray dog,' sometimes. If she was particularly drunk or pissed or both, 'Emma's social climbing little sad-sack.' No, Warren, Mummy didn't like you at all."

It appeared that after an almost sleepless night, Harry would also do penance for the adventures of the past twenty-four hours, for here, up in the clouds, Livy had Harry at her mercy. At least the third swallow went down with less effort.

"You don't have to take it so hard," Livy said, when he didn't answer. "You should have heard the things she called Daddy. She never let him forget she was a Shippen."

"I thought your..." He stopped. This wasn't going anywhere.

"You thought they got along," Livy said. She had him wrong of course. What he was going to say was that he thought her father's family was richer than her mother's and could have cared less about the Shippens. But Harry just nodded. Safety first.

"They did, I suppose, before Mummy started drinking, or stopped stopping," Livy frowned into her glass as she said this and drew her other leg up underneath her.

"Your mother did drink," Harry conceded.

"She always said it was because of Daddy's girls. Of course he always said, well, let's say he 'suggested,' that it was the other way 'round." Livy took a contemplative sip. "It's a chicken or egg thing, I suppose," Livy turned her head to the closed door at the front of the plane. "Daddy was so good-looking and horny and Mummy was already a lush."

"You're pretty tough on them." Ah, but that was the wrong thing to say.

She looked at him coldly. "What do you know? You married the princess in the tower. You're a pretty unlikely prince, Warren, but Emma thought you were and that was good enough for her. Of course, Perfect Emma couldn't be wrong."

He put up his hands to surrender, but too late.

"You think you've got us all figured out, don't you. Well, I got news for you, Warren. Thirty years and you still don't have a clue." She said this with such vehemence that he merely put his hands back down.

Seeing he wouldn't fight back, Livy got up from the seat across from him and went to the back of the plane. She made more noise with ice and bottles before she sat down.

Harry closed his eyes, and pretended to nap. He had worse problems than the posthumous judgments of Pippi Llewellyn. He had already dealt with those.

◆∆◆

THE LLEWELLYN FAMILY house at the Lake Wasoka Club had always been a Llewellyn house, built by the first Lloyd in the 1920s. With its ten bedrooms and wrap-around columned porches, only a club member would call it a "cottage." The first Lloyd had built it after a lonely season not being asked anywhere at Northeast Harbor. At least that's what Pippi Llewellyn had told Harry one drunken Sunday afternoon.

"The story he told was that he got seasick too easily to enjoy the ocean," she said. Pippi got a kick out of that, and a bigger one watching L.L. squirm as she told it. It was the only time Harry saw Lloyd Llewellyn show visible anger at his wife so he guessed the story was true. The Lake Wasoka Club and its members were rougher around the edges in those early days, like the Llewellyns, although no one would know it from the attitudes of their grandchildren.

"Oh Loy, don't be cross. Harry likes stories like that, don't you Harry?" Pippi Llewellyn held her glass out to Harry for a refill.

It was strange that Pippi Llewellyn had chosen to die there on the Llewellyn's home ground, a choice Harry never understood. She had always regarded the Club, this house and the Llewellyns' motives for coming here with amused disdain, an embarrassment that couldn't be extinguished by a mere sixty years.

It was June when she did it. Junes are full of hope in New Hampshire, and that one was brighter than usual. The sun rose ever higher in the sky. Leigh and Samantha were back from school. Emma had a new commission to restore a Rembrandt Peale. Harry found life was almost normal, with the added excitement of managing his still fresh adultery.

He was alone on the patio at Langdon House savoring the first really warm morning of the summer, scheming up a plausible excuse to get an extra night with Ephne the following weekend, when the cook opened the door behind him. "Phone for you, Judge. Hadley County attorney." Harry made a gesture of impatience. The woman was new and hadn't learned how to dodge calls from the county attorney.

"Says it's important," she said seeming to read his thoughts and holding the door open.

"Thought you ought to know, Harry," T.J. Carr's voice was surprisingly gentle. "We found your mother-in-law at her summer place this morning."

"Found?"

"Yah. She's gone."

Harry looked around for Emma. The cook was already cutting something up on the counter, listening to the radio. Harry lowered his voice as softly as he could, "You mean, dead?"

"About ten last night, the doc, thinks." There was a pause. "We're still here. I think you need to come over."

"Emma," Harry said into the phone.

"Maybe you need to come over," T.J. repeated, "before."

Harry arrived twenty minutes later to find a West Harbor cruiser, T.J.'s big Oldsmobile and a third car parked at odd angles in the Llewellyn driveway as if they had arrived at the same time in haste.

A large black woman opened the door.

"Judge, we sure glad to see you," she said in her softly accented voice. As usual Harry couldn't remember her name, though she had been with the Llewellyns since before his time, the lady who had always helped Pippi Llewellyn to bed.

"Of course, of course," was all Harry could think to say and held her hand.

"They won't let me call no one," she half whispered. "Don' seem right. Mis' Llewellyn ain't gonna like this." She seemed taken aback by the absurdity of these words and sobbed again, "Ohh."

He embraced the woman. "I'll see what I can do."

T.J. was unshaven, his hair was in the same state it had been when he had been called at six o'clock that morning. The doctor and a pot-bellied man in a blue uniform with stars on the collar were sitting on the stairway. They rose as he came in, but T.J. did the talking.

"Judge, you know Dr. Fleming? Chief Frye?" Harry shook their hands in turn.

"Thought you'd better have a look at this," T.J. said, all business, no preliminaries, and motioned Harry to the stairs. T.J. turned to the cop. "You keep everything secure down here, why don't you Melvin." The chief took his boot back from the first stair, gave them all a look, but went away toward the kitchen.

The doctor, T.J. and Harry then walked wordlessly to the top of the stairs, turned right and walked down the hall to a door which already stood ajar.

Pippi Llewellyn would have been pleased to know that she looked better than she had in years. Her carefully arranged honey-heathered-colored hair framed a tanned and almost unlined face. The relaxed half-opened eyes looked more bored than dead. Her mouth was open just enough to show part of her top teeth: a remarkably good looking woman.

The smell, however, wasn't one she would have chosen.

Having held his breath in the hall in anticipation, Harry inhaled reflexively and gagged.

"Th' muscles relax," the doctor said, nodding, without really looking at him.

"Uh huh." Harry stared. He had questions, but couldn't shed the feeling that she could still hear what they were saying. Some gesture was called for, so Harry went over to the bed. Turning to Carr he pointed to her hand. "Okay?"

"Sure, sure."

The hand was cold and dry. No life in it, but Harry held it for what seemed like a decent interval, longer than the living woman would have permitted. Then he let it go. She would have made no such effort for him, but Carr didn't have to know that. Harry rejected the idea of a goodbye kiss. That would have raised her up for sure.

"Well," he said at last.

"We've got a problem," T.J. said.

By way of explanation, the county attorney went over to the night stand. There was a half-empty carafe, a glass with an inch of water in it and a green plastic pill bottle with a pharmacist's label.

"Percoset," T.J. said, elevating it in a single motion with the eraser end of a pencil. "Thirty tablets prescribed in 'Powley' Penn…"

"Pay-oh-lee," Harry said.

"Pay…?"

"Oh-lee."

"Yah, well thirty, and filled six days ago. Doc says six or seven at once would probably be enough to finish a normal woman."

"Depending on tolerance," the doctor said.

Harry looked at the two of them in turn. The bottle was empty. The two exchanged glances but said nothing.

"Accidental overdose?" T.J. said at last, but he wasn't looking at the doctor, he was looking at Harry.

"Could be," said the doctor, "or might be stroke." He regarded Harry. Then he went on, "Prescription called for two at bedtime. Counting backward, there's eighteen pills unaccounted for."

"Course she might've spread this out," T.J. said, gesturing with the upturned bottle to make his point. "Not unusual to take an extra now and then." The two nodded at each other like kids in a high school play, then turned to Harry.

It took Harry a while to get into the spirit. Revelation came from the droop of the doctor's shoulders and the way his eyes returned to Harry when T.J. added, "Nothing says she took them all last night."

In the game at last, Harry said, "She did have high blood pressure."

The three nodded then and made noises like they were considering this new information.

Harry kept going, "She's not the kind of person to have a, ah, an accident, like this. Very careful lady, very precise." This brought more confirming nods first to each other then to him.

Pippi Llewellyn would have said *"Took you long enough. You, always thinking you're so goddamned smart."*

But she remained motionless, still gently smiling toward something at the foot of the bed.

"Well, stroke, then?" T.J. said.

"The family can request an autopsy," the doctor said, "I could be wrong."

T.J. looked at Harry and, when he didn't answer, began to redden with his famous impatience.

"No. No request," Harry said quickly.

"Well, call me if there's any change." The doctor turned and left the room. It was settled.

Outside, once Doctor Fleming had gone to his car, T.J. turned to Harry, speaking low, "You don't suppose there are any goddamned insurance policies, do you? Anybody who might raise hell about cause of death?"

"Don't know."

"Doc has six hours before he has to turn in his paperwork. He can't release the body without a 'natural causes' finding. You might want to make sure before he sticks his neck out." The last of this came quickly and sideways out of T.J.'s mouth. It was more than a suggestion.

"Sure, T.J."

"We understand each other on this, Harry?"

"Yah. Understood."

Harry could imagine T.J. telling the doctor, "For Christ sakes, call it a damn stroke. 'Accidental' doesn't do anything for people like them. The papers will probably put the words in quotation marks in her obituary."

Then Harry drove home to tell Emma her mother had died.

◆△◆

"A stroke, they think. She probably didn't feel it at all." Emma wiped her face with her hands, said "Mummy," and slowly began to weep onto the shoulder of a man who—until an hour and a half before—was planning to be unfaithful to her for as much of the following weekend as he could manage. Then they told the girls.

The depth of Emma's despair came as a surprise. As much as she adored her father, Harry didn't think she liked her mother much more than he did. After half an hour Emma seemed more composed. "I'm going up to lie down," she said. This was fine with Harry. He had two calls to make.

"Mr. Decker can speak with you now, Judge," the voice was just what an efficient secretary to a Wharton & Biddle's managing partner should have been. A click followed, then:

"Harry? Jack Decker here."

"Yes, uh, yes Jack. Have you heard?"

"Just heard from Rob Lefkowitz. He was with Loy at the audit committee."

"Yes, well, ah…" As usual, Harry knew where he wanted to end up, but not where to begin.

Jack Decker filled in the silence. "A stroke, Rob said. Tragic."

"Yes, looks that way." Harry hesitated as much as he dared on "looks."

"Uh huh?" In his mind's eye, Harry could picture Jack Decker looking up, suddenly alert.

"Well, uh Jack, like I said I was with the, uh, authorities at the home, at the Club,… at the 'scene' I guess you'd say."

Jack Decker didn't need a third clue.

"Scene," he said. Then, "Harry do we need to discuss this with Oswald?" Decker's tone became flat, matter of fact.

"No. Not yet anyway. The local people are satisfied to leave it at, ah, natural causes, but, well, there aren't any, well, insurance funded estate planning vehicles, are there? Nothing to… no one who might…"

He cut Harry off, "… okay, we've got it, let me check back with you. You at the Lake?"

"No, Emma's." Harry had said these last words before he considered their implication. Maybe Decker took it that way, too. There was a perceptible delay before he responded.

"You'll hear from us. Please give Emma my sympathy." The line went dead.

Of course Harry had one more call to make, and all he had to do was push the redial button, looking over his shoulder as he did.

Ephne's friend put him through.

"Hi," he said.

"You sound bright and cheery."

Harry lowered his voice. "Emma's mother died. Last night."

"Oh." There was a pause, then Ephne said, "Oh..." a second time.

"Yah."

"I'll cancel Friday then, okay?"

"Yes, look I've got to get off the phone."

"I miss you."

"Me too."

Twenty minutes passed and it was Oswald Popp who called back after all. As usual, Oswald wasted no time on preliminaries.

"I've been through the estate planning file here and there's nothing that would be affected by a cause of death," he said, his words sharp, matter of fact.

"Good."

"And no one is going to ask for a post mortem." This was as much a directive as a statement.

"Okay."

"Your people solid on this?"

"I think so." Then, "They're not 'my' people," Harry said trying to explain, "It's more of a favor."

All Popp said was, "Overdose?"

"Probably."

"There's a cremation directive in her will. Just get the body released. A plane is on the way. We should be fine."

Harry called T.J. "Just wanted to thank you again for your, uh, consideration this morning."

"It was nothing, Judge," T.J. said, his formal tone returning. Favor received and receipted, there was no more need for 'Harry.'

"It's always a relief when something like this doesn't bring up unnecessary complications," Harry added.

"I'm glad of that, too."

A moment passed. Then Harry said, "And nothing further is being sought at this end. The family would like the remains released for, ah, cremation as soon as possible, Windsor airport."

"Good. Good. I'll be sure to pass that along. There should be no problem."

Harry never knew what made Pippi Llewellyn choose that night to swallow her handfuls of Percoset. Maybe she had a final argument with Lloyd Llewellyn about another one of his girls. Maybe she just had a headache and said, "The hell with it." She left no note. She had made no threats.

She could, without any particular effort, have left a tablet or two in the bottle and put it back in the medicine cabinet. She was always careful about appearances in spite of everything. Perhaps the habit of having people clean up after her was just too deeply ingrained.

◆Δ◆

TWO DAYS LATER there was a dignified service in the church where Emma and Harry had been married with many of the same people in attendance. The woman who had opened the 'cottage' door was there. So was Tee Ingersoll. Lloyd Llewellyn carried himself throughout with conscious dignity and restrained grief. His indiscretions were too widely known to permit more than that, but display of emotion wasn't his style anyway. Two old school friends and a cousin of the deceased who had grown up with her in Unionville gave surprisingly light-hearted reminiscences of the laughing Foxcroft girl, the radiant bride, whose picture stood in for the absent coffin in the nave. This was a Pippi Llewellyn Harry never knew. He supposed that like everyone else, she let people see the side of her that she wanted them to see. Told them things that hid more than they revealed. The old stories brought the smiling girl briefly renascent. Relieved, grateful laughter came from old family servants and Harry's red-eyed daughters alike. Then a hymn and *finis*.

There are always unexpected consequences to death, but Pippi Llewellyn would have been particularly surprised at the positive effect her departure from this world had on her younger daughter's marriage. On the one hand, if Harry continued in his romance, he was bound to be caught and Emma might at last come to her senses. On the other hand ... well, for Pippi Llewellyn there may have been no 'other hand.' It was hard to say. Tough as divorce might have been on Emma, Pippi could have consoled herself with Harry's unhappiness.

Harry spoke to Ephne one more time after the funeral.

"How's it going?"

"Not great," he said. Harry simply could not tell his lover that for the past week his wife of nearly twenty years had clung to him in bed, that his daughters greeted him red-eyed in the morning. That he was nursing the illusion that, unexpectedly, he might be useful.

"I miss you."

"Me too."

"I guess you never thought of this?"

"Thought of what?"

"Thought that you were part of a family, that there was more to this than just you and me."

How was she so perceptive? "No, Ephne, I didn't."

"We're such loners, Harry."

"Yah, well..."

"No, I know you think that's different now. You're surrounded by your girls and ... well, your family, and you think they need you and that you can't let them down," she spoke rapidly into the phone.

"I don't know..."

"But remember you *are* a loner. You keep a big part of yourself for yourself. That isn't going to change. You know I understand that. They don't, those Llewellyns. They can't."

She was weeping. He heard her sniff. He wiped his own cheek.

"Ephne…"

"Call me, Harry. Call me when you decide."

The line went quiet.

But then, as always, Harry Warren took the coward's way out. One day led into another and there seemed always to be a reason not to call. Then it was a week, two. He liked to think it was impossible to say when he knew for certain that he wouldn't call, would never call. It was a month later, maybe a little longer, that Emma made a small joke that made him laugh. He didn't remember what it was she said, but did remember he took her by the waist and kissed her lightly. As she turned away he knew the choice was made.

Harry drifted out of sleep as the plane descended, and he did a quick mental inventory. He had the Martin file, with its copies of a family trust and amendments. He had a ten o'clock appointment with Wharton Biddle's managing partner, Rob Lefkowitz. Later, Tee Ingersoll would see him for lunch. One or the other might give him some reason why Ephne had come to see him, and why someone would want to kill her afterward. He might move a pawn or two in the game that, so quickly, had turned against him.

◆△◆

The Llewellyn jet reached Philadelphia a little after three and landed in a driving rain. Harry and Livy had to half run–half walk from the plane to the back seat of a waiting black car while two large black men got soaked collecting their luggage. Once it was in the trunk, one of the men climbed into the driver's seat and brushed the water from his face. The other waited in the rain outside.

Livy whispered, "For Christ sakes, Warren, tip the man." She gestured at the man outside. Harry got his wallet out but, before he could remove the ten he had his fingers on, Livy reached across him, pulled out a twenty and rolled down the window.

"Hey, Theo, thank you. Wet enough?"

He took Harry's money but smiled only at her before sprinting for cover.

"Uh-whee," the driver said, and gave them his most professional smile. "DeLancey Street, Miss Llewellyn?" he asked. Few black men did this kind of work now, a great loss because no one could fake good-natured deference better than a middle-aged black man. Edgar's crustiness and troops of monosyllabic Hondurans who ran Round Hill and Hobe Sound were what the Llewellyns had come to live with now.

"Please, Otis." Livy was giving the orders. "We'll drop Judge Warren off and I'll go on to Paoli."

"Yes Ma'am."

Well, he was this far. Harry settled back in his seat as they drove through the downpour. Perhaps it was the drink Livy had given him, but the hopes he'd built up on the plane had melted away. He was in a box. Ephne's death wasn't just going to ruin him, there was a chance now he'd be a suspect. A real chance. T.J. and the police thought she had been killed Friday or Saturday. All the time he had been alone at Langdon House letting the phone ring. Now *that* was an alibi. They didn't have a suspect yet, and if they still didn't have one before they found out about Ephne and him, and they *would* find out, they wouldn't bother looking any further. He had to find something to point them in another direction. But where?

All he knew was that Ephne's killing was tied up with the Martins, with powers of appointment, and with something she'd lost. He didn't know how, but he had to find out who else was in the crossroads of her story and the Martins. "*You lose something, you remember,*" she had said. Something she had lost or, maybe, just remembered, brought Ephne to that mountain side. Ephne had been on to something, and close enough to break those years of silence and call him. But whatever it was, it had begun here, here in Philadelphia, in that 'small town's' secrets Ephne was always trying to learn. And the only place he knew to start looking was the firm that drafted and amended the Martin trusts.

Grace had accepted his announcement of truancy with more fatalism than he expected out of a Sunday phone call.

"Monday's a light day. You' better be back by Tuesday, though."

And later Lloyd Llewellyn, once he forced the instinctive irritation out of his voice, had been more accommodating than Harry could have hoped as he promised him entree to Wharton Biddle.

"Of course, Harry, I can give Rob a call," L.L. said, displaying his usual lack of curiosity at Harry's activities. 'Rob,' Harry knew, meant Rob Lefkowitz who, when Jack Decker retired, had assumed the duties of family consiglieri. On those rare occasions when Emma wanted to dip into the principal of one of her trusts, it was now Rob Lefkowitz she called instead of 'Uncle Jack.' But none of this could be mistaken for intimacy with Harry himself. Without the Llewellyn calling card Harry knew he wouldn't get anywhere with Wharton & Biddle or the Martin trusts.

"You'll stay in the townhouse of course," Lloyd Llewellyn added. "You know that old headmaster of yours was quite complimentary of you."

"Mmm," Harry said, to hide his surprise.

"And I didn't realize your man Hannah had gone to Devon, too."

"Before my time, but yes."

"I think Livy's boy, Carter, may be happy at the Devon School after all."

Harry, like Livy and Otis, kept his separate, unworthy thoughts to himself as they drove in silence through the rain into the Philadelphia collection of warm wet smells that had first greeted him nearly forty years before. The distant skyline, dramatically altered since his college days by a surreal trio of new glass and steel towers, now looked artificial, out of scale. But once they turned off the expressway, onto South Street, he saw that little had changed at ground level. South Street was a little cleaner, not so many fried chicken places and palm readers, but basically the same little finger of ghetto it had always been. Then, two turns and three blocks north, they were on a tree-lined street of mixed brick and brownstone. The rain seemed to accelerate as they pulled up to the curb.

Livy flinched at a noisy lashing of large rain drops. "Otis, on second thought, I'd better go to Paoli tomorrow. Is that convenient?"

"I was hopin' you'd decide that, Miss Llewellyn," Otis said, showing every tooth. Oh, he was good. Otis must have been older than Harry thought.

"No reason to kill ourselves," Livy said. "Can you get our bags? Let me get the door."

Otis popped the trunk release, got out and half ran around the car. Livy fished in her bag for her key to the house. Her eyes met Harry's. "What?" she said.

"I didn't say anything."

"Jesus, Warren, you don't think I'm that desperate." Her eyes rolled.

"We all have our dreams, Olivia."

"Just help Otis with the bags, and remember it's a twenty buck tip, not ten. We have to live with these people."

◆△◆

HARRY HAD BEEN in the Llewellyns' townhouse only twice, decades before. Unlike the other Llewellyn places, the interior of this one was furnished with the severe simplicity much in vogue when Harry was still in school. Its bare brick walls held unframed abstract paintings and dramatic black and white photographs all lit with track lighting. The usual rainbow of primary colors and pastels of the other Llewellyn dwellings was missing from this house of olive, orange and beige. There wasn't much furniture, and what was there was severe, with glass, chrome, and bentwood much in evidence. It had an anachronistic air, a time capsule for 1970. Harry tried to imagine Lloyd Llewellyn in a Nehru jacket.

The conceit of Lloyd Llewellyn keeping a house just off Rittenhouse Square was that this was the place for Llewellyns to stay when 'in town.' Of course, there was no real need for such a thing. No need for Lloyd to stay 'in town' or any place else he didn't want to be. The trip to Round Hill was seldom more than a half hour, and Otis or a half dozen others were always available to drive. The real reason Lloyd had kept the house was that it was a place where Mrs. Llewellyn was not.

Emma had never discussed her father's infidelities while her mother was alive. She didn't bother to deny them if Lew or Livy were tasteless enough to bring them up in Harry's presence, but Emma made it clear that she did not consider this a topic for lighthearted banter, even from them. When, after her mother's death, Emma too began to mention them, it was only when incidental to some other question like whether it would be a good time to make a telephone call or when the Warrens might visit Hobe Sound. She never gossiped about her father, but she knew he enjoyed the company of numerous 'friends' and that it was to this house, mostly, that he brought them.

Harry wasn't sure that Emma, Lew and Livy's tolerance would have held if their father had come close to marrying one of these 'friends,' but Lloyd Llewellyn had much better manners than that. He had kept his romantic life and his family life plausibly separate, and his children, at least, had honored this by forbearing from any overt criticism. Now, nearing eighty, his romantic interludes were rare and the likelihood he would present the siblings with an inconvenient step-parent had become academic.

◆△◆

Harry reached Tee Ingersoll on the second ring to confirm lunch at one o'clock the next day at the Travelers Club. "God Harry. Twice in the same week. I forgot this was the day I usually take Prof to lunch. It's sort of a monthly thing. I hate to disappoint him."

"Well, why don't you bring him along. God, he must be ninety."

Tee seemed to consider this, then said, "Eighty-six, but you'd never guess." Tee paused for a moment. "Well why not? He'll enjoy it." Harry thought this was a lucky turn until Tee said, "Okay, Warren, what's up?"

"I'd rather tell you when we get together."

"Mysterious," Tee said.

Prof would be a distraction but it was worth it. If Ephne had any connection with the Martins it would have generated talk. If anyone had a better ear for gossip than Tee, Prof would.

"Ah, Harry, it would actually be a help if you could go over to Penn and collect Prof yourself. They've given him an alcove in the Van Pelt Library. He goes there to read and pretend he's writing articles. I'll tell him to expect you."

Harry hung up the phone and surveyed the bedroom Livy had assigned him. Like the rest of the house, it too was spare, spotless, anonymous, and impersonal. A canvas of what appeared to be scrambled eggs was the only adornment. He clicked on the television, then turned it off. The electronics at least were state of the art. He went into the bathroom and had a pee, emerging to find Livy knocking symbolically on the half closed door.

"You called Emma yet?" Livy said.

"Just about to."

"Maybe, after, after the other night, you'd better leave out the fact that we're bunking in together, huh?"

"I thought I'd just leave out the 'desperate' part."

"You know Emma," Livy said, giving him a 'do what you want' look.

Harry managed to deliver to Emma the news that he had arrived back in the City of Brotherly Love while omitting the information that Livy was spending the night under the same roof.

To his surprise Emma said, "You're all right, Harry?"

"Of course. Fine," he said.

"You just seemed so, so preoccupied."

"I'm fine. It's just a thing for the conduct office, the Bar Association. I'll be back tomorrow, promise."

Downstairs, he told Livy that he had made his call.

"She ask about me?"

"Just if we fought on the plane."

"And you said..."

"No more than usual. Nothing about..." He made a circular motion with his hand and gave Livy an insincere smile. She returned it and went into the kitchen to open a beer. She took this into the study and channel surfed. Harry took out the Martin case documents he had brought with him, and began to review them on a glass coffee table in the living room, stretching forward from a chair that seemed to have leather wings. It would be vital to show Rob Lefkowitz he had access to so much of the file already. Still it would be a long bluff.

After reading for two hours, convinced he had done as much as he could, Harry closed up his briefcase with a sigh.

At seven, Livy ordered Chinese take-out. The Eagles were playing and earning Livy's noisy disfavor. Harry decided to distract himself from his troubles for a blessed couple of hours, indifferent to the outcome of the game. They ate in front of the television and drank the rest of L.L.'s beer.

Like her sister, Livy could eat. Dumplings, mushi pork, duck in black bean sauce, General Gau's chicken all disappeared while she cursed the Eagles quarterback in particular and the team in general. A true Philadelphia fan, she heaped much more abuse on them than the other team. "Fucking Eagles, do *some*thing right!" When Harry looked up she said simply, "You take another one of those dumplings and I'll break your hand."

It was nine before she gathered up the half-eaten cartons and brought them into the kitchen. She returned yawning. "I'm dead," she said. "See you in the morning." Considering the probable exertions of her New Hampshire sojourn, Livy had stayed awake a lot longer than Harry thought she would.

Not that he lasted much longer.

The air conditioning in the house was central and Harry didn't know how to turn it on. The bedroom was warm and close, but when he opened a window the rain came driving in. He closed it again, stripped down to his underpants, and lay on the sheets.

Sleep came. Not a dreamless sleep. Confused images of Ephne and Emma, lovemaking and laughter, alternated with dark shadows of dread. Harry woke. The distant sound of the city, the sirens and bells, the distant traffic, once so familiar, now seemed alien, ominous. The scrambled eggs were still there on the wall. He turned on the television and watched the weekend news, mostly a President's increasingly unpersuasive denials of infidelity.

Harry drifted off again with the TV still on. Whether because of the news or in spite of it, his dreams took a decidedly carnal turn, the way dreams can when a love life has been interrupted as long as Harry's had been. But this was much better. He imagined himself hard and assertive, the bringer and taker of confident pleasure, and even heard his own approving groan as he began to grapple with a smooth female form, mindful not to interfere with the expert kneading and pulling that encouraged, welcomed.

Hot, sweet alcohol scented breath was in his face and he reached for and found his phantom partner. She made an answering sigh. They exchanged these favors, bringing sounds from each other that were equal parts surprise, gratitude and insistence.

But not Emma. Not Ephne.

Harry opened his eyes.

"Li... Livy?" He pulled back his hand.

"Who'd you think it was?" She squeezed again. Harry gasped, which she took for encouragement.

"As... Livy, Livy, wait." Her skin was like silk, but Harry pulled her hand away.

"Oh c'mon Warren, you're not going to stop with a little Dutch treat are you? Then she got close to his ear and breathed, accurately, "you know you want it" while she pressed a thigh between his. He made to move away, a show of reluctance, but half-hearted. Each cell, every corpuscle, was pointed in the same direction.

"C'mon Warren, let's settle this once and for all."

Harry didn't think Livy and he would ever settle anything and the husky insistence in her tone woke him up at last. This was not virtue. He was in enough trouble already.

"Livy, I don't think so."

Hearing his tone, she relaxed and in the half light from the doorway and the still flickering of TV screen seemed to shrug and smile. They rolled apart and lay still on their backs while Harry replaced his subsiding and very disappointed member in his shorts and thought of what the Phi Psi's would say if they knew he'd turned down Livy Llewellyn. There was no etiquette for a moment like this so Harry just lay still and practiced holding his breath while they learned that the weather was going to improve in the morning, a high of sixty-two. An update on the condition of the knee of an Eagle's linebacker didn't add anything to the moment either. Finally Harry found the remote and the TV went silent with a gentle plunk. It was then that he felt the bed move beside him and heard a deep intake of breath. Livy was crying.

He let her do this for a while then stood up and pulled a sheet up over her. She shook three or four times, then took hold of the sheet and turned her swollen face toward him. "Warren, you are *such* an asshole," she said. Then, later, "I suppose I should thank you."

"Livy." He sat on the bed and touched her shoulder.

She sat up then, holding the sheet with one hand and putting her other one on his. She made a determined sigh. "That little bitch Emma gets all the luck."

With that she motioned him away and stood up. She fluffed her hair as if she'd just played a set of tennis. Unconcerned with her nudity, she sighed and walked to the door. She stopped and turned there, framed in the hall light. She was still a remarkably beautiful woman. Harry's alter-ego twitched, now ready to answer the bell without him.

"You look glum, Warren."

"You'd look glum if you'd just blown your one chance to sleep with Livy Llewellyn," he said.

Livy considered this, and seemed to like it. Her silhouette shifted weight from one leg to the other.

"Well. Warren, this has been a day of surprises." She looked down and, before he could answer, she said, "And please don't be a complete asshole and say 'indeed'."

It was the very word forming in his mouth but he managed, "Surprises."

"For all of us. For instance, your dick's not half as tiny as I thought it would be."

There is never a good response to this and Harry allowed another involuntary twitch to suffice.

Livy made a sound like a sniff. "Well, I guess I'll just have to get off by myself," she said.

Harry felt his eyes widen.

"Oh don't give me that look. Don't worry, I promise not to think about you."

After she had gone Harry lay still, trying not to think of anything but being still. Yes, he had given up his chance to sleep with Livy Llewellyn. For what? When she threw him out, would Emma say 'thank you for not sleeping with my sister?' The other men on the cell-block, perhaps, would admire his self-restraint. He looked down at the diminutive thing now protruding apologetically just outside the fly-flap. At that moment 'tiny' seemed most appropriate. Indeed.

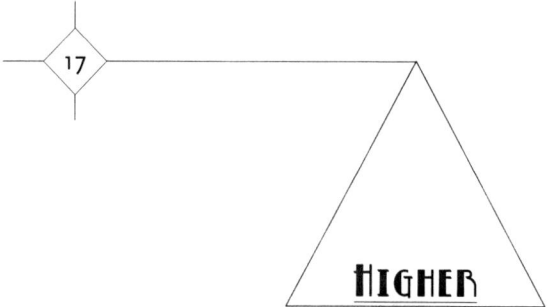

17 — HIGHER

Gregg bumped through the revolving door of a downtown Philadelphia Holiday Inn, set down the old briefcase that T.J. had loaned him and double checked the directions to Broad Street. He turned right and began to walk through the heavy sweet smell. Approaching the scaffold and shroud covered City Hall, he could see cream-colored patches emerging from a century of grime. Panhandlers importuned passers-by from doorways with lethargic menace. Nearby, glass and steel towers of overwhelming height disappeared above him into low clouds. They seemed designed to lift a fortunate few out of the dirt and clutter below. The heavy rain of the night before had done nothing to wash this city clean. It only made it wet. He hadn't thought it was possible but he'd found a place that was dirtier than New York.

Then again it may have been his mood. The drive from Hadley had been a nightmare. First, the van died on the North South Road. By the time Triple-A had arrived and got them going Erin was hysterical and Angela was agitating for a new car. As it was he barely made the plane. The flight down was worse. Thunderstorms diverted him to Baltimore where he'd sat for two hours before getting into Philadelphia after ten.

Gregg took the card from his breast pocket again, confirmed the address he had written down and turned into the entrance of one of the towers. A lobby sign board gave the list of building tenants, including

"Wharton & Biddle, Attorneys." He checked his watch, 9:45 a.m. He rode the elevator alone to the twenty-first floor.

◆△◆

T.J. HAD ORDERED the trip but after turning almost human on Saturday, he was back to normal Sunday, determined that Gregg get back in one day. "You do understand I have a budget, don't you. This isn't in it. What the hell do you think you're gonna find down there that'll take more than a day?"

Gregg had stared back at T.J. It was obvious he couldn't know what he'd find down there. This wasn't a serious suggestion.

"Yah. Okay," T.J. said, "You're right." T.J. handed him a folder. "The mother's eighty-four, but with all her marbles according to the home administrator. While you're gone I'll have some of your boys check the motels around Windsor. She had to stay somewhere. Maybe something will turn up. Don't get comfortable in the city of brotherly love."

"Comfortable." Gregg thought of the narrow hotel room and tired shower. That was rich.

◆△◆

THE ELEVATOR DOOR OPENED at the twenty-first floor onto a lobby paneled in dark wood and presided over by a perfectly beautiful girl wearing a headset and working a small switchboard that twinkled with lights. The girl's yellow hair was swept back and held in place by some sort of comb. She wore a simple white blouse with sleeves that stopped halfway to her elbows. A blue patterned silk scarf was knotted at her neck. She looked up at him, smiling as she spoke into the headset. Gregg wondered how she had found a scarf that matched her eyes so perfectly. Next to her a second girl, smaller, darker, sat in a typist's chair with her hands in her lap. He thought of T.J.'s office and Stacy. An antique grandfather's clock sat behind the two women confirming softly that it was nine forty-five. Well, there were lawyers and then there were lawyers.

"Wharton Biddle," the blonde said to no one in particular. She was English or something like it. She paused, listening, but made another smile at Gregg as she did so. "Yes, yes... of course, but Mr. Price is engaged. Shall I give you to his assistant?" Apparently that was fine because without another word she pushed a button and looked back up at Gregg. Her top teeth were white and perfect in a widening smile.

'*Engaged*,' Gregg thought. Not a bad way to say the boss was busy and couldn't be bothered to talk to you, especially the way she said it.

"I'm here to see Miss Shubert," Gregg said. "Miss Susan Shubert?"

"Ah," she said, her smile straightening. "Miss Shubert's expecting you. I'll ring her for you, shall I?" The switchboard made a soft humming sound and she motioned toward a collection of armchairs facing the elevator doors as she said "Wharton Biddle" into the headset again.

He took a seat and heard the girl field three more calls, two brush-offs and one "Ah yes, Mr. Morgan is expecting your call." A mechanical bell rang and a well-dressed couple came off one of the elevators and held a brief conference at the counter. After a moment the smaller girl stood and led them down the hall. The blonde girl started writing a note, paused, put the pen to her lips and inclined backwards, considering.

Gregg was admiring the way her breasts strained against the blouse and didn't see the tall grey-haired woman until she was standing next to him. "Sergeant Leavitt?" she said catching him in mid-stare. The elevator rang again and opened next to them. A FedEx deliveryman emerged.

"Mmm, yah, yes," Gregg said hurrying to his feet. He immediately recognized the newcomer as the other woman from the picture in Ephne Newsome's apartment.

"You musn't worry," Susan Shubert said. "I haven't decided yet what it is about Clarissa that reduces men to incoherence." She didn't look at the receptionist, but the girl heard it just fine. Her face hardened and for a moment she wasn't pretty any more, but she stayed quiet, and receipted for the Fed Ex package like nothing happened. As Gregg turned to follow, the girl said, "Wharton Biddle." Again, the elevator bell sounded.

Susan Shubert led Gregg down a hallway to a room marked 'Conference 12.' "I've got this for an hour," she said. "We won't need more time than that, will we?"

"No," Gregg said, following her in. He checked his watch. Exactly ten. She closed the door behind them and motioned him to the other side of a square conference table built for six people. Gregg waited until she sat down. Behind her he could see a bridge stretching across a black river below.

"Interesting voice," Gregg said, gesturing back to the hallway. "English?"

"No. South African. She also has interesting views on race and culture ..."

Miss Shubert seemed satisfied that she had the advantage. She looked at a small wristwatch on her left wrist. "Ten o'clock," she said, and folded her hands on the table in front of her, a school girl pose almost identical to the dark-haired girl at the reception desk. About fifty, Gregg guessed. A brown dress hung loose on her long, bony frame. Her eyes were a greenish-yellow and her now grey hair was cut simply with the same bangs she'd had when it was still brown and that picture was taken. Aside from the watch, she wore nothing decorative. Her hands, like the rest of her, were all length and strength. A woman who had never been pretty.

Gregg snapped open T.J.'s briefcase, took out a tape recorder and set it on the table. He removed a pen from his jacket pocket and clicked it, and laid it on the table next to a small pad, closing the case back up with a loud snap. He turned on the recorder then, looking up at her, he gestured toward it with his eyes. "Do you mind?" he asked.

Susan Shubert turned her head once to the left and returned it but said nothing. She wasn't going to help.

"Well," he started, "Ephne Newsome."

"Yes," she said.

"You knew her for how long?"

"Sixteen, seventeen years."

"She worked here? Worked with you?"

Miss Shubert took a long breath and said, "Ephne Newsome worked at Wharton Biddle for eleven years. She left seven years ago. She began as a paralegal in the general litigation section. After she had been here a year she showed she had considerable training in art history. The partners who worked with her found her a very valuable staff member for the fine arts group."

Gregg knitted his brows. "Fine arts?"

"Yes, this firm does a considerable practice in the transfer of ownership of picture art, historic pieces, antique furniture, document collections. We represent several local museums. There is also some litigation over title, authenticity, that sort of thing."

"What exactly did Ms. Newsome do for this, ah, group?"

"She researched provenances, arranged inspections, proper storage, transportation, insurance, translations of foreign statutes. Later she assisted with depositions, even trials, just about everything, really, except try the cases herself. She was quite good at her job, good enough for several other local firms to ask for her as an expert witness."

"And what is it that you do here, Miss Shubert?"

"I'm the firm librarian. I've been here thirty-one years. I was assistant librarian then. Ephne and I often worked together, particularly on the foreign law research."

"I thought that lawyers did that, you know, the research." Maybe the country boy approach would work.

Her weary expression told him, no. "Well, yes, in a general way, but someone has to find it for them in the first place. Even our associates charge hundreds of dollars an hour, Sergeant Leavitt. That's not time you can waste with errands."

"Can you give me an example?" Gregg asked. "You know, what would Ms. Newsome do on a typical case?"

Susan Shubert looked at her watch again and said, "Well, suppose a client, let's say a university or a public museum is in the midst of a purchase of a painting or a religious icon from another museum, or perhaps a private dealer. They're supported by charitable funds, so the purchase is publicized. An individual, or another institution or government reads about it and claims it was looted in war time, or sold illegally out of the country in violation of the Heritage Laws. Does the institution want to go forward? They need advice. Or, maybe the Museum's own connoisseurs decide the piece is improperly attributed..." Gregg looked puzzled. "A fake, Sergeant Leavitt," she said nodding for emphasis. "... And now they need to establish if, when and where the fraud was initiated. It was Ephne's job to make sure our lawyers had the documents, statutes and regulations translated, in front of them, when they began their research."

"Translated?"

"Even at Wharton Biddle we don't get many associates with a working knowledge of Romanian," she said.

"Ah, Icons," Gregg said.

"No Sergeant, Romanians are generally Catholics." The watch again.

"You were happy with her, I mean the firm was..."

"Oh yes. Invaluable. I hated to see her go." She emphasized 'I.'

Gregg made a note of this on his pad. When he looked up he was surprised to see tears starting out of her eyes.

"I'm sorry," he said.

She sniffed and fished a cloth handkerchief from a pocket in the brown dress, wiped each eye, and then blew her nose vigorously. She smiled for the first time. "I told myself I wasn't going to do this," she said in a younger, softer voice.

"Do you need a little time? If you..."

"No, no. I'd rather get it over with now. Really, please, I'm very sorry. It's just that, oh ..." and she fell into tears again.

Gregg turned the recorder off. He watched the woman's shoulders shake, her face hidden in her large hands. She sobbed involuntarily, clumsily. Someone not used to crying, more the way a man would cry. The spasm lasted a minute, then subsided. Susan Shubert wiped her eyes again. They were red-rimmed now. She sniffed and squared herself in her chair to face him.

"Miss Newsome, you knew her well?" Gregg said, when he thought she was ready. He turned the recorder back on.

"I knew her," the woman said, playing with the cloth in her hand. "But you have to understand, Ephne was, well, I don't think anyone knew Ephne well."

Gregg smiled what he hoped was encouragement.

"With Ephne, it was as if she had a secret, something only she knew. When she first came here, fresh out of grad school, she was so hopeful, so confident. She was very engaging."

"She was here eleven years?"

"Yes, eleven years," Susan Shubert said, her voice turning soft. She smiled at him across the table. "You know, I expected a sergeant to be much older," she said, gesturing at Gregg to let him know she realized she had changed the subject. "Someone with a big belly and a beat-up notebook."

"You have experience with police?"

"Of course I do. This is a law firm. You may think we do nothing but corporate offerings or estate planning, but I've worked with plenty of policemen in the last thirty years."

"Did Eph... Ms. Newsome?"

"No, she stuck pretty much to the art practice. Police were seldom involved."

"She was in New Hampshire, we think, to evaluate some furniture and pictures. She ever do any of that here?"

"Evaluation? I don't think so. She concentrated on documentation, authenticity. She was a very good expert witness, I'm told. We could never use her of course."

"When did she leave?"

"Seven years ago, in June."

"Why did she leave?"

"She never said. I never knew precisely why. One Monday I came to work and her desk was cleared out, people talking in whispers, that sort of thing."

"She was fired?"

"She said not, but yes, certainly."

"Any idea why?"

"I only know that payroll staff was told to prepare her severance immediately." She lowered her voice. "I heard that it was something about files she had taken out of storage."

"Files?"

"Confidential trust files. Ephne was given access to the firm's probate and estate files. She had such luck establishing provenances from things she'd found in old estate inventories right here at the firm that she was given unusual access to old files. She was always blowing the dust off this Pepper's probate or that Cadwalader's trust."

"Cad...?" Gregg held his pen up.

"I meant it as a figure of speech. Two old Philadelphia names. Don't try to spell it."

Her big hand reached over the table and touched his.

"But apparently she had been taking out files that had nothing to do with what she was working on for some time," Susan Shubert said. "I reached her that night and she was almost gay about it. 'Susie, it doesn't matter, relax, it doesn't matter,' she kept saying."

"Seems strange. Fired for picking up the wrong file."

"Apparently, this was one of Mr. Popp's files. Nobody ever touched Mr. Popp's files." She paused, "Popp," she said, "Three P's."

"His files were different?"

"Oswald Popp handled the black cases for the firm."

Gregg looked puzzled. "You mean civil rights stuff?"

Miss Shubert snorted, but gave him a look of real kindness and shook her head side to side. "You *are* young." She felt sure enough of herself now to put the handkerchief back in the pocket. "Mr. Popp was the man who was called when the college president was arrested in a gay bar, or the senator's son was caught with cocaine, or the wife of a major client needed an abortion after an encounter with a stable boy ... that sort of thing."

"Scandals."

'Uh huh, back when those things were scandals. Popp, Mr. Popp, handled those things for the firm. Oswald Popp knew where all the bodies were buried. He did some of the burying himself, and didn't want anybody knowing what he did."

"This Mr. Popp, the one you said handled ...?"

"Died two years ago." Susan smiled again, "Terrible man."

"You didn't like him."

"No one did. Me less than most. I loathed him."

"And you think he had Miss Newsome fired?"

"Certainly. Apparently he came in over the weekend and found her in storage with one of his files spread out all over the table. There wasn't any art in the inventory and nothing related to any case she was working on. She tried to talk her way out of it, but you could never fool Oswald Popp for long."

"Did you ever hear the name 'Martin' "? Louisa or Eleanor Martin? Heatherington Martin?" Gregg read off his card.

"No."

"Did she ever mention any of those names to you?"

"Not that I remember."

"Have you been in touch with Ms. Newsome, recently?"

"No. Not for at least two years."

"You know that you're the executrix of her will? Did you have a falling out?"

"I knew I was." She paused. "We just drifted apart. No, that's not right. She drifted away. Oh, we kept in touch for a year or so, after she moved. I met her for dinner or a show in New York, but only for a year or two. She called me whenever she came through Philadelphia at first. But—well I guess she just developed other interests."

"Any other friends? Women friends? Men friends?"

"Men, oh yes. Ephne didn't seem to have many woman friends. Except me."

"There was a picture of the two of you we found in Ms. Newsome's apartment. You're on a mountain, by a lake."

"She kept that?" Susan Shubert seemed genuinely surprised.

"The picture, yah. You remember it?"

"Lake Wasoka in New Hampshire. But that must have been more than fifteen years ago. We took a couple of trips and stayed at an old run down place. It was, ah, the West Harbor Inn. She'd gone to camp near there as a girl. You must go there all the time."

"Not really. but I grew up in Hadley just down the road."

"That awful little city?"

"Uh huh."

"I'm sorry," she said, and leaned forward to show she meant it.

"No. You're right," Gregg said. "Hadley's pretty rough, but it's home." He paused, then said, "Did, ah, Ephne have any local, ah, New Hampshire connections other than that camp, that you knew of? We found her bo... we found her less than a mile from the Lake."

"Connections, no. But she knew the lakefront from her years at camp. She could point out the houses from the tour boat. 'That's the Hamilton house... John Hamilton.'... like she knew them. Or 'There's the Llewellyns, you know, the people who bought the fake Homer.' She was always saying that sort of thing. She knew who they were, but she didn't *know* them, wasn't acquainted with them."

"Any local relationships, any romances here in Philadelphia?"

"Oh, always. Ephne was very progressive, that way. But never serious. Casual. One night stands, I guess you'd call them. But she always kept that part of her life ... separate."

"Anyone you can think of that she might have wanted to renew acquaintance with?"

"Well not here. I don't know about the Lake." Susan Shubert turned solemn. "Though there *was* one man from New Hampshire, but that was later, just before she left Wharton Biddle. She was pretty secretive about him, but you could tell it was different. Then, all at once, that was over, too."

"Name...?"

"I never knew his name."

"But you say this man was different?"

"Oh yes. Usually she'd just...." The woman's voice wavered, she hesitated, took the handkerchief out of her pocket, but then put it back again. "Usually with Ephne, well sometimes at the inn I could hear them in the next room, you know. But she'd just kick the boy, man, whoever he was, out in the morning, and be up and ready to climb a mountain or get in a canoe, like nothing had happened. This was different."

"What makes you think this man was from ..."

"Oh, because she asked me to bury some of the phone calls she made to him from the office. We couldn't just go making long distance calls from here, Sergeant. They have to be accounted for. I remember the area code. Like a wiseacre, I asked her if it was one of the boys she'd picked up at the lake."

"'No one would call him a "boy," Susan.' she said to me. Then she grinned ear to ear, and not the least ashamed of herself. When I asked her what the big secret was, she turned serious. 'You don't want to know, Susan. Let's just say he's sort of a client.'"

"This relationship last long?"

"For Ephne, yes. Two or three months. Then one Monday she came in, eyes red, unhappy, distracted. 'What's the matter, kiddo?' I asked her, and she just said, 'Came in second again Susie,' then she went to the ladies room. She cried a little. We never talked about him again."

"What do you think she meant by 'sort of a client'?"

"I wasn't sure. She obviously didn't want to talk about him so I didn't press. Probably someone who we once represented, perhaps a family member."

"This was after the picture, the picture of the two of you in her apartment?"

"Oh yes, about a year, maybe two. She never wanted to go back to Lake Wasoka after that, not with me anyway."

"And you still have no idea who this man was?"

"No, but I'm pretty sure he went to Penn." Susan looked up at the ceiling, searching her memory.

"Penn?" he asked. "Here in Philadelphia?"

"Uh huh, yes, the University. I'm almost sure of it. A few months after they broke it off, Effy and I were over at the campus at the fine arts department, pre-marking exhibits for an expert deposition. We went outside so she could have a smoke. I could never get her to stop. She looked around at the old buildings, the kids walking back and forth, and all at once she got wistful, not at all like Effy. She started talking about being 'trapped in time' and asked me if I'd ever been at Penn in the sixties. I told her I wasn't quite that old." The woman gave Gregg a defiant smile.

"Then Effy stamped out her cigarette and she tried to laugh it off. 'You just wonder if you'd met a guy at a different time in your life, a different place. I knew a man who went here.'"

"And that's when I said, 'That man in New Hampshire, the mystery man, the one you were calling?'"

"What did she say to that?" Gregg asked.

"'Just leave it Susie,' she said. 'I shouldn't have brought it up.' But she didn't deny it. It must have been him."

"Anything else she said about him?" Gregg asked.

"No."

"Anything you can remember that could help identify him?"

"Just the telephone calls."

"How do you…"

"Oh, mostly they were from him. When he called her, she had him do it through my office in the library. It was the ones she returned that I buried."

"I don't suppose there'd be a record?"

"There might be, but you don't think Wharton Biddle is ever going to let you look through their phone records, do you?"

Gregg said, "This is a murder we're investigating, Miss Shubert."

Susan Shubert smiled at him, almost tenderly now. "A murder of a paralegal who worked here a long time ago and was killed far, far away, Mr. Leavitt. Someone they fired. You think Wharton Biddle is going to let some out-of-state police department go through their confidential client phone logs for that?"

Gregg thought for a second but wasn't about to agree with her. "Did you keep a record of his number?"

She shook her head to say 'no.' The two sat silently, then Susan Shubert said, "Just the area code. You only had one in New Hampshire. I remember that."

"And you're sure of that?"

"Positive."

Gregg made a face and turned his palms up as if to say 'how?'

Susan Shubert took the recorder in her big hand. She pushed the stop button. "Jealousy, Mr. Leavitt. Pure and simple. I never had a friend like Ephne. I guess I thought she felt the same about me. You never forget the people who leave you, or who they leave you for."

They went on to review dates: when Ephne Newsome worked there, when she left, the year of the phone calls. Making sure he had her home address and phone number, Gregg explained to the woman that she might be needed to testify. In all, they took the full hour allotted.

◆△◆

SUSAN SHUBERT ESCORTED him back to the elevator and shook Gregg's hand as they waited for the car. He surveyed the lobby. The blonde was gone but the dark-haired girl was manning the phone. He turned back to Susan, "This is sure a beautiful office." As he spoke there was a commotion behind him.

Instead of answering him, Miss Shubert looked over his shoulder with a quizzical expression. Gregg turned. The blonde girl and an older man wearing bright suspenders were talking to someone turning down the hall from the lobby. Papers were on the floor and the blonde girl had knelt down to pick them up. The lace trim of her slip showed as she did.

The elevator opened behind Gregg with a soft bell.

Gregg and Susan Shubert then nodded their goodbyes. As the door closed Gregg heard the dark-haired girl say "Wharton Biddle" into her headset.

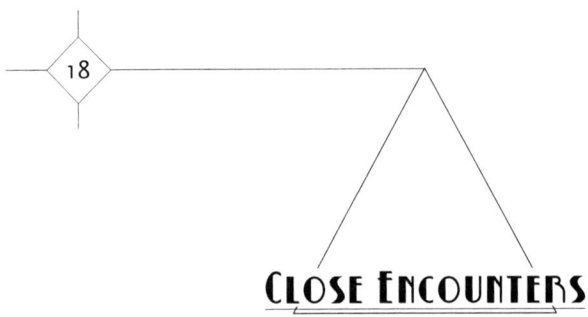

18
CLOSE ENCOUNTERS

The bigger the firm, the better looking the young woman at the front desk. Zach Hannah had taught Harry that, using different language of course, and Zach insisted that the woman greeting clients at Cruikshank be the best looking in the office. Everyone knew that Zach was more than a boss to some of these beauties, but he was right just the same. A client in a bad mood was less likely to take it out on a cheerleader. Wharton Biddle didn't disappoint. The girl Harry saw as he came off the elevator, briefcase in hand, was a heartbreaker, a sunburst of possibility to welcome the troubled, almost enough to make the visit worth the $12.50 a minute it would cost. The clock behind her confirmed it was just before ten a.m., the time for his appointment with Rob Lefkowitz.

But something was bothering the young woman. She was half turned toward a smaller dark-haired girl almost as striking as she was. She was speaking in a half whisper.

"... can't believe her. You heard what she..."

But the girl knew her business and fell silent to greet Harry with a smile that seemed to say 'You wonderful man, you're here at last!'

What she said was: "Oh yes, Judge Warren, just a moment." She punched buttons on the small keyboard in front of her. As she did this Harry exchanged nods with the second girl. There was something prim about the way she sat there, watching, her hands in her lap. Not bad herself, but definitely the second team, a clerical *duenna*.

"Rob," the first girl said into the mouthpiece of her head set, "Judge Warren is ... yes, yes, straight away."

The blonde punched a button and removed the headset. "Chloe, I'll take the judge down to Mr. Lefkowitz's office." As good as Harry thought he was at accents, hers eluded him. New Zealand? The dark girl took the headset without changing expression and rolled her own chair forward. Almost immediately she said, "Wharton Biddle, good morning." *Good muoning.* Ah, Philadelphia. He was back.

The blonde was tall, six feet in the heels she wore, but the bottom half of her was slightly more substantial than it needed to be. If she had a brother, he played rugby. For no particular reason, Harry was relieved to see this descent from perfection. She walked him around a corner to a single elevator which she opened with a key.

"Did you have a good flight down, Judge? Bad weather yesterday."

Bed Way..tha. Australia? South Africa, he decided.

"Yes, I did." he smiled up at her. They rode the elevator three floors.

She showed him enough teeth to let him know how gratifying she found this just as she said, "Here we are." They stepped out to face a desk of blonde wood where a moon-faced woman in an unbecoming purple dress was clicking away at her word processor. She was receiving recorded dictation through a larger model headset. This woman looked up and nodded wordlessly just as she unleashed a burst of dull clicks onto the keyboard. Neither woman spoke. These two were not friends.

THE OFFICE SPACE ALLOTTED to Robert, 'call me Rob,' Lefkowitz had grown considerably in the quarter century since Harry and he had first met. However, like all big law firms, Wharton Biddle now ran on unforgiving Darwinian principles so the opulence was rationed out. The view through the floor to ceiling glass wall to the Ben Franklin Bridge below was impressive enough but only one of the remaining walls sported the mahogany raised paneling that either Mr. Wharton or Mr. Biddle would have insisted on for the whole office when they ran the firm. The remaining two walls of this office were white sheetrock, back-lit by recessed fluorescence. One held a large framed cityscape of Philadelphia in the 1890s. Rob's Harvard diplomas graced the other. The fragment of paneling, the antique desk and a Tabriz on the floor were there as relics. An evocation of the past to let the client know he was getting—value *and* maybe a little tradition—for his $750 an hour.

Rob himself came from around the desk to greet Harry as he entered. "Judge, hello, hello. Can we get you something, coffee? A soda?"

Harry took his hand remembering no one says 'coffee' or 'soda' quite like a Philadelphian even after seven years at Harvard.

"No thanks."

Wordlessly the blonde closed the door behind her. Rob Lefkowitz hadn't lost any more hair but that durable remnant had acquired both the color and texture of a scouring pad. His face had filled out and he had been getting sun somewhere. Worry lines were etched into his face and competed with his smile, giving him that Talmudic look clients found so reassuring. The overall effect more than made up for the substantial paunch he had grown. This was precisely bisected by trousers held up by parti-colored suspenders, and draped to just brush the dull shine of his Gucci loafers. Rob Lefkowitz had grown up to be his own sharper, newer model of Jack Decker.

"How is judging?" he asked with feigned gravity, ushering Harry to one of two chairs arranged at oblique angles before his desk. He didn't go back to his desk, but rather took the other chair.

"It's fine, fine. All my jokes are funny, all my observations are profound."

Rob Lefkowitz laughed at this with just enough good-natured nodding to suggest he found the observation unusual, perhaps because most judicial self-deprecation was financial or confined to confessions of foibles only in worldly things.

"Thought about it myself from time to time," he said.

"Not for long I expect," Harry said, gesturing at the office with its vertiginous views of the city. 'Judge' Lefkowitz would have taken at least an eighty percent cut in pay.

Lefkowitz made a conspiratorial chuckle which sounded more

believable than his first one. Then he said, "You know, I never would have predicted you for the judiciary, not when we met."

Harry said, "You remember that do you?" He watched the other man's face settle into its worry lines then, to ingratiate himself, Harry said, "Was I that callow?"

"'I get to keep the pen, don't I.' You remember that?" Rob Lefkowitz beamed.

Harry shifted in his chair. Yes, he had said that. He shrugged to signal mild embarrassment and mumbled, "Not really."

"Well I do," Lefkowitz said, "and between you and me, I *loved* the way you stared down Oswald Popp. He wasn't used to that."

"It was that obvious?"

Lefkowitz giggled like a school boy at the end of a dirty joke. "Obvious? I loved it. Believe me you were a minor folk hero among the associates for that one. No one, I mean no one, treated Oswald Popp like that."

"He must be long retired."

"Two years dead and, may I be forgiven, not missed."

"I spoke with him, eight years ago, I think. He hadn't changed."

"Well, *Ni hil Nisi Bonum*," Lefkowitz said.

Harry made a shrug of assent. They fell into silence which was taken as a signal to get down to business because Rob Lefkowitz leaned forward, an elbow on each knee, his gold cufflinks catching the glint of the overhead lights. Tee would have warned him about cufflinks.

"So, what can I do for you? Mr. Llew … Lloyd said it had something to do with a project you're working on up in …"

Harry removed some papers from his briefcase, careful to make sure Lefkowitz could see the Wharton Biddle logo. "A case, a probate case I'm reviewing for our office of bar discipline, actually."

Rob Lefkowitz hadn't risen to managing partner of a five-hundred-man law firm by being stupid. Nor was he susceptible to having smoke blown in his eyes. He was, after all, in the smoke blowing business himself. But Harry knew Lefkowitz *wanted* to do whatever he asked. As long as Harry was careful not to lock eyes with him—he'd flinch for sure—there was a very good chance he'd give Harry what he wanted. Lefkowitz had a small mole on his cheek opposite the midway point of his nose and Harry concentrated on that.

"A case...?"

"Well, it's complicated and, for reasons I can't fully reveal, quite sensitive."

"Ah, well." He smiled. One legal statesman to another. "Well, how can we help?"

Harry began his tale.

"Some years ago, Wharton Biddle established a trust and did estate planning for a client." He pulled a three-by-five card from his pocket and pretended to consult it. "Heatherington Martin," he said. Harry gave Lefkowitz the card with the name and date of the trust and amendments. When the man looked up, Harry kept focused on the mole and continued.

"There's a series of suits in Hadley County, New Hampshire, involving the administration of the Martin trust, some loans to two of the surviving beneficiaries and a series of mortgages, ah..." Here Harry felt his throat going dry and his voice took on that constricted, strangled waver he had heard from god knew how many lying witnesses "... and, frankly, we have concerns that there may have been some improprieties in their representation."

"Improprieties?" Rob Lefkowitz frowned at the word. "You don't mean here in Pennsylvania, nothing wrong with the instruments?" Harry had anticipated a frisson of concern and made a placatory wave at him before answering.

"No, no. The, ah, wrongdoing we suspect arose long after the family moved to New Hampshire from Haverford. The investigation concerns their..." Here Harry paused for half a second and lowered his voice to impart the need for discretion. "... subsequent representation."

"You have the trust instruments?" The cuff-linked wrists turned upward.

"It and two amendments." Harry leaned forward and lowered his voice even further. "But evidence in our proceeding indicates that there may have been some nonrecord provisions and possibly one or more contingent beneficiaries. Additional heirs."

"Addi...?" Lefkowitz didn't finish. He got up from his chair and went to the window before he turned around. "But why you, Judge? Why are you...?" He let the obvious question hang in the air. "*Why is a sitting judge involved in evidence gathering?*"

Harry had tried to prepare for this question, but predictably, now that he was out on the limb, the familiar flinch emerged. When he swallowed, he actually heard himself make a sound. He re-focused on the mole and made the leap.

"New Hampshire's professional conduct proceedings are confidential, Rob, at least up until a formal complaint is filed, but the attorneys in question have, well, a certain reputation." To punctuate his concern Harry pretended to consult the copies he had with him. I can't go any further than say there's a pending, ah, proceeding." Harry let the word hang in the air, giving his best imitation of manly discretion.

"Well, isn't this discoverable?" Rob Lefkowitz wasn't a litigator but he knew enough about trial practice to know that a motion for discovery and a subpoena could accomplish what Harry was asking him to give up.

"Yes, yes," Harry made what he hoped was a convincing sigh of mild despair. "But the adverse parties to ongoing litigation of course have no interest in identifying additional beneficiaries."

Lefkowitz said, "There's no guardian ad litem?"

"Ah," Harry said, shaking his head slightly. "Now you've identified the problem." Lefkowitz would conclude, now, that the guardian too was on the hot-seat. He thought of Zach. "*If it's their idea, Harry, they believe it.*"

"Mmmh," Lefkowitz said, "I see." His eyelids sunk in pleasure. Even smart guys like Rob Lefkowitz liked reminding themselves how really smart they were. Now he had enough. He didn't need anything further and, more to the point, he didn't want any. A guardian cheating his wards was nasty business. No lawyer wanted in on another lawyer's disciplinary case, busy lawyers least of all. As for the wild-west procedures enforcing New Hampshire's lawyer disciplinary rules, well, Rob Lefkowitz now had the word of a sitting judge. He had all the cover he needed to grant Lloyd Llewellyn's request, but Lefkowitz still hesitated. Harry gave the last little nudge.

"New Hampshire proceedings are more inquisitorial than adversarial," he said. "I'm sure the Pennsylvania bar has independent staff for this sort of thing. But New Hampshire is a small bar, Rob. Our discipline office is practically all volunteers. We do appreciate the help." He chanced a look now at the other man's eyes.

"Uh, huh," Lefkowitz said. His eyes went out of focus while he balanced the dubious propriety of giving Harry access to client files against the unpleasantness a refusal would cause with Lloyd Llewellyn. The one thing Harry knew Lefkowitz wouldn't do was call Lloyd himself. Lloyd wouldn't want to be implicated in the details of an impropriety if there was one, and if Harry's request was within bounds, Lloyd wouldn't look kindly on doubts focused against even his least favorite son-in-law. Lefkowitz was paid to handle things, not to look for absolution from the client.

"So, just research then, background?" Harry relaxed. That was a "yes."

"Just ... background. Exactly. I know it's a little unconventional." Harry stood up to squelch any second thoughts. "Lloyd *said* if anyone could help me with this you could," and rose smiling as he said this. Rob Lefkowitz, the family retainer.

At this Lefkowitz also stood, made a rueful smile and crossed to his desk.

"This stuff must all be in storage, you know, if we've still got it." He fingered a couple of buttons on his phone. When it was answered he got right to business. "See what files we have on Heatherington Martin. Yah, yah, no. Estate Planning and Trusts, uh huh…" He looked up at Harry, put down the phone and said, "All this stuff is indexed on the computer now. I can't even turn the damn things on." Harry rewarded him with an answering scowl of resignation. As they waited, they made small talk, the changing face of Philadelphia, the Harvard-Penn game coming up the next Saturday. Throughout, Rob Lefkowitz tapped the index card on the desk with his free hand.

After an interval, a voice came over the intercom and Lefkowitz made a quarter-turn away to pick up his phone. "Yah, uh huh. Really?

Well, uh yes, yes we'd better have that too. Thanks. Oh, still there? Yah, when can we have it?" He put his hand over the mouthpiece. "It's out in storage, but she thinks they can have it here this afternoon."

Harry hadn't counted on a long delay but nodded as nonchalantly as he could. "Great, can I check back, about ..." He looked at his watch. "About three?"

Lefkowitz turned away. "Three o'clock?" he said into the phone. He looked back, eyebrows up. Harry nodded to show three was fine. "Yes. Okay, good. Really? Oswald's too? Well, let me know when you've got them copied." He hung up the phone.

"Tell you what, Rob, just so there's no question, why don't you have one of your people prepare a certification that the file's complete. I'll receipt for it."

Well, why not? After breaching half the known Canons of Judicial Ethics what was a phony receipt and an unnecessary certification?

"Happy to, but no publication? All *in camera*."

"Oh, everything stays under seal, for discipline purposes only. Put that in your transmittal, of course." Harry said this with more assurance than he felt. These papers would probably be Exhibit 3 in Harry Warren's trial, after some phone records and the warrant, but at least they'd see he had the balls to try.

"Funny," Lefkowitz said, gesturing toward the phone. "Speak of the devil, it seems Oswald Popp, your old friend, did some work for the Martins."

◆Δ◆

AS THE SON-IN-LAW of Wharton Biddle's largest client, Harry got the full ceremonial exit, Rob Lefkowitz himself accompanied him down the private elevator piloted once again by the glorious South African amazon. Harry was feeling almost light hearted, it had been so easy. All he had to do was get back by three...

"Clarissa will set up a conference for you; you can leave your things there if you want."

As they turned the corner to enter the paneled lobby, Harry found himself gazing upon the profile of Sergeant Gregg Leavitt, fifteen feet away. To the surprise of his escorts the New Hampshire judge seemed to do an immediate one-eighty-degree turn and start back round the corner. Rob Lefkowitz, mouth open in surprise, stopped first. Only then did the girl turn back as well. "You okay, Judge?" she asked.

Harry had managed to open the case by then and spilled his papers onto the floor. He looked down helplessly as they went in all directions. Ever the helpmate, the girl knelt and started gathering them up. Harry joined her, careful to stay on the far side of the corner. Rob Lefkowitz hadn't retrieved a dropped piece of paper for at least a decade, even for a Llewellyn, and didn't now.

Eventually, the sheets were collected and Harry had them in hand again. "Thank you, thanks, sorry, sorry about that," Harry said as he stood.

"You're all right, Judge?"

From Rob Lefkowitz's expression, Harry guessed he had rubbed deeply enough into that veneer of good humor for one morning. There could be no further delay. They set off again and Harry turned the corner leaning slightly forward, as if expecting a strong wind.

Leavitt was gone.

Harry almost skipped to the elevator door.

"Well, Rob, thanks again."

"Any time." Just was a hint of impatience. Second thoughts?

"I'll be back at three and, ah, why don't I leave this with Clarissa," Harry said unnecessarily. He handed her the case. The girl's smile now showed diminished radiance appropriate to her boss's declining enthusiasm.

"I'll try not to drop it," she said.

"Great. Well, goodbye," said Rob Lefkowitz. He had the look of a man whose prejudices had been recently shaken but later confirmed.

The elevator behind Harry opened. Of course. That's where the policeman had gone.

Harry, entered, gave a final wave, and pushed the button marked 'L.' The elevator descended in a lurch making soft clarinet chirps on its way down. On a whim Harry pushed the button marked 'M' just above 'L.'

When the door opened, Harry poked his head out and saw he was on a wide C-shaped balcony, almost empty of people. He approached the edge and scanned the lobby floor below as it led to the front entrance. There, three quarters of the way to the door, he saw the young policeman again, his closely cropped head inclined down, checking what looked like an address book. A battered briefcase was at his feet.

Harry backed to the rear of the balcony, almost to the wall. There he turned and pretended to study the grain of the blue-black marble while making sideways glances at Leavitt. He watched the policeman close the notebook, pick up the case and make his way to a guard. From the guard's gestures he was asking directions. Then Leavitt turned, walked out onto the Market Street sidewalk and disappeared.

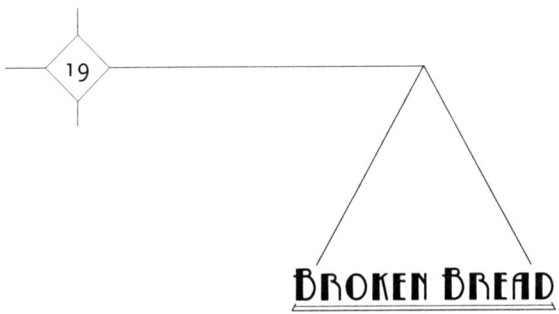

19 — Broken Bread

Another twenty dollar tip was required for the cab driver to agree to wait on Walnut Street, but after the close call at Wharton Biddle, Harry didn't want to spend five minutes on any sidewalk hailing a new cab. There was no one there when he emerged, certainly not a New Hampshire state police sergeant, but Harry still hurried up the walkway that traced the route of the long discontinued Woodland Avenue until the bulk of the Van Pelt library stood between him and the street.

Slowing until he stopped at the library steps, Harry turned and surveyed the campus foliage, now yellowed on trees that had been little more than saplings when he was an undergraduate. Streams of students spilled down from the walks that had once been 36th Street and Locust Street. No one would confuse Penn for Princeton or Dartmouth, even now, but it was a far cry from the gothic slum it had been in Harry's day. He supposed that in its reclaimed glory his alma mater would now have no room for Harry Warren. It had taken some doing for his daughter Leigh to be moved off the wait list six years earlier and she had been a much better student than Harry.

"You're far more punctual than you were for class, Mr. Warren."

Harry turned toward the familiar voice only to see a fragile, white haired 'Prof' Rush coming down the steps to greet him. Despite the years, Prof was still turned out with all the care of a male model he once could have been, his tie just slightly off center, his negligently folded pocket handkerchief standing in his breast pocket like a flag, as Livy would say. Of course, when Dr. T. Lippincott Rush wore it that way, it looked perfect.

"Good to see you again, sir."

The old man gestured at the campus. "Care for it?"

"Quite a transformation."

"A miracle. In my day of course it was still in decline. Street cars, football players with unpronounceable names, the impossible Mr. Stassen, but now, well, you see."

"I've got a cab over on Walnut," Harry said.

"Ah," Prof said, and the two set out. Except for his curious bow-legged gait typical of old men, it could have been thirty years before. The thought must have come to Prof as well because he said, "You remember your senior Spring?"

"Of course."

"You were rather hard on Cleveland Amery and Digby Baltzell but very kind to me," Prof said. "I loved your paper, but you know how those things go." He cocked his head at the library. "I still have a small office off the rare book collection. They indulge me out of guilt. Haven't let me near a classroom for twenty years."

The two regained Harry's cab, rode in silence to Market Street, and were crossing the river by 30th Street station when Prof said "So, Tee says we have to sing for our lunch today."

"Well, I hope so."

The older man seemed to adjust his cuffs. "Tee felt the need to warn me, you see. Such a good boy. My second cousin, once removed, but he's much more than that to me."

"I'm sure its mutual." Harry surveyed the collapsed flesh beneath his companion's chin, the small pouches under each eye. The forbidding, distant Prof Rush had become another lonely old man, grateful to be asked to lunch.

"Perhaps. He's kind enough to do this once a month and I enjoy it. When you get to my age, contemporaries tend to thin out and the ones that survive live in places with impossibly precious names. My favorite is 'The Elms at Bala Cynwid.'"

Harry lifted his eyebrows and smiled.

"After all, they've all died, haven't they? The elms I mean, not the people. What will they do when there's only one left? Call it "'The Elm at Bala Cynwid'?"

The cab pulled up at the Travelers Club and a man in a black suit came down to open the taxi door.

"Good afternoon, Dr. Rush," he said.

When Harry emerged from the car after paying the fare the same man nodded a silent greeting.

◆△◆

Harry had found that people, after fifty, generally have the appearance they deserve. Greedy children could work their excess off with sports and games. An undergraduate could drink for days at a time, but a shower, shave and one night of sobriety was usually enough to put the shine back in his eyes. However, after a half-century of excess, the glutton's belly swelled—on a woman, the bottom—and the veins in a drunkard's nose will have burst into a tell-tale magenta. The grey cheeks and deep creases in the faces of smokers of ten thousand packs of cigarettes were more revealing than a CT-scan.

Judged by results, Tee Ingersoll could claim a blameless life. Except for the disappearance of hair from two small parabolas of skin that now defined his hairline, the years had left no mark. Unlike Harry, he appeared to weigh exactly what he had at eighteen. As he strode into the Travelers Club, a minute behind them, Tee said something to the man at the door who laughed and nodded to him. He could have been talking to the house man at his old fraternity. The few members present gave no indication that the famous 'Ted' Ingersoll was in their midst.

"Well, well, well, Harry Warren at the Travelers," he said, but not loud enough for anyone else to hear; he took Harry's hand.

"Tee," Harry said watching as his old roommate jerked his head slightly. There was no more hair to shake off his forehead, but the youthful gesture remained.

"You know, I've always liked it here," Tee said, letting go of Harry's hand and looking around.

"Prof's in the men's," Harry said. "Watching you now, I wonder, you must miss the old days."

"How do you mean?"

"The doorman, you'd have left him your hat and gloves if we ever wore hats and gloves. You were always good with ... with servants."

Tee stood very still as Harry said this, but instead of responding, smiled and talked past him. "There you are, Prof. Did you show Harry the campus?" The old man made a smile that said 'of course not' and instead ushered them to a table. Anyone watching would conclude Harry was the guest, not the other way around.

After they sat, Tee returned to Harry's unanswered question. "You always were observant, Warren." He snapped open his napkin and laid it on his lap in a single motion. Having squared his chair he brought his eyes to meet Harry's. "And of course you're right," he said. "I miss the old days very much. I go to the damnedest places now."

"I'm not a member, you know," Harry said, thinking this would explain his presence there. "They have a reciprocal deal with the Wasoka Club." It was better than that. L.L. had an arrangement for the whole family. All bills went straight to his office.

The Prof watched them and made an exaggerated motion with his hands to signal that the mystery was solved. "Of course, of course." Then very softly, "The Llewellyns can do no wrong. Though it wasn't always that way."

"Drink?" Harry asked as a waiter approached. Most times he would have loved to hear gossip about the Llewellyns, but not today.

"Many, I hope," Tee said. "We don't start production until next week. We're all going to Vegas," Tee smiled with mock pride. "Yes, Las Vegas. We found a blackjack dealer who 'sun lights' as a faith-healer. We're calling the episode 'Danke Schein, Jesus!'"

It had been three years since Harry was last in the Travelers but the dining room captain approached and greeted him with the warm pretense that he was recognized. "Welcome back, Judge," he said handing him a wine list. Then he tendered menus to "Dr. Rush," and "Mr. Ingersoll."

"Jeffrey," Prof returned the greeting with one nod of his head.

Prof raised his eyebrows in approval after the man left. "'Judge' is it still? Well, Jeffrey is the best of a vanishing breed."

"I always envied you two for that." As he spoke, Harry handed Tee the wine list.

"Envied? For what?" Prof asked with an echo of his old *froideur*.

"The way you always know their names."

"Mmmm."

"No, I mean that sincerely."

"Oh God, Warren," said Tee. "Sincerity? Between us?"

"Sorry."

"No, no." Tee waved his hand. "I'm prepared to forgive anything. The *sole meuniere* they give you here is to die for. Montrechet all right with you, Harry? Prof?"

"I'm allowed one glass," the old man said.

An Asian man with a dark complexion brought their wine and then for half an hour Harry allowed Tee and Prof to go on about the comings and goings of their numerous cousins. While they talked they moved through *foie gras*, endive with mustard vinaigrette, and sole with asparagus and *pommes dauphine*. Prof was careful to ask ahead for a small souffle with *Sauce Anglaise*. They were waiting for that when Jeffrey came to see how they were doing. Tee asked if the Sandeman 1978 had been opened yet that day.

"I know that's your favorite, Mr. Ingersoll," Jeffrey said. Then, more softly, "We'll uncork a new bottle. The same, Dr. Rush?" Then, remembering, he turned to Harry, "Anything for you, Judge?"

"Ah, why yes. The same, please."

"It's very good of you, Jeffrey," said Tee, as the man turned to leave.

"Thank you, Mr. Ingersoll."

Harry shook his head slowly at Jeffrey's retreating back. These two would never want.

"All right, Warren, why the weary incredulity?" Tee had just replaced the bottle of Montrachet, now empty, back in its cooler.

"I'm just surprised.," Harry looked into Tee's placid eyes as he savored the last of the crisp yellow wine. "Surprised that there are still people who can step back into the old ways. Maybe a little disappointed. I never really got the hang of it."

"Ah, there, Tee," Prof said. "I told you, Harry would never be comfortable with his little impostures. It's always much more fun being Pygmelion than the statue." He spoke as though Harry wasn't there. His color had returned with a second, forbidden glass. He was once more his old self.

"Oh... ohh, that," Tee said. "Ahh, well don't worry, Harry. You never will. Get comfortable, I mean. Nothing to be alarmed about. It's part of your charm. You seemed so, so *teachable* when we were boys, but of course after a certain age you can only *imitate*. You never really learn."

Prof nodded, his eyes twinkling.

Harry leaned toward the old teacher and said, "You were always saying that it wasn't about 'class' anymore, it was ..."

"Caste, Mr., excuse me, I know it's late in the day, but shouldn't I call you 'Harry'?"

"Of course."

"I always ask. No, there's no such thing as class in America any more. We forfeited that some time ago. We wasps are just one of the tribes now."

"Little tricks we learned, Harry, that's all," said Tee. "Incidently, it's 'staff' at a club unless they're from Borneo or some other godforsaken place."

Harry acknowledged the renewal of his education with a nod.

Then Tee said, "But enough of that. What's so important that you shake us from our settled habits?"

"Would you believe that I'm suffering from an incurable disease and making peace with my old friends and mentors?"

"You lie. For your kind, Warren, when the time comes, you'll slink off to some quiet cave and expire. I'll be genuinely sad. I always liked you. I even forgave you for those verses you wrote about St. Mike's." Tee said this without insouciance and Harry didn't banter. But after a short interval Tee said, "Well, hell, you're not going to humiliate us with silence are you? After my confessions? What's up? What gives?" Prof also leaned forward.

"Okay," Harry said. "I need your help. Your memory."

Both men put their napkins to their lips at the same time and sat back in their chairs. "How wonderful," Prof said, "Will this be a contest?"

"Let's see." Harry leaned forward and said quietly as he could, "Do you, did you know the Martin sisters?"

"Louisa and Eleanor?" Prof smiled like a contented chess master who had just said "mate." *'It's a small town Harry, that part of Philadelphia.'*

"The same."

"Louisa would be about eighty, ah, eighty-two, three. I went to her party. Eleanor, a little younger? Used to live in Haverford? Disappeared about twenty years … ah, Lake Wasoka." Prof seemed very pleased with himself as he made this second connection.

Harry nodded, a small bow to undisputed genius.

Prof turned to Tee, beamed, then made a small, dismissive wave. "You knew their father at Merion, Tee. Tony Martin, pretty good doubles player right up until the end, so it was a bit of a fluke." Prof paused and turned back to Harry. "Had a stroke playing squash downtown about five years after you two left Penn. He was on Court 3. I was on Court 5. The kind of thing you remember. Wife's name, Margaret, though everyone called her Mazzie… I can't remember her family name. Tony lingered on for two, three weeks before he died. Terrible."

Tee nodded. "Now I remember. Louisa was still a bit of a wench right into her fifties. The other one, Eleanor, always looked liked an unmade bed. Lipstick on crooked, hair flying around, you know the kind of thing." Tee leaned forward and added softly, "Louisa had a re-pu-ta-tion."

Prof, listening, nodded and rolled his head back in recollection.

"Tony Martin, I think, did something downtown, respectable, but I don't think he prospered particularly. It was Mrs. Martin who had the money, wasn't it?" Tee put his thumb forward like a pointer. "Chestnut Hill?"

Prof nodded but he was staring at the ceiling. They were back in College Hall, Sociology 207, 'American Elites.' "No, Haverford," he said. "After Tony died, the daughters sold the house in Haverford and moved away."

Tee shrugged, turned back to Harry and asked, "Why the interest in the Martins?"

Harry had rehearsed for this.

"Well, you're right. They, the daughters, Eleanor and Louisa, still live up near us, near the Llewellyns, on Lake Wasoka. There's a case I've got going, and I need some family background." Harry spoke as the dishes were cleared. Jeffrey came and poured purple wine into small glasses while a waiter brought a dark souffle with a small pitcher of yellow sauce. Prof poured the sauce and broke the crust releasing a small puff of aromatic steam. He savored it then spooned some onto a plate. Harry watched him have two fork-fulls before he broke their contented silence.

"Do you think the mother's family, Margaret's, was weal... rich?"

"My, my you are curious," Tee said, as he ordered coffee. When the man had left Tee added "...and you're ever so casual." Tee shared a glance with Prof before continuing, "Yes, I remember now. Prof's right, Tony's father had been something with the Provident. Top rung job but, you're right Prof, nothing dynastic, if you catch my meaning. His wife I didn't..."

Prof put up a hand. "No, no, I've almost got it." He gazed into the middle distance. "Shippen," he said.

"Who?"

"The mother, the Mrs. Martin, was a Shippen."

"Emma's grandmother was ..."

"Different branch of the family," Prof interrupted Harry quickly with a small, dismissive wave with his hand. "One of the Shippens married down. That was Mrs. Martin's branch of the family. Nothing so grand as Kaye Shippen Newbold. That's how Kaye always insisted on being called, you know, with the emphasis on 'Shippen.' Thank God she lived in a civilized age, before hyphens."

"Granny Kaye," Harry said.

"C'mon Warren, don't pretend you knew her," Tee was laughing.

"No, no. It's what Emma calls her. All I ever knew was a picture."

"Quite the grand dame," said Prof, "but before your time, Harry. Right into the '50s you couldn't pick up the *Bulletin* "Country Life" pages without seeing her blazing away from her wheelchair. He took another spoonful of his dessert, then gestured with his spoon much the way he had once done with pieces of chalk.

"But back to the Martins. I forget the details, but one of the Shippen men, Mrs. Martin's branch, took up with a housemaid, or the nanny or someone equally unacceptable. Nineteenth century stuff. Mazzie Martin was the product of that side of the family. My aunt Polly could never see the Martin girls without remembering *that* story. Naturally, she attributed Louisa's later proclivities to the genes of the libidinous housemaid."

Tee snorted at this. "But of course we know differently, don't we Harry? Take the amorous career of your father-in-law—your sister-in-law for that matter—no one blames any of that on a saucy young thing from Armagh." Tee paused. "I haven't offended you, have I."

"Not at all. But just so we're clear, I neither confirm nor deny a thing." *'Come on Warren. Let's settle this once and for all.'*

Prof and Tee exchanged neutral looks.

"Would they have had valuable things?" Harry asked, "The Martins?"

"What an interesting question," Prof said. "I don't know. It's too bad my aunt isn't around. She could have given you the whole story."

Tee shrugged again. He accepted coffee in silence when it came, but made just the right amount of appreciative sounds when two additional glasses of port were delivered again by Jeffrey himself on a small silver tray.

"There's something special about the '78," he said. They drank it in silence. Harry had a vision of L.L.'s secretary whistling over this luncheon tab in a month's time.

"You know, they might have," Prof said when Jeffrey had left.

Harry risked a 'go on' gesture with his hand.

"Now don't rush me," Prof said. "Yes they might have. The ancestor didn't prosper after his dalliance and the house—it had a name..." He held a spoon stationary in his cup, then began to stir as he spoke. "Something to do with sycamores, or was it chimneys? No, I can't think of it, I'm sure they had many of both. Those evoked 'Elms' have driven everything else out of my brain. Well, it doesn't matter. It was one of those great gothic revival things off Germantown Avenue that they pulled down when Chestnut Hill became suburban. There was a bit of a stink. The real money was tied up in a trust and stayed with the children of the first family, but the child from the second family got all the family candlesticks, furniture, things like that."

"Mrs. Martin's people?"

"Uh huh. Her father, I think. Of course, by the time Louisa and Elaine..."

"Eleanor."

"Hmm?"

"It's Eleanor."

"Yes, yes, Eleanor," the old man seemed to lose his train of thought. But he put a finger to his nose and continued. "By the time they came along, all was officially forgotten, you know. Both members of the Assembly. By then no one was good enough for Louisa, except for, how shall I put it, recreational purposes. I seem to remember talk later of a child, but that was probably nonsense."

"A child? A father?" Harry didn't think to get this lucky.

"Oh, no one in particular. When there are lots and lots of friendships, it's difficult to say, isn't it. There was a six month period of 'travel' when the two sisters disappeared. Auntie Polly used to smile when she talked about how 'well' Louise looked after her 'vacation.' It was not a friendly smile, Mr., er, Harry." He blotted his lips with his napkin.

"So you think she, Louisa, had a child? But any idea whose?"

"Who can say? In those days such children were handed off. But I have to warn you, Harry, I think Lloyd Llewellyn's name was mentioned in connection with Louisa. So were several others. It does seem careless of Louisa to have let herself get caught that way. My my, this must be some case for you to want all this old tittle-tattle, must be more than forty years ago." Prof turned his head in a questioning way.

Harry pressed on. "So, L.L. ...?"

"Just tittle-tattle, Harry. They were 'great friends' as we used to say, but that was no more unusual for her than him."

"Anything else about a child?"

"No, just rumors. You could do that then. No loose ends, if you get my meaning."

Harry nodded. "Like everything, the story changes when you know the background."

"Mmm," Prof said. "Well I'm afraid that's all I can give you. Once the sisters moved off to New Hampshire, well..." The old man opened a hand to indicate he knew no more.

Tee drained off the last of his port, glad to change the subject. "Funny, you calling me like this. I was talking about you just last week. Meant to tell you last Friday. You remember the boy across the hall our freshman year, Cary Hymerling?"

"Cary? Sure I remember him."

"Hell of guy, Cary. My internist. Doesn't like the feel of my prostate. Always asks after you."

"You see Cary a lot?"

"Every time my PSA goes up." Tee began to shake his head. "What? Your eyes are wide open. What *are* you thinking?"

"I"m just surprised. You, ah, knowing Cary Hymerling."

"Dr. Hymerling. Actually, he's a hell of a nice guy, and like I say, asks after you. You should stay in touch."

Harry opened his mouth but Tee closed his eyes and brought his chin up. "Oh, I get it. He's a Jew. You think I don't have Jewish friends?"

"Well, you never did."

Tee dismissed this with a sniff. "A long time ago, Warren. The past. I spend most of my time with Jews now as a matter of fact. They're the only people with any talent."

"I'm sorry, I didn't mean..."

"Sure, no problem. Shouldn't have got on my high horse. It's just that, well, Cary's a nice guy and that has nothing to do with him having his finger up my ass every other month." Tee regarded the table. When he looked up he said, "You know, Harry, you've become a terrible snob."

"Boys, boys," Prof said to his middle-aged companions, "no fighting at the table."

PROF WAS UNSTEADY as the three left the Traveler's. Tee stationed himself by his elbow, though he never actually touched him. Harry watched as Tee settled the old man in a cab and then give a mock salute as the cab pulled away into traffic. The yellow car disappeared.

"Old age is a shipwreck," Tee said, frowning.

"He didn't seem bad at all."

"Mmm. He'll go back to that retirement home now and be sick for two days." Tee grimaced and put his hands in his pockets.

"Retirement home?"

"Wissahickon Pines," Tee said.

Harry shook his head slowly but Tee was no longer thinking about Prof.

"Now. Really, what's going on? Don't tell me 'nothing.' You must read my reviews. I'm world-renowned for being understanding. I am *trained* to empathize."

Harry blinked. "That obvious?"

"Yes." Then, "Look, I'm not the most sensitive guy in the world. You want to talk?"

"I guess I do, but right now I've got to read some old files."

"Tonight then?"

"Okay."

"Don't overwhelm me with enthusiasm."

"Okay, yes please, Harry said.

"Call me at home."

◆Δ◆

As promised, Rob Lefkowitz had the Martin family files waiting on the table of a conference room two floors down from the suite of offices reserved for senior partners. Harry was led there by the dark-haired girl. The golden haired Clarissa now favored him with no more than a perfunctory smile.

Even vestigial luxuries had been shorn away down here. This room was all utility. Harry was grateful for the chromium carafe of coffee with its nest of different colored packets of sweetener and a small bowl of ice stuffed with miniature plastic containers of cream and milk. He was particularly pleased not to encounter the young policeman.

Sharpened pencils, a half dozen felt tipped pens, green with 'Wharton-Biddle' in gold letters on the barrels stood at attention in a steel cup. A yellow legal pad, three contrasting blocks of colored post-it notes and a small calculator were arrayed next to four bulging manilla folders that rose a foot and a half from the table. The barest whiff of mold came from the folders.

"Just let me know if you want any copies, Judge." The second string receptionist stood alone in the small room with him so she knew the middle-aged visitor had 'dined well' at lunch. He took her neutral manner for disapproval. "Just dial 310 on the telephone," she said.

The files were arranged in chronological order, the oldest on top.

The first file concerned and included a 1928 prenuptial agreement between Heatherington Martin and Margaret Shippen. Miss Shippen had been the 'client' then as the owner of about two hundred thousand dollars in securities. In a document remarkably similar to the one Harry signed nearly a half century later, Mr. Martin disclaimed any right to these. Martin himself brought little to the marriage beyond his Penn diploma and a job with a Philadelphia bank Harry had not heard of. Apparently, however, he had expectations from his father, which Miss Shippen agreed to forgo. Ah romance. Harry wondered if Margaret Shippen's father had brought young Mr. Martin to Wharton Biddle for lunch.

Next was the thin probate file for Heatherington's father. The filing system number showed a file was opened in Montgomery County in 1937. Whatever Heatherington's expectations had been, all his father left him was a summer house on Lake Wasoka and a heavily mortgaged house in Haverford. There was some unpleasantness during estate administration over a due-on-death clause in the mortgage of the Haverford property, but after some correspondence back and forth, the bank had relented. A fiduciary deed to Heatherington and Margaret Martin as joint tenants was recorded and a new reduced mortgage agreed to. The original of this deed and a carbon of the mortgage were in the file. Harry said "Ah" out loud when he saw that Mrs. Martin had contributed to pay off the mortgage debt and that the value of her portfolio had fallen to less than one hundred thousand dollars. It occurred to him that by 1937 the Warrens in Hadley might have had as much money as the Martins in Haverford.

The third file was a litigation file four inches thick, with stiff, white on black photostats. It began with an inconclusive 1948 consultation with Mrs. Martin about a cousin complaining about a long-ago Shippen Family probate. The Prof had been dead on. But instead of 'candlesticks' they were arguing about a pair of portraits and a set of Eakins drawings. The portraits appeared to have gone back in exchange for some cash, but the drawings had stayed. There was an exchange of letters with a suburban law firm, some interview notes and a nasty handwritten note on light blue paper from Margaret about the bill. The file closed with an apologetic letter on bank letterhead from 'Tony' Martin to 'Butch' Detweiler, the addressee of the note.

The fourth file, with six inches of paper, was the thickest. It contained the Heatherington Martin trust documents and was opened in 1956. A net worth statement showed that by then Mrs. Martin's portfolio was back up to three hundred fifty thousand dollars and Heatherington had accumulated almost as much in securities himself. Since the family had prospered, and appeared likely to continue, Mr. and Mrs. Martin had executed a family trust with all the usual provisions for avoiding federal estate tax, as it was then written. The early part of the file contained a new exchange of 'Dear Tony' and 'Dear Butch' letters, the Dear Tonys on onionskin carbons but typed now on electric typewriters. Harry wondered if Butch Detweiler knew that Tony Martin had been transformed from interloper to be watched to one of the faithful to be protected? What a wonderful country.

The trust's schedules identified the usual securities for solid Philadelphians from the era, Pennsylvania Railroad, U.S. Steel, Philco and Dupont. The Eakins drawings were listed along with pieces of silver and porcelain valued at twenty-six thousand dollars. Miscellaneous furniture and furnishings had been given a nominal value: one thousand dollars in the schedule. That seemed to close out Emma's theory about the furniture, but only the silverware and Mrs. Martin's jewelry had been professionally appraised.

A file copy of a 1972 letter from a partner in the estates and trusts group to Heatherington was the first piece of photocopied paper. Yellowed and brittle, it was clear in its intention.

> *Dear Mr. Martin:*
>
> *Confirming our conversation of this date, you wish to amend the Heatherington Family Trust as per the enclosed draft despite our recommendation of this morning. You understand that, while it is unlikely, a claim could be made by a natural child of a descendant under the terms of this amendment.*
>
> *It is always difficult to revisit certain events from the past, but given recent trends in the law of New Jersey regarding confidentiality, adoptive proceedings can no longer be presumed immune from inspection.*
>
> *If, upon reflection, you wish to address the matter further or should your situation change, please let me know. The provision with which we're concerned is attached. Please accept our thanks for your kind words concerning George Detweiler. He was a great mentor and will be missed.*
>
> *Yours sincerely,*
> *Michael Stokes, Esq.*

A file copy draft of a page from the Heatherington and Margaret Martin Revocable Trust was next.

> SIXTH: Upon the decease of the surviving settlor this Trust shall continue for the benefit of settlors' children Louisa and Eleanor or for the legitimate issue of any child who may not survive the settlors, per stirpes. The Trust shall continue for the benefit of said named beneficiaries until the death of the survivor of said children of the settlors and thereafter to whomsoever the settlors' said children may unanimously and acting together appoint. No appointment by either child acting alone shall be effective whether or not it occurs after the death or disability of the other beneficiary. In default of such unanimous appointment, the Trust assets shall be distributed free from trust upon the death of the survivor to the legitimate issue of said children per stirpes and in default of issue, in equal shares to The University of Pennsylvania and The Philadelphia Historical Society.

A letter from Mr. Martin responded.

> Dear Mr. Stokes:
> Thank you for yours of the eighteenth. I understand your concern, however, Mrs. Martin and I am more concerned over my daughter' Eleanor's improvidence than the remote possibility of such a claim being made.

Just behind this was an onionskin copy of a single letter, December 1976, from Harry's old friend Oswald Popp to Mr. Martin.

> Confirming our discussion of this afternoon, you have decided to take no action to amend your estate planning documents despite the possibility of future claims based on pretermitted status. Should you decide to act on our recommendation, please contact Mr. Wood in our Estate

Planning section and he will prepare the amendment we discussed.
Sincerely,
Oswald Popp

Even Harry could read behind the red flag of the insertion of the word 'legitimate.' Prof had thought there was a child, and now Harry was sure of it.

Before tackling the fifth file, Harry went in search of a men's room. He regarded himself in the washroom mirror and thought on the contrasting conversational styles of Messrs. Stokes and Popp. The florid face in the mirror was slack. That man, with his disordered greying hair, his eyes barely able to face his own reflection. Did that man really think he could save himself from people like this? He splashed cold water into his eyes.

The fifth file was untitled. It had only a number, '768' and the words 'Absolutely Confidential' stamped on its grey cover. A second copy of Popp's letter to Heatherington Martin was stapled shut in a sealed envelope inside the fifth file, which was tied with string. The envelope was also stamped 'Absolutely Confidential.' On the cover were the words 'The Pines Manor, Cotuit, N.J.' Inside were the original birth records of Eleanor Martin, not Louisa Martin, and a 1962 letter from The Pines Manor to Oswald Popp. "Eleanor," Harry said out loud.

Dear Mr. Popp:
Thank you again for your referral of Miss Martin to Pines Manor. We have made the necessary financial arrangements directly with Mr. Heatherington Martin who, as you assured us he would, assumed all responsibility for his daughter's financial obligations. She is somewhat older than our typical resident but is now fitting in nicely here. It is a misfortune that she allowed matters to become so advanced before taking appropriate action. We did not find her sister's presence to be helpful and after some discussion with family members she has left. She will, however, return, if requested, for her sister's delivery.

When the time comes—we expect it to be as early as mid June—we will contact you to initiate proceedings in the Court of Chancery to facilitate proper placement.

Our consulting physician assures us that, despite Miss Martin's relatively advanced age for a first pregnancy, there is no reason to expect anything other than a routine confinement and delivery. As you predicted, the idea of having her sister accompany her here was a bad one. Miss Eleanor Martin is really quite nice when left on her own.

I have the honor to remain,
Very truly yours,
Marcia Holt, Director

An envelope, also sealed, was next. In for a dime. Harry took a pair of scissors from the tray of office supplies and cut the top off.

Inside were old white on black photostats of notes on checkups and surgeons notes on a caesarian delivery at a placed called Maple Grove Hospital, a baby girl safely delivered, after some difficulty, of Eleanor Martin.

"Eleanor," Harry said again, and shook his head as he tried to think of the tired, disorderly woman locked in carnal embrace with, well, with anyone. Still, there it was.

There followed, in June as predicted, the usual consent forms and adoption petitions on pre-printed forms. Father "unknown," including a mother's waiver of parental rights signed in Eleanor's neat schoolgirl's hand. A lawyer named Myron Katz represented Eleanor and one named Dennis O'Connor was guardian ad litem for the child.

In the midst of the forms and applications was a second letter from Miss Holt.

Dear Mr. Popp:

We will, of course, try to comply with your telephoned request at next Wednesday's hearing. However, as you know, we cannot absolutely assure success.

It is most unusual to nominate an adoptive family without informing them of the particulars of the adoptee's back-

ground, especially since it now appears that the birth mother's family intends to follow this child's progress into the future.

As you know, I have strongly advised against this course of action.

I have the honor to remain,
   Very truly yours,
     Marcia Holt, Director

He turned to the decree of the New Jersey Court of Chancery. It awarded custody of Baby Girl, unnamed, *sub nom* Pines Manor Home, to Reginald Newsome, 'Shop Supervisor,' and Carol Newsome, 'RN,' of West Chester, Pennsylvania.

"Jesus Christ," Harry said.

So there it was. Ephne's holy grail. She was one of these people after all. Harry tried to imagine the look on her face if she had read this, but found all he could conjure up was the photograph of her next to that tree, her last picture.

"Oh Ef...," he started to say, but instead, with the sound of that first syllable, he began to sob uncontrollably. Deep groans came and went as he struggled for control. "How could I?" he murmured, "How could I?" over and over until he settled into exhausted silence.

Once he was still, Harry set the Confidential file aside. With a deep breath he turned to a thin sixth file for Margaret Martin's estate, including a death certificate: "Metastasized carcinoma; liver failure; esophageal."

The 1972 date of death was a week after 'Michael Stokes, Esq.' had written to Heatherington Martin. '*If your situation changes...*' Harry noted that Mr. Martin's date of death came right after Popp's letter. Well, lawyers were never a beloved profession.

The bottom file, like the fifth, had no title. The words 'Absolutely Confidential' again appeared on the folder and the number '1076' was on the tab.

On top was a short letter to Oswald Popp on Mr. Martin's office stationary but hand written with the downtown Philadelphia address crossed out and a Haverford post office box written in.

> Dear Mr. Popp:
> Thank you for the report from your assistant on the young person we spoke about ...

A letter from a man who didn't want it read back to him later.

> ...enclosed is a check for $800 to Camp Abenaki. As discussed, please make arrangements with the Camp for the upcoming summer.

There were two more of these, one for each of the following years. A fourth letter, this time on plain white paper written in a wavering hand, said:

> Dear Mr. Popp:
> Thank you again for making the arrangements at St. Agatha's School. The tuition for the coming term is enclosed."

Next, a yellowing photocopy of a letter from Popp to Louisa Martin:

> Dear Miss Martin:
> I understand from our telephone conference that no further tuition assistance will be forthcoming for the young woman at the St. Agatha's School and that you do not wish to continue your late father's practice of paying her fees for Camp Abenaki in New Hampshire.
> I have communicated this to the parents. The girl was suspended from St. Agatha's during the Spring term as a disciplinary measure for stealing. The parents have concluded that this was the reason for termination of tuition assistance. I have made no comment and have, of course, not revealed either the identify of your family or the fact of Mr. Martin's decease.
> They have been informed there will be no further communications from this office.
> At your request, I have enclosed our final statement for services and will close our file.
>   Sincerely,
>   Oswald Popp

There was a final letter from Popp addressed to Louisa Martin in New Hampshire:

> *Dear Miss Martin:*
> I have not been able to recover the ring you spoke of during our telephone conversation and it does not appear likely we will be able to do so. If you had alerted me to this wish earlier, it is possible that we may have been able to persuade the girl's parents, but not now.
> Sincerely,
> Oswald Popp

There was no follow-up, and no administration of Mr. Martin's Estate. There was only an untitled folder containing of a copy of a transmittal letter to Louisa Martin enclosing a copy of the trust to her and confirming that there had been no Pennsylvania probate for either Martin parent, and a final piece of paper, dated only six months earlier, addressed to Cruikshank and Hannah:

> *Dear Mr. Hannah:*
> As per Ms. Martin's telephoned request, enclosed please find a photocopy of The Heatherington and Margaret Martin Trust with those Amendments prepared by us. A check of the Montgomery County Probate Court confirms that no administration of Heatherington Martin or Margaret Shippen Martin was undertaken there. We cannot affirm that further Amendments were not made.
> If we can be of any further assistance, please let me know.
> Yours sincerely,
> Michael Stokes, Esq.

Well, that would follow, but why was it in this file? Zach would want everything, but why had he asked so late?

Harry rang extension 310 as instructed. When the young lady arrived, Harry kept his back to her and pretended to be taking in the view. He motioned to the pile of documents he'd pulled from the trust file to cover his tracks. He hoped this would make it less obvious that he found the petitions, orders and file numbers of the New Jersey adoption proceedings. When she had gone he returned to the men's room and put more water on his face.

There was no need to guess what had kept Ephne at Wharton Biddle for so long. '*When you lose something, you remember.*' The unopened envelope proved that she never found it, but the fact that Popp caught her showed she was looking in the right places. Whatever had finally brought Ephne to the Martins' house, there, they had killed her for it. While Harry waited for his copies, Harry could picture the two old women confronted by Ephne for the first time, knowing what they'd done to her. Which one had reached for the shotgun?

CONFIDENT THAT HIS reddened eyes had recovered enough to get him through a brief interview, Harry waited for the dark-haired girl to bring back his copies. While he was waiting he called Grace.

"Not back tomorrow!" She was obviously furious. "You realize I now have to get your good friend Judge Stevens to cover. It's almost five o'clock, I ..." She subsided into angry silence.

Harry swallowed, almost nostalgic for the time when all he worried about was professional precedence. "Sorry..."

But Grace was onto something else. "Listen, you think of any reason why T.J. would want to know who called us a week ago Friday?"

"No."

"Ordinarily I'd tell him to stuff it, but he said he needed to 'exclude' us from a call made by the victim of that Green Mountain shooting. Funny thing, though, I checked next door, and he didn't ask Judge Stevens."

Harry couldn't do anything but swallow.

"The only call I remember was ..." Grace began, then she too went silent.

"Well, ah ..." Harry began.

Grace cut him off, now sharp tongued and positive. "The nerve of that guy. A judge's chambers. I'll just tell him we didn't get any such call."

Desperate, Harry had to risk it. "And, ah, did it have anything to do with Mrs. Baker?"

"Well that's what I mean, Judge. Family business. Nothing to do with T.J.'s victim." Harry could hear the conviction leaking out of her voice.

Another silence, then finally. "I can be in tomorrow afternoon."

"I wouldn't," Grace said. "Wednesday's soon enough."

"No I'll be there."

To HARRY'S SURPRISE, as he hung up, it was the blonde Clarissa who appeared with his finished copies. "I promise not to drop them," Harry said.

"You are okay, aren't you Judge?" He hadn't amused her. Her gaze was level, skeptical and devoid of sympathy.

"Of course."

"Well, are you all settled here?" She gestured at the files. "Need any further copies?" She asked this as she set a letter on Wharton Biddle stationary down on the table.

Harry read the two paragraphs quickly, saw that they confirmed he would be burned at the stake if he delivered the copies or divulged what he'd read to any third party other than in the course of attorney discipline proceedings, and scrawled his signature.

"Thank you, ah …"

"Clarissa." *Klehrissa*

"Of course."

◆△◆

TEE'S TOWNHOUSE IN the Society Hill neighborhood, only a few blocks from the Mask and Whig club, was a twenty-minute walk in the twilight. Tee greeted him at the door.

Oblivious to the gentrified throng moving behind him on the brick sidewalk, Harry looked up and said simply, "I'm in trouble."

"Obviously," Tee said. "I hope this means you're not going to shovel the same bullshit you gave us at lunch."

HARRY CARRIED ONLY ONE certainty with him the next morning as he and Tee boarded the smallest Llewellyn plane toward a noon-time landing at the Windsor, New Hampshire airport. Ephne didn't just stumble into the Martin house. She'd been headed there all her life.

Tee agreed with his second conclusion as well: That somehow those self-important, empty women had killed her for the impertinence of reminding them of who she was, who they were, what they had done to her. That Tee Ingersoll should agree, 'Ted' Ingersoll, for that matter, shouldn't have mattered, but Harry felt heartened by it just the same. He'd told Tee everything and with the ink still wet on his promise to keep Wharton & Biddle's files confidential, Harry had shown him those as well.

But how? Louisa, they agreed would shoot Ephne out of hand, but the crazy old woman in the deposition had looked like she could barely get out of bed. Eleanor was healthy enough, but who could imagine her doing anything so decisive. Then again, who could imagine her with her legs wrapped around someone who left her in need of the services of Oswald Popp? More to the point, why would Ephne have told them? She must have just come across something: the trust documents, perhaps, maybe some of the originals of the copies he had just read. After all those years going through probate files, Ephne knew where and how to look through people's papers. She had learned enough to have come and asked him about powers of appointment. But he couldn't imagine Ephne telling the Martins any of this or them listening if she had! Something had set them off, but what?

In the small hours Harry had devised a plan, not much of one, but something anyway. If he could get Eleanor on the witness stand, he might get her to blurt out something. It would just be Zach and the Bank's lawyers. Zach would give him an opening. He'd have to put up a show of resistance, but it wouldn't be more than that. The Bank's lawyers wouldn't give a damn. He laid his idea out for Tee.

"You can do that? Make her answer questions?"

"No, of course not, but if she gets knocked off-balance, blurts out a wrong answer, I may get the county attorney to focus on them and leave me out of it."

"And what do I do?"

"Just watch. You'll see a slip before I would, some mistake that you'd catch. Something I wouldn't notice."

"Pretty thin, Warren."

"Tee, I'm out of options. He's already questioning my clerk."

"Maybe they'll give us adjoining cells. It'll be like old times. Hell, I don't have to be in Vegas until Thursday. I can give you two days." He turned serious then. "Look, Harry, I don't know much about these things or how they work, but has it occurred to you that if this doesn't work, they'll forget everyone else and just turn to you? Not just for the warrant you signed, but for the shooting?"

◆△◆

PICKING THEM UP at the airport, Emma, lonely from her days alone after a week of refereeing Harry and Livy, tried to strike up a conversation, but both Harry and Tee were too deep in thought. Finally she said, "You two are pretty communicative."

"Mmm." Harry patted her knee to avoid saying anything further.

"Well what did you learn from two days in Philadelphia?"

"A little about port wine," Harry said, "Not to mention a short sharp lecture on anti-semitism from my friend here."

"If the shoe fits, Warren."

"Sorry. I shouldn't have brought it up," Emma said. Harry knew that desperate as she was to know when Tee was leaving, she would never ask.

Harry looked at his watch. "I'm going to run up to court," he said. "Take Tee with me."

"Take Tee?" she turned toward him.

"Research," Tee said from the back seat.

"All right, don't tell me," Emma said. "You know how I like mysteries."

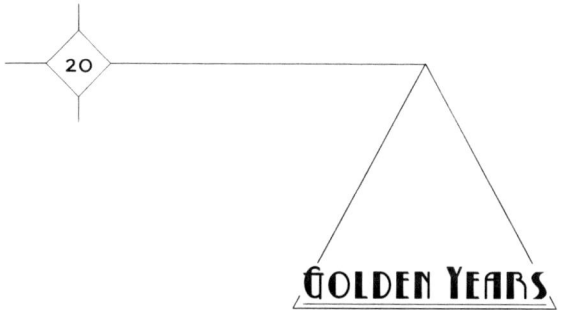

20 GOLDEN YEARS

As Harry Warren began his survey of the stack of Wharton & Biddle files, Gregg Leavitt was inspecting a sign that announced the "Brandywine Presbyterian Retirement Home." It was weather-streaked and faded, and the overgrown lawn around it testified to better days now past. Even so, the three-story gothic grey-stone building with its newer spoke-wings of single story grey brick were an improvement on the Hadley County Home. Gregg left the rental car in the otherwise empty parking area marked 'VISITORS.' A second lot, just visible beyond, held a dozen older vehicles in varying states of disrepair.

Entering through a heavy oak door, Gregg was met by the thick, sweet heavy smell of institutional food, industrial strength cleaner, and very old people. He was in what looked like the living room of a large private house. A woman with thick glasses sat behind a desk at the opposite end of the room and watched him cross the worn maroon carpet.

"Help you, hon?"

Gregg made what he hoped was a sympathetic smile and held her magnified eyes with his. She seemed to soften. He saw a tray with the remains of what looked like two lunches on a small table behind her chair.

"I'm hoping to speak to Mrs. Newsome."

"Carol?" The lady's eyes widened further behind the lenses.

"Yes, Carol Newsome." Gregg put both hands on the desk.

"Well, you're in luck. We're just finishing lunch." She gestured to her tray. Then she leaned toward him and asked in a near whisper, "This have something to do with her daughter?"

Gregg nodded.

"Terrible thing, terrible. 'Course you'd hardly know it from Carol. They told her day before yesterday but all she wanted was to get back to her bridge game. That's the way it is with the old. Some of them. They lose interest."

Gregg tilted his head to show interest, not wanting to interrupt the flow.

"The girl never seemed to care much either, ya' know. Comes around—came around—twice a year, tops. 'Course its like that with the adopted. Blood is thicker than water, so they tell me, anyway." The eyes turned up at him. Gregg wondered whether he had earned a category.

"I'm sure it is," he said. "You said they were finished, uh, Mrs. Newsome was finished with her lunch?"

"Sure, hon, sure. Let me go get her." She bumped the tray as she rose. She was almost normal size above the waist, but huge from the hips down. He was surprised she wore slacks, but as she walked toward an open door and the sound of plates and silverware being handled, Gregg saw that her legs remained enormous down to her shoes. She had a rolling rhythmic gait, but the top half of her was not synchronized with the bottom. Two people rather than one. Her breathing was labored. Well, that's how it was with the pear shaped.

◆Δ◆

THEY FOUND MRS. NEWSOME arranged in a wheelchair with her back to a three-windowed alcove. The afternoon sun revealed the transparency of her skin beneath dangerously thin white hair that had been bent into a fragile imitation of a wave. Her hands were busy in her lap. She didn't smile or offer her hand when introduced.

"Let me tell you, first, Mrs. Newsome, how very sorry we are," Gregg began.

The woman's dark brown eyes regarded him. 'Yes, yes," she said, then looked back down.

Gregg waited for something further. When nothing came he gestured to the chair opposite her as if to request permission to sit. She made a slight shrug and gestured with one of the busy hands. "Why ask me? You're going to do as you damn well please."

"I'm the investigating officer," Gregg said.

"Some man of hers. You'll see." Mrs. Newsome said, and made a snuffling sound of disapproval.

"Some man?"

"She had lots of men. Always did."

"Well, of course we want to follow up on every possibility, Ma'am. Do you know anyone that we might..."

"Know? Know! Hah, that's a good one." The old lady's eyes glowed. There was a click of dentures. "As if *we'd* ever know any of them."

"You weren't ac..." Gregg began.

"We didn't know *any* of them. She was either ashamed of them or ashamed of us. One or the other." Mrs. Newsome turned her head away from him toward two black women coming up the hall, their melodic contralto laughter contrasting with her sharp tone. They mistook her turn for interest in them.

"Af-noon Carol," they said in unison pronouncing her name as a single syllable.

She waved toward them, but dismissively, and turned her eyes to the floor.

When they had passed, she spoke more softly. "Ashamed of them or us. Mostly us, I think."

Gregg felt this needed a response and started to say "Well..."

"Oh yes. Since she was old enough to walk. It was like she looked around the crib and knew she was adopted and couldn't believe she'd landed in Chester, PA."

"That's where you lived? In Chester?"

"Reg and I lived in the same house for forty-nine years. I did, anyway. Reg only had forty-six."

"That's Mr. News..."

"No, *my* boyfriend." The old woman turned back to him after almost barking out this interruption. Her teeth clicked again. She swallowed. She took a deep breath and then, to Gregg's surprise, she smiled. In the ruins of her face he could see at least one set of lines from long ago laughter and thought she should smile more.

"They warned us, of course. Told us to expect that she'd be proud. That's what the agencies did in those days. 'Personality Traits, Indicated' they called it. Assertive - nine. Defiant - ten. Ten on a scale of one to ten mind you."

"I didn't know that."

"It's not like you can take them back. Not like a puppy from the pound. Believe me, there were days when I would have if I could."

"She was a—difficult child?" Gregg thought of his own daughter and the impossibility of such a thought.

"Difficult," Mrs. Newsome snorted. "You could say that, difficult. If you call staying out all night when you're fifteen 'difficult' or getting expelled from prep school for stealing 'difficult.'"

"She had trouble at school?"

"No, no, she was smart enough. Got good marks, especially when she got out to State College. Came easy to her. She couldn't keep her hands off what wasn't hers is all."

"I understand she was an expert in antiques, art."

"Yes she was. I have to say that for her. She was good at that. She was happy with that, least I think she was."

"You didn't see a lot of your daughter, then. Recently I mean?"

"Twice a year. Called once a month. Ever since she moved to New York."

"She ever mention anything that would bring her to New Hampshire, Lake Wasoka?"

The old lady leaned forward, suddenly interested. "That damned place? They told me she was on a mountain. They didn't say anything about that damned Lake."

Well yes, but we're pretty certain she had been at one of the lake houses. She was ... found only a mile from the Lake," Gregg said.

"I always told Reg that place, that snooty camp, would be the death of her."

"Camp."

"Camp Abenaki. That man from Philadelphia, the lawyer with the funny name, Popp. He gave us the money to send her there. 'Course when she was expelled from school, all that stopped."

Gregg felt himself straighten. "Oswald Popp, Oswald Popp from Wharton Biddle?"

"Like there could be *two* Oswald Popps," she said.

"So Os... Mr. Popp gave you money for your daughter. He did this on behalf..."

"Of her people. His 'principals,' he said. And, no, he didn't give it to us. He paid the camp, paid the school."

"But he did have a client?"

"Of course he did. But that was the point. They didn't want us to know who they were. We never knew the name. Popp was the man we dealt with. Till he cut her off."

"We know that shortly before her death she was appraising property at the house of some people originally from Philadelphia. Martin. Does the name 'Martin' mean anything to you?"

"No."

Her expression softened. "She begged and begged and somehow Reg got enough together to send her back to camp for half a summer. Then when we went up to get her, end of July, she just cried all the way home. Never said thank you, just kept saying 'Why can't I stay? Why can't I stay?'"

"Do you think your daughter's, ah, death, had anything to do with camp, Camp Abenaki?"

"No, probably not. The camp closed. Good riddance in my opinion. But that lake's where she always wanted to go every summer. One day she sat here, right in that chair"—she pointed at Gregg's lap—"and told me those were the only happy days of her childhood. Only happy days." The old woman contorted her face and showed a different, deeper set of lines.

"And, it was Oswald Popp's idea to give you the money to send her to Camp Abenaki?"

"No, he just paid the bill. Nasty man. Rude. Came in and told us his 'principal'—'principal,' I remember the word—had instructed him to enroll 'Miss Newsome' at Camp Abenaki. He was real specific. It had to be that particular camp. Later this 'principal' told him to enroll her at St. Agatha's.

"Not like they asked us," she said in a sing-song cadence. "After all, what do a shop foreman and a nurse know about the daughter they raised that the 'principal' doesn't know better."

"So Popp also provided the money to send her to school. St. Ag...?" Gregg was writing the name of the school.

"St. Agatha's."

"Yah, St. Agatha's as well as the camp?"

Mrs. Newsome nodded. "Course she didn't have the right clothes, she didn't live in the right neighborhood. She learned that quicker than anything else they taught her in that damn school. God. I wish we'd never laid eyes on that man, Popp."

"Why? Wasn't it..."

"A good deal?" She cut him off. "Sure, it was, or would have been for anyone else, but not our Ephne, not the little princess. Little thief. Got caught taking money out of the other girls' lockers spring of her freshman year. Expelled. Popp found out, must have told his 'principal.' Never a dime after that. Back to public school. Didn't she love that."

"This Mr. Popp contacted you about the expulsion?"

"I contacted him," she snorted again. "I called him that summer. The school said they'd take her back, so I called, called him at that fancy law firm downtown, Wharton something."

"In Philadelphia?"

"No, Paris, France," the old woman said, mocking him. "That's when he told me that his 'principal' wasn't going to make any more payments. 'The "experiment" hasn't worked out' was what he said."

"He called it an experiment?" Gregg shook his head. "You're sure he never mentioned a name? Did you ever hear the name 'Martin'?"

"That's what he called it, an 'experiment.' Then he said, 'You are not to call me again.' I tried to talk to him about the camp, how she had her heart set on it, but while I was trying to talk to him he just hung up on me in mid-sentence, and no, he never mentioned any names."

Surprisingly her eyes shone and large tears came out of each at the same moment. Her voice rose, a girl's voice.

"It wasn't our fault, you see. She had it in her head that there was a big family out there. She even had names for them. They were going to take her back, that we, Reg and me, we were just some terrible mistake." She wept then, her shoulders trembling.

Then she looked directly at him, eyes red and wet but with the beginning of a smile and said, "He was sorry he did that, though. Hanging up on me the way he did."

"Sorry?"

"He called back a week later and wanted the ring back."

Gregg remembered the glint of gold from the closed hand. "The ring, plain gold, with a crest of some kind?"

"A St. Agatha's ring. He gave it to us for her when she was accepted. Belonged to 'one of the principals,' he said."

"So you..."

"I told him he could go to hell."

Gregg waited. He looked away at cars arriving in the parking lot beyond the window, old cars, coming and going. He looked at his watch, 3:45, shift change.

"Nothing more recent? Nothing she said that would connect her with anyone in New Hampshire?" Gregg asked.

But Carol Newsome's mind was elsewhere. "School was bad enough, but that damned camp," the old woman said with sudden ferocity. "Some camp counselor filling her head with ideas about her *real* mother. She heard two of them talking about how she looked just like *her*, whoever that was.

"From that moment on, we never got a moment's peace. 'Wait till I find my real mother,' she'd say whenever something didn't go her way. Then she got that ring! As if that was ever going to do her any good, abandoning her the way they did. 'Real mother!' What did she ever do for her?"

"Did your daughter know about Mr. Popp, Oswald Popp? I mean, she worked at Wharton Biddle. She had a run-in with him there, much later. That couldn't be a coincidence."

Carol Newsome gave Gregg a sharp look. "You're smarter than I thought, young man."

Gregg stared back.

Then she said, "Well, she never said so, but of course it wasn't a coincidence. Somehow she found out, probably heard Reg and I talking. I asked her when she started there, even warned her, but she'd get all airy with me. Said she didn't know what I was talking about. But they must have found out, put two and two together. They fired her, didn't they?"

Gregg tried to give the flood of words the attention he thought she wanted for them. Then he asked, "Did you ever meet Susan Shubert?"

"No. Heard about her, of course." The woman stiffened in her chair. "We weren't good enough to meet her."

This new anger seemed to compose Carol Newsome. She produced a crumpled tissue and used it to dry her cheeks. Then she released the brake and tested the wheels. "There are only five other women in this place with sense enough to play bridge. Can you wheel me into the rec room?... she pointed. "I don't want to be late, lose my spot."

Gregg rose, moved behind her and began to push.

As they rolled, he tried again. "But anything more recent? About New Hampshire? Since she left Philadelphia?" The old lady only pointed at where she wanted to go.

They passed door after door as they moved down the hall. The opened ones revealed the spare double rooms. One doorway held a surprisingly beautiful woman who looked about ninety. She wordlessly reached up from her wheel chair to touch Gregg's arm. She stared with uncomprehending eyes.

It was then that Carol Newsome said, "No, thank God, she hadn't talked about New Hampshire or that damn camp for seven or eight years, not since her big romance didn't work out."

"Big romance?" Gregg leaned down toward the white hair.

"Oh, well, that was another big secret. That was about a year after Reg died and a year before she pushed me in here. 'This one is different,' she said. *He* was from New Hampshire. She thought she was going to marry him."

"You're sure of that? Your daughter told you this man was from New Hampshire?"

"Some big shot. She never said who, just that it had to be a secret because he held some kind of public office."

"Any idea what kind of office?"

"No. I asked of course. That's all she would say, 'Public Office,' like he was the governor or something. Then she got all coy and said she had to be discreet, New Hampshire being such a small state. I assume that meant he was already married. I told her he didn't sound like such a catch to me, sneaking around to see her."

"What did she say to that?" They had entered a large well-lit room. Gregg could now see three other ladies at a card table, one, like Mrs. Newsome, in a wheelchair. One of the other two was expertly shuffling a deck of cards.

"Oh she got all high and mighty then. 'You can't talk about him like that,' she said. 'He's a wonderful man.' Well, they're all wonderful when you've got the itch." Carol Newsome made a little bark of a laugh and two of the card players looked up.

"Did she tell you his age? Anything about him at all?"

"Funny thing," she said. Gregg stopped ten feet short of the group.

"Funny?"

"She would never talk about her boyfriends, just change the subject but she wanted to talk about that one, even though she made such a secret about who he was. The way she stood up for him. Once I asked, 'What's so great about Mr. Wonderful' and she said he was a war hero. Got himself wounded in Vietnam."

"Wounded?"

"Almost crippled. Had a limp, she said." Carol Newsome motioned him forward. "I guess he couldn't have been all bad, after all. A veteran and all."

"This was eight years ago? You're pretty sure?"

"Yes. Next time I saw her, she didn't want to talk about him. Said it was all in the past and why did I keep bothering her about it. We had quite a row. That's when she told me the only happy days of her childhood were up at that damn camp and now she would never go back there. It wasn't long after that she stuck me in this place."

Even as she talked, Carol Newsome's eyes were fixed on the table. The player shuffling said, "Carol, Agnes needs her meds at five thirty. Are we going to start?"

"Yes, yes" Carol said. "Goodby Mr, Mr. uh—goodbye." She dismissed him with a wave.

Gregg maneuvered her into the table. He considered introducing himself but saw that the others, like Mrs. Newsome, were much more interested in the cards. They didn't greet each other.

"Well, thank you, Mrs. Newsome," Gregg said.

Gregg left the four at their table. He glanced back at them framed in the light of an upright lamp, a feeble assist to the grey twilight from the window behind them. He knew he was forgotten before he was gone.

At his car Gregg saw the two black nurses from the hall get into the same car in the next lot over. He felt a sharp and unexpected longing to be in Hadley that night. He checked his watch. There was an eight o'clock flight to Windsor. If he missed it, he would have to spend another night here. He looked back at the building and shivered but not from the cold. Because, of course, he knew now who had killed Ephne Newsome.

◆△◆

STACY TOOK HIS call from the Philadelphia airport. "I hope you got good news. He's been on the warpath all afternoon."

"Now what?"

"I don't want to spoil the surprise."

Gregg made a sound of impatience.

"Okay, something about that Newsome woman's cell phone," Stacy said. "Look, don't get him goin,' huh. I gotta get out of here. My daughter's got basketball tryouts tonight."

After a click and silence T.J. came on. "Jesus, Leavitt, you ever think of checking in?"

"Sorry, I ..."

"Well, don't be sorry, be smart. That cell phone call to that Applebone..."

"Applebaum."

"... Yah, Applebaum, him. The call that showed up on her bill looks like it got routed to Judge Warren's chambers."

"Jesus, T.J., ah, Mr. Carr, we're sure of that?"

"Uh huh, Brittany, the girl in the clerk's office who takes the calls to the main number, she remembers one coming in about that time, female caller and, like she always does, she tells the caller that judges don't take calls on pending cases. Woman's voice on the other end tells her it's a personal call. She starts to leave her name, 'but I told her we don't take messages,' Brittany says. Says she remembers it because the caller got snotty and she tries Warren's chambers. There's no one there, of course, being Friday afternoon. Brittany tries to tell that to the woman and she hangs up on her."

Gregg could feel himself swelling up as he listened.

"Look," he said, when T.J. had finished, "Newsome had a boyfriend in New Hampshire, sometime ago. Seven – eight years at least, and accordingly to Newsome's mother the guy held some kind of public office *and* had a serious war wound."

There was a long silence. Then, "You're shitting me, right?"

"Oh there's more. The other woman I interviewed, the friend, Shubert, she works at this Wharton Biddle law firm. She's sure this guy, it has to be the same guy, he lived in New Hampshire. She says he went to Penn *and* made a bunch of calls to Newsome at the firm. How many guys in New Hampshire fit that ..."

Before he could finish, Gregg heard T.J. yell. "Stacy! Sta... shit." Then, "Gone, everybody's gone around here. Look, you see what happens when you wait until six o'clock to check in?"

"Sorry Mr. Carr."

"All right, all right. Dammit, I thought Grace was getting cute with me. Look, you know and I know what this means. But we got to be careful, right? I'll get the clerk's office on it in the morning. If Warren called her from here, they may have records downstairs. And look, I'm not going to bother you now but we did okay checking the motels around the Windsor airport. It didn't make sense before, but now ..." He exhaled into the phone, and his voice turned soft. "Look, Leavitt, uh Gregg, I suppose since we're both about to implicate a county court judge in a murder case you can start calling me 'T.J.'"

◆△◆

UNCLE RUSS WAS WAITING at the nearly empty Windsor terminal when Gregg's plane landed at 11:30. The old man said nothing, only showed him a grin as he shifted his cup of Dunkin Donuts coffee into his left hand and took Gregg's bag.

Once through the automatic doors to the street the shock of a New Hampshire November night came like a slap in the face. Gregg pulled his sport coat closed and bent into the wind.

"Turned cold this afternoon," Russell said. He motioned toward his car in the short term lot. "Step on in, will you. If I get out of here in seven minutes, I'll save two bucks."

They'd gone five miles before Russell spoke again. "Erin's got a temperature. Angie seemed pretty tired, pretty stressed." It was his explanation for meeting the plane.

Grateful for the break in their latest contest of silence, Gregg knew he had to say something. Ever since he'd left the nursing home he'd run the story over in his mind. He knew, knew in his heart that Judge Warren was tied into this. Yet, deep, deep down, he wanted him tied in; that he *wanted* to poke a hole in that world of big houses and expensive cars, where they looked right through you, and nobody worried about fan belts and credit card bills. These people who thought this made them different, better.

"Uncle Russ...," he said. When he didn't continue Russell turned toward him for a moment before returning his attention to the road.

"Look," Gregg continued. "There's no easy way to say this so I'll just say it. There's evidence, good evidence, that the woman on Green Mountain, Ms. Newsome, Ephne Newsome, was mixed up with someone, someone we both know."

Russell didn't answer but pursed his lips to show interest.

Gregg stared straight ahead. "We, I believe Judge Warren may be involved in this, that he knew the victim."

Russell prided himself on not showing emotion or surprise but he knew his mouth fell open as he searched his nephew's profile for something other than the weary unhappiness it showed.

"You got to be kidding."

"I wish I was, for your sake, if nothing else."

"Harry Warren. C,' mon…" In spite of himself Russell's smile of disbelief gently faded away.

Then Gregg said "You got any vacation built up, this might be a good time to take it."

Russell felt concern for Harry Warren, but more than that, he didn't like the new righteous tone in his nephew's voice. He stared straight ahead. They were on the part of Route 16 that had once been concrete. No matter how much asphalt was laid over it, a rhythm of 'bump-bump' … 'bump-bump' sounded through the car at one second intervals. After a dozen or so of these Russell said, "You think I'm made that way?"

"No, but I thought you deserved a chance."

"Just checkin.'" After a silence Russell said, "You know, a man turns prick just 'cause he thinks he's right, is still a prick. Lots of ways, he becomes a worse prick than the guy who's just getting by."

They made eye contact again, but both knew better than to take it further.

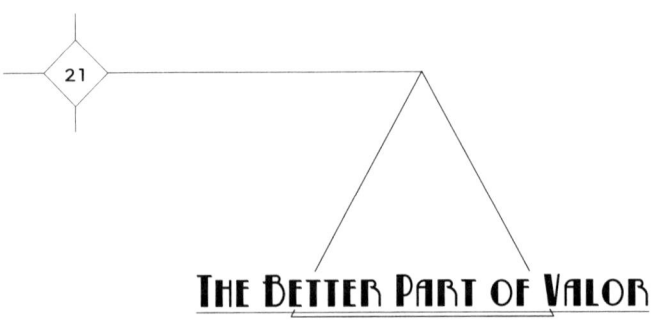

The Better Part of Valor

Prof Rush had always been fond of saying "Legitimacy is what you fall back on when things go wrong." This was much on Harry Warren's mind when he re-entered the Hadley County courthouse Tuesday afternoon, a brown Wharton Biddle expand-file containing the Martin papers under his arm. On his drive north, leaving Emma and Tee, uneasy in one another's company, he concluded that legitimacy—and innocence, of a sort—was about all he had left. He was still a sitting county court judge and T.J. would have to remember that.

But even a paranoid can have real enemies, and Harry wondered if it wasn't perception rather than paranoia that took hold of him as he approached the metal detectors and sheriff's deputies at the courthouse door. Ordinarily, judges were waved through a with a smile.

Today was different, or was it? Did he imagine it, or was there a certain hesitancy, a failure to meet his eye? Perhaps that deputy opening brief cases, who waved him through only after being told to do so, was a new man. Perhaps he read too much into the silence of the single deputy escorting him around the waiting line and across the floor to the door marked 'County Court Chambers.' Whatever it was, when the door shut behind him, Harry felt winded. It was then he realized he'd been holding his breath.

"Grace, I need you to bring your book in," Harry said without preliminaries as he walked by her uplifted face.

Her mouth opened slightly, then closed. Displays of decisiveness from Harry were unexpected. With a rueful glance at the pile of unfinished court work, now risen to the height of her shoulders, she nevertheless followed him into his office. Unusual for her, she closed the door and waited for him to turn around.

"Look, I can't explain," Harry said quickly, "but now I need you to clear the decks for the rest of the week." Grace surprised him by remaining silent. "... and we need an expedited hearing in the Martin case scheduled for tomorrow."

"Tomo ..." She broke off. There was a five-day rule for hearings. She would have to bully everyone into submitting to the judge's latest whim.

"Good," Harry said, trying to sound all business as he sat behind his desk. "Look, I think there's a connection between the Martin case and that woman who was murdered on Green Mountain."

"Okay...?" Grace dragged the word out into a question. *'What business was it of yours?'* She seemed to ask.

"Don't tell anyone this when you call, but I have to make sure we can still go forward with the probate appeal. If we can't, if it gets all bollixed up in the criminal case, it won't be ... ah ... fair to the bank." So far, so good, Harry had delivered the line he'd rehearsed in the car.

"The Martin case mixed up with ... Ephne's ... or should I say, Jordan's case?" Grace said.

With a sinking heart Harry let his eyes rise to hers. Having paused, then pronouncing the names with such care, Grace didn't need to say anything else.

"I do take a lot of messages," she continued. "Since I began working for you I find that I *dodge* a lot of messages. Hundreds in fact. People forget things, especially at my age. But, Harry, do you think I'd forget a woman who walks in unannounced and calls herself Jordan?"

His resolve was melting. It always did, and he had no doubt it showed. When he said nothing, Grace explained. "Stacy brought in the return of the warrant you gave T.J. on Saturday, it was the same woman."

He looked away. "Look, Harry. I picked my side a long time ago. I'm seventy-two years old and they can't do anything to me. Nothing that matters anyway." Harry only nodded and looked into the middle distance.

"It gets worse," she said. "T.J. came in here this morning and started asking me if I'd gotten any calls lately from someone named Miss Ephne Newsome."

"This morning?"

"Oh yah. Cute bastard. Pretended to be wondering if *I'd* got the message." She rolled her eyes. "Told him we get lots of messages but I didn't remember that one. He gave me that spider to the fly smile of his, pulled at his nose for a while, and wished me a Happy Thanksgiving. Then, just as he's leaving, asks me, real casual, could he and young Leavitt have an appointment with you today? "New matter, he says."

"Today?" Harry repeated. He knew it would come to this, but thought he might have a week, a couple of days at least. There was no possibility he could get through an interview with T.J. today with anything less than an obstruction of justice charge by the end of the afternoon.

"You sure you want in on this?" Harry asked.

"I am in." She took a memo book out from under her steno pad. It was made up of sequentially numbered double leaves, pink for the original sheets which were divided by perforations into three separate message slips a page and white carbonized copy pages which were not perforated. "This is a new book. I seem to have lost the one I was using last week." Neither of them had to dwell on what T.J. might later make of such a "loss."

Harry weighed what she said and nodded back, but couldn't meet her eyes. "You want me to tell you about it?" He owed her that at least.

"Not particularly." She put the new message book down. Then, more gently, she said "Maybe later. Maybe now's a good time for me to be as stupid as T.J. thinks I am."

"All right." Harry looked up. Then, as if there had been nothing said, "Expedited hearing on Louisa's competency with a follow-up status conference in court on, let's call it 'asset preservation' tomorrow, clients and counsel?"

"Done," she said.

"Okay then. I've got to make myself scarce. Right now I can't let myself be interviewed by T.J., and I think he knows that. He isn't going to sit around and wait."

"You've got that right," Grace said. "Stacy's already called this morning to confirm that appointment in ...," she looked at her watch "... twenty two minutes. 'Follow-up on the warrant' she called it. You want me to tell them anything in particular?"

Harry thought this over. T.J. wouldn't be using a subterfuge if he was positive. He was confident, but he wasn't quite sure. Yet. "No, as soon as I get out of here tell him I was taken sick. Give him a new appointment for tomorrow, after the hearing. He won't go nuts if he thinks it's just one more day. Just get me until after the hearing with the Martins. I've got to get some answers first. I need the time, Grace."

"Well, you want to write out an administrative order?" Ordinarily, when away from the courthouse Harry appointed Amanda to act on his cases in his absence. That would, no doubt, be Exhibit 4 in any future trial.

He thought for a moment. "No, let's keep it vague. Just make sure Zach Hannah and the bank's lawyers are here early. I want to walk right onto the bench." Harry looked at the clock. "I've really got to get out of here. T.J. may just decide to say the hell with it and come in here. Wouldn't he love to make an arrest?"

"Ar... " The old woman's face fell and one shoulder sagged. "That bad?" Harry went over and put his hands on her shoulders.

"Look, thank you for not asking, but no, I didn't kill anyone. I'm not guilty, not of that anyway. But I'm not particularly innocent either. I've done enough in the last seven days to end five careers. And my marriage. I probably won't ever be able to prove it, but I think, no, I'm pretty sure, the Martins killed Ephne Newsome. I don't know how but I think I know why. T.J. is trying to rope me into this and, what's worse, he may really think I did it. I'm just scrambling now, Grace. You can see that, don't you?" Harry hoped this came out all manly and decisive, but even he could hear his voice rising as much in tone as in volume. In the movies he had loved as a boy, this would be the scene where the supporting actor was shaken by the leading man. 'Get a hold of yourself, Warren.' Something like that.

What Grace asked was, "Where *are* you going?"

He smiled at her. "Stupid, right?"

"Ok."

As she said this, Grace began to look every one of her seventy-two years. The rims of her eyes turned red and they had acquired a wet shine. She seemed to shrink. Harry took her in a clumsy embrace. Beneath her suit she was all bones. They stood together, two frightened people, frail in their different ways.

There were two discreet knocks on the door then but it was opened almost immediately by Russell. He took in the scene.

"I can come back," he said.

"Naw, we're done," Grace said. She sniffed wetly and tried to make a roguish smile. Failing, she moved away from Harry toward the door. "Good thing you came when you did, though. His Lordship was starting to enjoy himself." She seemed to recover at the sound of her own voice. "I suppose you'll want the rest of the Martin files?" she said to Harry.

"Uh huh."

Russell let her by him, then turned to Harry. He was carrying his own coat over an arm and a small glass jar of sugar. He set the jar down on Emma's silver tray. He didn't move, but seemed to slump over as if studying a detail on the coffee pot.

"I suppose you know everything, too?" Harry said.

Russell straightened. "I don't know, Judge. Do I?" He turned around.

"Look Russell, you're a cop, a good cop. This," Harry made a circular wave with his hand, "You don't want in on this."

"No, I don't suppose I do."

"So, you know, it's best if you..."

Russell interrupted with a tone Harry hadn't heard before.

"You know, it wouldn't kill you to ask once in a while. Just ask."

"Ask?"

"Yes, ask. Climb off that cloud you float around on just for once. I don't know who you think you're foolin."

Russell moved forward. Harry was reminded how much bigger he was, and for a moment thought the man might hit him. He felt his eyelids flicker, waiting for the blow.

But as Russell moved closer, he only spoke more softly. "Judge, I know you got trouble, but I'm not walking out on you unless you tell me to."

"Okay, okay" Harry said. "But let's be clear. I'm not *telling* you to do anything." He paused. His voice was suddenly hoarse, "I'm asking, Russell."

"That wasn't so hard, was it?" Russell stepped back and shifted his weight back against the sideboard, then put his fingers on the bottle. "I take it you won't be needing coffee today?"

"No, I'm, ah, going."

"That nephew of mine spoke to me last night and again this morning. Tells me T.J. has his pants on fire now to take your statement," Russell said. He held his hand up as Harry started to answer. "A statement you won't be wanting to make, I expect, but seeing as you're a sitting judge at the Hadley County Court, it's a fair guess you don't want to refuse to give a statement either. I'm just guessing, of course."

"Of course."

Russell nodded several times. "Well, then you're right about goin.' Course, I'd hate to see you drivin' around in that shiny new Mercedes of yours, no snow tires and all. Why don't you let me take it over to Hadley and get them changed for you. Won't hurt for them to think you're still here. Meanwhile, you can borrow my car. It's parked around back." Russell pulled a ring of keys from his jacket pocket and pulled off a single car key. Handing it to Harry he said, "Probably take me two, three days to get tires for a car like that. That be convenient?"

Harry took the key and nodded. "One day, actually ..."

Grace's phone rang and they both heard her say "Stacy, sweetie, I told you I'd call..."

"Get what you need. We'd better go," Russell said quickly.

Grace had gathered the Martin files in a box. She pointed to it as she spoke into the phone. "I know honey, he's impossible. And I *am* sorry." She gestured insistently in the direction of the hall as she said this. Russell stepped out to check. Harry started to follow, but the big man reappeared in the doorway and motioned him to wait. Harry could hear shuffling feet. The door to Amanda's courtroom squealed on its hinges, and there was a far-off cry of "All rise," and the noise of scraping furniture before the door closed on the gentle din of another day of justice. A similar roomful of people awaited him. They were soon to be disappointed. Or relieved.

"...uh huh," Grace said, "Well, you just missed him. Came in here looking like death warmed over. I just sent him home. I was about to call you." She paused, saw Harry's look, shrugged, then motioned at them again to get going. "Oh, I guess, ten or fifteen ... well don't get in a whirl about it sweetheart." Harry gave her a long look from the door. Grace rolled her eyes. "Look, honey, I know we can get T.J. in for a nice long session tomorrow afternoon, this is probably just one of those twenty-four-hour bugs. The kind you get on airplanes."

As Russell and Harry made their way down the hall, the last words Harry could hear her say were, "Well, how about two o'clock tomorrow?"

Russell took Harry down the service stairs and through the basement. At one end of the hallway a ground level door led to the rear parking area. Russell pointed through the dirty glass to his car. "See that blue Bel Air?" Then Russell's face turned doubtful, "You drive a standard?" Harry nodded.

Russell opened the door while Harry carried the box of files through. As he did this, Harry could hear another door opening further back in the basement, so he ducked outside quickly. He turned back to Russell to thank him, but the big deputy only waved his outside hand for him to go. Then Harry heard him call out, "Lionel, you old bastard. I've been looking for you. Thought you'd snuck outside for a smoke."

"Well, what's it to you?"

"We got to get those lights changed, Lionel. Grace can't work in the dark."

"I told' ya, I work for the Coun..."

The door clicked shut on the rest of Lionel's answer.

◆Δ◆

AS USUAL, RUSSELL'S CONCERNS were well placed. It had been a while since Harry drove a car with a clutch and it showed. The car bucked and the gears ground, but he finally managed to get it out onto the highway without stalling or actually hitting anything.

Out of instinct, he turned right at the highway and headed west toward Route 93. In truth, he had started off with no fixed idea of where to go. Half a lifetime had been spent dealing with problems on his own schedule. He could no more deal with an emergency than a cat could swim. But he knew he had to get out, get away from the net T.J. was spreading for him. He adjusted the rear view mirror and checked it as the courthouse shrunk from view. No one had followed.

At the Ashland intersection with Route 93 the giddiness of escape subsided. He turned south. Langdon House was his only refuge now.

When he reached home he found Emma just returning from walking Abigail. The dog greeted him with her usual thoughtless rapture, indifferent to Emma's half-hour of attention to her needs.

Emma, however, was tolerant of the treacherous affection of dogs. It was people who disappointed her.

"I don't know what whim brought Tee Ingersoll back so soon," she said. "But the next time perhaps, he can leave the office behind. He's been up in the guest room since you left on some conference call. And the phone's ringing non-stop. Something about a 'story conference.'"

"I'm sorry."

"Uh huh."

"I'll talk to him, but right now I need to get ready for a hearing on the Martin case." She stared at him. "Look, Emma, I'll explain all this later. Promise."

Once settled at his desk Harry tried to get ready. After the third call, he turned off the bell on the extension.

Harry had never acquired the preparation habits of a good litigator and knew his skills as a cross-examiner had never been better than average. Despite this he thought he might have a brief opportunity, if he could just get Eleanor Martin on the witness stand and start her answering questions about the trust, just enough to show that she had reason to fear Ephne Newsome, maybe blurt something out about that long ago stay at Pine Manor. He would have all the courtroom props every judge had and would be free from objections and interruptions—at first. It wouldn't take much to remind T.J. that she, more than anyone, had the opportunity to kill Ephne and let the prosecutor know she had a motive as well. He knew he had to make Eleanor's revelations look accidental—a surprise—but if he did, it might send T.J. down that trail, not Harry's. To do this, he had to have some plausible questions to ask her.

The Hadley County probate court file contained an inventory with an appraisal of the house and land ($1.29 million) miscellaneous personal property including "a matched set of monogrammed Purdy shotguns, a 12, 16, 20 and a 410-30-30 over-under." There was an entry for "Anatomical sketches (att. to Thomas Eakins) value: $100,000 (est. E. Newsome)." He could imagine Ephne's little girl's delight in finding these treasures hanging in the Martins' wreck of a house. Still, the total inventory of personal property was only one hundred sixty-two thousand dollars, including a "1931 Gar Wood 32-foot commuter power boat (poor repair) - $5,000." The guns, some old silver and a five-year-old car, were the only items given specific values. A final note read "miscellaneous household furniture: less than $5,000 (est. E. Newsome)."

Harry groaned. *"E. Newsome."* Why hadn't he read the inventory? A lifetime of cut corners rose in a single reproach.

Harry pulled out the Martin trust. There was a reason for the expression 'Philadelphia Lawyer,' and nothing was more 'Philadelphia' than Wharton Biddle. There was nothing that could be said in ten words that couldn't be said better in a hundred. No one would call it elegant prose, but there would be no blunders either. After re-reading the trust, now for the tenth time, Harry knew no one would ever accuse the good grey men of Wharton Biddle of neglecting to identify—precisely—who could exercise the limited powers of appointment, what would happen if they didn't, and who was responsible for the taxes when and if they did. Margaret Martin may not have liked the size of her bills, but she got her money's worth.

What nagged Harry as he went back through the papers, was Popp. The cover-your-ass letter. Why write a letter like that without something to prompt it? But no note, no memo. "The matter we discussed..." and sent ten days before Heatherington Martin died.

"Never recovered consciousness." Prof had said.

Of course. Word would have spread quickly through the little village that included what was left of 'Old Philadelphia' about 'Tony' Martin. Certainly that would include someone in the estates and trusts section of Wharton Biddle. Yet here was correspondence, obviously sent to someone who could no longer read it, announcing for posterity that he had rejected the sage advice of Wharton Biddle. That would be a job for Popp.

Then Harry re-read the Charitable Remainder Trust.

This trust, with Eleanor, Louisa and Zach Hannah as successor trustees had been prepared a year and a half earlier on the Cruikshank and Hannah stationary.

> 18. *Pursuant to the power of appointment set forth in Paragraph SIX of the Heatherington and Margaret Martin Trust, as amended, the undersigned, acting together do hereby publish and declare this Trust for the purposes, inter alia, of exercising said appointment.*

Harry compared the signature page to the copy of the New Jersey adoption release. Eleanor's school-girl writing was remarkably unchanged from her days at The Pines Manor. He had no early example of Louisa's handwriting, but by the time they exercised the power, it had descended to a careless scrawl. Oddly, for someone as careful as Zach, Harry saw that he had witnessed their signatures himself. Not a defect, since he wasn't a beneficiary, but not good practice. Not up to Zach's standard. The line below was witnessed by

"*Sydney Smith   Windsor, New Hampshire*"

Smitty.

Harry made a time-line of dates. The remainder trust was dated more than a year earlier, between the dates of second and third mortgages. Harry checked copies of the mortgages in the file to see if the third mortgage made any reference to the new trust. No, but then no Cruikshank lawyer was involved in the mortgage. Still, the Martins hadn't told the bank about the new trust. The copy of Zach's letter to Wharton Biddle, oddly, was dated after the date of the charitable trust.

It was like Zach to follow up, to cross check what his clients gave him against what was in the file, but it was more like him to check it out ahead of time.

Harry felt himself drifting. How could he tie this to Ephne?

When the Martins hired him, Zach couldn't have known about Eleanor's child. He'd have covered that if he had. He was too good a lawyer to omit a child born out of wedlock, and of course he would have seen how important the double exercise language was. After all, Ephne had figured it out. Why would she have those questions about powers of appointment if she hadn't? He debated a phone call to Zach again, but decided against it. He was the Martins' lawyer and there was a limit to what even Zach would do for him.

The shadows lengthened. The hall clock struck four. Harry turned on a lamp in the room and dialed the courthouse instead. The clerk's office put him through to his chambers.

Grace got right to the point.

"T.J. marched in here at lunch time and demanded, demanded to know your whereabouts."

"And?"

Grace seemed flustered over Harry's lack of outrage. He had concluded, sadly, they were both going to have to get accustomed to a loss of status, but didn't have the heart to tell her.

"I told him, 'What do I know?' You came in sick. You left sick."

"Uh huh, he buy it?"

"Well, he had to, didn't he. Then, next thing, her Ladyship, Judge Stevens to you, sails in here wanting to help. Any motions need attention? Wants to know what your temperature is. So I guess we know where T.J. went after he left here."

"And what did you say to her?"

"Nothing, though I did give her a foot of your pending motions and a 'God bless you my dear.' She's been talking to T.J. about something more than the weather. You could see that a mile away."

"Well, if that's all, we, I, ought to be good until tomorrow." Harry let the statement hang in the air, a question.

Grace responded with, "Zach Hannah wants you to... call him." Harry knew the reason for her hesitation. If he returned Zach's call, Zach would know that Grace and he had spoken.

"He say what about?"

"No, but he asked if he could get you at home. I said I guessed so, I was sure Emma could take a message."

As if Harry could use Emma as a messenger now. Well, Zach would know better than that. "Anything else?"

Instead of giving him an answer, Grace's voice changed, "No, ah, well, I'll have to run that by the judge."

"Someone just come in?"

"Yes, of course, but he was white as a sheet. I hope we'll see him tomorrow." He had to give Grace credit. Her performance was seamless.

"T.J.?"

"Of course, of course."

"Thank you, Grace."

"Don't mention it, good bye."

Harry knew the danger of calling Zach but finally gave in to curiosity and the need for a friendly voice. Twice he picked up his phone to hear Tee's voice. The third time he got a dial tone. The Cruikshank front desk put him right through. A week hence and secretaries might be more circumspect when Harry Warren wanted to speak with their masters.

"Harry?"

"Hi Zach. Grace said something was urgent."

He made a soft chuckling noise. Harry could picture him stretching back, pushing his glasses to the top of his head.

"Yah, well, sick as you are, we shouldn't even be having this conversation."

"What conversation?"

"Exactly. Look, you know that Ephne Newsome was our expert in the Martin case?"

"Uh huh, yah." Harry cleared his throat, knowing what was coming.

"Look, ah ... Harry this is tough to say so I'm just going to come out with it. You had no actual knowledge about her role in the civil case, but now, well, I assume that's why we're having that hearing tomorrow. It's just that T.J. Carr has called me in twice and today he's been calling every half hour and, believe me, all he's asking about now is you."

"Me? What..."

"Yah, you. This morning, he wanted to pin down when we filed a copy of the probate inventory with the county court. That was September in case you're interested. Then this afternoon he wanted to know when Ephne's name went on the pre-trial witness list. Fifteen minutes ago he wanted to know if you'd made any comment when that got filed."

Harry groaned inwardly. He would have to deny reading it. He could add dereliction to his list of sins.

"Look, Harry, I didn't know. For what it's worth I just want you to know Ephne didn't tell me about you two until after you were assigned to the appeal. I'd have never let you..."

"When did she, uh, talk about...us?"

"After we got the probate order and I told her we were appealing. She asked me all casual, no big deal, 'so who's sitting on the appeal?' I gave your name and she turned red as a tomato. Well, you know Ephne."

"Yes I know, I knew, Ephne," Harry said. Then, understanding what Zach really meant, "I didn't realize that you... you and she..."

Zach sighed, "Uh, well we both know I'm a hopeless case, but here's the important thing. It's obvious T.J. has figured out about you two."

"Ah, shit Zach."

"No, not from me. I had to fess up about myself, of course, but I didn't see any need to bring you into it."

"So, what makes you so sure he, ah, suspects, ah..."

"Oh for Christ sakes, Harry, wake up. All he asks me, he and that starched-collar police sergeant, is: 'When did Judge Warren know this? When did Judge Warren know that?' Trust me, he knows. You didn't write her any letters, did you?"

"No, no letters."

"Well, watch your ass. What there is left of it."

◆△◆

TEE KNOCKED SOFTLY on the library door. Harry hadn't heard him approach. His chin was resting on one hand and he didn't look up.

"You off the phone? I've got to call Nevada again." Then, seeing Harry, "Any decisions?"

Harry shook his head slowly and just as slowly turned to face him, leaving the unfinished question hanging in the air. In a curious way Zach's voice over the phone had freed him. All the possibilities were gone now, but one. He had one more card to throw on the next morning. Until then he could only play hide and seek with T.J.

Tee went over to the part of the wall that held Harry's diplomas, his thirty-year-old picture of the Phi Psi's. "God, look at this," he said taking the picture off the wall. "I always told you that was the place for you, didn't I? I'll bet that was the time you were the happiest, before you decided you could make it one better, make it all the way to this." Tee gestured with the picture before replacing it on its hook.

"You're right ,of course," Harry said. "You usually are. I've spent thirty years trying to fit in with the Llewellyns. Too much time. Maybe that's why I... Who knows? But was it so awful? To try to be something different from what you are? All right, *better* than what you are? From the time we're kids we're told we can be anything we want to be. Well, did I do anything more than that?"

Tee snorted. "No. You're not the first guy to fly too close to the sun."

"And now I'm going to pay for it. But believe me, I'm not going to gnash my teeth and call it all a 'mistake'! Everything I did, I did on purpose."

"Okay, okay," Tee said. "You come up with any ideas?"

"Maybe. As I explained last night, Ephne Newsome is, was, the daughter of Eleanor—not Louisa—Martin. Somehow she figured this out, probably going through papers over at the Martin house. At the same time, she could see that Louisa was delusional, almost certifiable. The Martin family trust requires both sisters to agree to any distribution otherwise it's not valid. Ephne must have read this because she asked me about the same very unusual provision just before she was killed."

"So?"

"So she must have concluded that anything the Martins had in the trust *had* to go to her. There was nothing they could do about it."

A smile of ironic satisfaction spread over Tee's face.

"Except, except the sisters amended the trust *before* Louisa became incompetent."

"So ..." Tee began.

"There had to be some kind of confrontation," Harry said, "there at the house and one of them, probably Eleanor, shot Ephne with one of their antique shotguns."

"Okay, I'm sold, but how do you get her to..." Tee spread his hands.

"Confess? I doubt I can, but all I've got to do is get her flustered, make a mistake, blurt something out. Hell, maybe she'll take the Fifth. That's if I get that far."

"What's to stop you?"

"Nothing, at first, but I've got to get on the bench, get her started. If the prosecutor gets to me first, he can do pretty much the same thing to me, make me take the Fifth, or lie."

Tee said, "So why hasn't he?"

"He's not quite sure. But tomorrow he'll go next door to the judge I told you about."

"The one who hates you? The pretty one, blonde?"

"Yeah, she was at the dinner, and she'll give him a warrant to start asking for things. She'll give it to him because, once she does, she knows I'm done for. That's why I have to get through the hearing first."

Tee turned thoughtful. "So she needs a reason not to give him—this T.J. character—that warrant."

"That's right. Unfortunately, I can't think of one."

"It's so like you, Warren."

"What?"

"To assume other people may not want things. Just as much as you did."

◆△◆

THEY WERE A GRIM threesome at dinner that evening with Tee getting up every ten minutes to answer another call on his cell phone while Emma pretended to make conversation. As always, she put hospitality first, and while Tee was in the room they spoke only of Philadelphia things.

When Tee stepped out after coffee, however, Emma changed the subject to Zach Hannah.

"Have you seen much of Zach lately?"

"Aside from the dinner, no," Harry said. "We talk on the phone."

"Didn't you think he looked awful? He had to leave yesterday's Museum Board meeting early and..."

"Not like Zach," Harry said. "You said 'and...'"

"Oh nothing, never mind. Could you get a couple more sticks of firewood?" She pointed to the dying embers. "Two's enough."

Harry left the dining room and walked by his friend.

"No, two, maybe three more days..." he was saying into his phone.

In the garage, Harry found he had parked Russell's unfamiliar car too close to the woodpile. Squeezing between the cars and the logs stacked against the wall, Harry dislodged a small cascade onto the floor. He swore and picked one up. When he replaced it, he shifted it to his left hand, but in the half light, something moved making a metallic sound. Peering down he saw a silvery scrolled pair of metal tubes. He moved the logs aside and pulled at the object which revealed itself to be a double-barreled shotgun. He turned it over and was not surprised to see the letters 'H M' etched into the plate that held the rear sight. Just beneath, in plain arabic numerals, was the number '16.'

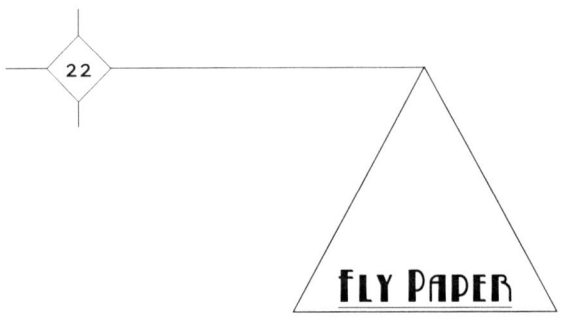

22

Fly Paper

Gregg covered his impatience with silence as he watched the high voiced county court clerk and Lionel Whitcomb try to face each other down in the gloom of the courthouse basement. Complaining all the while, Lionel had finally moved his tubs of floor wax and urinal tablets, his mops and brushes, snow shovels and God knows what else away from the door marked 'Records/Storage,' but the door was locked and he was damned if he was going to look for the key. Only after Gregg suggested that a sledgehammer might do the trick did Lionel discover he had it on his key ring all along.

"Commissioners gonna hear 'bout this," Lionel announced as he turned the key to reveal a long room filled floor to ceiling with boxes of paper. A narrow aisle ran down the middle. Lionel went inside, snapped on a naked lightbulb and leaned against the stacked boxes. He folded his arms.

"Okay Lionel," said the clerk. "We'll call you when we need you." Gregg set his teeth at the note of official satisfaction in the man's falsetto. Some people could piss you off just saying 'hello.'

"Nope, this here's county, not court," Lionel announced.

Gregg could see the custodian intended to stand there while they looked. Nothing the clerk could say would dissuade him now.

"Look, ah, Mr. ah, Whitcomb," Gregg said. This is a police investigation, okay?" Gregg took a step toward the man to be able to look down at him from a steeper angle. "And these sure look like county court records." Lowering his voice he added, "You stick around, you'll have to testify, be cross-examined." Everyone knew about Lionel's ongoing angry divorce. The last place he wanted to be was back on a witness stand.

Whitcomb shifted his gaze up to Gregg but almost as quickly he looked back down. "Well, why din't you say so?" He gestured permission to Gregg to come into the room, but still seemed hesitant to leave.

Gregg said, "Before you go maybe you can help with some of these boxes?" It was hard to make out what Lionel said to this with all those keys bouncing off his hip, but Gregg was satisfied that love had nothing to do with it.

"Key?" Gregg said, as Whitcomb reached the door.

The custodian detached a key from the ring and held it up. "I'll get it back?" The Clerk nodded impatiently and held his hand out.

Lionel eyed him and then handed the key to Gregg.

"Uh huh," he said and shuffled away.

"Surly bastard," the clerk said when he was sure that Lionel could no longer hear him. "He's been even worse than usual since his wife threw him out. Fired his lawyer, right in open court. Called Judge Stevens awful names, not to her face, of course."

"Awful," Gregg said.

The clerk gave him a long look, then seemed to remember why they were there as he surveyed the room and began shifting and tilting the boxes. "I'm sure the phone bills are... no, not there," the clerk said. Gregg sneezed twice and received two soft spoken 'God-bless-you's'.

T.J. had hustled him down here the minute he'd arrived. "That Shubert woman says she took phone calls during work hours so they probably came from here if your hunch is right. Clerk's office say they've got phone records going back more than ten years. Go get 'em, but don't let that nosy bastard know why."

"You don't want to interview..."

"You like your job? You think anyone will be interested in hiring you if this turns out to be a dead end? You find me some calls to a 215 area code, confirm they went to the Wharton Biddle law firm and we're off to the races. Till then, go slow." T.J. went over to his window and fingered the Venetian blinds. "Little Harry's here I see. There's his fancy car. We'll visit him after. When you get done I hope to have another interesting piece of news by them."

◆△◆

"Let's see ... no, just cancelled checks in there." The clerk pushed a box aside. "Payroll... let me tell, you that was a pain in the ..."

The clerk seemed to sense that Gregg was not in the mood for discussion of his administrative challenges. Not that he shut up, but he stopped expecting answers. As they worked down the aisle, the clerk identified and rejected box after box with a sing-song cadence: "Service contracts, nope, bailiff's time cards, nope." Twenty minutes passed.

"You sure they're here?" Gregg tried to keep the irritation out of his voice.

"Oh sure. We don't throw anything out. Unless Lionel there–" at this he gestured at the open door, "threw them out to make room for more soap powder."

Eventually the clerk grunted, "Think ... yup, got 'em." Gregg could see boxes marked, 'Bell Atlantic' sitting in a recess behind a carton of discarded copy paper.

The clerk rooted around and found the months for the year Susan Shubert said she had routed calls to Ephne Newsome from New Hampshire. Gregg winced as the squeaky voice cried out 'got 'em' again and began pulling bundles of records to make a pile on the floor. "January, February," he said. The pile fell over. He looked up at Gregg, "Here's March and April... You can help, you know."

The phone bills were easy to sort. Each month contained one set of sheets for New Hampshire in-state calls, one for out-of-state, mostly Massachusetts, a few for Maine and Vermont. Then, in the middle of the page, a call to area code 215. Gregg checked his card, yes, the Wharton Biddle number. Then, again, eight days later. And again. In all, he found fourteen calls between March and June, just as Susan Schubert had remembered. There were no calls after June.

"Anything that would tell us who placed a particular call from here?

What extension?"

"No," said the clerk. Our office and each judge's chambers can get an outside line any time they want. There's no protocol for it. You know it would help if you told me what you're looking for." When he got no response, the clerk gave Gregg a look that was supposed to convey insight. "This is about Judge Warren isn't it?"

Gregg narrowed his eyes. "That's none of your business yet. But if I start to hear any courthouse gossip along those lines, I'll know where it came from, won't I." He gestured with the records he'd separated from the rest. "We'll take these."

As they left, Gregg pulled on the storage room door to close it. It stuck. He pulled again. Finally he opened it and closed it with a vicious crash. "Fucking thing!" he heard himself shout, but finally it pulled shut. Getting control of himself, he re-locked the door.

"Don't worry, Gregg," the clerk said, adopting a 'there, there' tone. "You've got all you could, and don't worry. No one will hear anything from me." The man knew a lot more about the investigation than he'd let on.

◆Δ◆

WHEN GREGG, WITH the clerk in tow, delivered the bills to T.J., the prosecutor gave them a greedy look.

"Okay T.J., here's the bills," the clerk said, scuttling around Gregg to face T.J. "You going to finish telling me what this is all about?" He looked defiantly at Gregg as he spoke.

"All in good time," T.J. said, grabbing the papers.

"No. First you bother my deputy about some call she put through to Judge Warren's chambers last week. Now you've got me crawling around in the cellar. This is court business, court records, and I need to..."

T.J. looked up. "I said, you'll see. In the meantime go fuck yourself." But T.J.'s body language was gentler than his words and the clerk seemed to sense this, especially when the prosecutor went to the window and smiled at something he saw in the parking lot.

"Now listen here, T.J. ..." the clerk began.

Gregg had heard enough from the clerk for one morning and decided this was as good a time as any to find Lionel Whitcomb and give back his storeroom key. Crossing the courthouse lobby, he saw his uncle.

"Hey Uncle Russ, you know where I can find Lionel?" He held the key up by way of explanation to his uncle's questioning look.

"Sour-faced bastard hides out in the furnace room most of the winter," his Uncle said. He looked out the window. "I saw him downstairs a few minutes ago."

The two stood together, not speaking, still feeling the distance between them from last night's conversation.

Then Russell said, "Take a left at the bottom of the stairs. Big room with the slidin' door. I think he's down there now."

Gregg started toward the door to the basement but his uncle called after him. "See you tonight?" Gregg turned, puzzled. "Practice field," Russell said. The two had promised the Hadley High School coach they'd look in on his practice. "Sure," Gregg said, and took this as the beginning of his uncle's capitulation on the matter of Judge Warren. It had to be done. It might as well be now. In the meantime, life moved on.

Following Russell's directions, Gregg walked down the basement corridor to a sliding metal door with 'Furnace' written across it. He knocked.

"Yah, come in."

He rolled the door open.

Lionel, he saw, had made himself a nest of sorts in a torn upholstered chair. There was a stack of girlie magazines on the floor but Lionel was reading *Field and Stream* just then. An ancient coffee maker stood on a table against the inside wall together with dirty cups, boxes from fast-food places and other trash. The smell, a mixture of fuel oil, cigarettes, and Lionel, was strong.

"Yassuh." Lionel said without getting up. Gregg knew this was New Hampshireese for 'What the hell do you want?'

"Key," Gregg said, holding it up and putting it down on the table. The room had been built for coal storage and an old coal furnace, wrapped in asbestos stood against the wall. A newer, much smaller oil furnace sitting next to it roared to life as if cued by the key striking the table.

"'Bout time," said the man in the chair.

Gregg slid the door closed behind him. He breathed deeply of the comparatively fresh air in the hall.

GREGG RETURNED TO FIND the clerk gone and T.J. newly enraged, his voice almost breaking as he yelled.

"Goddamn it to hell! Jesus, Mary and goddamn Joseph, can't we catch a break around here?"

Stacy for once had decided that this was not the time to plead delicacy and received Gregg's questioning look without expression. "Ask him," she said, leaving. "If he doesn't have a stroke first."

Gregg had assumed the phone bills would have cheered T.J. up. The night before he had received Gregg's call with something approaching joy.

"*I knew it, I knew it. As soon as he dropped his pen... you remember?... as soon as he looked at those pictures, seen what he'd done.*"

Gregg didn't think he'd ever heard T.J. happy, really happy, before. But now the red-faced prosecutor looked ready to get down on the floor and start chewing the carpet.

Emboldened by his own recent tantrum with the storage room door, Gregg pointed to the bills on the desk. "Hey, we found fourteen calls. They all correspond to the time period Susan Schubert talked about. What are you getting all worked up about?"

T.J. looked down at them, "Uh huh." He ran his finger over the statements. "Good... good. Fourteen you say? Thank you, Sergeant Leavitt, for pointing that out." He closed his eyes and turned his face to the ceiling. On a fly strip just above him an insect was making deliberate clawing movements amidst the remains of many dead comrades.

"So, I should be able to just walk in on little Harry with these right now, shouldn't I?" 'Say Judge, you know anything about these fourteen calls from the courthouse to Wharton Biddle in Philadelphia?' Watch him crumple like a wet Kleenex."

Gregg said. "So why don't we. You've got an appointment don't you?"

"Well sure I could, unless, *unless*, he's already skated out of here 'sick' before I get to him. While I'm waiting for you two geniuses to find these bills, watching his fancy car in the parking lot, only to find out that damned uncle of yours has lent him *his* car. He's been gone for a half hour. 'Getting snow tires put on,' Russell says." T.J.'s eyes narrowed. "Say, you didn't tell Russell..."

"No, of course not." The lie came out smoothly.

T.J. looked at him hard, but almost instantly seemed to deflate as he waved an apology. "Ok, no offense," he said, mistaking Gregg's reddening face for anger. "We'll just have to get him tomorrow."

T.J. sat then and creaked backward in his chair. "You speak to those boys of yours I sent down to Windsor yet?"

"No. Message I got was someone was going to the Department of Motor Vehicles."

"Yah, well we're looking for a hit on a silver Range Rover, Land Rover. There can't be that many of those in New Hampshire."

"Range Rover?"

"Desk clerk at the Burgoyne," T.J. said. "You know, that hot sheet place just outside of Windsor? Desk clerk thinks our lady was in there a week ago. Could have been Friday, Saturday or Sunday. He's ninety percent sure it was her but he can't be sure which day 'cause when they pay cash he doesn't keep records, avoids the state rooms tax."

"Anyway, he remembers she got picked up next morning by a big SUV with 'Rover' written on it. He didn't get a look at the driver but, whoever it was, it was clear from the woman's expression the driver was some pissed off...

'Course, your rookies can't leave well enough alone. The guy keeps talking and says later, he *thinks* it's the same lady he saw again last Friday night, except now she's all dressed up fancy in a navy blue dress. He'd remember that blonde hair anywhere, he says. Of course *we* know the second sighting can't be our lady. She's safely tucked in the medical examiner's refrigerator."

Gregg lowered himself onto a chair. He knew only that the next minute and half would be important.

"We'll have to eliminate the second sighting. That won't be hard. The clerk got a good look at the guy with the second lady. Drove off with him in a blue or green van. Says it's hard to tell color at night under that neon sign but he saw the driver." T.J. had become quiet, now. Confiding.

Gregg nodded. He knew about the sign, of course.

"What makes you think it was Newsome either time? Couldn't it be another lady both times? He closed his eyes as the nightmare unfolded.

"Sure," T.J. said, "That's why I'm waiting on the DMV. You fallin' asleep over there?"

"No, just ah, no." The moment had come when Gregg knew he could still take the middle course: tell T.J. whose van it was. T.J. would explode. He'd be pulled off the case, the job with the Governor gone forever. But he'd keep his job. He'd put in his twenty and end up teaching driver's ed and maybe coaching football at Hadley High. But the seconds ticked off and still he said nothing, and with each second of silence, the decision congealed around him.

Stacy put her head around the half-opened door. "You want that fax from DMV?" She flourished a piece of paper.

"You bet," T.J. said, reaching out for it. He made a low-pitched three syllable laugh. "One of your rookies is romancing an IT lady down at DMV. You may have to pay him overtime for last night."

T.J. studied the list, then gave a low-pitched whistle. "Four silver Rovers in Windsor County," he said. "Look at number three." He pushed the paper over.

The third name on the list was "Irr. Trust f/b/o Emma L. Warren, P.O. Box 187, North Windsor."

Gregg looked up. There was no going back now.

T.J. seemed to sense his reaction. Quietly, he began to speak. "You can see this does it, can't you?"

"Sure, it's ..."

"Exactly. That's one coincidence too many," T.J. said. He waved Stacy away.

After a full minute of silence T.J. turned all business. "All right," he said. "I've tried enough cases to know how much can go wrong. What we want, what I think we can get is a confession. Our little Harry—you saw him when he signed that warrant—our Harry will fold if I catch him right, but we can't pussy foot around on this any more. I'm going after a warrant from Judge Stevens. We'll search the Rover. We know he gave her a ride, so there's something, a hair, a thread, something. That's all we need."

T.J. poked the paper with his finger, "And, we can ask for little Harry's phone records too, something to push him over the edge if he gets tough on us."

"You said something about him being sick."

"Yeah, but they've got a special hearing scheduled in the Martin case tomorrow. Something tells me he'll be well enough by then."

T.J. put both hands behind his head and returned to his familiar balancing act behind his desk. "You know, that guy could have stopped my discipline hearing. One goddamn phone call... but he didn't raise a finger. I knew the day would come when he'd need a friend."

Keeping his voice as level as he could, Gregg said, "Ah, T.J., about the Burgoyne business, how are we going to handle that, ah, second sighting?"

"What second sighting?" T.J. grinned.

"Then you're not going to go into the business with the Warren's car, the SUV?" Gregg knitted his brow, not understanding.

"Of course I am. Look, just because some desk clerk *thinks* he saw her a second time... Hell, it's not like we don't now *know* it's the wrong girl. The car proves it. It's obvious, the guy made a mistake."

T.J. looked at the troubled policeman, with something that could be mistaken for compassion.

"I know. I know." His voice dropped, "You're worried about withholding it. Don't. As long as we don't have solid information corroborating the clerk on the second sighting, we're in the clear. Besides, picking her up in his wife's SUV, that's the clincher!"

T.J. savored the moment, sighed, and then leaned forward, "Stacy!" he yelled. Then to Gregg he said, "Go on. Get out of here, I'll get the new warrant drawn up. We'll serve it tomorrow."

◆△◆

IT HAD NEVER been easy for Russell to sit in the bleachers at Hadley field "Home of the Bulldogs." As a boy, he had played thirty-one games for

Hadley High, starting every game after Marcel Huppe was hurt early in his freshman year. He caught a few passes, ran two fumbles back for touchdowns and was captain his junior and senior year. One of a small number of players who weren't French-Canadian on the Hadley team—in some of the other cities the chant would go up "Bull Frogs! Bull Frogs!"—Russell was often the biggest man on the field, a blocker and tackler. There was some thought that he might go to college, play at the University of New Hampshire, but with a widowed mother and three sisters, it was just impossible.

He caught sight of Gregg on the track that surrounded the field and gave a wave of recognition through the familiar haze. There were no practice fields in Hadley and, by November, the playing field had grass only in the end zones and along the sidelines. It had been dry for two days. In the twilight the team kicked up dust. This and the steam of their breath and evaporating sweat rose together into a darkening sky.

Gregg sat next to him. "What do you think?"

"Well, they ain't big, but they certainly are slow," Russell said.

Gregg nodded. He had also played, but not on a championship team like his uncle's. A team more like this one. Hadley had limped into the playoffs and was likely to have only one more game, but Gregg was grateful for the distraction. They returned the coach's grateful wave. Something, anything, to get his mind off tomorrow. They would go to Judge Stevens and T.J. would hold back on the Burgoyne Motel desk clerk's memory of the second date. Nothing would move T.J. away from using Mrs. Warren's Range Rover to get a warrant. T.J. was convinced it was a slam dunk.

"It's the clincher, for chrissakes!" was all T.J. would say. "We pivot from the car and go right to the morning he signs the warrant! The case proves itself."

"But the ..."

"We never put the clerk on. We don't need to. It's peripheral."

"*Peripheral.*" Well, T.J. was right, technically, but Gregg knew once any defense lawyer looked into it, it would all come out. The 'second woman' was Mrs. Warren's sister, and he... "*Oh, I'm going to miss you General.*"

Even worse was T.J.'s new-found solicitude. "Look, Sergeant Lea... Gregg, you're so worked up about this? You go run it down, go talk to the desk clerk." Gregg remembered the yawning clerk, how their eyes had made contact, him standing under the neon thinking the sister didn't look so young any more.

"... Nope, no chance 'tall." Russell's voice swam out of Gregg's imagined interview with the desk clerk.

"Yah," Gregg said.

Russell fixed him with a concerned expression. "You still worked up over Judge Warren?"

"You know I am, but ..."

"... but? You didn't have no 'buts' last night."

"Lot's happened since last night." Gregg grinned at his uncle. "Snow tires, for chrissakes."

"It is November." But Russell returned the smile.

Gregg shook his head, then added "No, something more than that." Russell caught the quaver of fear in his voice.

"What?"

"You were right about Carr," Gregg said.

"Want to talk about it?"

"Yeah, you're not going to like it." Gregg was right about that. As he laid out the story about the clerk, his uncle's frown grew deeper. He decided to leave out his own part in the "second" sighting.

"So Carr's decided not to tell Judge Stevens about the clerk seeing the Newsome woman, or I guess I should say someone who *couldn't* be the Newsome woman, that second time."

"That's right."

"Well what do you think? Was the clerk right the first time or the second?"

"Maybe neither," Gregg said. "How do I know?"

"Judge Stevens issues that warrant and it comes out later that you didn't tell her, it's your ass. You know that don't you?"

"Why do you think I'm such a bundle of joy?"

"Mmm. Look, is there anything else?"

Gregg raised his head to see his uncle's heavy frown. In the distance thirty-five adolescent voices cried "One - two - Three, Bulldogs!"

"Well, shit," Russell said, "I guess all you can do is hope she doesn't issue that warrant."

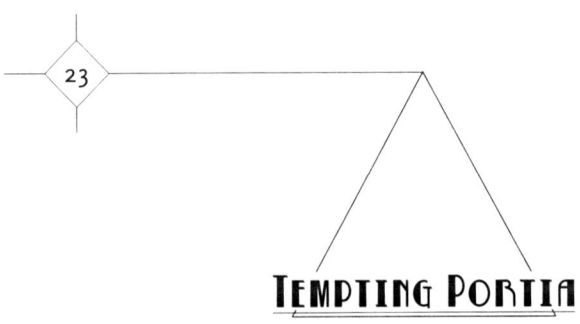

23

TEMPTING PORTIA

As he drove into the long shadow thrown by the Hadley County courthouse, Tee frowned at the untidy patch of lawn. He parked in a lot half filled with cars, pick-up trucks, and police cruisers, and walked between two knots of smokers gathered at opposite ends of the wide stairs that led up to the front door. It and the portico and columns that framed it were a year past due for painting. Anyone standing next to him would have heard him say then, "Oh Harry."

He and Harry had decided to arrive separately. Tee's appointment with Amanda Stevens was for ten o'clock and Harry would arrive forty-five minutes later. He hadn't wanted to risk sitting around for an hour waiting for the eleven o'clock hearing in the Martin case.

Inside, a metal detector greeted Tee with an accusing ring. A second try required the deposit of glasses, keys and a cell phone in a plastic tray proffered by a deputy who made no effort to hide his irritation. Once through, Tee replaced these items in various pockets, straightening his camel hair top coat as he did so. "Where is Judge Stevens holding court?" he asked.

The deputy had returned to his newspaper and didn't bother to look up as he said, "Courtroom three." He gestured vaguely with a thumb toward the furthest of three sets of twelve-foot-high double doors across the lobby.

Tee went to the doors indicated, opened one slightly, and peered in.

The courtroom itself was nearly empty. Two men were arguing something to an attentive woman in a black robe with lots of yellow hair. Below her, a stenographer typed silently on a small machine and a third woman with a mannish helmet of short gray hair kept busy with papers at a smaller version of the judge's bench behind her. A balding man in gray sat at a small desk halfway up the room. Tee knew he was a Bailiff because that word was stenciled on the front of his desk. This man raised his eyebrows at Tee in a not unfriendly way. Tee supposed he had been mistaken for an out-of-state lawyer up from Boston because the man looked down at a sheet of paper then back at him, an unspoken question in his eyes. Tee gave a faint negative shake of the head, removed his coat and sat down, crossing his legs.

Judge Stevens be-robed was even more striking than she was in evening dress. She acknowledged Tee with a small nod and smile of recognition before returning to the argument going on before her. One of the disputants turned, stared for a moment, then faced front again. The other simply kept talking. As he watched, Tee saw her begin to exhibit the stilted mannerisms of a person on audition. Her posture stiffened, she presented what she thought was her better profile. The hand that had been so gently twirling a strand of hair fell to the bench before her.

The dispute was over a building contract, but Tee was far more interested in the cadence of the argument. The harsh enunciation, particularly from the lawyer who Tee guessed was representing the contractor, revealed an atonal emphasis on every fourth or fifth syllable; not gentle the way it was in Maine, near the coast. Harry fell into the same rhythm when he was excited or unhappy.

Tee had never pretended to understand Harry's determination to return to New Hampshire, and the morning had done nothing to enlighten him. When Harry married Emma, the ultimate debutante, Tee assumed Harry would stay in Philadelphia, settle in, blend in, the way he learned to do so well. But for some reason they had come here, and here Harry had made a dangerous enemy of this girl judge. Tee looked around the shabby room. Why would anyone fight over this?

Yesterday he watched Harry move from giddy optimism to despair and back again. There was a local monster, someone who went by the soubriquet of 'T.J.' who was pursuing him, but it was this woman that he feared. Amanda Stevens, he insisted, was implacable. She couldn't be swayed or persuaded. "She's a damn force of nature! She'll make it her business to hang me and she'll dot every 'i' and cross every 't' while she does it." It was hopeless.

It was at this low point that Tee asked, "Isn't there something she wants more than your scalp?"

"Sure. She wants to sit on the Supreme Court and right now I'm in the way."

Tee had thought for a while, then said, "Maybe we can show her something she wants even more." He tried to sound convincing as Harry shrugged assent. What did he have to lose?

◆△◆

FROM THE BACK of her courtroom Tee noted the care Amanda Stevens seemed to take as she made notes, occasionally interrupting to interrogate or correct one man and then the other. On one occasion she quoted, accurately, a longish complete sentence back to the man who appeared to be losing the argument. Tee couldn't tell whether the point was important or not, but he admired how the young woman could project the tone of an earnest undergraduate while she remained in complete control of the two middle-aged men in front of her. Like himself, each lawyer was old enough to be her father. She had stopped resisting the habit of curling a strand of hair around a finger as she listened and wrote. She nodded from time to time to show that she took in this point or that. She had learned the non-verbal trick of expressing approval with warmth and disapproval with mild disappointment. If he cut the tape right, she could be a hit.

Judge Stevens brought the argument to a close. "Thank you gentlemen. You'll be informed of the court's decision." Then she stood and the bailiff startled Tee to his feet with a loud bang of a gravel. "All rise!" If they did the show, someone would have to teach the old man to drop his voice and leave the gavel at home.

Amanda leaned over the bench and said something to the gray haired woman. This woman looked briefly at Tee then back to the judge and nodded. Judge Stevens then disappeared through the door behind the judge's bench.

◆△◆

WHILE TEE WATCHED Amanda, Harry drove down the empty Wasoka Club roadway past the now shuttered 'cottages' and clubhouse toward the shore of the blue-black lake in the distance. He guessed that the Llewellyn's cottage would still be open since Lloyd had been there as recently as Saturday, and he was right. When he got to it, he found none of the winter shutters had been screwed on and the house, while locked, was easily accessible.

Emma still spent part of each summer here and the girls had lived here from June to September until they went off to college. As Harry got out of Russell Chase's car to reconnoiter, the memories of those years came back: the images of his girls, tanned and confident with their sun-streaked hair, as they moved between tennis courts, sail boats, and the golf course, followed, at first by a pack of devoted girls similarly disposed and later by an even more devoted pack of boys with other things on their minds. Leigh, the oldest, won all the contests for the girls at first. She looked more like Harry than Emma, and was blessed with pale blue eyes that contrasted with her dark hair. Watching her, Harry had regretted his own solitary boyhood. He had never been good at games, even when he was asked to play. Then, when Samantha came along three years later, she won all the contests for the boys and the girls. Taller than her sister, she had her mother's red gold hair. Where Leigh had tried, persevered, Samantha found everything effortless. Harry divided his days at the Llewellyn 'cottage' between a bit of golf, reading in the shaded arcade that faced the lake, and watching his daughters have the childhood he never had.

He rounded the corner of the house to receive a blast of air off the lake and went to a French door that hadn't closed properly for a decade. As he suspected, it hadn't been fixed and opened to a gentle push.

Once inside he proceeded straight to a smallish pine-paneled room where Lloyd Llewellyn maintained a small gun cabinet. Confirming that there were three empty slots and that the case was unlocked, Harry went to the front door, unlocked it and surveyed the neighborhood. No one.

Pulling on a pair of gloves, Harry walked quickly to Russell's car, removed the shotgun and retraced his steps. As he walked he heard a distinctive clicking sound coming from the gun, as though something was rattling around inside. Time enough to check that later; right now it was essential that he not be found with the gun on him. He knew, of course, that someone had planted the shotgun in his garage. He had known it last night. Now he would wait to see who pointed T.J. and the police in that direction.

He opened L.L.'s cabinet, moved one gun over and put this one in with the rest. Closed up in the cabinet, the gun looked much the same as the others. Not that it mattered. No one would have the courage to search the home of L.L. Llewellyn. The gun was as safe there as it would be at Fort Knox.

Harry checked his watch. He had just enough time to get to the courthouse and start the hearing in the Martin Case.

◆△◆

THE WOMAN CAME OVER to Tee while he gathered up his coat. She walked with a clumsy gait, almost rolling, like a sailor. She stretched out her right hand in greeting. Tee took in the built-up shoe without letting his eyes pause. They would show her seated, always seated.

She pulled the spring-hinged gate open for him then led him past the two recently contesting lawyers, now conversing pleasantly, one shaking his head in sympathy as the other recited the serial misfortunes of a high school football team on which a son or perhaps a nephew named 'Lucas' was playing. Tee followed her across the business part of the courtroom then up two steps to behind the judge's bench and through the door he had seen Judge Stevens use.

Crossing a hallway, the woman led him through a door labeled

'CHAMBERS,' crossed a small office, and hesitated at a second door. She gave a perfunctory knock, then ushered him inside.

Amanda Stevens was finishing up a telephone call but gestured him inside while she spoke into the phone. She smiled at him over her conversation. "Of course ... well, I'd have to know more about it..."

Tee turned away to learn from a wall covered with framed certificates that six years earlier she had been "New Attorney of the Year" according to the New Hampshire Bar Association. Before that, she had been an editor of the *Cornell Law Review*. She was admitted to the First Circuit Court of Appeals, the Second Circuit Court of Appeals and the U.S. Supreme Court. She had performed some act that Windsor, New Hampshire Rotarians thought constituted 'Distinguished Service' and she owned a Phi Beta Kappa key from Bowdoin.

"No, not an automatic conflict...," she said to the telephone then listened. Then she said, "Of course, it's sensitive ... bring in what you have at ..." She turned away from the phone to look at her wristwatch. The masculine turn of her elbow only emphasized that she was a truly beautiful woman. She glanced briefly from the watch to Tee catching his half-smile, a woman accustomed to being found desirable.

"No, still today, let's say, ah, ten-thirty?" she paused. "Yes... uh huh." Then, "Well, no. No, affidavits are fine. I mean, T.J., you don't plan on bringing a shotgun in here do you?... Oh ... sorry, I thought you said you had it... Well, eleven then." She had turned her gaze away and didn't see Tee start at the word 'shotgun.'

She hung up the phone and came around the desk to shake his hand. "I'm sorry Mr. Ingersoll. Business."

"Not at all," he said. "And please, Judge, call me Ted."

She said nothing to this but motioned for the two of them to sit down in the two chairs that almost faced each other across a conference table set in front of her desk. "Well, ah, Ted," she seemed genuinely curious, "what brings you to Hadley County?"

"Judge, I..."

"Please, 'Amanda.'"

"Of course, Amanda. Well ..." He made a tent with his hands under his chin and sat silently meeting her eyes. "You know that I'm in the television business."

Amanda felt the glow of anticipation she'd been nursing since getting his first call. She thought he'd been interested at the Crowninshield dinner on Friday night. Men were so transparent, even famous men; no, especially famous men. Nevertheless, now at the words 'television business,' a drop of perspiration darted down from her left armpit. She managed a low, conspiratorial giggle, "Well, ye-es, I had heard," she said, smiling, knowing that it was working, like it always had, even now.

◆△◆

Tee had done this more than thirty times. Occasionally he found himself in the presence of a true innocent, someone genuinely oblivious to who 'Ted' Ingersoll was and why he was there. Someone with no idea of what was about to happen to him. '*Me? Watcha wanna put me on TeeVee for?*' Even less often he encountered the practiced reluctance of the already-famous, people who knew that the conceit of "Profiles" was to provide a new perspective on its subjects, one not necessarily better and, quite possibly, much worse than the reputation they had already won—or stolen.

But most of the people who had faced him, as Amanda Stevens was now, were like her. They had achieved something, sometimes much, in their little corners of the world. Some were loved, some were hated. They were not fools. Some had become rich, others powerful. Nearly all were respected or feared by the people they worked and dealt with in their daily lives. They had become People of Substance.

But they weren't *famous*, not yet. Thus far that delicious feeling of being *known* had been denied them. They hadn't yet heard the subtle but still perceptible drop in the volume of conversations when they entered a room. They hadn't experienced awkward sidewalk encounters with complete strangers who greeted them with the presumption of old friends; who just wanted to say…

With 'Ted' Ingersoll in front of them, people like Amanda could just see the first faint gleam of celebrity, the dawn of that final confirmation of worth, the finishing, confirming gloss that had, so far, just eluded them. At last, at long, long last, this, even this, was going to drop into their hands.

Rarely, Tee saw this greedy, expectant look soften into gratitude. Usually, it was only glazed contentment. Amanda swallowed and her color deepened. Her eyebrows and ears rose ever so slightly. Her lips parted. They would get that shot, the beauty that both hid and abetted the ambition. The people in their living rooms wouldn't really like her in the end. Tee almost felt sorry for her. Still, he made her wait.

"I thought you might have," Tee said. They sat without moving, the silence hanging in the space between them.

"Would you consider," Tee began slowly, "consider being one of Profile's subjects for next season?"

SUCCESS HAD BEEN proffered to Amanda before, and she knew better than to wait. "It would be an honor," she said immediately. She exhaled and made a short involuntary laugh. "And a pleasure," she added.

"You understand that it's a pretty intrusive process," Tee said. "Camera people will follow you day and night. It's about four months. We snoop, ask questions."

"Ted, I assumed as much," Amanda felt her own wide involuntary smile, a six-year-old on Christmas morning. She knew this wasn't her best look. Her lips came together and she looked down.

"Well, don't be so quick, uh Amanda. Remember, we'll be interviewing grade school teachers, colleagues, old flames." He raised his eyebrows. "Nobody who's going to feel the need to go public with that wild weekend in Daytona is there?" He delivered this with his soft dark laugh, his eyelashes sinking then moving up slowly to reveal the direct gaze.

Amanda looked up quickly, but responded to his laugh with her own. "No - no, my personal life is disappointingly uneventful," she said.

Tee made a mental note, 'Check on college behavior' but nodded back to her with mock sympathy.

"And we'd like to build the story around a case you preside over. Any problem with cameras in the court?"

"Not usually. The parties would have to agree," she said.

"Oh, they always agree." Tee paused, then added, "Back here?" He made a small circle in the air with his hand at the room.

"I'm sure we can work that out," she smiled.

"Great, great. He surveyed the room. "Always liked that scene," he said pointing to a framed nineteenth century print on the wall behind her where a pre-Raphaelite beauty was lecturing a small group of men in Renaissance costume.

"Portia and Shylock," Amanda said without turning around. "*The quality of Mercy is not strained.*"

Tee nodded, looked at the picture again, and said,

> "'*It droppeth as the gentle rain from heaven.*
> *Upon the place beneath. It is twice blest;*
> *It blesseth him that gives and him that takes.*'"

Amanda looked at him directly. She was accustomed to being the smartest kid in class. "I'm impressed," she said.

"Sorry," Tee said. "You'd think at my age I'd learn to stop showing off my memory."

"No, no. It's really quite remarkable."

Tee sunk back into his chair, hooking an arm over its back. Well, she'd taken the bait. Now let her feel the hook. "Always been a failing. My biggest, Harry says."

"Harry." She said it positively, but it was a question.

"Harry Warren." Tee regarded her.

"You know Judge Warren, ah, well?" Two circles, almost red, blossomed inside the pink of Amanda's cheeks.

"Oh, for years. We were roommates at Penn." Tee said this as he retrieved an appointment book from an inside pocket and pretended to consult it. He closed it and smiled at her brightly.

"Roommates," Amanda said trying but not quite able to manage a smile.

"Small world isn't it? Harry always said I was a damned show-off. Still does, but, hell, you know what Gide said about friendship."

"No, I don't," said Amanda.

"The only real ones are the ones you make before you're eighteen," Tee said. "Lot of truth in that when you think about it."

"I suppose ... suppose there is."

Amanda straightened some papers on the table. She looked up, made a quick smile that faded quickly, deciding.

"Stroke of luck, really," Tee said. "Meeting you on Friday."

'How is that, uh, Ted?"

"Well, it's the perfect lead in. You know, the older judge with the protegé. I did something similar last year with two dancers at the Joffrey. Did you see that one?'

"I think I've seen them all. The older dancer had M.S."

"ALS. Tragic. I see this one playing out differently of course. You're the story, not Harry. America has lots of middle-aged judges."

"Oh, of course."

"I mean, I love Harry like a brother, but we can't very well show him as a giant losing his powers. We can't claim that for our Harry, can we, much as we love him." Tee made a low, disloyal laugh and his eyelids dipped once. He heard the relief in her response.

"Uh, no. No, I don't suppose you can," she said, her laughter joining his, her voice even lower, confiding. She had seen the net, thought to resist, but now, as usual, like the rest of them, was allowing herself to succumb.

Tee gave the last pull.

"Look Judge, Amanda, I know you've got a lot to do and I've got a plane to catch. The production people will call you next week and start up with some kind of shooting schedule. We'll need releases, that sort of thing. Be thinking of a signature case now, won't you?"

"I'll have to clear all this with our Chief Justice," she said quickly, rising to take his outstretched hand which she held as if fearing to let him go.

"Of course," Tee said. Then to be sure she understood, "I can't tell you how happy I am about this. Harry Warren is my oldest friend and the chance to work him into the background of one of these pieces, even in a bit part, well, it will make a great story even more special for me."

He took out a pen and notebook, turned to a new page and wrote, then ripped it from the book and handed it to her. "Look, there are always questions that come up. My assistant can be reached at that number any time," he said.

They stood in silence; then as if signaled, both moved to the door together as Tee spoke. "A wistful older man watches the young protegé sail by him. Not envious, not resentful, just wistful as he watches the younger 'him' become what he might have been. Having you be a woman gives it an extra twist of the unexpected, don't you think?" Tee turned a palm upward.

"I've never thought of Judge Warren as being, well, wistful." Amanda said, looking down. "Certainly not wistful about me."

"But that's exactly what he is, Amanda. He even suggested you. And as for admiration, well, 'force of nature' is the phrase he used. 'She makes me aware of my own inadequacies. She can't help that, of course. But she leaves me comfortable with them.'" Tee shrugged inwardly. Well, Harry could have said it.

Amanda straightened and made a face of skeptical surprise. Tee nodded at her and quickly added, "He *was* wistful at eighteen. We learn to hide it at our age."

"I didn't know he knew you at all," Amanda said. It was obvious she didn't think of Harry Warren as a source of charm. That idea would take some getting used to.

The intercom on Amanda's phone went off.

"Yes." The judge turned away quickly, irritation in her voice.

"County Attorney and Trooper... Sergeant Leavitt here to see you."

Amanda looked at her watch, ten forty already. "Duty calls," she said to Tee and saw him through the door. A well set-up young man in a green uniform was standing just beyond. Behind him was just about the ugliest man Tee had ever seen. Tee smiled at the policeman.

◆△◆

ONCE DELIVERED TO the lobby by the limping clerk, Tee put his coat over his shoulders leaving the arms empty. He whistled the opening bars of an Italian symphony as he walked, causing the deputy, still engrossed in his paper, to look up. "Ciao," Tee said, delighting in the surly man's startled reaction.

Tee stepped through the courthouse doors back into the November chill. It was 10:45. Now he had to drive around for a half-hour, and return to Harry's courtroom just after the hearing began. Harry was afraid Eleanor would recognize Tee if he sat with her beforehand in the courtroom. Tee would tell everyone later how gray and peaceful it all seemed, how he just missed all the excitement. Everyone loved the part about the look on the deputy's face. They knew about the rest.

24

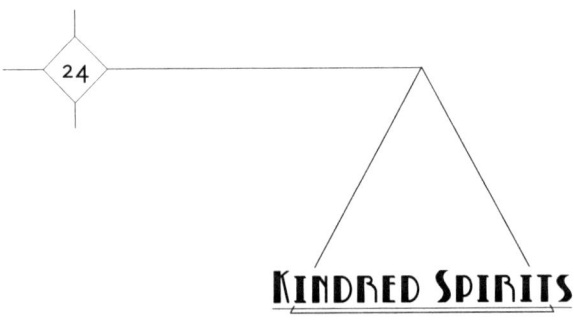

KINDRED SPIRITS

Amanda's clerk offered her cheek to T.J. as he stopped at her desk. He leaned over to kiss it.

"Loretta, when you going to get rid of that damn husband so we can run off together?"

"Big talker. I'm free at five if you want to do anything about it."

"Loretta, darlin', you're many things, but surely you're not free," T.J. said. He motioned toward the closed door and raised his eyebrows.

"She's expecting you. What's the big mystery?" Loretta's voice dropped to a whisper as she pushed the intercom button. T.J. just put his finger to his lips.

Judge Stevens' voice came over the intercom.

"Yes?"

"County Attorney and Trooper..." Loretta looked up at Gregg, unsure.

"Sergeant Leavitt."

"Sergeant Leavitt, here to see you," Loretta said.

A moment later the door opened.

"Okay. Have them come in, Mr. Ingersoll is just leaving."

Gregg recognized the man from the banquet as he exchanged goodbyes with the judge. He then gave T.J. and Gregg a bland smile before he walked past them. Judge Stevens stood at the door to her inner office, her eyes on the departing visitor until he reached the hall. She motioned with her chin to her clerk to go with him and the woman jumped up quickly, her feet making an arithymic cadence on the floor as she skipped to catch up. After she had, the judge turned back, looked down and seemed to take a deep breath.

◆△◆

GREGG CAUGHT A FAINT SCENT of perfume. He hadn't been this close to Judge Stevens before. She shook both their hands and sat down opposite them across the table that was drawn up perpendicular to her desk.

"So, T.J., what *is* the big mystery?" Judge Stevens asked pulling up a chair.

"Judge, I might as well get right to the point. This is a hell of a thing. We've got an affidavit and a request for a search of Judge Harry Warren's house, chambers and phone records. You gonna have a problem with that?"

The judge's mouth opened slightly, then closed. She gave them each a long look, provoking a nod of confirmation from T.J. She looked up at the ceiling and made a gesture of impatience.

"I guess that depends," she said looking down, her voice lower than before.

"This is related to the..." T.J. paused for emphasis, "homicide of Miss Ephne Newsome, sometime between Friday, October 30th at 3:45 p.m., and Monday, November 2nd at 8:00 a.m." T.J. said, all business now, reading from Gregg's affidavit.

"Homicide? Harry Warren?" Judge Stevens said this sharp and quick with a "wait a minute" note in her voice.

"Yah." T.J. pushed the affidavit and pictures across the table toward the judge. "That's the lady."

She ignored the papers and Gregg thought she seemed strangely reluctant to touch them. The three sat in silence. Then with a sigh, she pulled her hair behind an ear, leaving a strand with the width of a thumb which she began to twist around a finger. She looked down at the pictures, winced, and picked up the affidavit and began to read. Gregg followed her eyes and consulted his copy.

> 1. I am Sergeant Gregg Leavitt of Troop H of the New Hampshire State Police. I have been a state police officer for six years and assigned to the Hadley County Barracks for three months as watch commander.
>
> 2. I have supervised the investigation of the wrongful death of a female subject who has been identified as Ephne Newsome, a resident of 78th Street, New York City. The Hadley County Medical Examiner has confirmed that this woman (hereinafter, the victim) met her death from wounds inflicted by a shotgun between October 30th and November 2nd.
>
> 3. During the course of this investigation, I was able to determine that the victim placed a telephone call by cell phone Friday on October 30th at 3:45 p.m. to the Hadley County courthouse, #603-555-4000 which call may have been routed to the chambers of Judge Harry Warren as per Verizon Wireless records appended hereto.

Gregg saw the judge turn to the appendices, then back to the affidavit. She reached the end of a page and initialed it.

> 4. Our investigation confirms that Miss Newsome was not personally acquainted with either Ms. Grace Carroll or Mr. Russell Chase, who are the only other persons regularly employed in the same office suite. I have also determined that the only other person who regularly utilizes the dedicated line at that number is Judge Harry Warren.
>
> 5. I have determined from information given to me by reliable informants acquainted with the victim that eight years ago the victim was involved in a romantic relationship for a period of about three months with an adult male who then resided in this state; that the

victim described that individual to these witnesses as holding "high public office" in New Hampshire; as suffering from the effects of a war-time gunshot wound to his leg and that this individual was a graduate of the University of Pennsylvania.

6. I have confirmed that Judge Warren was a sitting judge in the Hadley County Court on all dates pertinent to this investigation; that he has a noticeable limp from a leg wound sustained in Vietnam and that he is a graduate of both the University of Pennsylvania Undergraduate College and Law School.

7. I have reviewed the phone records of the Hadley County Court and determined that between January and March of the year in question at least fourteen telephone calls were made to the law firm of Wharton & Biddle, telephone #215-555-1776 in Philadelphia, PA, where the victim Ephne Newsome was then employed. The clerk of Hadley County Court has confirmed there is no record of that law firm being counsel of record in any case before that Court during the period in question.

8. I have further confirmed through a reliable third party informant, who was employed together with Newsome at the law firm of Wharton & Biddle, that she received a number of telephone calls at that number from a person identified by her as the same person with whom she was then romantically involved.

9. On November 6th of this year, before this information became known to me, I sought a search warrant from Judge Harry Warren to search the premises of Louisa and Eleanor Martin in West Harbor for evidence related to this homicide. As part of that

> application, the identity of the deceased victim was made known to him and photographs of the deceased victim were displayed to Judge Warren.
>
> 10. Judge Warren became visibly and inexplicably agitated upon viewing the photographs. I now believe this to be because he recognized the victim. Nevertheless, he failed to reveal this fact.

Amanda looked up from the papers. "You *believe* he recognized her? You read minds, Sergeant?"

"Well..." Gregg said.

"Did Judge Warren say anything? Anything that expressed recognition?"

"No, Judge."

T.J. moved his gaze from Gregg to the judge and back again. He started to speak but the judge raised her hand and turned back to the affidavit.

> 11. Despite the fact that, as I believe, Judge Warren had been intimately acquainted with the victim, and probably had spoken to her by telephone within a week's time, he did not then reveal to the undersigned that he had been intimately acquainted with the victim as I now believe he was. Although the victim's remains as depicted in the photographs shown to Judge Warren were disfigured, I have seen photographs of her taken contemporaneously with the period of the relationship which I believe took place between the victim and Judge Warren and believe she remained clearly recognizable from these later pictures. (See Exhibits 1 and 2)

Gregg knew when Judge Stevens was at this point because she stopped reading and turned to the smiling photograph from Newsome's apartment. Her shoulders moved slightly. Then she compared the two, pursed her lips and looked up at the two of them across the table. T.J.

nodded silently at her. She turned back to the affidavit. When he was sure the judge was reading again, T.J. made a face at Gregg that was half question and half disapproval. His first inkling this wasn't going the way he expected.

> 12. The search of the Martin house pursuant to the above referenced warrant revealed that a 16-gauge Purdy double-barreled shotgun was missing. Its earlier presence has been confirmed to police by Eleanor Martin, a resident of the house.
>
> 13. I have confirmed from airline records that Ephne Newsome flew from LaGuardia Airport to Windsor Intl. on Friday, October 30th; that she rented a Ford automobile from the airport Alamo agency and that she has been tentatively identified as a guest at the Gen. Burgoyne Inn in Windsor on either the 30th or Saturday the 31st of October. The following morning she was seen entering an automobile (a silver Range Rover SUV) with New Hampshire registration. A silver Range Rover SUV matching this description is registered to a member of Judge Warren's family and he is known to have regular access to the vehicle.

Judge Stevens' eyes closed momentarily when she read this. Gregg could see her reaction and glanced at T.J. who had only nodded back to him as if to say "See?" He was right. The car was the clincher. But as she read on, Gregg wondered why she didn't ask any questions. In his experience they always did, especially if they thought the subjects were guilty. She turned the page without comment.

> 14. I have reason to believe that information within the possession and control of Judge Harry Warren, including telephone records, credit card records and physical evidence will lead to the acquisition

> *of material evidence related to the commission of the crime of homicide by a person or persons unknown against the life of Ephne Newsome.*
>
> 15. *If Judge Warren executed a search warrant with actual knowledge of his relationship to the victim, Miss Newsome, then there is reason to believe he knowingly jeopardized the investigation of a capital crime.*
>
> 16. *There is probable cause to believe that the search will reveal evidence material to the commission of the crime of obstruction of justice and or hindering prosecution by Judge Warren."*

The judge silently turned to the 'prayers' page, a laundry list of documents sought, including phone records, credit card bills and a search of the Warren home.

Amanda Stevens put her initials on each page and laid them in turn upside down on the others until she had finished. Symbolically, she asked, "Sergeant Leavitt, do you solemnly swear this is true, accurate, and complete to the best of your knowledge and belief?"

"The information is, ah, accurate," Gregg said. T.J. turned quickly toward him but said nothing. Ordinarily he would have said something like "I so swear," and the judge would have signed the warrant then. But this judge heard the hesitation he had meant to convey. She pushed the papers forward, tapped the pen on the table and then put the tip of the pen in her mouth. She exhaled audibly. She looked past them for a full thirty seconds without saying a word and not inviting any. Then she stood and walked past them to the windows which looked out over the parking lot at the empty woods beyond. Gregg stared at the paperwork she had left on the table and regarded the wet end of the green pen she'd had in her mouth. Gold lettering ran down the side. 'WGBH Ch. 2,' it read. When she turned back to them she smiled and shook her head.

"What you're really saying, Sergeant, is that you actually believe Judge Warren *may* have killed this woman?"

T.J. spoke before Gregg could answer. "No, not yet. We aren't making that accusation yet, Judge. This is a material evidence warrant. We do think he has material information which may assist us in our investigation, certainly on the obstruction..."

"... and destroy the reputation of this court while you're at it," the judge interrupted him quietly and firmly as she turned around. T.J. raised one eyebrow in response.

"Well, I can't speak to..." T.J. began.

"Come off it T.J.," the blonde woman said raising her hand. "You've got Sergeant, ah ..." She flipped a page over. "... Leavitt ... Sergeant Leavitt as much as saying Judge Warren killed the lady." She came back from the window and leaned on her hands at the head of the table. She turned to Gregg. "Is that what you're saying, Sergeant Leavitt? That what you think?"

Gregg felt his stomach tighten.

"I certainly believe the subject ... Judge Warren ... may, may have material evidence, Judge," he said. "Further than that..."

"May?" She angled her face toward him. Their eyes met. There are many ways to say the word 'may.' Gregg guessed he had used the right one.

T.J. jumped. "He doesn't have to show probable cause for an arrest, just probable cause to find material evidence. This is a search warrant, not an arrest warrant."

"Thank you T.J. Your analysis is always cogent. You realize this is a sitting judge of this court? Perhaps you'll forgive me if I linger a while on detail?" She tapped the pages. Gregg watched T.J.'s face redden in its uneven, unhealthy way.

"Well, Judge" T.J. said, "if you feel there's a conflict, that you can't..."

She cut T.J. off. "Don't put words in my mouth. I'm not saying that at all." She turned to the warrant. "What about Mrs. Warren? Won't you be looking at her phone records, too?"

"That's likely," T.J. admitted.

"A little broad isn't it?"

Judge Stevens picked up her pen. T.J. hadn't responded so she pointed to the papers for emphasis. "Then what you've got is some phone calls to a big Philadelphia law firm from someone, someone in this courthouse and some ten-year-old gossip. You think its possible that a five-hundred-to-one-thousand-man firm might generate at least one case up here in Hadley County? Might use local counsel?"

Gregg heard himself say "Well the clerk says…"

The judge interrupted him. "When was the cell phone call made? The recent one?"

Gregg consulted his notes. His hand shook. "3:45 p.m. Friday the 29th," he said at last.

Judge Stevens leaned forward across the table. "Well, I happen to know—know for sure—that Judge Warren wasn't *here* that particular Friday afternoon."

T.J. blinked. "Uh, you *know* that?"

"To a certainty." She gave them a smile now. Gregg saw the life rope hurtling toward him.

"Well, there's the pictures," T.J. said, "I was there, too." He nodded at the papers for emphasis. "When he issued the warrant. Judge, it was clear to both of us that he recognized her."

"What time of day was it?" Judge Stevens asked.

Gregg referred to his notes, "Just before noon," he said looking up.

"On a weekend?" She gave them a weary smile.

"But…" Gregg added. T.J.'s eyes now went dead, but stayed on him.

There was silence. The radiator began to complain.

"So what you've got is an incomplete call, some gossip, some decade-old phone calls to a five-hundred-man law firm…" Judge Stevens sounded like she was summing up for the defense, but she kept her eyes on the warrant seeming to miss the exchange of looks between the two.

T.J. made a nodding gesture with his head toward Gregg. "Say something," it said.

When Gregg didn't speak T.J. took his copy of the affidavit from him. "Judge, we have the testimony of the law firm employee that the person in the romantic relationship was a University of Pennsylvania graduate who was a public official in this state, and a wounded war veteran."

The judge looked at Gregg. "This state? The victim actually said 'New Hampshire?'"

Gregg knew he had to be careful. "Well, no, not to that witness." He said as if considering it for the first time. "She wasn't reported as actually saying 'New Hampshire.'" He let the words hang in the air. T.J. looked at him as though he'd been slapped.

"You know how many people attend Penn, T.J.?"

"Not many from here."

"About twenty thousand," she said, ignoring him. She shook her head slowly from side to side. "And how many state employees do we have here in New Hampshire? Another twenty thousand?"

The judge put both her hands back on the table and leaned toward them. A pair of bracelets slid down her wrist and made metallic sounds.

"And this Burgoyne business and Mrs. Warren's car? Look fellas, I live in Windsor. I know all about the Burgoyne. There are people in and out of there all the time. Well, we all know what kind of place it is. You have a positive I.D. of Ms. Newsome or not?"

"Well..." T.J. started to say.

"No," said Gregg, interrupting. "'Pretty sure,' was what the desk clerk said."

T.J.'s mouth stayed partially open but he said nothing further.

"Look, ah, Sergeant Leavitt? Now look at me," the judge said. "Tell me. Do you really think Judge Warren is guilty of murder? You ready to bet your career on this? You're asking me to do that, and I will, but only if you really think so. Are you that sure?"

Gregg saw now that a little reluctance would go a long way. "Well..." he said, trying to show just the right level of concern, "...it seems more likely than not that..."

"Not good enough, Sergeant. Yes or no?"

They had always said Gregg Leavitt had great peripheral vision. He could see the tacklers coming and feint and dodge away just as he seemed in their grasp. So without diverting his gaze from the judge he was perfectly aware that T.J.'s narrowed eyes were focused on him.

"No," he said drawing it out.

At this T.J. almost pushed his chair over getting to his feet, but he caught it. He was several shades of bright pink and breathing audibly. Still he managed a smile, the look of a prisoner who realizes the pardon from the firing squad isn't coming after all. "We'll see if we can't get a little more for you, Your Honor." There were other judges, after all. He reached across the table for the package of papers, but the judge's hand got there first.

"No, no. I'll have Loretta log this in," Judge Stevens said, her voice turning soft. The two touched different ends of the documents at the same time. Amanda looked up.

"Well ... uh ... okay, Judge, if you say so," T.J. said, withdrawing his hand.

"I know you wouldn't show this warrant around to another judge, T.J., but given the gravity of the case we'd better establish a time line. You know I have to call the Chief Justice on this."

T.J. seemed to swell. There'd be no fixing up the affidavit now. For a moment Gregg thought the county attorney would start shouting.

"Thanks for your time, Judge," was what T.J. said. He gestured to Gregg with his chin and saying nothing further, turned and walked to the door.

"Thank you, Judge," Gregg said, getting up to follow.

She didn't answer them until they were almost out the door. "Call in about an hour. Loretta will have it logged in by then." The door closed before she finished. Amanda Stevens then stood over the papers in silence. She looked down at the green pen and reflected on how perishable good news could be.

"Well, shit," she said.

◆Δ◆

Gregg clicked the door closed behind him as they emerged into the lobby. T.J. was walking fast so Gregg had to run a step to catch up to him.

"Will someone tell me what the hell is going on here?" T.J. whispered hoarsely as he plowed across the floor.

"Maybe ..."

"Shit, 'maybe.' She could've given us that warrant like that," T.J. snapped his fingers. "Like that..." He took three more steps. "God damn it," he said pushing the door open to the county attorney's office. He stopped suddenly, then turned and regarded Gregg. "And what was all that 'Gee, I never thought of it that way' bullshit? After I softened everything up for you? I thought I could count on you, Leavitt. Thought you had a backbone."

The two stood as T.J., in his distraction, pulled a pack of cigarettes from his pocket, catching the looks of two passersby. Remembering he couldn't smoke out there, he pushed the pack back into his pocket and stared at the door to Harry Warren's courtroom.

"Well, she didn't say 'no' and no one says I can't go ahead and ask little Harry a few questions myself." T.J. started across the lobby to Judge Warren's courtroom. "Go back to my office and get the whole file from Stacy. Meet me in there," T.J. said over his shoulder. "And, Leavitt, see if you can please grow just a tiny pair of balls before you get back?" T.J. turned and walked through the courtroom door. As he did so, Gregg heard him call out, "Zach, what brings you up here?"

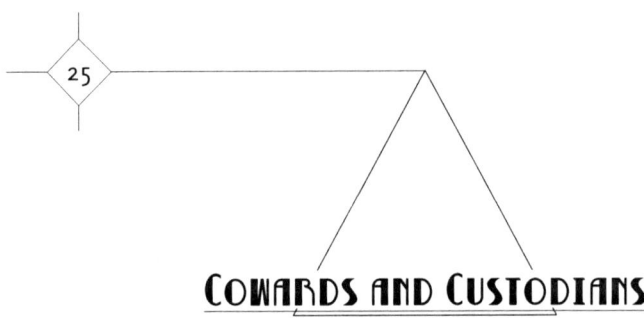

Cowards and Custodians

Amanda knew she had one choice and one chance. This wasn't going to go way. She had to call the Chief Justice. More to the point, she had to call him when she knew he wouldn't take it. She needed time to think.

Fortunately, she knew his schedule. During her year as law clerk, she had learned this, as well as how to avoid his bad breath and fragile ego, his after-hours appearances in the law library while she tried to torture yet one more of his decisions into coherence. The Chief never quite worked up the courage to try anything with her, nothing beyond the occasional avuncular hand on the shoulder. Then he made a too-casual suggestion for a "working" dinner, and Amanda had found out where his wife took exercise class. Just coincidence, of course, that the two became such good friends.

Still... her thoughts turned back to Ted Ingersoll. No one wore suits like that in New Hampshire. Her hand rested on the phone. The man was right. They would have been great. She looked at the warrant papers again. She knew about T.J., and how he could be about warrants. Maybe she was right to wait.

No, she couldn't sit on this. Harry Warren ... Harry Warren ... that weak, lazy little show-off. How could he get himself mixed up in something like this? Just when he looked like he might be of some use after all.

"Loretta," she said into the intercom, "get the Chief for me." Late mornings on Wednesdays were always case conferences. No call would be put through. She felt the safe narrow universe of the New Hampshire courts opening its arms to her, the good girl, doing the right thing. The great bright world of "Profiles" receded into the distance.

"Dammit!" she said while she waited. Her lips compressed and her cheeks swelled, the skin around her nose was pinched. For a moment she was less than beautiful.

Loretta's voice came through the box, "The Chief is hearing oral argument. It'll be about an hour. Shall I leave a message?"

"No," Amanda said. "Tell them I'll call back."

She sat back and made a sound between a puff and a sigh while she calculated. She had made the call. She was covered. That would give her a least the afternoon. Maybe she'd think of something before then. There was always something.

She heard a pop. Then the sound of furniture moving. Then another pop, and another. Through the walls she could hear shouting.

◆△◆

AT ALMOST THE SAME MOMENT Amanda decided to make her call to the Chief Justice, Harry Warren mounted the steps into his courtroom. Harry felt a flash of anger as his toe caught the hem of the still untailored robe. Lifting it, he emerged frowning behind his bench and heard Russell shout the same words he had heard thousands of times before.

"All rise! Hear ye, hear ye. Now comes the county court for the county of Hadley, the Honorable Harry Warren presiding. Draw near and you shall be heard. God save the State of New Hampshire and this honorable court!"

This might well be his last time in a courtroom, at least at this end of one. He had timed his arrival to leave no time for T.J. to get to him before the Martin hearing and had only seen Tee in the distance, turning out of the parking lot in Emma's car. The two had no chance to speak, and he had no idea whether he had made any headway with Amanda.

The walk to his chambers had left Harry terrified that T.J. would intercept him, and the false cheer that Grace tried to display as she hustled him out of chambers and toward the courtroom was, in its way, even more frightening than that.

Harry stood until Russell knocked down the gavel, got to his chair and mumbled, "Please be seated," into the microphone before him.

Harry's stomach lurched at the sight of T.J. Carr standing in the front row of the spectator's section. When Carr resumed his seat, he slouched, looking at Harry with a half smile. Two rows behind, Zach sat with two of the young lawyers from Cruikshank, their black trial cases open in the aisle next to them. Eleanor Martin was on Zach's other side and, beyond her, Margie Tuttle. A metal walker stood in the aisle. Of course. Zach would have Margie help Eleanor to the witness stand, whether she needed it or not.

Eleanor looked this way and that, the way small birds do in the presence of bigger, stronger cousins. Zach had his arms draped over the back of the bench in front of him. He turned and said something to the associate that made the younger man smile. If T.J. was in his courtroom already, then Tee's ploy probably hadn't worked. Harry tried to imagine how it would go. Would there be shouting?

Grace handed up a file and turned to the room to announce the caption.

"*Whitcomb v. Whitcomb*," she said. "Pending motions."

Harry tried to focus on the cover of the file, realizing only then that this was not the Martin case. It was Lionel Whitcomb's endless divorce.

He cupped his hand over the microphone. "Grace."

She stood and came to the bench. "I thought Amanda took care of this last week," he said. "We're doing the Martin..." In the distance T.J. was becoming visibly impatient, craning his neck toward the wall clock, squinting as he checked it against his watch. No, Harry wouldn't be able to bluff him.

"She did," Grace said, bringing Harry's attention back to the Whitcombs' file. "This is just for entry of the final order." Then, standing on her toes she put her hand over the microphone and got herself close enough to whisper. "The S.O.B. fired his lawyer so no one's bothered to object. And," she turned around and scanned the courtroom. "...and he's not here, so just announce the decree *nisi*. We can close this thing once and for all and get on with..." Her raised brows finished the sentence for her.

Harry saw that the long suffering Mrs. Whitcomb was already coming forward with her lawyer. They were followed by a guardian *ad litem* for the Whitcomb children, a mannish lady Harry knew to be Hadley County's 'battered women's' counselor. "One good deed before I go," he thought.

He turned the cover and tried then to read Amanda's handwritten order, but couldn't stop his hand from twitching. He tried to steady it on the bench. In the back of the room he saw Russell's nephew come in with a sheath of papers. The policeman leaned over to T.J. who gestured back sharply. Both men then looked up at the bench, saw Harry was looking at them, then turned back to one another.

The policeman nodded to T.J. and went back out the public door, closing it softly behind him. The bank's lawyers in the row across from Zach were gathering up their paperwork. They knew they were next and could see the marital matter would be short and perfunctory. They both looked up at the policeman with polite lack of curiosity as he passed.

When Harry had finished pretending to read the Whitcomb order, he leaned forward and spoke into the microphone for the record: "Lionel Whitcomb?" There was no response, though Mrs. Whitcomb made a wary glance behind her. The counselor took her hand.

"Has outcry been made for Mr. Whitcomb?" Harry asked, "I thought I saw him here this morning." But of course he had only imagined it.

Russell stood and made an open palm gesture with the motion list in one hand. "Hasn't shown, Judge," he said. Then Russell's eyes moved to T.J. and back again to the judge before he sat down with a gesture of resignation.

"Okay," Harry said. "Please have a seat, Mrs. Whitcomb, and I'll finalize this order for you." With his still trembling hand he began to write.

He finished the words, "Hearing having been scheduled, the defendant not having appeared, and no objection being fi–" when a loud noise made Harry look up. The door at the back of the room was now wide open but moving shut again, apparently after banging against the rearmost spectator's bench. The bank lawyers were looking back at the door in attitudes of surprise and reproach, but Zach and the young Cruikshank associates had their eyes fixed on Lionel Whitcomb who was striding up the aisle between the rows of seats, a half smile on his face. His keys rattled metallically with each step. Harry had never seen him move so fast.

Russell started to get back to his feet as Whitcomb's strangely rapid and purposeful stride brought him to the swinging gate between the spectator seats and counsel tables.

Mrs. Whitcomb had turned then and at the sight of her husband, gave a sound midway between a cry and a moan and dropped her head down almost to the table. The gate flew aside swinging on its spring-loaded hinge. This brought Russell all the way up, one hand at his hip, his eyes on Whitcomb.

But Lionel already had something silver and shining in his hand. From six feet away he shot Russell once in the chest and the big man staggered and sat back down heavily in his chair, his own pistol clattering to the floor. Smoke rose with the shot. That's a big gun, Harry thought. It made a great noise and kicked in Whitcomb's hand.

With this Mrs. Whitcomb's moan turned into a wild, keening scream and she broke away from her protectors, running forward around the table and toward the bench. One of the lawyers with Zach started out into the aisle but tripped heavily over a briefcase and Eleanor's walker. This made enough noise for Whitcomb to whirl around and fire a second shot in his direction. It was high. Plaster flew off the back wall.

"Mr. Whit–" Harry started to say.

"Oh fuck you, fuck you," Whitcomb shouted turning to walk past the lawyer and guardian now scrambling under the counsel table. Whitcomb raised and fired the gun right at Harry. Harry's microphone exploded and something caught Harry in the face. The world turned pink.

Up to that moment it could be said Harry was standing his ground, but that would make no allowance for the lethargy of the true coward. Even that interlude was short-lived, because the bullet in Harry's direction shocked him into the next two phases of every other Harry Warren response to danger: panic and flight. Whatever else, it was time to go.

He kicked back his chair and turned, crouching—cringing, really—and tried to make for the door behind him. Mrs. Whitcomb had reached the front wall by then and for an instant Harry thought she would come up the stairs and try for the door along with him, but she only turned in despair and slid down onto the floor next to the bench. Her hands were palm out in front of her. "Poor lady," Harry thought as he stretched for the door knob and safety.

HARRY HAD OFTEN SUFFERED dreams of trying to get out of a confined space without effect, or of hurrying to get to some appointment yet, for some inexplicable reason, never quite making it. The revenant goal hovered just out of reach while some malign force weighed down his arms or feet as he tried to navigate a kind of cosmic Jell-o. This time, as he lunged for escape, Harry knew it was no dream, but the more he stretched, the more the familiar force pulled him the wrong way. In fact, he'd again stepped on the hem of the new robe, and worse, done so with his good leg. Between the weakness of his other leg and the pull of the robe on his shoulders, his fingers only grazed the knob of the door.

He staggered, did a little hop and, though off balance, was almost free. Harry had no faith in epiphanies. He knew as his hand grasped the knob that his nature was and would remain what it had always been. Fear and shame had been his primal urges. They still were, and at that moment he feared the safety of the hallway as much as Lionel's gun. So Harry Warren did what he had always done best, he hesitated. With that, the weak leg gave way. It was only physics from there on.

Harry felt himself pitch and fall toward the pleading woman. Whitcomb had reached her now, gun up, as Harry's free foot found only air and he sailed forward in their direction. Whitcomb must have seen the black-robed airborne figure out of the corner of his eye because he jerked backward in surprise.

Harry landed hard on the first step and rolled into a sideways somersault. He came to rest sprawled face down on top of Mrs. Whitcomb.

Her terrified eyes shrunk with shock at the sight of a bloody face suddenly nose to nose with hers. Harry struggled to roll over to get back to his feet, but the best he could do was turn himself to where, half sitting, half lying on the wailing woman, he found himself face-to-face with Lionel Whitcomb.

And his very big gun.

Perhaps Lionel wanted to savor the moment. Or maybe he could see from Harry's expression that he was only trying to get out of the way and decided to wait for the better shot. Whatever it was, instead of just firing, Lionel raised the gun further up and cocked the hammer theatrically before bringing it down on Harry again. He was saying something like "Aaww" when his chest seemed to explode and he pitched forward into the wall above them. His gun went off and at the same time Harry felt Lionel kick him in his good leg. He must have kicked Mrs. Whitcomb too because she made a yelp of surprise in his ear. Then Whitcomb, and separate wet, warm parts of Whitcomb, fell on them in a heap.

The next few seconds were filled with Mrs. Whitcomb's screams, piercing, continuous and loud. Then the young Sergeant Leavitt stood over them as he kicked away Whitcomb's gun making it slide along the floor. Whitcomb himself seemed to recover. He made a series of loud snoring noises and crawled about a yard through the blood pouring out of him before he collapsed and fell still for good. Leavitt tested Whitcomb's limp form roughly with his toe, then seemed to inspect Harry. Harry saw that the trooper's gun was a bigger, duller, more substantial version of Whitcomb's and was distressed that it seemed mostly pointed at him while the Sergeant performed these errands.

"You wounded?" Leavitt asked, his eyes going back and forth between Harry and the man he'd shot. Mrs. Whitcomb just screamed louder while Harry looked back dumbly. Then, tired of all the noise, Harry hoisted himself up onto the stairs he'd just fallen down. He saw he was covered with blood and grayish bits of tissue which looked purple on the black robe. Mrs. Whitcomb's contorted face and one shoulder of her white blouse were covered with a spider web of spattered red. More importantly, she was spurting bright red blood from her thigh. It had about the same flow as the water fountain Harry remembered from grammar school. This time, though, it came and went, came and went.

The pandemonium in the room became general. Cries of *'911! 911!'*

and warnings, belated, Harry thought, of *'Stay down, stay down'* echoed through the room as brown-shirted deputies and grey-shirted bailiffs rushed in, weapons raised.

Then Grace was with him, shouting herself, "Harry! Harry! Did he get you?" He regarded her haggard face as she inspected his forehead. Then, "Jesus, he just missed you." She made a reproachful smile.

By then Harry could see that Zach was also next to them, facing down a nervous bailiff, whose drawn gun was moving around in quick jerking motions. "Easy, easy," Zach said as he pulled off his necktie and began to tie it around Mrs. Whitcomb's very large, very white thigh. She wailed as he tightened it, but the fountain of blood subsided to an ooze. The bailiff and Zach then supported Mrs. Whitcomb's head and lowered her to the floor.

"Well," Harry thought, "some guys are good in a crisis." Harry felt good enough to stand up then, and it seemed time to go back to chambers. He tried the second step. As it had been with the door, nothing seemed to work. He looked down to curse the untailored robe again only to see blood coming out of his shoe. Strange, his foot felt fine. Grace saw this as soon as he did and pulled up his robe like a curtain. The indecency of the old woman lifting his robe for a look made him smile. He looked down to see a small, almost perfectly round hole in his trouser leg, just above his knee.

"Not quite," Harry said to Grace and sat, or fell, down again.

"Oh Jesus, Mary and Joseph," she said. "Don't you ever know enough to duck?"

◆Δ◆

Harry was given the third ambulance, Mrs. Whitcomb and Russell being much more seriously wounded. Lionel Whitcomb had no immediate transportation needs and lay where Sergeant Leavitt had rolled him, temporarily forgotten in the middle of the drama that would get them all, briefly, on the six o'clock news around the nation. Lionel didn't seem to mind. He had that dead-eyed look a drunk gets just before he passes out. Well, Harry had seen that before.

The Hadley EMTs weren't army medics and they certainly didn't have any morphine for him, so Harry's primary impression was one of numbness which steadily resolved itself into excruciating pain. They cut his pant leg right up to the crotch and applied a big padded bandage to the back of the wounded leg, where the hole was apparently somewhat bigger than the one in front. Enough bigger to elicit an "oh shit" from the EMT. Unlike Mrs. Whitcomb, Harry's blood was coming out purple and, happily, much more slowly. He lay there on the stretcher hearing the snatches of conversation.

"... Judge ... saved her life..." one Cruikshank lawyer was saying to the tie-less Zach as the EMT's finally rolled Harry past them out of the courtroom. Outside as they bounced him down the courthouse steps, he thought he heard some ragged clapping but was more conscious of an interval of bright sun in his eyes. For a moment he was sure he saw Tee still perfectly dressed. Was he dreaming, dying? Maybe Emma would buy him a camel hair coat for Christmas. Suddenly this was shut out by the roof of the ambulance and the hearty enforced cheerfulness of the ambulance attendant, a girl with crooked teeth and hair that had tried much too hard, and some time ago, to be blonde.

She started to urge Grace out of the ambulance as she put a blood pressure cuff on Harry's arm.

"Don't even fucking think about it, honey," Grace said. After seventy-two years, Grace had learned to say this in such a way that people listened. The blonde shrugged and moved over as she finished putting the cuff on. The siren came on and the vehicle jumped into motion. Harry watched Grace try to smile. "Hang on, hang on," Grace was saying, softly squeezing his free hand.

Then he heard the attendant shout, "Preshahs' droppin,' step on it!" The ambulance lurched to a higher speed.

"You grow up in Hadley?" he asked the attendant, but he didn't hear her answer.

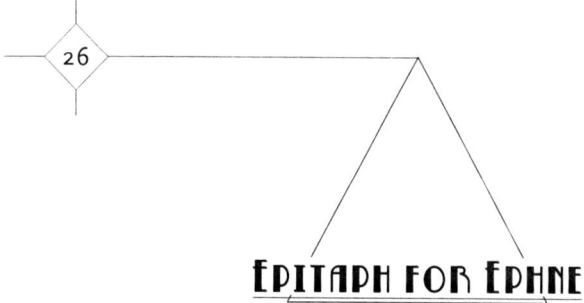

26 EPITAPH FOR EPHNE

Harry was not one of those people who hated hospitals. He always found them to be warm, dry, and undemanding, with cornucopias of pharmaceutical-quality drugs on demand.

Deprived of pain killers during the twenty-minute ride from the courthouse to Hadley Regional Hospital, Harry was rewarded with two glorious opiate-soaked days in the ICU before being transferred to a floor room. By then he was ready for the change. He enjoyed the drugs, but ICUs were too open for his taste. There were half the usual number of walls, and even these were half window. 'I see you' seemed a more appropriate name. Recurrent visions of T.J. rattling a pair of handcuffs at one of those windows didn't help.

The move to a floor room meant Demerol *and* privacy. They also had TV's in these rooms, and it was on one of these that Harry saw himself reborn as 'hero.'

Harry knew that the kindest description of his behavior was that he had stumbled down two stairs. On television, however, he was the *"North Windsor jurist, who threw himself between the deranged gunman and his intended victim, was upgraded from critical to serious this morning..."*

One of these reports spoke of his "gallantry." The state police sergeant, Russell's nephew, who had saved them all, had to be satisfied at first with "quick thinking," though, inevitably, he too was elected "hero." If there were any doubts, they were dispelled by the eyewitness accounts of Grace

Carroll and Margie Tuttle. Grace's sharp assessment of her boss: *"just like him,"* with its hint of affectionate disapproval, put the final stamp on Harry's credentials.

Others, it seemed, had harbored secret suspicions of Harry's valor: *"In short, a selfless act of quiet courage that comes as no surprise to these long time Hadley residents."* Classmates from grammar school, one of whom had beaten him up as a boy, attested to his bravery. Grace usually had the last word, her always emphatic *"just like him"* played again and again until finally, *"This is Moira Baxter, Action 8 News."*

◆△◆

REJOINING THE WORLD, Harry saw that Emma, Leigh and Samantha, after their initial terror, had maintained vigils each in her own way. His initial interludes of consciousness found Leigh cross-examining doctors like she was going to take the place public. She took names and numbers and made lists, as if she could will her father back to health through sheer efficiency. Emma concentrated on the nurses. She established first name relationships with everyone on all three shifts. *"Pauline, I hate to be a nuisance, but is it time for Harry's IV? I have so much trouble keeping track. I'm so glad you're doing this."* Samantha, seeing the staff vetted by her sister and mollified by her mother, did what she had always done best. She wandered about allowing the doctors to fall in love with her.

The press proved fickle soon enough. After four days the reporters tired of his and Gregg Leavitt's praises and their attention shifted to the foolhardy exemption of the "deranged" (Channel 8) or "distraught" (*News & Observer*) Lionel Whitcomb from the usual courthouse security checks. As far as could be determined, Lionel had simply let himself in by the basement door that morning like he always did, fortified himself with half a quart of Three Feathers down in his cellar room, put the gun in his pocket and walked upstairs to the courtroom avoiding the metal detectors at the front door. When it came out that one commissioner was Lionel's cousin, the ritual assignment of blame was complete. There was no appeal from the raised eyebrow of a local news-anchor.

Harry's daughters were struck by the number of people in the Hadley

Regional Hospital who remembered their father. Not the doctors, of course. Like Harry's own mother, these were bewildered strangers, cast up in Hadley by twists and turns of fate. But the clean-up people, the CNAs, the technicians, the kitchen staff—these were all Hadley born and bred, and Harry, it seemed, had been everyone's best friend.

"Daddy, you could run for mayor of this place," Leigh said to him after watching Margie Tuttle's testimonial to his "guts."

"Okay, just as long as I don't have to run against your mother."

"You're safe there. We were just downtown, picking up your car." Leigh made a face, "I thought Windsor was grim." She adjusted the grey suit, blue blouse and sensible blue pumps expected of Brown Brothers traveling investment bankers. Having satisfied herself that her mother was meeting minimal standards of competence and convinced that her father would live, she was to return to New York later in the day. Leigh was all Llewellyn when it came to business. But not about him. Since childhood she had known her father was brave, known it since the day Emma had given her the newspaper story to frame. She had been shocked by what happened, but not surprised.

Emma spoke to her from the other side of his bed. "Don't worry darling, your father will get over this. We'll be hearing about his loveless, solitary childhood again soon enough." But as she said this she took his hand, the one without the tubes, and squeezed it to show she was prepared to indulge him.

A technician came in then, flicked the IV bag and wrote something on a clipboard. Shyly she asked Harry if he remembered her from their days in grammar school. Harry smiled and lied.

"Okay it wasn't entirely loveless," Harry said when she had left.

"See?" Emma said.

Leigh said, "Oh my God, you don't mean..."

"I didn't say I knew her biblically."

"Imagine my relief," said Emma.

"Can we talk about something else?" As Leigh said this, Samantha turned into the room, her abundant red-gold hair gathered in a braid over one shoulder, trailing two doctors like hooked fish.

"Speaking of love," Leigh said, showing sudden interest in her wrist watch.

Samantha, since infancy had affected ignorance of the effect she had on others. She looked from face to face and said "What?"

This exchange between sisters made one doctor self conscious enough to pretend to review Harry's chart. He would have done more, but the only bit of routine maintenance that needed looking to was Harry's catheter bag. The healer was smitten, but not that much. The other white-coated man smiled at the lion with his cubs. A lot he knew.

◆△◆

A MAN HARRY'S AGE couldn't get shot in the thigh without side effects. One of these was infection, and despite the antibiotics this led to a persistent fever. In the days that followed, therefore, Harry was permitted visitors, but also suffered to fall asleep in the middle of their sentences without insult or apology. He found himself emerging from dreams, not once, but four or five times in a given day. They were vivid dreams, in which he played an active role.

On Harry's fourth day in the hospital, he woke in mid-sentence. He had been back at Phi Psi greeting a new crop of freshmen during Rush Week.

"... *Harry Warren*," he heard himself say and saw that his right hand was out while an insincere smile ached on his unshaven face.

As he awoke he realized the extended hand was offered to Russell Chase who, as always, was surveying him with well-placed concern. Not that Russell looked very good himself. Russell's bathrobe and hospital gown were askew, his own right arm in a sling. He seemed much too big for the wheelchair.

The nurse who had pushed Russell in said, "It's the meds." Then to Harry in that heightened decibel level permitted only to nurses, she called out "Harry, Harry, you awake, dear?"

"Yes, yes, uh Har, uh, yes."

As he willed himself back to consciousness, Harry saw that Emma was crouched down by Russell's chair holding Russell's free hand in both of hers.

"Just a few minutes, Russell," the nurse said.

Emma stood then. "You two wounded warriors mind if I get some lunch?" She walked around the bed to put the call button on Harry's lap, kissed Russell and took the nurse's arm. "Gladys, can you point me to the lunch room?"

When they were alone Russell turned from the sound of retreating footsteps to Harry. "You back?" His eyes searched Harry's for confirmation.

"Yah, it's just, well. Except I'm thirty years older than I was a minute ago."

"Well, you almost didn't get to thirty-one."

Harry shrugged, then winced. "You either," he said.

"Yah, he tagged me pretty good. Felt like I'd been pole-axed." Russell pointed to his sling. "Couldn't move. All I could see was you and Grace. I thought he'd got you, too." Russell gestured toward his own forehead, but he was referring to Harry's wound. For some unknown reason, Russell seemed to be explaining himself.

Harry fingered the bandages over his eye. The doctors had told him that hadn't been a bullet. The microphone housing had hit him at the hairline and left a three-inch gash. Eight stitches, but not life threatening. "I hope that's not an apology," Harry said.

"Keep thinkin' I could've been a little quicker."

"No, Russell."

The big man leaned forward in the chair, looked behind him, then more in whisper than voice, he said, "But you got up. You got to the door. I saw you. You could've gone through."

Harry knew better than to embellish or lie. "For what?" he said.

"Oh." Russell seemed to consider this. "I suppose. Yah."

They shared a short silence.

"Good thing that nephew of yours is a good shot."

"He's a good-un." Russell nodded and shifted himself carefully in his wheelchair, glad to change the subject.

"How are you doing?" Harry nodded toward Russell's chest.

"I'll live," he said. He pointed to a spot just above his slung arm. "Went straight through. Didn't hit a rib, only nicked the shoulder blade. Lucky."

Harry let his head fall back and watched some drops descend into his IV.

While he looked away, Russell said, "Gregg, I guess you know, he got that assignment down to the governor's detail. Changeover in two weeks. They'll make the announcement Saturday morning once they clear him in … well, about Lionel."

Harry turned his face back toward him. Russell saw the question there because he added, "He's off the Newsome case. Movin' to Windsor right away."

"I suppose T.J. will wait a decent interval," Harry said.

"For what?" Russell made a close mouthed smile.

"C'mon, Russell."

"You think he's comin' after you on some bullshit obstruction charge? You? The hero? Sure, T.J.'s just dyin' to do that."

"We both know he has more in mind than that."

"Maybe he did, but he'll never admit that now. Hell, I hear he couldn't even get a warrant to search your office."

"I'm not following you, Russell. Who…?"

Russell settled back in his chair. "Never mind that. T.J.'s problem is that they're pretty sure they know how and where that girl got killed now. You're not a good fit."

The Demerol fueled lassitude was breaking up, and Harry's wounded leg had begun to remind him why he was still there, but he pressed on.

"Fit?"

"Well, Omer, you know Omer Pouliotte, Fish and Game? He was helping Gregg with the crime scene package and, nosy bugger that he is, Omer sees that the gun that's missing is a double barrel 16-gauge but all the ammo loose in the gun cabinet is 20-gauge. Only one box open and just two shells gone. Ever since they found her, they've been trying to figure out how a little girl like that could take a tight shot group in the belly and still run up a mountain afterwards when Omer says, 'suppose the shooter put in the wrong shells, the twenty gauge.'"

"I don't…" Harry squinted, then winced.

"Muzzle velocity would go way down," Russell said, turning his left palm down, but wincing himself as he thought better of the gesture.

Seeing Harry was still frowning he added, "The smaller shell. It wouldn't build up enough compression." Harry remembered the rattling just before he put the shotgun in L.L.'s gun cabinet.

"So how does that rule me out?"

"Well it's pretty sure the gun missing from the Martin house was the murder weapon. The others haven't been fired for years. Gregg didn't think you, bein' in the army and all, would've been dumb enough to put the wrong size shells in the gun.

"They can place her, the victim, at the Martin house when she made her last cell phone call. That call was made to the courthouse. They thought it was to you, but there's some question whether you were there to take it. Some order you didn't sign. I asked Grace and she thought that was pretty funny. Anyway, she didn't make any more calls ... to your house, for instance."

"Uh huh."

"Even after the excitement, T.J., he goes over to the Martins with your picture, see if he could place you there. They both swear you were never there. The older one, she don't think much of you, by the way. Margie Tuttle? The shoplifter? She says she never saw you there either. They all remember Miss Newsome and a bunch of lawyers being there, but never you. Well, he pressed her a little and Margie Tuttle starts hollerin' that they're tryin' to do something about her probation."

Harry remembered Margie in her sweatshirt. He started to laugh but ended up coughing.

Russell took this in. "Yah, it was probably quite a sight, but Gregg says Margie called her public defender, that little red-haired girl, and then she started raisn' hell. 'Course T.J. just blamed the poor cops."

"So, where does that..."

"Look, the woman's not local, got no family except a mother in some nursing home down in Pennsylvania who don't give a damn. The only guy besides T.J. who ever liked you for this is off the case and seems to have reasons now to hope you're innocent. I'm tellin' you, nobody cares, no one's pushing."

Harry let his head fall back on the pillow. "*Nobody cares.*"

"Not that T.J. didn't try, the bastard. He's got a hard on for you, Judge. What you ever do to him?"

By now Harry's interest in the story was losing out to the pain in his leg. He reached for the pain pump and it yielded a series of clicks. Ten seconds later a sense of well-being flowed over him. He clicked again, but he'd used up his allotted dose and the pump sat silent.

Russell leaned closer. "You did all right, you know."

"Russell, I got hung up is all. I just didn't know which way to run." Demerol, liquid truth.

"Sure, coulda, woulda. Bullshit. It's what happened that counts."

The fog gathered around Harry, already exhausted, as he heard this. He closed his eyes. When he looked up again, the light coming through the window signaled a different time of day. Russell was gone. Emma was back next to his bed, attentive but silent while Harry puzzled over what would make Eleanor—it had to be Eleanor—pick up the bigger gun and put the wrong ammunition in it. But he didn't puzzle long. Emma smiled, took his hand and the darkness, warm and soft, welcomed him back.

◆Δ◆

WHEN HE NEXT AWOKE, Emma's back was to him. Black windows told him it was night time. Her hand was on Zach's arm.

"... sorry about the mortgage, Zach, but ..."

"Look, I'm a big boy, Emma, I understand. It's only money. I'll just have to find someone else."

"You understand, don't you?"

"Not really, but ... Emma," Zach could see that he was awake and nodded in Harry's direction to get Emma's attention.

"He's back." Emma said this with an almost artificial levity and stepped away quickly.

"Darling, Zach wants to talk with you." She threw a sharp look at Zach, then back to Harry. "Alone."

"Uh huh." Harry watched her turn and give Zach a hard look, a warning of some kind, before leaving. Good loyal Emma. Always worrying about him.

"I was wondering if you'd ever wake up," Zach said after Emma had gone.

Harry tried to pull himself up on the pillows. As he did, Zach said, "I was just telling Emma about my first case up here in Hadley County. Thought you were listening, you said 'indeed' three times."

Harry stared, still gathering his thoughts.

"One of your predecessors, sanctimonious bastard," Zach said, returning to his story, "let in a chiropractor—a damned chiropractor—as an expert, in a slip and fall." He grinned. It might have been the old days except Harry couldn't summon the energy to smile.

Zach moved from the window and sat down next to the bed. "No, Hadley County was never lucky for me," he sighed. "You remember the election? I won big in Windsor but I never carried Hadley County.

Harry still said nothing. He just stared. For one thing, he was sure Emma and Zach hadn't been talking about Zach's old cases. For the first time in their lives, Zach looked away.

"Funny," Harry said, "I though you two were talking about money."

"Little short, that's all," Zach said at last.

"I'm sorry to hear that," Harry said. "Can I help?"

"No. Shorter than that." Zach waved away the question with a smile. "I wonder ..." he started to say. Then, suddenly grinning over his glasses, "Hey, I gotta know. That business at the bench." The familiar face turned friendly and skeptical at the same time. Harry remembered how he ran up to put the tourniquet on Mrs. Whitcomb.

"I tripped," Harry said, knowing what the question was. "I stepped on my robe, the hem. Too long for me. First thing I knew I was on top of her."

"You tr–?" Zach's eyes widened in disbelief.

The absurdity of it all got them both laughing in a guilty, laughing-in-church kind of way. Harry caught his breath long enough to say "She was some surprised." With that they both gave way again. After a bit more of this they caught their breath. Harry wiped tears off his cheek with his free hand. He felt warm again and knew the fever would return.

"You bastard," Zach said, shaking his head. "Tripped." But his smile faded and he winced from a pain of his own.

But Harry had seen how Emma had pulled away.

"Zach, how much does Emma know, you know, about…"

"Oh nothing. Not from me anyway. She did say you were 'terribly worried' about something, 'weren't sleeping.' She asked me what it was. Actually, I wasn't sure I knew." Zach smiled and raised his eyebrows.

"Uh huh," Harry said. "We keep it that way?"

"Sure, sure," Zach said, nodding, making a small burping sound, his color returning.

"That's good, because she was showing some interest in the Martin case." Harry heard his voice as if someone else was talking.

Zach cocked his head then, alert, interested, non-committal. He arched his eyebrows in his 'what-are-you-getting-at?' way. "Interest?"

"You remember the videotape, Zach? The Louisa Martin deposition?" Zach nodded once, but still silent.

"Well, Emma saw a chair, a settee—whatever you call it—you were sitting on it. She was pretty impressed with it. In fact, she was pretty impressed with *all* the stuff she saw in Louisa Martin's bedroom. She ask you about that?"

"Emma," Zach said simply. They exchanged a long look. Then, changing the subject, Zach said, "That what the hearing was going to be about?"

"A little," Harry said. "mostly it was some bullshit idea of mine … that I could get Eleanor Martin to confess to …, well, something … but, that was then. You see, lying here with tubes running in my arms and out my dick I've had time to think. Think about 'why.' Why does Ephne Newsome call me after seven years? Why is she interested in powers of appointment? But mostly: Why, why wasn't she asking Zach Hannah—Cruikshank and Hannah? He'd have told her it didn't matter any more. They'd already amended the Martin trust."

Zach's scalp seemed to shift on his head at the word 'appointment' but he only smiled indulgently. The patient was rambling. They were back in the office again while Harry worked up an argument. *'Good, good. I like it,'* Zach would have said.

Harry took a breath. "And why all the litigation when all they have to do is sell one chair to Winterhur or the Peabody or some dot.com millionaire with more money than sense?"

Zach said, "What are you talking about, Harry? What's this Winter... whatever ...?" He trailed off.

"That's what Ephne would be good at, wouldn't she, selling those things?"

He was guessing, bluffing, but Zach watched him carefully before saying, "Sell what? The sisters wouldn't even let me sell that old boat. Too much pride."

"Sure, pride. 'Better a lawsuit with some rude bankers than sell off a family treasure.' That's what I thought before I read the file, but why would they hesitate to sell a couple of sticks of old furniture if it got them out of the woods?"

Harry reached over and took a sip from a glass of water, confirming that the call button was still handy.

"The only thing that makes sense is: They *didn't* know—about the furniture anyway. You've got it listed as 'miscellaneous furniture' on the inventory, just some junk they must have brought up here when they sold the house in Haverford.

Zach cocked his head backward. "I didn't know you were an expert in..."

Harry interrupted. "I'm not, but Emma is and Ephne was. And if Emma could tell from a videotape, Ephne must have known the second she walked into Louisa's bedroom. Even if she was wrong, she'd have looked into it. She'd never let it go as 'miscellaneous furniture.'"

"Harry." Zach held his hands up in a dismissive, 'please-stop' way. When they had worked up a case for trial Zach had always told him, *'Don't paint yourself a picture. Don't try to go further than the evidence takes you.'* Zach began to play with his gold pen, turning it this way and that, holding it between his two index fingers. He was smiling but Harry had never seen so many of his teeth.

"But, of course, Ephne wouldn't stop there. She would have wanted to know more, wanted to see the Wharton Biddle trust documents, and she couldn't resist playing 'do-you-know?' with Eleanor, maybe even Louisa?"

Zach gave a small jerk of recognition at this.

"I expect the Martins probably enjoyed going over the good old days, even with Ephne. At first. Until the coincidences piled up. Camp Abenaki? St. Agatha's? Oswald Popp?" Harry was out of breath.

Zach snorted. "Who the hell is Oswald Popp?" he asked. Harry waved his hand. Even Zach couldn't know everything.

"No, at some point, either Ephne or the Martins, who knows which, figured out they were living different halves of the same story."

"The painkillers must be pretty good in this place," Zach said, and tried to laugh again. Harry had never heard Zach laugh unconvincingly before, "You're not suggesting that Eleanor or Louisa …?" He let the question trail off.

But Zach had a point. The machine dispensing the pain medication whirred softly just then and clicked on its own. Harry felt the wash of second-martini well-being flow through him. The tips of his fingers tingled. Perhaps he wasn't making sense after all. Still, he kept on. "Yah, but there she was. What was it? She figure out about the adoption? She ever complain to you about the life they stole from her?"

Zach didn't speak or move, but he stopped pretending to smile.

"You tell me, Harry, you tell me." Zach now looked at him like a man who knew the answer and was mildly disappointed at how long it was taking Harry to get there. Then again, he could just be an old friend waiting for the patient to fall asleep.

"They'd have been some pissed off wouldn't they, Eleanor and Louisa, presented with this miserable bastard child? Or maybe even more pissed off to find they'd amended their trust to hand off all their property to their lawyer. Pissed off enough to do something about it? Louisa's mean enough but she could barely get out of bed, and I don't see Ephne walking upstairs just to give her a sporting shot. I suppose Eleanor could do it though, she's mean enough, too, under that ditzy, helpless school-marm act she puts on. She *could* shoot her own daughter.

"Daughter?" Zach began.

"And here's the good part, the Amendment, the one witnessed by you and Smitty. Ephne knew about that. That was how she was going to sell the stuff. But then she finds out she's the heir. Well, the trust isn't much use to her, is it?"

"Harry, this isn't funny."

"No. No it isn't. And of course, there's the other thing."

"Other thing?"

"Yeah, if either Martin did it, she'd know how to do it right. All that 'shooting' they do down there. Even Eleanor would know which gun to pick, how to load it and what to load it with. But someone not used to guns, someone who never used guns ... who never got a hunting license... he could make that mistake easy enough, he could put in the wrong sized shell. Someone ... Christ, this is hard, Zach ..."

Zach's eyes moved quickly to the side; considering, confirming, before returning to stare steadily at him.

"And you know ... what?" Harry said. "Neither one of them could have put the thing in my garage."

Zach smiled at this and made a shrug. How many times had Harry seen that gesture? *'You may say that, but what can you do with it?'*

"You were always good at theories, Harry." But Zach's voice now had the tone of a man who knew a New Hampshire jury, when it heard this, might just understand. "Do you know how many times I've covered your ass the last week?"

"I know, I know. But T.J. and that cop, Leavitt ... Someone, someone's going to figure it out. They won't get it at first, but they will eventually."

Zach regarded him without affect, but colder now. He shifted in the chair.

"It's going to narrow down fast now, Zach. T.J.'s not the sharpest knife in the drawer, but even he's going to figure out that Ephne was Eleanor's kid. Even he can figure out the Martin trust residue would have passed to her instead of the trust. Then people in your office will compare notes. 'Remember how that appraisal information got changed?' Then it will be 'where's that first draft?' You all friends down there at Cruikshank these days? A few young studs looking to change the stationery?"

ZACH GOT UP from the chair and went to the window. He rocked back and forth on his feet. At last he said, "Actually, let me tell you a different story." He spoke in the kindly understated language of a Hannah opening. "You see, there's this judge. He's not much of a judge, but he's all right. Married up. No one's quite sure how he pulled *that* off, but he knows he's lucky so he's a good boy, loyal and dutiful.

"Then the years go by, and the leash starts to tighten up on him, all that 'yes dear' stuff, until one night he finds a new lady. She shows an interest and he remembers for a few days that he's a man again. One thing leads to another and ..." Zach shrugged.

"But after a couple of rolls in the hay he wakes up one morning and remembers he's already hit the jack-pot. No broad is worth what he'd have to give up, so he dumps the new girl. He thinks he broke her heart. He's wrong about that. The little bitch doesn't have a heart. Oh, an itch or two to be scratched, but mostly this is a girl with needs, a girl who wants.

"A few years go by and he forgets all about her. He's home and dry. Then, out of nowhere, the lady calls him and says 'let's get together.' Wife's out of town, why not? That's when auld lang syne turns into 'I'm gonna tell.'"

Zach turned and shrugged. "You can see, can't you Harry? You saw the rest of it all right. I'm sorry about the gun, but T.J. seemed to be floundering. You know how it works. Once he indicted you, he couldn't go ahead later and chase someone else. That's all. You know I, well, it wouldn't have played out to the end."

It was a reasonable analysis and given with soft emphasis; bad news given to a client with a weak case.

Neither spoke. The silence was broken by the sound of the hospital loudspeakers. "*Dr. Jones, dial 386, Dr. Jones...*"

"Two stories," Harry said at last.

"Yah, two stories."

"But why me, Zach? After all you've done for me?"

"You mean the judgeship. Well, let's say that was always a consolation prize, wasn't it."

The two of them stared at different spots on the floor, like they were mourning something that had happened to someone else.

"Well," Zach said at last, suddenly, effortlessly changing tone and smiling with what looked like the old secret warmth, "between us, I don't think either of us is much interested in telling his story, do you?"

"Maybe not, Zach, but, the furniture... you can never get the money now. How much..."

"Three million," Zach said, shaking his head. "That's what she thought."

"Three million what?" Emma came into the room. She took in the men's expressions and stopped. "I, ah, I can come back?" she asked. "I'm not interrupting?"

"Nope. Just leaving," Zach said. "Good luck, Harry."

"Zach?" Emma said to his back as he brushed by her. She turned back to Harry. He couldn't read her expression, probably because it was the first time he ever saw her afraid.

"What did he...?" Emma's voice trailed off. When Harry didn't respond, she said, "He's certainly in a rotten mood. Do you think he feels okay? He looks awful." But the man in the bed had gone back into the dark.

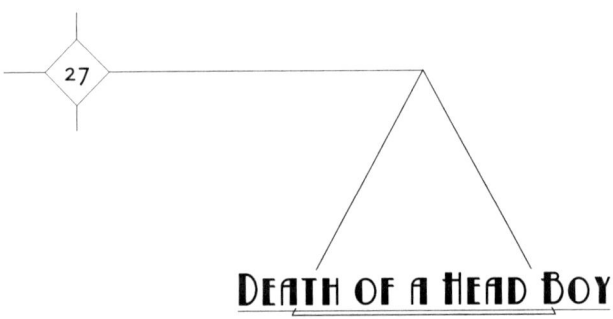

27

Death of a Head Boy

From habit Zach Hannah began to reach down to lock his car door but, after pausing to consider, he tossed the keys on the front seat and, using both hands, gently pressed the door closed.

It had been warm for Thanksgiving and that morning, Friday, had begun like Indian summer. But he had grown up in the mountains and knew warmth in November was a fragile thing. The temperature had now dropped into the forties and was still falling. As if to remind him, a chill gust rolled down the mountain and raised his hair away from his head. He already missed the warmth of the car, but the cold would go away once he started to climb. It always did. He checked the laces on his boots and swung a small backpack over his shoulders. Then he tightened the strap that held his glasses and set out on a hollowed out path past a 'Summit' arrow. The 'Trail Closed' sign the Appalachian Mountain Club put up every November first came fifty feet later.

The old rhythms returned as he walked the trail upwards through the familiar wind-stunted spruce and fir. His boots gripped the rutted muddy path, and splayed roots served as steps where they emerged from the eroded soil. As predicted, his body warmth returned as he climbed.

How many times had he started up this trail? Twenty? No, forty times? Man and boy at least that, but seldom at this time of year and never at this time of day. The late afternoon light slanted at an unfamiliar, ominous, angle. No sound came but the wind, the scrape of his boots and the rhythm of his breathing. The last time he had been here—ten years ago? twelve?—there were crowds of hikers. He hadn't come back after that. Well, that had been August. There wouldn't be a crowd tonight.

At the tree line the air sharpened. The moan of the wind rose an octave as it came with increasing force down through the narrow crevices of the boulder-strewn slope rising before him.

That new pain in his side was throbbing now, reaching out in little shoots and starts into his lower gut. It came and went but each time, just a little further, a little longer than the time before. Most of October he'd thought he had the flu. Then he thought it was an ulcer.

Breathless, he stopped to let the pain recede. He fingered the pill bottle in his pocket and confirmed the water bottle in the backpack. But he wasn't high enough, not yet.

Breathing deeply, he turned back to take in the narrow valley, the notch, already filling with shadow below. A lettuce-green web of ski trails traced the side of the grey-green mountain across the notch. He regretted the grey-yellow scar of bulldozed earth next to one trail that signaled the beginning of yet another condominium. He wondered if his office had created this one. Then the pain jumped into his belly again and made him groan. Well, one couldn't hurt. He took a pill, placed it on his tongue, unscrewed the bottle and washed it down. He rested, still out of breath, waiting for the pain to subside.

When it had, he set off again, making his way steadily upward, not hurrying, picking his steps one at a time through the boulder field the way the Head always did, until just above he could make out the 'table rock' where the Devon boys always had lunch on Headmaster's Day. Whether it was the memory or just the pill, the pain had all but disappeared by the time he stopped and regarded the wide flat boulder. He stood, panting in the wind. God, that first time he sat there with the others. Hadn't that been just about the happiest day of his life? The only sophomore on the Rock.

He walked around it, then sat on the Rock, on the very spot where the head boy always sat, just beneath the shelf that was the Head's place. That first day the Head had put his hand on the head boy's shoulder as he stood up to start for the summit. Two years later it was his shoulder the Head had used. A good day, too, but nothing like the first.

The pain returned and erased the memory. "*Normal activity, no hard exercise.*" The pale, watery-eyed oncologist had spoken to him with patient annoyance, almost a whine. "*Take two of these when the pain increases. Two at a time. Don't wait. Take them at the first twinge.*"

He thought now that 'twinge' seemed hardly the word for the stabbing pain that seemed to start in his ass and reach out of his navel, especially now that both he and the doctor knew what was causing it.

"*When*"—He didn't say 'if,' the little prick—"when" with just enough emphasis to let him know he didn't really give a damn. And later: "*When it gets to where the pills don't help, two an hour, we'll have to go to intramuscular. You'll just get nauseous if you take too many orally. Oh, and no strenuous exercise.*"

"Injections?"

"Mm-hmm." The doctor's tone suggested he would probably find these injections a great inconvenience.

He assumed the doctor was still sulking because he had laughed at his big announcement.

"*I see many reactions Mr., ah, Hannah. This is the first time I've seen hilarity.*"

"It's all right, please, I'm sorry. It's just that you'd have saved us all a lot of trouble if you'd given me this news three weeks ago."

"To you, you little prick," Zach said out loud as he took two more pills. Then, when he turned to leave the Rock for good, he patted it goodbye, the way he would a favored dog.

He continued on for another quarter hour. He still wasn't quite high enough. It would take ten more minutes to put him over four thousand feet, maybe twenty, the way he was slowing down. But the pain came back and seemed to settle in. Apparently this was what the doc meant by 'strenuous exercise.' He sat down beside the trail until the spasm passed. Then he said, "Fuck this," out loud.

He twisted the top off the water bottle and set it down. No reason to wait any longer. This would have to be high enough. He wedged the bottle between boulders and pulled out the container of pills. He popped off its white top. He was about to flip it into the wind, but thought better of it and put the top in his pocket. Whatever they would say about him, no one would call him a litterer. The solitary man laughed aloud a moment, then winced and held his mid-section before he sat back quietly.

He took the white pills two at a time, a pair on his tongue and a swallow of water. Two more and two more until the water was gone. He hadn't counted so he spilled the remainder in his hand. Four pills left. He'd started with twenty-two. Eighteen should be enough, he thought. He put the others back, recapped the pill bottle and buttoned his pocket. "Ambiguity," he said aloud.

He prided himself on being able to assess the odds. They were still good that if he turned around now, right now, and put his finger down his throat, he could still get down, get to the car. The floor of the narrow valley was black now, but the trail was wide enough. Down there, life still waited.

Life. Sure, maybe three, even six more months of it. Just enough time to lose what he had left. T.J. had started calling again, a note of wariness came from the telephone now and no more talk of Harry Warren.

Warren! How had he figured out so much? Smitty had been so sure. *"We'll put ...I'll hide the shot gun in his garage while you're in there. You still think she'll loan you the money? Stop worryin.' Leave this part to me. You know Warren. He'll panic and go to Carr and then Carr will be all over it, thinkin' he's fuckin' Sherlock Holmes. You're sure he was, fuckin' her?"*

Well, now even Smitty knew it hadn't worked. Better that way, he'd know enough to keep quiet.

A new light-headiness began to come on. He smiled at the sensation and made a small grunt of satisfaction. A very small tide running out, but quickly. He recalculated his odds. Too late now.

He faced the orange sun, neatly cut in half by the purple loom of

Stark Mountain. Across the valley shadows were advancing across the Blue Ox Trail.

He had learned to ski over there, won his first race on Blue Cow, the gentler longer trail that fanned out from the vertical slope. It was supposed to be a stroke of luck for him that they held the Junior Nationals here in the East on the 'steeps' of Blue Ox. The Colorado kids weren't used to ice.

The shadows advanced. He wanted to think about skiing, snow, but faces kept coming.

"I'm sorry Zach, but no, it's more money than the building's worth." Emma, of all people, turning businesslike on him.

"But I'm finished Emma. I can't get anymore from the bank. The firm has voted to move out of the building. I'm broke."

"I'm sorry Zach."

"But ... well, Samantha ..."

"Don't bring that up Zach. We agreed."

"I didn't mean ... it's just that ..."

"No. No, she doesn't know and she never will. I'll do whatever I have to make sure of that. You know I will."

A burst of wind made him shiver. He had known she would. She was a Llewellyn after all.

Then the new face appeared. She had been too perfect, so hungry,

"I'll need to have the glue analyzed. The finish is Eighteenth Century, but the glue will be definitive. I'm positive they're authentic. The bed, the settee, the chairs. The chest is English, but the rest is Philadelphia Chippendale. I'll need her asleep to get the samples. She's crazy, Zach, but..."

"Can you give me a ballpark number?"

"Depends, but if everything checks out, two and a half to three million. Let me go over the family papers next week."

Enough. Enough for both of them, but her tone had changed.

"I told that health care aide, Margie, I'd take care of them tonight. She's got a court date next week, and wants a night out. It's better this way though. Come up about eight. We need to talk."

But later, when he got there, more than her tone had changed.

"You don't understand. It's off, Zach."

"Off? What the hell..."

"Look, I'll explain later, after I talk to them. But our, our arrangement has to be off. Don't you see, it would be like stealing from, from family."

"Talk to them? Wait a min.... What do you mean 'family'?" He remembered hating the desperation in his voice.

"You're being irrational." She had looked up at the staircase then, pretending to be concerned, as if she hadn't just drugged them. *"They'll hear you."*

And finally.

"Don't you see? They're stuck with me. They can't throw me away now. It's the way my grandfather wrote the trust."

"Your grandfather? What are you talking about?" And then she told him. As she did, he saw that she was right.

"I'll pay you. Do you understand? But I can't lose it again."

"Lose what?"

"This." She had waved her hand at the shabby room around them with its tarnished framed pictures of little girls at camp, bigger girls with lacrosse sticks. She picked up a silver framed portrait of a severe unsmiling woman as a bride. *"I keep telling you, but you won't understand. That's my grandmother. This is mine."* Then she looked upstairs again. *"Or it will be, soon enough."*

She went over to the cluttered desk and picked up an old yellowed letter. He could see the Wharton Biddle letterhead. *"This settled it."*

"Settled what?"

"You wouldn't understand. It's a copy of Oswald Popp's letter to my folks about my ring. I remember when it came." She waved her hand at him then, a small gold ring on her little finger. *"He sent a copy to my grandfather. God, it feels strange to say that."*

"What?" She said then, a new tone when he stepped toward her. *"You going to hit me? You think that will change anything?"* She flashed her brave smile, the same one she showed that first night in his office, afterward. The same smile she'd shown when they'd decided what they'd do with the furniture.

He tried to reason with her, but he had felt so sick. However many aspirin and antacids he took, he just couldn't keep anything down, couldn't concentrate. The partners meeting that morning had been a nightmare. The newly cold stares, the young partner saying, *"This lease, Zach. It doesn't make sense to renew."* He'd hired him, trained him, but it didn't matter. They were going to stick him with an empty building, a two million dollar mortgage, and Suzanne demanding separate maintenance of ten thousand dollars a month. Now this.

"Look. I'm going outside to have a cigarette. When you calm down, we'll figure out where we go from here. I know this sounds pompous but I think I need legal advice, don't you?"

He remembered actually running his hands through his hair. He had to do something, anything. Anyone could understand that. The guns were right there. It took forever to get one open, then the shells spilling in the drawer as he fumbled with the boxes. Outside in the wind, her back to him, she hadn't heard him coming. She turned around. Her expression, a frown of concentration, didn't change. She didn't have time to be surprised.

He pulled one of the triggers. The gun jumped with a loud explosion and smoke seemed to whip around the porch. She bounced backwards, then looked down and saw blood. She started to run. He pulled the trigger again. Nothing. Then he pulled the other trigger and the gun went off again, but she never broke stride and disappeared into the dark. He had looked down at the still smoking gun in his hands. She was gone. Nothing worked. Nothing.

◆Δ◆

THE SEATED MAN squinted at the mountain across the notch. The shadow line had reached the spot, there, right by the steeps where it all began to go wrong. The race he was supposed to win. The thirteenth gate, two red poles with ruts up to his knees, *push, push ... breathe... shift... breathe... breathe.* Then the world upside down, the ground above and sky below, the crack of the Kastle GS breaking and the second crack.

The line of shadow hung there and then it was past. Moments later, the last orange sliver of sun sank into the ridge beyond.

The wind softened. Now it was a child's face, laughing under the braided golden hair. *"Mummy, I won, I won."* And then still laughing, *"Pretty good huh, Mr. Hannah?"* Her arms briefly around him as she jumped with excitement. *Mr. Hannah.*

The man made motions to rise but only rolled over.

He heard someone make an 'uhhn' sound and felt grit and small pebbles coming into his nostril.

Well at least Smitty had stood by him. *"She was no good, Zach. C'mon, pull yourself together."*

He'd have never made it through the night without him. Then the waiting. One day, two. The fear as Carr got close, then elation as he turned to Warren, and just as Carr was convinced, that stupid janitor... Oswald Popp! What a name... Warren asked about him, too... who the hell was Oswald Popp?

His head rolled back, the pink and blue of the sky turning orange, then nothing but orange and black. He could feel himself shivering. But only the motion, he wasn't cold.

"Thank gaw for sm... fav..." The man said. He closed his eyes. He breathed regularly for a while as the darkness became total and the wind rose again. His head was propped against the crevice of a boulder that had split cleanly down the middle ten thousand years before. It had settled and waited through the centuries to provide just the right angle to constrict his windpipe as he leaned back against it. His breathing turned into a series of damp snorts and jerks of the shoulders while something other than will struggled on. His glasses now lay diagonally across his face, the edge of the frame ticking against the rock with the movements of his head. The man became still. He was alone with nothing but dark and wind, because sometime before that, Zach Hannah had made his way past the red gate through the ruts and onto the sun-lit straight-away toward the people cheering for him below.

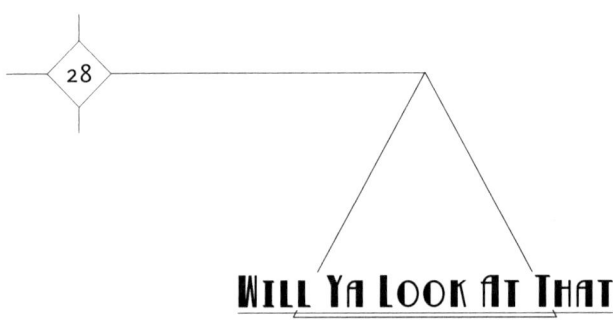

28
Will Ya Look At That

Oscar Leighton switched off the engine and let the backhoe cough a few revolutions until it shuddered still. He'd been at it for two hours now, dressing the side-slope of the leach field for the Alpine Ridge Condominium, Phase I. He was good at this. Even his uncle would say, "You c'n be a dubba' Oscar, but you're a fuckin' artist with that backhoe. I'll give you that."

Tori hadn't liked it much, him working the Saturday after Thanksgiving. She wanted to go Christmas shopping over to North Conway and hit the outlets. But his uncle promised him double-time, and they had to get the leach field in before the ground froze. It went down into the teens the night before and there wouldn't be many more chances.

On the slope above him they had cut the trees and scraped away the topsoil leaving almost two acres of grey granite and yellow earth, now traced with the lines and angles of grey concrete walls and footings. Brush was stacked in conical piles, waiting for snow cover before burning. By Monday the foundation would have set up enough for backfilling. Might even get the rough landscaping done after that if they didn't get an early snow. Come spring, the carpenters would be far enough along for them to spread the loam for lawns and gravel the parking lots and walkways. He'd marry it all into the ski trail below him. A little loam, a little grass seed. Oscar could picture it all in his head and he felt good about it, knowing.

Oscar never understood skiing, especially when a man could ride clear to Canada on a snow-machine. People said they paid half a million dollars for some of these condos just so they could ski out the door right onto the trail. Well, he guessed it was their business.

Oscar inspected the corner of the leach field where an outcrop of ledge marked the boundary between earth and stone. He squatted and eyed the top of the sloped sides. It had taken a week to bring in enough fill to build up it up to the string line. Satisfied the top of the field was now level, Oscar calculated his double-time pay again. Six hours at $44 per hour, take home near two hundred. He'd take Tori shopping tomorrow.

A pair of cardinals glided into the clearing. The male, bright red, pulled something out of a brush pile. The birds then made for a clump of trees where the male darted from branch to branch, still holding his prize. The rust-colored female seemed to shadow her mate on branches just beneath his.

Oscar kept his eye on them. The tree tops stood out against the steep slope of Mount LaFarge across the notch. Still watching, he fumbled his binoculars out from under the seat of the back hoe, careful to keep sight of the flashes of red. It didn't seem possible, anything that bright could live in this world of browns and greys.

Sometimes if they stood still long enough, he could make out the cardinals' bright yellow beaks, but this morning, just as he got the binoculars focused, the pair fluttered upward. Oscar tried to follow but they bounced in and out of view until finally he lost sight of them completely. Hoping they might drop down again, Oscar swept the binoculars back and forth taking in the tops of the line of trees. Nothing but a glint of reflected light from Mount LaFarge. It was above the treeline, up in the rocks. Probably a broken bottle. He refocused. He watched for a bit, took the binoculars away from his face and rubbed his eyes. Then he looked again.

"Oh shit," he said.

They'd rode him something awful after that poor woman over on Green Mountain.

"Pissed on her foot. Thought he'd got her mad."

"Heard that weren't th' only thing got pissed on."

Even the deer he'd killed the next weekend hadn't made things any better. He knocked it down with the first shot, but it struggled up.

"Four times. No shit, 'Sure Shot' got her four times. We were an hour dressing her out. What a mess."

"What happened, Oscar, she catch you pissin', too, or you just like hamburg?"

Behind him, his uncle's jeep whined up to the condo site above. Oscar heard the door slam. He made one last pass with the binoculars at the mountain across the way, brought them down and scowled. The older man took his time to make his way down the broken ground.

"You gonna stand here all day, Oscar? Thought I paid you to dig, not look at your damn birds." But the old man smiled to show he didn't mean it. Oscar had worked fast that morning and they both knew it. He wasn't complaining. Just passing the day. Just his way was all.

Oscar pursed his lips, looked down, and then with the look of a man who's decided something once and for all, handed the binoculars over. "Eyes are kinda sore today. Can't quite make out, well..." He pointed toward the spot up on the mountain. " See that flash cross the way that seems to come and go?"

"Uh huh."

"What do you think that is?"

His uncle raised the binoculars to his eyes and began to adjust the focus.

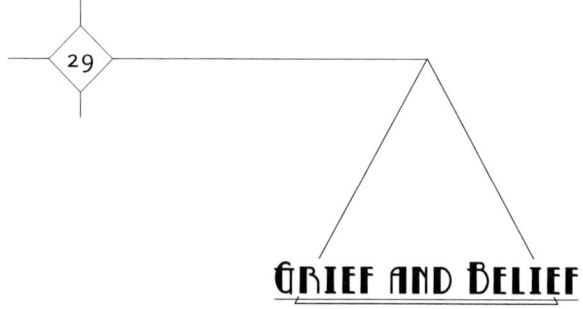

29 Grief and Belief

The Saturday morning after Thanksgiving began in fog that sat like a pearl-colored blanket on the slopes below Langdon house. By ten o'clock the breeze had freshened and scattered the mists, finally leaving only bits and pieces that clung like plumes of smoke to the tops of distant hills until they too were gone.

Life at last was almost back to normal. Emma puttered in her studio making noises with a small vacuum. Harry, wheel-chair bound, his immobilized leg stretched out in front, swathed in bandages and a soft cast, had been parked next to Emma's floor-to-ceiling studio window so he could take in the view. Recuperating at Langdon House wasn't an uncomfortable confinement, though he longed for a real shower and knew he would never grow accustomed to sitting down to pee. His daughters, Leigh and Samantha, home for the holiday, had become bored with rolling him around the house, and indulged him with only a short stay on the patio to admire the clouds before they parked him to bask with Abigail next to Emma's studio window.

Emma put away her vacuum and began to polish a federal period commode. The gentle smells of oil and wax filled Harry's nostrils.

"What would you like?" Emma asked and gestured toward her sound system to show she meant music.

"I don't know, something Teutonic." Harry waved at the vista of mist and conifers.

The overture from *Parcifal* filled the room. Well, what could be more Teutonic than Wagner?

Leigh and Samantha's renascent companionship had been quickened by Samantha's weekend guest, Benjamin, an understandably self-conscious young man of thirty, too old for the ponytail he sported, even for an instructor in the Eastport Wooden Boat Project who was obviously bedding his new 'mate.' Harry feared that Samantha had inherited the Llewellyn libido along with their red hair. Much in love, she seemed simultaneously to have rediscovered affection for her big sister. Benjamin, ponytail or not, was decent enough to pretend to occupy a bedroom two doors down from Samantha. Leigh's husband had left for New York early the day before and the sisters had been left to a gentle competition to amuse Benjamin and, when they had time, Harry.

So far, it seemed that Russell's hospital predictions were coming true. Grace daily confirmed there were no further calls from T.J., no more requests for records. A week earlier, the day he came home, Harry's tormentor-turned-savior, Gregg Leavitt, had moved on. He was pictured in that morning's *News & Observer* with his very pregnant wife and a small daughter with a direct stare and her hand at her nose.

**Hero Cop Assumes New
Duties in Statehouse.**

Harry had skimmed the story to get to the good part. "...Leavitt was compelled to shoot down deranged gunman, Lionel Whitcomb, as he fired on his estranged wife, Judy, and county Judge Harry Warren who shielded her..." The newly promoted Lieutenant Leavitt would be running the governor's security detail for the rest of her term.

Tee had called from the 'wilds' of Las Vegas.

"I suppose now I'm really going to have to go through with that show," he said, with no preliminaries.

"I'm sure Amanda will expect it."

"Mmm, you know when they carried you out of there, you looked so bad I was sure I wouldn't have to. Ah well, be careful what you pray for," Tee said.

Harry knew that was as much an expression of concern as he would ever receive from Tee Ingersoll.

As the days passed, lassitude had turned to hope. It had been three weeks now since the courhouse shooting and nothing but congratulatory letters had arrived. Perhaps Russell was right. At idle moments Harry made vague plans for a nighttime visit to the Wasoka Club to retrieve the shotgun from L.L.'s cabinet. He even daydreamed of a second bout of televised celebrity on Tee's show.

Parcifal ended precisely at eleven o'clock, just as the chimes of three different house clocks struck the hour. That was when the phone rang. Harry could hear Samantha's voice answering the phone.

As she answered, Samantha's voice made the descent from bright greeting to cautious confirmation and then to something grave indeed. Harry and Emma didn't need to hear the words, her tone said it all. Emma exchanged glances with him and wiped her hands on her apron. She pushed her special magnifying spectacles up on her head.

Leigh also had heard because her footsteps sounded down the hall. Samantha put down the phone then and came to the door. She gave a long look to her mother but turned to Harry. "Daddy, I've got really bad news."

'*Barbara,*' Harry thought, a thrill of fear going through him, but said nothing. He supposed Emma had similar thoughts about her father.

"It's Mr. Hannah, Daddy. He was climbing on Mount LaFarge yesterday. He, he died."

Samantha said this softly, her eyes bright, and walked toward him to comfort him as she did. Samantha's first instinct was to comfort her father, but after the years of ski racing, Samantha had become attached to Zach and she might have been seeking comfort as well.

It was not a surprise to hear Leigh convey something close to relief as she said, "Oh, that's just awful," after hearing her sister's message. Leigh had just finished with racing when Samantha started, and was never a strong enough competitor to capture Zach's attention. Like all first-born children, she had, and would, spend a lifetime keeping track, keeping score.

Considering the way Zach and he parted, Harry had little difficulty receiving this news. Nevertheless, he had fashioned just the right frown for manly grief when Emma made a noise beside him like she'd stubbed her toe. Not a cry, just a short sharp groan, as much anger as pain.

The three of them then saw her take three tentative steps and sit heavily in the newly repaired Windsor chair. "Zach," she said, but she wasn't speaking to them.

◆Δ◆

FEW WOULD HAVE APPRECIATED the irony of Zach Hannah's memorial service more than Zach himself. The son from his first marriage was there, positioning himself between wives one and two. Wife number three had recently alleged mental cruelty and serial adultery to begin the latest case of *Hannah v. Hannah* in the New Hampshire family court. She skipped the service at Windsor's St. Mark's Episcopal Church.

New Hampshire's great and near great, however, were there in force. The Head had actual tears in his eyes. The governor looked appropriately grave as she stopped often to greet and console. Her new head of security stood at the back of the church with two troopers stationed in the side aisles about halfway up the nave. While the officers were there for her, their presence along with the governor's lent a certain institutional dignity to the proceedings that Zach Hannah would have liked.

The Cruikshank office was, of course, out in force, lawyers and staff. Harry estimated at an average of $250 an hour—a good rate for New Hampshire—it had cost them at least sixty thousand dollars in billables to fill those pews for their namesake. This must have rankled the Management Committee. Rumors had already spread through Windsor of how much Zach was overdrawn on his partners' account.

Three Supreme Court judges, there with spouses, shared the governor's front pew just opposite the family. Behind them were six past and present county judges. There was an angular quartet of grey- and white-haired men who could only be from the Dartmouth ski team. Two of these, Harry deduced, were Devon boys from the way they went over and embraced the Head. There was even the ex-congressman who had beaten Zach in that long-ago campaign.

The rest of the pews were filled primarily with New Hampshire lawyers, a few truly Zach's peers, but mostly only pale copies of the man they had hoped to be, had wanted to be. In the middle of this group sat T.J. Carr.

And Smitty was there. He glowered at Harry. He had reason to, because Harry owed his perfect view of all the proceedings—and Zach would have loved this best of all—to the fact that Harry had been asked to give the eulogy!

There was no way Zach's son could have known, of course. What he did know was that there was ongoing trouble with the Cruikshank partners and that Harry, after all, had been with Zach at the office in happier days. He too had gone to Devon and, of course, Harry was still big news. A logical choice. Harry accepted the offer not for any of the right reasons. A decent showing would make any judge there shy away from any future warrant.

A busy man with busy friends, Zach's service had been delayed until mid-December to allow people to clear their schedules. Having graduated to crutches by then, Harry had been given a convenient perch opposite the altar and consulted his notes as the chapters of his late mentor's life filed into the pews below. Emma had circled around and was about to sit with the other county court judges, but the Chief Justice intercepted her and placed her next to him in the front row. Emma then took her revenge on the man by carefully introducing herself to his wife though Emma knew her perfectly well.

Harry covered his mouth with his notes. He had been given two weeks to prepare his remarks, two weeks to think. The service began.

I am the Resurrection and the life. Whosoever believeth in me...

The service ran at a good pace, the old words familiar enough to the plurality of non-Episcopalians in the room for them to make the appropriate responses to the young priest with his surprising baritone.

He did an excellent job, the priest, and soon had them in the spirit of the thing. It wasn't easy. Like most contemporary funerals, the principal was absent, reduced to ashes only hours after his discovery on Mount LaFarge. This assembly had to make do with a photo of a smiling Zach accepting the skimeister award at a long ago Dartmouth winter carnival.

Still, by the time they sang the Navy hymn, one they sang often at Devon—*Oh, Lord our father, strong to save...*—and got through two gospel readings using the old Prayer Book and King James Version language, he had them sounding like enthusiastic converts. Then it was Harry's turn. As he hobbled to the lectern Harry heard the pleasant murmur of a dozen or more whispered assurances from the pews. Yes, *that* Harry Warren.

By this time word had gotten round of Zach's diagnosis. The consensus was that, as usual, he had handled the death sentence of metastasized pancreatic cancer just right. No lying around a hospital trying to wheedle a little extra morphine from the night resident for Zach Hannah. No, he'd picked the clean, quick exit you'd expect. He was that kind of guy.

Of course, Harry knew he'd gone up on that mountain with a little more than a diagnosis on his mind. He *had* killed Ephne, after all. Then there was the small matter of trying to pin it on Harry.

What Harry Warren said was:

> "Zachary Thomas Hannah did not believe much in monuments. In part, this was because while he always lived in the future, he did so with confidence that the past, and his role in it, would take care of itself.
>
> This, I think, was because he knew that monuments are only aids to memory, reminders in stone. And he knew that the accomplishments of some need no such assistance; as a student, an athlete, as spokesman for political causes that yielded more honor than success, as the builder of a great law firm that yielded both and, most memorably, as the teacher of scores of new lawyers—he left those who knew him with memories that need no prompting. As lawyers, we will always remember that no client of Zach Hannah's

ever lost a case because his lawyer was outworked by the other side, and no young attorney at Cruikshank and Hannah was ever left to flounder alone on a difficult case."

The platitudes flowed over the assembled mourners who fixed their expressions in postures of appropriate gravity. Harry knew it was no sin to be a bore at such a time.

"He was a father and a leader, good at getting other people to do the right thing because we all knew Zach Hannah stood for right things.

He was never one for excuses. He chose his last path the way he'd chosen the others. He was not a man to waver and, when he got to the end, at a place he loved, who can doubt that he was content with the destination? Because in this, as in so many other things, he had chosen his own course and stayed with it, no matter how hard, cold, steep and dark it became."

Having done the expected Harry caught Emma's eye. She stared intently, unwavering. She hadn't wanted him to do this, and he couldn't very well explain why he wanted to. Perhaps it was the way she said "Zach." When she had seen he would insist, she had turned distant, cold. But her disapproval was silent. She said no more.

"Our religious training tells us we cannot expect always to be good. We need forgiveness because our sins do not befall us; we choose them. 'Don't knock sin, Harry,' Zach used to say to me. 'Without sin, where the hell would we be?'"

This got a decent laugh. Good thing. The 'steep, dark path' business had been a bad choice. Too close to the bone.

"Much of what a lawyer does is to intercede. To weigh up a hidden good against the more apparent wrong. A good lawyer learns how to do this. A great lawyer already knows. A good lawyer knows that some of the wrong that men will choose is made thus by what fate has chosen for them ...

Harry paused.

"... but also that there are some clients who simply need a great lawyer."

More laughter, but nervous.
Harry returned to platitudes.

"We all knew how great a skier Zach was. He knew that one racer can hit the ice just so and make it to the finish and glory. Another hits the same ice a millimeter further down and flies into disappointment. There is no sin, no morality, no justice in that, only fate.

Zach recognized that it is what we do at the intersections of fate that matters. For some, their nature is to accept defeat and disappointment with as much grace as they can manage. For others, impatient with the cards fate deals, new cards are dealt from hidden places.

Zach Hannah was dealt many good cards. He was intelligent and always succeeded at his studies. His body did what he told it and he was the supreme sportsman. Men and women alike loved him and loved to follow him. He was even good looking."

This earned a ripple of nervous amusement. Both ex's shifted in their pew at the very instant Harry said 'loved.'

"But he had his bad cards, too. Disappointments, losses, some too deep to acknowledge and none much worse than the last hand he was dealt. We remember him today the way we, too, will be remembered, for how he played them all, good or bad. I submit he played to win, but always dealt off the top. He didn't gloat when he won. He didn't cry when he lost. I suspect he turned the last card over much like the first and looked the consequences straight in the eye."

The lie flowed out as sonorously as the rest. Harry saw no stir, no shudder of dissent, though in a sea of upturned faces both T.J. and Smitty looked down.

"As a lawyer, Zach was also a receiver and keeper of secrets. He knew there are times when, in this world at least, men are to spare others from truths too painful to bear. I never knew him to breach a confidence or reveal a truth even when it would have been to his great benefit. Never."

Emma seemed to shift her weight in the front pew though her gaze remained steady.

Harry turned then to the priest.

"Padre, I've already brought gambling into this lovely church. I hope you'll forgive me for a touch of heresy."

The priest favored him with a helpless smile, the kind given to those past hope of redemption, but he had a sense of humor and made a faux gesture of absolution which their audience enjoyed.

Harry waited for the church to quiet.

"It's an embarrassment, but I believe in an anthropomorphic god. True. No cosmic intelligence lurking in the ether for me. God's a big guy, who wears robes, sounds a lot like James Earl Jones and speaks Elizabethan prose with an American accent. He too is a baritone."

Both priest and congregation appreciated this and Harry paused again.

"So I've had this image for two weeks now, and its pretty clear. God is seated and he's got all the files on Zach...

Harry made his voice as deep as he could...

"'Well, Hannah, you've done this, you've done that, all the evidence is in ... Do you have anything to say for yourself?' That's when Zach gets to his feet..."

Harry squared his shoulders and moved his glasses down his nose as Zach always had:

"Actually…"

That too was a success, but when the church quieted down Harry knew to return to safer ground.

"And who could have a better advocate, or be more deserving of it. I suggest that this final, unappealable, decision will be a final, famous victory. For our wonderful departed friend. May the God of each and every one of us see it the same way."

Somewhere Harry's anthropomorphic God rolled his eyes and made a new notation in an already crowded ledger.

◆△◆

Emma's eyes were red. She touched his check. "Old silver tongue," she said.

"I have my moments."

"Yes, Harry, you do."

They stood at the front door to the almost empty church. The Head was just inside with the last to leave, his arm around one of the old skiers. The old man's eyes met Harry's and to his surprise the Head moved with remarkable speed across the landing towards him, hand out.

"Harry," he said "That was magnificent. Magnificent."

"Thank you, sir, Mr. Buck. You're very kind."

After the Head departed in some confusion, Emma said, "Really, Harry."

"What?"

"Don't pretend to be stupid. I thought you resented not being able to call him 'Head,' the way Zach always did. The man was trying to make up for …"

"You're unusually insightful today, darling." He didn't think it was he who had told her about the Head's rules for how he was addressed.

Emma breathed out. Perhaps she remembered then where she *had* heard it. They stood in silence. In the distance Edgar had maneuvered the SUV to the edge of the pavement below. A light wet snow was falling. The plan was for Edgar to take the Warrens to a reception at the first Mrs. Hannah's home.

Emma's voice came then from beside him.

"Insight, that's your thing, isn't it?"

"Yes, Emma. It takes me a while. Years in fact, but in the end insight is my thing." Harry said this looking straight ahead. There was no response.

He knew it all by then. All those days Zach had stood in the snow and watched Samantha. Emma's rage over Zach's girlfriend as his campaign fell apart. The year Samantha was born. The year Harry became a judge, his "consolation prize." His memory—now—of Zach's every comment, every expression when Emma's name was spoken, hers when she learned he was gone.

Their heads turned toward one another and their eyes met. 'Zach,' she had said, and, yes, of course, that was the moment when he knew. Zach, the man he had just praised and commended to the Deity. Zach and Emma. Zach and Samantha.

Harry had always believed the human iris to be the most beautiful thing in nature. Its colors fold into one another, better than any flower, any jewel. But not color alone. He held the conviction that this was a tiny gorgeous window, for looking in as well as looking out. The blue-green of Emma Llewellyn's eyes seemed to pulse, the black pupils to shrink, to close, then open again. Emma nodded then, but maybe not.

AND COULD HE COMPLAIN? After a lifetime of making use of others, could he really object when they made use of him? If Emma wasn't perfect she was better than he deserved, better than he had ever been. For a time the piece named Harry Warren had been slated for sacrifice from Emma Llewellyn's chessboard. Had he done any less? And what sacrifices would he have required of her if Lionel Whitcomb hadn't kicked over everyone's board as he made his own last, mad, desperate move?

Then Edgar was there. Emma walked ahead of Harry as he hobbled down the stone steps. She got the car open, waving Edgar away as she took charge of the crutches.

As they pulled away, Harry said, "I'm not up to the reception Emma, do you mind?"

"Me either," she said.

"Home then?"

"Yes Harry, home."

And so his game, their game, two pieces sacrificed, went on.